Revelations

Revelations

Charlotte Phoenix

Library of Congress Control Number:		2014910102
ISBN:	Hardcover	978-1-4990-3114-0
	Softcover	978-1-4990-3115-7
	eBook	978-1-4990-3112-6

Rev. date: 10/25/2014

Contents

To my family

While this is not our story, the main characters and narratives were inspired by anecdotal accounts I heard as a child when "grown folks" talked nearby and by the love, faith, values, and traditions I learned living in multigenerational households.

Acknowledgment

I gratefully acknowledge the support and encouragement I received from friends and family who urged me to "write down" some of the stories I told them or who gave me honest appraisals of earlier drafts. Special thanks are affectionately extended to Sylvia, Maria, Emma (1917-2014), Gayna and Beth, as well as to Eric for invaluable technical support. I am so appreciative of my daughters, Tina and Cherie, for always believing in me and for being my sounding boards throughout this project. Most of all, I am indebted to my beloved husband, Chris. I am blessed to be his wife. For forty years, his love has inspired me to pursue my dreams with confidence and passion.

Part 1

EXCERPTS FROM THE JOURNAL OF CLAUDIA REYNOLDS THORNTON

Saturday, November 27, 2004
4:00 a.m.

I can't sleep. Jason is sleeping serenely in our bed with a soft smile of complete satisfaction spread across his face. I'm tempted to awaken him so that he can share the anger and frustration that are causing my restlessness. Yet I know that talking to him would only make me more upset. He went to sleep reveling in memories of hosting a totally successful event and would not appreciate my letting a brief encounter in the ladies' room diminish my enjoyment of it. I would present to him the latest evidence that Delia is a bitch. Then he would once again make excuses for her inappropriateness and wonder why I care about it at all. I admit that I'm disgusted with myself for letting her shenanigans disturb my peace. I'm sure that, like Jason, she is sleeping soundly without the slightest concern for my feelings. In fact, if she knew that I was upset, she'd probably derive pleasure from it. I need to get over my loathing for her. She has only a peripheral existence in my life, and I should not allow her to influence my relationship with my husband.

Last night, I was excited about beginning the third trimester of my first pregnancy. When I stepped out of the limousine in front of the Plaza Hotel, my body, mind, and spirit were filled with joy. I was excited about this year's *BUMPN* Holiday Gala. Held annually the Friday night after Thanksgiving, it is the first big celebratory event of the Christmas season, drawing a potpourri of black and white journalists, publishers, entertainers, politicians, business moguls, and media executives in and around New York. The paparazzi were camped out on both the Central Park and hotel sides of Fifty-Ninth Street, so flashing cameras greeted each guest as they arrived. I actually smiled at the cameras, proud to show off my "Baby BUMP," which is the nickname Jason has given my ever-expanding tummy. It is an affectionate and symbolic play on the title of the magazine he founded ten years ago and has always served as editor in chief: *Black Urban Male Professionals' Network (BUMPN)* magazine. We learned last month that we are having a son, and Jason knows that in addition to being the heir to the magazine, he is destined to become a black urban male professional, a BUMP. This was my fifth *BUMPN* party, my third as Mrs. Jason Thornton and my first as a mother-to-be. All of these affairs are wonderful, but this one was so very special. I wasn't able to enjoy the sour apple martinis and cosmopolitans that I usually accept from the waiters serving various hors d'oeuvres and cocktails throughout the evening. Instead, I enjoyed sipping ginger ale from champagne flutes.

Jason came toward me as soon as I entered the room. His eyes and his smile were both wide with joy and pride. He greeted me with a warm hug and a sweet kiss on my cheek as he asked, "How was the ride down?" I told him that there was less traffic than expected and that we had made the trip from New Rochelle to Midtown Manhattan in under an hour. Then after telling me that I looked beautiful, he looked at my tummy, rubbed it, and grinned, commenting, "And you, Baby BUMP, are lookin' good as well." He proudly pointed to Baby BUMP as we spoke to every guest along our way to his clique, the four couples with whom he had been talking when I came into the room. The husbands in the clique were his closest friends from his undergraduate years at Howard University. Except for Greg, they were all part of the class of 1986. Greg was in a five-year engineering program and graduated a year later. They have remained close through the years and all now live in New York. Greg, a vice president with IBM,

and Bob, who owns four McDonald's restaurants in Brooklyn and Queens, married their college girlfriends, Alicia and Carol respectively, shortly after they both graduated in 1988. Alicia is a certified public accountant who handles all of our personal and corporate taxes, as well as those of several other celebrity clients, and Carol is a research chemist who left the cosmetics industry in 2001 after the birth of her fourth child. Marvin, a gynecologist and fertility specialist in Manhattan, and George, a brilliant criminal attorney in Brooklyn who has never lost a case, both married their spouses later, after they graduated from their professional schools. Marvin and his wife, Janice, met in Boston in 1990 while he was in his last year at Harvard Medical School and she was a sophomore at Emerson. They married in 1994. Janice, who humbly and humorously refers to herself as a "working housewife," is a successful author-illustrator of children's books and talented part-time actress who has appeared in independent films and recurring roles on various New York-based soap operas. George met Paula, an architect, in 1998 when a friend recommended that he hire her to renovate his brownstone in Park Slope. They married in 2000. She has designed primary and vacation homes for a number of high-profile clients, many of whom were present at the *BUMPN* affair. She also designed the remodeling of the kitchen, family room, and master bedroom suite at our house.

I get along with all of the husbands. As for the wives, I'm closest to Janice and Paula. We came from outside the Howard clique, to which our husbands and the other two wives belong. We didn't know them in their undergraduate years. Alicia and Carol are cordial enough to us, but they remain closer friends with our husbands' college girlfriends and invite them to social events. There are times when they share stories and jokes about their good old days that remind us that Alicia, Carol, and the old girlfriends see us as outsiders or, at best, the neophytes in their unofficial sisterhood. They make a show of including us in their conversations and inside jokes, but their glances to each other remind us that we do not share their intimate bonds, forged through shared experiences of campus life and first loves.

Jason and I were the last of the five couples in his clique to tie the knot, having done so less than two and a half years ago in the summer of 2002. Our courtship was also the shortest. We first met in 2000 but didn't get to know each other until a year later when I did a feature piece on Jason and *BUMPN* during the weekend news. As is my style, I also interviewed his mother and siblings, as well as childhood and collegiate friends, business supporters, and rivals. The day after the feature about Jason aired, he sent me a dozen roses. A week later, he called to invite me out for dinner. We were mutually attracted to each other. We talked and laughed for hours while dining and dancing during that first date. Deeper emotional connections between us built quickly, and within three months, we were engaged. A year and a half later, we married.

I dated in high school, college and afterward but my first serious relationship was with Jason. Before we hooked up, he shared a ten-year love connection with Delia which began a week after she arrived on Howard's campus in 1983, a year ahead of Alicia and Carol. Delia graduated with honors as a psychology major and was also homecoming queen her senior year. She is a classic beauty: five feet ten inches tall, thin but shapely with flawless dark chocolate complexion, and thick wavy black hair. To earn spending money while at Howard, she did some modeling with a small agency in DC. Pictures of her appeared on calendars and in department store ads in local papers and she walked the runway in several local fashion shows. When she graduated in 1987, she enrolled in a graduate degree program in psychology at New York University. It was a strategic choice. New York was where Jason lived, and it was the ideal place to pursue her studies and her goal of becoming a fashion model. She continued dating Jason but did not accept his first proposal of marriage because she wanted to be free to follow a career path in modeling wherever it might lead her. Two years later, she had successfully completed her master's degree but had been less successful getting consistent work as a model. After struggling three more years, she decided to give up on a modeling career and to accept Jason's second proposal of marriage. But a month later, she learned that she had been selected to be an Ebony Fashion Fair model for the 1992–1993 season, "Living the Fantasy." Delia said that she could not pass on that opportunity to tour nearly two hundred cities modeling haute couture and ready-to-wear fashion in the world's largest traveling fashion show. She knew that the show's creator, Eunice Walker Johnson, was a formidable woman who had overcome resistance and racism to become a dynamic, respected figure in the fashion industry. Mrs. Johnson had to work hard to convince European designers to sell her their fashions for her first show in 1957. But by 1992, she was recognized as the biggest buyer of European haute couture. Valentino,

Pierre Cardin, Yves Saint Laurent, and other major designers jumped at the opportunity to be included in her shows. Ebony Fashion Fair had raised more than $50 million for various nonprofit groups and had served to springboard careers of black supermodels, actors, and television news anchors. Delia was positive that she would find the success she imagined for herself as a result of being an Ebony Fashion Fair model. So though she remained engaged to Jason, she put their marriage plans on hold to go on tour.

After the 1993–1994 season, Delia left Ebony Fashion Fair to work in Europe, where she found the international success of her dreams. In 1997, when Delia was at the top of her game, she agreed to appear for free on the cover of an early issue of *BUMPN*. She used her fame and appeal to help promote the magazine and fashions by a young black designer featured in that issue. However, she declined Jason's third marriage proposal, since she was not ready to settle down yet. They mutually agreed to end their engagement, freeing them both to move on and see other people. They continued to see each other occasionally when her career brought her to town. Jason dated many prominent and lesser-known women after he and Delia separated, but he was not involved in another serious relationship during the four years before we began dating.

Jason explained to me early on that while he would always regard Delia as a good friend, he realized that his romantic feelings for her had begun to wane long before the actual breakup. They do not share the same core values. He is a man who firmly believes in serving God and his fellow man. He generously shares his time, talent, and resources to serve others and support various causes. He is determined to be a good provider and role model for his family, and he wants a family very much. Jason sees marriage as a journey two individuals take together, sharing each other's triumphs, trials, and setbacks as they follow their individual paths to success. He wants a wife who is, like he, a Christian and has her own interests and ambition but who will prioritize her marriage and family ahead of material success. Delia is more self-directed and shows limited interest in church and public service. She views marriage and children as things that inhibit her freedom to do whatever she wants to do as an individual. So over time, Jason realized that despite their strong attraction, they were not compatible and could not be happy married to each other. Jason has told me many times that he knew on our first date that I was the woman he had prayed to find. He also shows me in so many ways that he loves me and finds me beautiful, even more so now that my waistline is almost as big as my booty.

I have never felt jealous of Jason's relationship with Delia. I am confident that it was part of his past and that I am at the center of his present and future. I jokingly describe Jason's life in two parts: BC—Before Claudia and AD—After Delia. I'm not bothered by his feelings for anyone he knew BC because I know that his love for me in the present, AD, is stronger than anything that came before. However, I'm not sure that Delia and her friends understand that. At thirty-nine, her modeling career has peaked, and she is working a lot less and being paid less than in years past. Recently, she appeared as a "mom" in a couple of commercials, advertising vitamins in one and a minivan in the other. So she has returned to New York, supposedly to get a doctorate in psychology, modeling just enough to support herself while taking classes. However, I suspect that her decision to return to New York is motivated by the fact that she has done everything that she wanted "to do as an individual" and is now ready to settle down in a marriage, preferably with Jason. I trust Jason and his feelings for me, but that doesn't mean that I am happy to have Delia as a part of our intimate circle of friends. The few times we have interacted, I found her sarcastic, condescending, and untrustworthy. But Jason always defends what I consider to be her inappropriate manner by saying, "That's just Dee. She's doesn't mean any malice, and she's a good friend."

Last night, I saw Delia staring at me several times as Jason and I moved around the room, chatting with as many guests as possible. However, I wasted no attention on her. Two hours and a couple of ginger ales later, I required a pit stop in the ladies' room. It was there, behind a closed stall door, that my suspicions about her were confirmed. A small group entered talking and laughing. *That's Carol's voice*, I thought to myself before hearing her ask, "So, Dee, how is it being back in New York, so close to Jason? I thought that out of all the couples on campus, you and Jason were the one most likely to make it last forever."

Alicia chimed in, "Yeah, and he still looks good, Dee! Does it ever bother you, wondering if you made the right choice to walk away?"

Delia laughed before responding, "It's been a long time, and we've both made choices. You know that I don't believe in looking back.

Besides, if I were still into Jason, I could get him back, but I'm not interested so—"

Carol interrupted her, "I always did admire your confidence, but he seems really happy with Claudia and their 'Baby BUMP.' He has a perpetual smile on his face these days."

Way to go, Carol, I thought, quietly listening, hidden from their view in my stall.

"He's always wanted to be a father, and I know that he's happy about having a son," Delia retorted. "But Jason is too much of a man to be genuinely satisfied with that . . . girl. He would prefer a real woman."

I was not surprised that she revealed her claws. She did not fool anyone with her feeble attempt to hide her insecurity about aging in a youth-driven profession. Still, I was beginning to get angry.

"And you know this, how?" asked a woman with an unfamiliar voice.

"He said as much when we had dinner last week. It was like old times. He asked me to model spring fashions in the March issue of *BUMPN*. I agreed to do it, and we talked about other possible 'collaborations' between us," Delia said, laughing snidely. "It's obvious that he still wants me, but he is excited about that baby."

The strange voice inquired, "Are you saying he's unhappy with her?"

"No, I wouldn't say that he's unhappy but maybe unfulfilled. A man like Jason needs a mature woman who is his emotional equal, one who constantly stimulates his mind, body, and soul. I'm sure she loves him and is giving him what he says he wants, but she doesn't understand him, so she can't really please him."

I became angrier every time Delia spoke, and I had just about reached my limit. But before I could bolt from my hidden place to confront her, Alicia surprisingly came through, sarcastically responding to her friend.

"I'm really surprised," Alicia said. "He seems to have been genuinely pleased, even ecstatic, since he first introduced her to us. I just never thought he was that good of an actor."

"C'mon, Alicia," Carol offered. "I admit they seem downright blissful, but you can't always tell from outside appearances what's going on underneath. How many couples do we know who couldn't keep their hands and eyes off each other one minute then filed for divorce the next? I'm just saying, you never know. This is Dee. She and Jason had something special. Maybe it just never went completely away."

That was the final straw. I flushed the toilet and opened the door to see three surprised faces and Delia's, which had more of a smug look as though she was conveying an insincere "Oops!" The room remained quiet while I approached the sink, washed and dried my hands, and applied a fresh coat of lipstick. As I returned the tube of lipstick to my purse, I looked directly at Delia and said with confidence, "I understand my husband well enough to know that he is so over you. He'll always be your friend, and I'm sure he asked you to appear in *BUMPN* to do you a favor. He has plenty of models more popular than you clamoring to appear in the magazine. I'm appalled that, after all you once were to each other, you accept his invitation to this event for his friends and supporters when you are clearly neither."

All eyes were focused on Delia as I moved toward the door. She shrugged her shoulders, shook her head dismissively, and said, "Whatever," as I left the room.

I returned to Jason's side and continued to smile as we worked the room. I don't know when Delia left. I didn't see her the rest of the night, not that I was looking for her. I was enjoying the positive attention, well wishes, and compliments from everyone else, especially Jason, who held me close to him at all times. Finally, we sat with the clique, talking and laughing for about half an hour after the last of the other guests left around 1:00 a.m. Neither Carol nor Alicia spoke about the earlier incident in the ladies' room. It was obvious that Paula and Janice were clueless about it. We all left together to summon our vehicles just before 2:00 a.m. Jason and I were the last to leave. In the limo, I decided not to tell him what had transpired with Delia and the others earlier. I was tired and didn't feel like talking about it, especially with a third party present. I laid my head on Jason's shoulder, and he put one arm around me, resting the other on Baby BUMP. For most of the ride home, we were both quiet. He laughed a couple of times when he felt the baby kick, and I laughed at his reactions. I was happy to get some rest in the limo and even happier to lie down in my own bed when we got home. Jason fell asleep almost immediately, but as tired as I felt, I only managed a brief restless slumber. Now finally, I'm yawning and feeling drowsy enough to sleep. It's almost 6:00 a.m.

Saturday, November 27, 2004
11:30 a.m.

Jason woke me up around 10:00 a.m. to serve me breakfast in bed. He didn't realize how little sleep I had, and I didn't tell him. I smiled as I saw how delighted he was with his flawless presentation. In the center of the mahogany bed tray sat a china plate with a single poached egg resting atop a lightly toasted slice of twelve-grain bread and a petite medium rare filet mignon surrounded by slices of mushrooms, green pepper, fresh garlic and onions sautéed in olive oil. Slices of fresh fruit in a crystal bowl and a champagne flute filled with apple juice were beside the plate on the right. A silver service wrapped in a white linen napkin and a single red rose in a crystal bud vase were on the left.

"Good morning, my love," he said as he replaced the pillows under my head with a satin-covered foam wedge to support my back when I sat up. "Did you get enough sleep?"

"No, not really, but I'm hungry now, and I can nap later," I said. "Why did you do all of this?"

"I wanted to make you as happy this morning as you made me last night. I know that it was a long evening and you were on your feet for hours. You were amazing with everyone, and you helped me host *BUMPN*'s best event ever. I just want to be sure that you get the rest and relaxation you deserve today."

It was a loving gesture, vintage Jason at his considerate best. My husband is very romantic and often surprises me with royal treatment. Yet I wondered about the timing of this particular surprise. I decided to tell Jason about my brief encounter with Delia and to find out about the dinner she mentioned having with him last week. But I surmised that Jason already knew what had happened and had prepared this surprise to keep me calm and positive during the inevitable discussion he was anticipating about Delia's latest faux pas.

Going straight to the point, I began, "I spoke briefly with Delia last night. Have you talked with her lately?"

Matter-of-factly, Jason responded, "She called me this morning."

"Oh, what did she have to say?" I asked.

"She said that she was afraid that you might have misunderstood something she said and she wanted to apologize if it had upset you." He added, "She hopes that we can all stay friends."

"She has got to be kidding," I said. "There was no misunderstanding. She announced that she was going to appear in the March issue of *BUMPN* because you asked her. She said that you took her to dinner last week and you are hers for the taking if she wants you but she doesn't. She surmised that you are happy with me now because of the baby but I can't really please you for long. It would have been impossible for me to misunderstand those declarations. I don't trust her and could never consider her a friend."

Jason tried to evoke my sympathy, explaining, "Dee is going through a rough patch now. She is insecure and vulnerable. She was trying to save face in front of longtime friends. I'm sure she had no idea that you were in earshot. She asked me if I could feature her in an upcoming issue of *BUMPN*. I agreed to return the favor she did for me appearing for free in one of the early issues. The rest of that was her taking things I said out of context."

"What did you say that she could have taken out of context?" I wanted to know.

"Dee asked at one point if I thought we could ever get back what we had together. I told her that I would always care about her and value our time together but that it is too late to revisit our relationship. I am married to an incredible woman whom I love, and we are expecting our first child. Dee knows how important family is to me. And I stated emphatically that I have no desire to break up my marriage or my family."

I feel no compassion for Delia. Either she was lying and I have no tolerance for liars or she was confused by Jason's explanation. I have no patience for a college graduate who cannot understand what sounds crystal clear to me. "You do realize that I just happened to be the one they didn't see. It could have been anyone, including someone who would have used Delia's words as fodder for tabloid, television, or Internet gossip. Neither of us needs that kind of publicity. She spewed her venom at an event swarming with journalists. It was the worst possible venue for her to discuss our personal business, truthfully or falsely."

Jason acknowledged her indiscretion. "I told her that, and she apologized. Look, she was wrong on several counts. I'm not going to defend her. If you don't want her around us, I won't invite her to anything else we give. I can't promise that Alicia and Carol won't invite her to their gatherings but—"

"I don't care if she's around," I interrupted. "Just don't expect me to ignore her lies and insults. I will call her out if she speaks inappropriately about you, me, or us. I don't like Delia, but she's just not that important to me. What matters more to me are your actions. You are my husband, and I need to trust you."

"Of course, you can trust me. What are you talking about?" Jason queried.

"Really? Why didn't you tell me that you had dinner with Delia last week?" I asked, finally getting to the heart of the problem.

"Because it wasn't important to me," he responded. "It was a business dinner. I don't always tell you when I meet with a colleague or one-time contractor. That's what the dinner was all about: figuring out an appropriate feature for Dee to appear under contract in a single issue of the magazine."

"Delia is not just a one-time contractor," I asserted. "You proposed to her three times during a relationship that lasted ten years."

"But it's over. I don't love her now. At this point, she is a contract model and a friend."

I tried to make him understand. "Even if you thought it was not important to tell me beforehand, after she hit on you during the dinner, you should have told me. I have a right to know if someone we know is trying to undermine our marriage. Last night, I wasn't hurt by her insinuating that you still had feelings for her. I didn't believe her. What hurt me was that you had taken her to dinner and kept it from me. You say the dinner was not important. However, you gave it importance because your secrecy makes me wonder what there was about it that you felt you needed to hide from me. Withholding information is the same as lying. So you lied to me about your dinner with her."

I could tell that Jason was sorry that I was upset. But he didn't apologize because he didn't seem to understand that he had done anything wrong. Because he had not told a lie, he didn't believe that he had lied. He wasn't hiding anything from me. He just didn't think he needed to tell me about every business meeting he had. I wondered for a moment if he was right. Maybe I was making too much of this because of my feelings about Delia. I was about to concede when he made the mistake of saying that he thought my extreme reactions were brought on by the extra hormones from my pregnancy. What? His implication that my feelings were irrational made me furious. Jason realized too late that he had said the wrong thing. He tried to apologize, but I was too upset to hear anything else he had to say. I needed some distance from him while I calmed myself. He understood and went downstairs to read and watch television. However, as I write these words, I realize that I also want to vent to someone who understands my values about honesty and marriage. Who better to understand and advise me than the one who instilled these values in me in the first place? She knows how to maintain love and trust in a marriage. Hers has lasted joyfully for over thirty years. So I'm heading northward twenty-five miles to my parents' home, where I grew up, in Appleberry Hills, New York.

Saturday, November 27, 2004
11:55 p.m.

I can hardly believe all that happened today and how it has turned my whole world upside down. I've been feeling so many emotions all at once: anger, hurt, confusion, and compassion. The result is a cacophony pounding in my head and heart. So I am channeling my professionalism as a reporter to record the facts as objectively and dispassionately as possible. But I probably cannot avoid expressing emotions and biases in the telling, since I am too intimately involved. I drove here against Jason's wishes, but without his objections, to sort through my feelings about honesty in our relationship. Instead, what I encountered has made me question my ways of thinking about so much more than that.

Jason understood my need to relax in a calm, peaceful setting. We agreed that I would spend tonight with my parents and meet him at church in the morning. He smiled and told me to drive safely as he carried my overnight bag and placed it on the backseat of my car. "I love you" was all he said as I turned the key to start the engine.

"I love you too," I responded then pulled out of the driveway.

During the forty-five-minute drive here, I reminisced about my childhood and how I still feel that all is right in my life whenever I come "home." My dad, Claude Reynolds, bought the thirty acres of land as a thirtieth birthday present for my mother, Sarah, in 1977 when I was two and my brother, Claude Jr. (CJ), was one. There was a ten-acre farm with a small orchard of apple trees and cherry trees, strawberry bushes, cabbage and pumpkin patches, a sweet corn field, and a vegetable garden where lettuce, onions, carrots, cucumbers, peppers, and tomatoes grew. The other twenty acres were open hills and grassy areas where cows used to graze. Hank Millsom, the widower farmer who sold the property to my dad, retained five additional acres with his farm house, a barn and stable with two horses, as well as his pet dog, some chickens, and a few pigs. He loved his home and wanted to stay there for the rest of his life, but he had neither the stamina to maintain his land nor the money to hire farmhands to help him. He wanted to see the thirty acres he sold be put to good use and kept beautiful and productive. My dad agreed to hire a couple of workers whom Hank could supervise in maintaining the farmland. He also assured him that the remaining acres would be put to good use.

Dad challenged Mom, who was pursuing her doctorate in education at the time, to use the land to build the ideal educational environment based on a proposal she developed as a candidacy project. There were many obstacles to overcome, which CJ and I were too young at the time to understand. Yet, she persevered and attracted influential supporters and investors who believed in her academic vision and financial plan. Her Appleberry Hills PEACE Academy opened in September 1985, in time for me to enter fifth grade, CJ the fourth grade, and our baby sister, Cara, the first grade. We commuted from our house in New Rochelle Mondays through Fridays until our house on the grounds was completed in 1988. After that, we walked about three hundred yards down the flower-lined path from the back door of our home to the front door of our school. So from the age of thirteen, Appleberry Hills has been the site of my home and school, my haven from stressful situations in the outside world.

Because my mother was responsible for my development at home and in school, the values I learned in both settings were consistent and intertwined. Children of different ethnicities and cultures commuted on private buses from Westchester, Fairfield and other counties to learn together in an environment designed to "*p*romote *e*ducation and *a*ppreciation of *c*ultures and *e*thnicities." We studied and mastered foreign languages and used them on extended educational trips to different parts of the world. More important, we developed lasting friendships as we learned to respect one another's ethnicity and culture while retaining pride in our own heritage. We performed farming chores with Farmer Millsom and our science teachers as part of an enriched science curriculum that literally brought plant and animal science to life and taught us to respect nature and the environment. I remember how much fun we had watching the beautiful pink and white blossoms on the trees in spring being replaced by cherries and apples that we picked and ate in summer and fall. I remember how proud we were to prepare and eat salads made from the vegetables that grew from the seeds we planted and how exciting it was to watch piglets and colts being born and to help care for them as they grew.

What I remember most about my childhood and youth is that I was happy and surrounded by love. My dad loved my mother so much that he bought her all that land to help her fulfill her dream, and my mother loved me and my siblings so much that she built a whole school campus so she could give us the best education and keep us near her all the time. Love, respect, honesty, and excellence were the values stressed at school and at home. We were expected to act and speak with integrity, fairness, and compassion. We were taught to accept responsibility and to strive for excellence. Our teachers and staff exemplified those values, especially my mother, the director. Dr. Sarah Ann Reynolds is loved and admired by students and alumni, parents, faculty, and staff. But I love her more. She is my "she-ro" and my most trusted advisor.

At home, I learned that faith, trust, and love are the cornerstones of the foundation upon which marriages and families are built. I always wondered if any couple in history or in fiction ever loved each other as much as my parents do. Their love filled our home and covered their children like armor, protecting us from whatever negative forces confronted us outside. We were disciplined with love in a culture of expectancy. We were expected to always be honest, loving, respectful, and respectable. When we lied or behaved inappropriately, we had to seriously reflect on our dishonesty or misdeeds in order to explain aloud to ourselves and to the rest of the family why we went astray. We all hated those "sessions" because we felt so ashamed. So as we grew, we learned it was easier to tell the truth and do the right things as much as possible. As adults, we chose careers that reflect the importance of truth in our lives. CJ is an artist who expresses his truth on canvas. Cara promotes truth as an attorney with a consumer advocacy group, representing consumers victimized by fraud or deception in advertising, sales practices and/or product warnings. I investigate and report truth as a television journalist. That is why I wanted to see my mother today. She and Dad instilled these values of love, family, and truth in us. And they've sustained a happy marriage for over thirty years. I trusted her to help me sort through my feelings.

As usual, it only took me forty-five minutes, door to door, to arrive at Chateau Reynolds. Driving slowly around the circular driveway, I looked through the living room and dining room windows along the fifty-foot front of the house before I finally stopped in front of the attached garage. It had been less than forty-eight hours since a dozen of us gathered around the extended dining room table to enjoy a Thanksgiving feast fit for royalty. But everything was back to normal. The fancy linen, sterling silverware, china, and crystal were washed and put away. The leaves were removed from the dining room table. So it was back to its normal length for seating six and only a cornucopia centerpiece was on top of it. I saw the family pictures once again on the baby grand piano in the living room, replacing the sheet music that was there on Thanksgiving when Cara played hymns and holiday songs that we sang together after dinner. I recalled how Mom had tried to teach each of us to play when we were children, but Cara was so much better than CJ and me. CJ much preferred to play drums. I inherited just enough of Mom's singing ability to serve as lead singer. So in our teens, we often entertained our parents and their guests by harmonizing as the Reynolds Three. We didn't have the talents of the Jackson Five, but we had a lot of fun performing back then. We still sing at family gatherings and lead everyone in singing carols at the annual Christmas Eve party.

I couldn't see the kitchen, but I knew it bore no visible signs of all of the extra cooking and serving that had occurred. My mom is the best cook I know, and she makes all of her best dishes for the holidays. Jason and I have not yet finished the leftovers we brought home. We ate the crab-crusted salmon and sautéed baby spinach leaves with the eggs I poached for breakfast Friday morning. Before Jason left for the *BUMPN* affair, we consumed most of the appetizers in our stash: fried and cocktail shrimp, Buffalo wings, deviled eggs, homemade cheese pastries, and Swedish-style turkey meatballs. We haven't yet unwrapped our share of turkey and stuffing, leg of lamb, macaroni and cheese, sweet potato pudding, black-eyed peas, yellow turnips and string beans with almonds. Our plan was to use those items for today's lunch and dinner so I wouldn't have to cook. I guess that's what Jason ate in my absence.

Mom maintains a well-stocked pantry and full-sized freezer, so she is always prepared and delighted to cook for any size group of visitors. She says that if people are willing to drive this far to see her, then she should be willing and able to provide them with a decent meal. Of course, the meals she prepares are so much more than decent. We all took her cooking for granted growing up but now realize how extraordinary even her everyday meals are. I smiled as I thought about how in warm and hot weather, Dad steps up as the master of the grill, barbequing whatever meat Mom marinates in one of her special homemade sauces. Summer is my favorite season, and I love smelling the aroma of well-seasoned meat, poultry, and seafood cooking on the made-to-order oversized grill while I play tennis and dive or slide into the swimming pool. We all love it when there are enough visitors to enjoy a spirited game of volleyball as well.

Turning my key to open the front door, I could hear the sound of the college football game playing on the television in the den. I left the overnight bag by the door in the living room, hoping not to have to explain yet why I was planning to spend a night away from Jason. Dad was pleasantly surprised to see me and immediately rose to give me a kiss, looking behind me to see if Jason had come also.

"How's my firstborn?" he asked after he kissed my cheek.

"I'm fine, Daddy," I said. "Good game?"

"Not really," he replied with a disappointed tone as he sat down in his favorite lounge chair. "It's 27-zip, and it's only the second quarter. I hate runaway games when the teams are so obviously mismatched. How was the event last night?"

"It was great: great crowd, great food, great fun! I even think the baby enjoyed it." I laughed, rubbing my tummy. "He was the center of attention with his daddy pointing to him and patting him all night."

Dad chuckled. He didn't ask why I had come alone, but I knew he wanted to know. Since Jason learned that I was pregnant, he has either driven me or hired a limo to drive me whenever I am traveling more than fifteen to twenty minutes from our home. Not yet ready to discuss the reason for my visit, I changed the subject.

"Where's Mom?" I queried. I had seen her car through the window of the garage as I pulled up. I assumed she was home but I hadn't seen or heard her since I arrived. That was odd because she usually spends Saturday afternoons in the kitchen, making snacks for Dad to nibble while he watches the games, preparing Saturday night dinner, and marinating the roast or preparing the dough for the rolls to be served at Sunday dinner. It felt strange not seeing or smelling the aromas from my mother's culinary masterpieces. There were just two buttered biscuits in a baking pan on top of the stove and some coffee in the percolator. I also wondered why there was one set of breakfast dishes in the sink. My parents almost always dine together, and Mom washes all of the dishes as soon as she and Dad finish a meal.

"She's upstairs," he answered. He looked sad but tried not to show it. That fueled my curiosity and my concern.

I inquired, "Is she all right?" If she was in the master bedroom, she would have seen or heard my car when I arrived, and if everything was all right, she would have come downstairs to greet me. Of course, I should be the one to go to her, but she always comes to greet any of her children when we come to the house.

Dad responded somewhat vaguely, "She got some disturbing news yesterday about an old friend she knew in Michigan, and she's trying to decide what to do about it."

I grew more curious because whenever Mom is sad or upset, Dad comforts her. He holds her, listens to her, and takes care of her. So I wondered why he wasn't with her.

"Is the person a friend of yours as well?"

"No, I knew him, but we were not close. I do owe him a lot though."

"Is that why you seem upset?" I asked, certain that he wasn't telling me all that was going on. I knew that Dad would answer honestly if I posed a direct question.

He thought for a moment then said, "I kept something important about him from your mother a long time ago. I should have told her when it first happened, but I didn't do it then, and I never did. When she heard that he was sick, she also learned what I kept from her."

I was confused and stunned. My dad kept a secret from my mother? Preposterous! They tell each other everything. "Who is this man, and when did this all happen?" I needed him to explain his uncharacteristic behavior.

"He and your mother were . . . together. After they broke up, she and I started dating, and she agreed to marry me a couple of months later. She didn't know all the circumstances regarding the breakup. I knew, but I didn't tell her, and I should have."

"I can't believe that Mom is upset with you about something that happened over thirty years ago. What did she say to you about it?"

"She said last night that she understood, but she has barely spoken to me since then. She's acted pleasant enough, but I know when something's bothering her. The bottom line is we both know how important honesty is to her, and I've had thirty years to tell her the truth. After we got married, I didn't think it mattered, and over time, I didn't think about it at all. But that doesn't change the fact that I broke the promise I made to your mother to never keep secrets from her."

"Mom is probably just upset about her friend being sick. If she had a problem with you, you know she would talk to you about it. Mom always stressed to us how important it is to communicate our feelings honestly and not to hold negative feelings inside." I didn't wait for Dad to respond. I immediately went upstairs to talk to Mom.

Mom was in the master bedroom. The bed was already made, complete with the overstuffed shams and decorative pillows. She was dressed in her habitual Saturday leisure wear, a colorful caftan and jeweled wedge thongs. She was sitting in a lounge chair, looking out of the window overlooking the driveway. I knew she must have seen me drive up and linger in my car a bit before coming into the house. So I was even more surprised than before that she had not come downstairs or called down to greet me. She turned to look at me, and she smiled broadly when she saw me. Still, she was more subdued than usual. She stood as I approached her, and we hugged tightly before she spoke.

"Hi, Claudia," she said warmly. "What's wrong?"

"I'm concerned about you. You didn't come downstairs when I arrived, and Dad said that you received some unsettling news yesterday." I wanted to hear her description of her relationship to the man who was sick, and I wanted to find out if she was upset with Dad.

"No, what's wrong with *you*?" She clarified her previous question, avoiding my probe and taking control of our interchange.

"I'm okay," I replied, "What about you?"

"You are here with an overnight bag and without your husband. Jason hasn't let you drive yourself this far in months, so either he didn't know where you were going or he found out too late to arrange for your transportation. Either way, something is amiss. So what's causing trouble in paradise?" Mom knows me too well, and despite whatever might be bothering her, she is always most concerned about her children.

I realized I would have to talk about my feelings if I was going to get her to talk to me about hers. "It's not *what* that's causing trouble. It's *who*, and the *who* is Delia."

"Now you know that other people can only cause trouble in your marriage if you or Jason gives them the power to do so."

"I know, Mom, but Jason gives her power. No matter what she says or does, he makes excuses for her. He took her out to dinner last week, and he didn't tell me about the dinner or the fact that she hit on him. And he doesn't understand why his secrecy about that is a problem for me. You taught me that withholding information is the same as lying."

Mom seemed taken aback by my memory of her words to me. She thought for a moment and then spoke slowly like a classroom teacher explaining a previously taught lesson that her pupils had misunderstood. "I meant that when a person deliberately withholds the truth in order to create a false impression, it has the same effect as making a false statement." Then she focused directly on my issue with Jason. "Do you think that Jason didn't tell you about the dinner because he wanted to give you a *false* impression of his relationship with Delia? Do you think he was hiding a bourgeoning affair with her or some residual feelings of love?"

"No," I answered confidently without hesitation. "I'm sure that all he wants with her now is friendship. He respects what they had. He still cares about her, and he's grateful to her for things she did for him in the past. But *her* feelings are a different matter. I don't think she loves him, but I think she wants him back or at least wants to think she could get him back if she wanted him."

"Why did he say that he didn't tell you about their dinner?"

"He said that it was just a business dinner. She needed a modeling gig, and he offered to feature her in an upcoming issue of *BUMPN*. He says that he didn't think it was important enough to share it with me."

Mom smiled. "If you believe him, then you are the one who is giving Delia the power to affect your relationship. Her feelings are not important to your marriage. His feelings are the only ones that matter. If you trust his feelings for you and his explanation about the dinner, you need to move on. Jason's a good man, better than most. Don't give

Delia importance or power that she can't get on her own. Don't let her drama hurt you or lead you to hurt Jason."

I was confused. "Are you saying that you think he was right in not telling me about her advances to him?"

"I understand that you feel you had a right to know what she did, and I'm sure, knowing you, that you made your position clear to Jason. Knowing him, I'm sure that he won't make that same mistake again. But I can understand why he didn't want to tell you. I'm not saying he was right not to tell you, but I understand his reasoning. He knows that you don't like Delia already, and if you found out that she came on to him, you'd be justifiably furious with her. That would probably be the final straw for you. Since nothing happened and he set her straight, he just wanted to 'keep the peace' with his wife. There is no doubt that you are much more important to him than she is, and I'm sure that he would cut all ties with her if you asked him to do so. However, he would probably prefer not to have it come to that."

"Well, I did find out about it," I said. "He said he wouldn't invite her to anything else if I asked him not to, but that she would be invited by Alicia and Carol to their events. I told him I was okay being around her, but I will never be her friend. I don't like her, and I don't trust her with good reason. Still, I didn't ask him to end his friendship with her."

Mom challenged me again. "So why are you here away from your husband, and how long do you plan to leave him alone?"

"I just needed a peaceful place to relax and calm down. I'll call him later and go back home tomorrow after church. As always, talking with you helps me clear my head and feel better." I hugged my mother tightly and then suggested, "So maybe I could help you feel better if I knew what is weighing so heavily on you. Dad said that you are upset with him because of something he didn't tell you thirty years ago about a man you used to love. How can you expect me to understand and forgive Jason for not telling me what Delia did last week when you are upset with Dad for not telling you something so long ago?"

Mom bowed her head momentarily. When she looked at me, I saw her eyes were filled with tears, and a single tear was rolling down her right cheek. She shook her head and sighed deeply before she spoke. "I'm not upset with your father. I know why he didn't tell me what he knew about Moody. My feelings were so confused back then that I might have hurt all of us by making bad decisions based on the wrong things.

I had a long complicated history with Moody, and I could never have knowingly hurt him, even if it meant denying my love for your dad. Believing what I did back then, I felt free to follow my heart and marry Claude. It was the best decision I ever made, but I might have handled things differently if I had known everything back then."

I was relieved but puzzled. "Then why aren't you talking to Dad?" I asked.

"Like I said, I was confused, and my life was complicated. I deliberately withheld information from both of them because I wanted them to believe what I needed to believe. In time, I came to believe it myself and forgot the truth. I thought that nobody else knew, but I was wrong. Now I have to tell them, and I'm ashamed. I've just been procrastinating, trying to figure out the best way to tell your father before I fly to Detroit to tell Moody. I feel like such a hypocrite, demanding honesty from everyone in my life when I've told lies and kept secrets of my own."

I could not fathom my mother lying or keeping secrets. Not Sarah Reynolds! What would she have to lie about? Still, I had never seen my mother appear so sad and guilt-ridden. I wished I could reverse roles and comfort her like she always used to comfort me when I felt bad about my mistakes. "Mom, I know you," I offered. "You could never have done anything that would make Dad, or anyone else, turn away from you. Dad loves you so much. He'll understand and forgive you in a second. You're such a good wife, a good mother, a good person, and you hold yourself to impossibly high standards. You need to forgive yourself as easily as you forgive everyone else."

"I know that he'll forgive me," she acknowledged. "But he's going to be hurt, and I never want to hurt him. It's funny. I thought that I was protecting everyone, but now I realize that I should have told the truth back then. The truth will eventually come out, and people will be doubly hurt—first, by whatever you thought would hurt them and second, by the fact that you lied."

"I know that I'm your child," I said, "and just a third party to your marriage, but we've always been friends too. Can you tell me the secret? I just can't bear to see you like this, and I want to try to help."

"Actually," Mom said, looking like she had just experienced an epiphany, "you have a right to know because it concerns you." She sighed. "First, you need to know that I love you more than I love myself.

I always have since the day I knew that you were inside me. That love has grown deeper and stronger through the years as I watched you mature into the magnificent woman that stands before me, filling me with unbelievable joy and pride. Your dad feels the same. He loves you more than you can understand until you are the parent of your grown son. That will never change, no matter what. But the truth is that Moody might be your biological father."

"No! That's impossible!" I exclaimed. I did not, could not, believe that. "I look like you, but I act just like Claude Reynolds. You know it. I know it, and everybody says it all the time. I have more of his personality than CJ or Cara. Dad and I are like two peas from the same pod. There's no way we could be that much alike without being father and daughter."

"I know, baby. But are you two so alike because of genetics or environment? I'm just not sure. I can't be. Back then, I—"

"You did what?" I interrupted. "Cheated on Dad? You wouldn't have done that. You couldn't have. Mom, I don't believe what you're saying." Then desperate to make sense out of her outrageous supposition, I asked, "Did this Moody rape you or something? You keep repeating that it was complicated. Please help me understand what was happening to you."

"No, Moody is a good man. He would never hurt me in any way. He loved me. I loved him too and still do in a way. I owe him so much more than I could every repay. But I fell in love with your dad. I tried to fight it and pretended that it wasn't real, but it grew to be much more than I could deny. I never cheated on Claude, but I did cheat on Moody with him. In order for you to understand everything, we'll need to talk for hours because it's a long story that goes back to my childhood. I'll tell you all of it, but first, I have to talk to your dad. I don't want him to think I'm angry with him because I'm not."

"Okay, but I have a question for you. I know that my dad is my biological father, but if you have doubts, why haven't you ever done a paternity test to find out for sure?"

"Things were happening so fast. Claude had to move to New York right away and wanted me to come with him as his wife. It would be months before I could have a paternity test, and I wanted to marry him right away as much as he wanted to marry me. I told him that I was pregnant, and he assumed that he was the father. I let him believe that he was because I wanted him to be. As time passed, I just accepted that he was, and any initial doubts I had vanished. So I didn't need the test. I didn't tell Moody that I was pregnant and he might be the father because he told me he was glad we never had children and he didn't want one with me. So I didn't want him to be your father. I wanted you to belong to a man who loved you and wanted you as much as I did. But now that I know what happened with Moody, I know that I should have told him the truth then, and I must tell him now."

"But what is the truth? You don't know what it is without a paternity test. You haven't been untruthful, and you don't need to say anything unless Moody is my biological father. If it turns out that Dad is my father, as I know for certain that he is, then you have no reason to feel guilty and no reason to tell either of them what happened more than thirty years ago."

"Maybe I don't have to say anything to Moody, but I have to tell my husband the truth. He needs to know why I've been acting so distant since last night. And we agreed long ago to never keep secrets from each other. He feels guilty about not telling me about his experience with Moody, and he needs to know that he was not the only one who withheld information. That way, we can ease our consciences, forgive each other, and decide together what to do when we get the test results. Don't worry about us, my darling. We love each other and you much too much to let whatever we learn hurt any of us. We are your parents, but if Moody is your father, you two have a right to know each other. He is a good man, and he would be so proud and happy to know that you are his daughter." Without another word, she stood and headed downstairs to talk to Dad. Turning to me, she added, "I know you have questions. I promise to tell you everything after I talk to my husband."

Questions? I thought. *Is she kidding? This is not another news story I'm investigating. This is my life! Everything I think I know about who I am is suddenly being questioned.* This is all so incredulous to me. Mom and Dad have a solid marriage which they say is built on love, faith and honesty. It is hard for me to believe that they both entered into the marriage withholding truths from each other and that they have not revealed those truths until now, seven months after CJ, Cara and I surprised them with the romantic celebration of their thirtieth anniversary.

We arranged for a limo to take them to spend a romantic day while we readied the grounds and ourselves for a beautiful ceremony and reception. After lunch at Yvonne's in New Rochelle, they went to a matinee performance of *A Raisin in the Sun*, starring Sean Combs and Phylicia Rashad, at the Royale Theater. When they returned home around seven, their final surprise was the formal "wedding" with CJ serving as best man, Cara as maid of honor, and me as matron of honor. Mom looked so beautiful in the gown we had bought for her, and Dad was stunning in his tux. Their love was evident in every word, glance, and gesture they exchanged during the renewal of their vows and all through the night. When the last guests left, Dad said this was the best surprise because we gave our mom the wedding she deserved but didn't get the first time. Mom said that she honestly preferred having their wedding at this time because she loves Dad even more than when they eloped and because the children they both love so much were the best attendants they could ever have. After Thanksgiving dinner, just two days ago, they were still beaming as we looked at the picture album and video from that night in April. So it's hard to fathom how the mention of some man whom I have never heard discussed in my life has caused such stress in their marriage. And to make matters even worse, I am supposed to entertain the possibility that my whole existence is a lie and that the mysterious man could be my—I can't even think the word— father. Claude Reynolds is my father. There is no question about that.

I didn't want her to say anything to Dad yet, but I expected her to do it. I was beginning to realize that I knew very little about my parents' lives before they were my parents. Aside from a few childhood pictures and anecdotal information they had told me, most of what I thought I knew about their experiences before I was born was probably what I had imagined to fill in the gaps. However, whatever I don't know about my mother thirty years ago, I do know very well the woman she has become. That woman would have to tell her husband the truth regardless of the test results. She needed to tell him immediately to spare him from any more feelings of self-recrimination for his part in the events of the past and to let him know that she understood and forgave him. I agreed to wait upstairs so that she could speak with him privately in the den. Yet I couldn't help sitting on the stairs, trying desperately to hear their interchange. I rationalized my eavesdropping by considering it my right to know, given my stake in the outcome.

I couldn't hear every word, but I gleaned from the sounds of their voices that my dad was relieved that Mom was not upset with him. He didn't seem to be upset with her either. There were long pauses when I surmised that they were embracing each other. After one such pause, I heard Mom say "Moody" and "DNA Test." Dad sounded agreeable. They moved to the kitchen, where Mom was preparing snacks. I could hear them clearly as they continued to talk there. Dad said that the results of the paternity test would not change how he feels about me. He will always be as much my parent as he is CJ's or Cara's. What took minutes nine months before I was born wouldn't alter the feelings he developed over the nearly thirty years of loving and caring for me ever since. Mom said it was going to take a long time to explain everything to me. Dad offered to help if she wanted him at any point. She said that she might come for him later but wanted to start the conversation with me alone. She left him a snack and said we'd take a break to make dinner for him. She knew my baby and I would be hungry by then too. I returned to the master bedroom and waited there for her. She brought up a tray with two sandwiches made with leftover Thanksgiving turkey, microwave popcorn, and a pitcher of orange and cranberry juice mixed. She filled our glasses with the juice and took a sip of hers before she began.

For the next six hours, I listened intently to everything she said. She began to tell me all about her years in Parkersville, Michigan, a suburban company town near Detroit. That was where she lived her first twenty-seven years before she married my dad and moved with him to New York. I was anxious to hear about her relationship with Moody, but she started by recounting incidents from her life long before the circumstances that led to her doubts about my paternity. Despite my desire to get to the facts about that issue, I respected her need to tell me all the things that she wanted to get off her chest. Besides, I was coming to realize how very little I knew about my mother's past. I know from experience that knowing about one's past is crucial to understanding their behavior. So I listened intently, limiting my comments and asking only a few questions, as she told me her story in her way. This is what she said.

The Oral History Recounted by My Mother
Sarah Anne Morgan Reynolds
(April 1952–June 1963)

I have always related so well to Countee Cullen's poem, "Incident," published in 1925. It tells of one of his earliest experiences with prejudice and the profound effect it had on him. He was a happy eight-year-old enjoying an extended stay in Baltimore, Maryland. One day, he noticed a white boy about his age looking at him. When he responded with a friendly smile, the white boy stuck out his tongue and called him a nigger. Cullen reflects on how the incident affected him, relating,

> I saw the whole of Baltimore
> From May until December;
> Of all the things that happened there
> That's all that I remember.

My recollections of my childhood are a lot like that. I know that I was happy the first ten years of my life. I have general memories of growing up in Parkersville. I recall the joys of family celebrations and traveling around the state, across the U.S., and abroad. I remember feeling loved and protected by my parents and my maternal grandparents who lived just two blocks away. But my most vivid memories are of their funerals and the increasing sense of loss, abandonment, and anger I felt after each one. For years, my sleep was haunted by dreams of those funerals. Even now, I remember them all in great detail like they happened yesterday. Until last night, they were what I remembered most about my youth. But since then, I have been remembering a lot more, especially about the one person who was always there for me, through all of their funerals and for years afterward. That was Virgil Moody. Before my sixteenth birthday, my parents and grandparents were all gone, and I turned to Moody. He did all I asked of him and asked for so little in return.

I was five years old when I attended my first wake and funeral. They were for my great-grandmother Priscilla, whom I called Grannie. She lived two blocks away from me and my parents with my mother's parents, Bea and Papaw to me. Grannie was Bea's mother, and she had come to live with her after she became blind and left her home in Meridian, Mississippi. I was very close to Grannie and enjoyed the stories she told me about her parents and about living in Mississippi. Before she died, she asked me to remember the stories she told me about my heritage and to use them as lessons about life as I grew older. Grannie was a faithful Pentecostal, what some folks called Holy Rollers, and she used to say how much she looked forward to going to be with Jesus and her parents in heaven. When she died, I was happy for her and imagined her being on her way to a big welcoming party in heaven. At her wake, she looked so beautiful in her exquisite silk and lace peignoir. I was surprised by how cold she felt when I kissed her cheek and stroked her hand, but it didn't frighten me. That night, I could hardly sleep, excited because I thought that I would see her rise up to heaven the next day. Nobody knew that I was expecting to witness her ascension. Everyone thought I understood that it was a spiritual journey, not a physical one. So I was not prepared for what would take place the next morning.

At the church, I sat in the front pew between Mommie and Daddy and with Bea, Papaw, Grannie's other living children and the granddaughter she raised, whom I called Aunt June. Grannie's open casket was just a few feet in front of me. My joyful heart sank when the coffin was closed at the start of the service. I was horrified to see Grannie locked inside a metal box with no holes in it. When I yelled, "No!" and began to cry uncontrollably, Mommie kissed me and Daddy held me close to his chest. They thought that I was starting to miss my beloved great-grandmother. They didn't realize that I didn't really understand death until that moment. I had learned in Sunday School that the spirit lives after the body dies, but I had never thought about what happened to the body when it died. My exclamation and tears were motivated by fear, the fear that this horrible treatment of Grannie would someday be inflicted on Bea, Papaw, Mommie, Daddy, and, eventually, me. I was too frightened to pay attention to the service. In fact, I continued to cry quietly until I fell asleep in Daddy's arms.

After the church service, I walked with my family behind the casket. I was relieved when I learned that we were riding in the limousine to the cemetery. I thought that meant that they were going to open the casket to free Grannie so she could rise up and fly to Jesus. Yet once again, my hopes were dashed when instead of opening the casket, it remained closed, and it was lowered into the bottom half of a concrete vault six feet below the surface of the ground. As Reverend Gibson prayed and read scriptures, family and friends threw rose petals on top of the casket.

My fear and confusion were fueled when Bea's elder sister, Pearl, became hysterical, screaming, "No, Mama, no! Don't leave me. I want to be with you." Pearl's husband, George, and her brothers, Genie and Billy, grabbed her to keep her from jumping on top of the casket. Reverend Gibson and others looked on in shock. Bea looked angry.

"Let her go," she said firmly to her brothers. They turned to look at her, and she repeated resolutely, "Let her go!"

As Genie and Billy complied and stepped away from Pearl, Pearl backed away from the open grave, holding on tightly to George. She looked at Bea then lowered her face. She returned quietly to sit in the folded wooden chair next to Bea's eldest sister, Birdie. Reverend Gibson concluded his remarks. Then the top of the concrete vault was lowered, encasing the casket. I was bewildered, grief-stricken, and terrified, seeing Grannie's body trapped inside a bronze box that was enclosed in a cement one. Jesus' body was placed in the tomb sealed with just one heavy stone. So I understood how He could get out and go up to His father, God. Grannie wanted to go there too, but it seemed that everyone who said they loved her had conspired to make that impossible by locking her inside two heavy boxes and preparing to cover them with all the mound of dirt next to the hole she was in. Once again, I cried, not quietly that time. When the graveside service ended and people started to return to their cars, I pulled away from Daddy. I didn't want to leave Grannie alone, locked up, and buried there. I didn't want to jump in the grave, but I wanted to stay beside it for a while. Mommie tried to comfort me, and Daddy picked me up and carried me back to the limousine waiting to take us back to Allen AME Church, where the women's club would be serving a meal they had prepared for the family and mourners.

I never spoke about my true feelings that day. For the next few weeks, whenever I went to bed at night, I would pull the covers over my closed eyes, lie perfectly still, and hold my breath as long as I could, trying to imagine what it felt like to be dead. Eventually, I decided that it would be a long time before anyone else in my family would get old and die. How wrong I was! I still had four funerals ahead of me over the next ten years. I was never again as frightened as I was at Grannie's. But each one made me sadder and angrier than the one before it.

****

I met Moody in November 1955 when I was eight years old. He was our paper boy. Back then, our daily newspapers were delivered by teenage boys who rode bicycles and threw the papers at our front door Sundays through Fridays. Every Saturday, they rang the front doorbells of all of their customers to hand-deliver the papers and to receive the weekly payments for their services. Both my parents' and my grandparents' houses were on Moody's route. Usually, Mommie or Daddy answered the door to pay Moody at our house. But Daddy's health had been deteriorating over the past two years, and it was difficult for him to walk without assistance. Mommie had just started singing professionally on Friday nights, and she was sleeping late on Saturday mornings when Moody came to collect. The first time I paid him, he asked me my name. I told him that I was Sarah Ann Morgan. He laughed and said, "Oh, S-A-M—Sam." I corrected him, but he repeated it. I said that Sam was a boy's name, and I was not a boy. He said that was the point: I was a very cute little girl, who would probably grow up to be as pretty as my mother. So he told me I didn't need a pretty name. I had pretty eyes, pretty hair, a pretty nose, and a pretty mouth. I had enough pretty things about me. He told me unattractive girls needed pretty names so that they could have something pretty about them, but pretty girls could be called anything. I told him that what he said made no sense and I did not like him. Once again, I told him my name was Sarah, and I slammed the door in his face. That became our pattern. Every Saturday, I would give him his money, and he would say, "Thanks, Sam." Then I would scowl at him and slam the door.

Mommie took a leave from teaching to go on tour promoting her first hit record in January 1957. So Daddy and I were alone much of the time. He became progressively weaker. When Mommie was away, she paid for a home health attendant. He came to bathe and dress Daddy every morning. He fed him and helped him get around during the day, and he put him in the bed before he left in the evening. I made coffee for Daddy and admitted the attendant before I went to school in the morning. Bea came over every day before I returned from school. She cooked dinner and ate with us. In the evening, when the attendant left, he took her home. Then, I entertained Daddy when I practiced playing piano, singing, and reciting pieces for church and school programs. Before I went to bed, I put cookies and milk by his bedside. I never resented caring for him because I loved him so much. Even when he became too weak to get out of bed, he made me feel safe and loved. He told me wonderful stories about his life, and we played cards and board games. I was always happiest when Mommie was home, but when she was away, I had fun being with Daddy right up to the end.

November 3, 1957, four months after I turned ten, Daddy died. I attended my second funeral four days later. Daddy was in the hospital almost three weeks before he died. It was ironic to me that I was capable of seeing and helping care for him at home but was deemed too young to be allowed to see him in the hospital. Mommie was out of town when Daddy was admitted to the hospital. When she returned, she spent every waking hour there with him until he died. So I stayed with Bea and Papaw. When Moody came by to collect his payment from Bea, he tried to make me laugh and always asked if there was anything he could do to be helpful. Sometimes, Bea asked him to take the garbage out to the alley or rake the leaves. She offered to pay him, but he wouldn't accept any money. After he left, Bea and I would read her paper then watch television while Papaw was visiting Daddy in the hospital.

A few hours before Daddy died, Mommie persuaded the doctors to let me see him. I only spent a few minutes with him. I could tell that he was in pain and really tired, but he kept smiling, trying not to let me know how bad he was feeling. I told him that he should try to nap and I'd come back after he woke up. He told me to get Mommie so we could both kiss him before he went to sleep. When we both returned, he smiled, and we all said, "I love you." Then he closed his eyes and was asleep in less than a minute. Bea and Papaw took me to the hospital cafeteria, and Mommie stayed by his bed until he died peacefully an hour later.

There were more people at Daddy's funeral than at Grannie's, and I remember the details of the service much better. The entire congregation of Allen AME came. So did some of his friends from the Ford factory and some of Mommie's friends from the schools where she used to teach and from Atlantic Records. Daddy's only living relative was there, his elder sister, Sadie. Rev. Hardeman preached an uplifting eulogy based on Daddy's favorite scripture, John 3:16. The choir sang "Precious Lord, Take My Hand" and "The Last Mile of the Way." The church served a wonderful repast in the banquet hall after we returned from the cemetery. Throughout the day, Mommie mourned with quiet dignity. Like her mother, Bea, she didn't believe in public displays of hysteria. She didn't need to put on a show for other people to try to judge how much she loved her husband. He knew and God knew that she was in deep despair. And she knew that God would comfort her and take wonderful care of Daddy, his faithful servant. She held me close throughout the services at the church and at the gravesite. I cried as much at Daddy's funeral services as I did at Grannie's, but I didn't cry myself to sleep that time. By then, I understood about the eternal life of the spirit, and I was not afraid for Daddy's body to be closed in the coffin and buried in the ground. The tears I cried were because I missed him and felt a profound sense of loss.

I was sad about losing Daddy and about how devastated Mommie was. Despite her desire to stay strong in front of everyone, especially me, I knew how miserable she was. I could hear her cry herself to sleep nightly for the next few weeks. She called Daddy's name, Alvin, as she wept. When I came to her, I saw her holding Daddy's pillow in her arms. She set it aside to hold me, and we fell asleep together. I can still remember vividly the warmth of her arms around me and the moistness of Daddy's tear-soaked pillow beneath my head. We mourned together and comforted each other until Christmas when she had to leave to perform at some holiday shows out of town. We continued to grieve separately.

When Mommie left that time, I moved in permanently with Bea and Papaw. Moody was their paper boy also, so I continued to see him weekly. He had stopped teasing me after Daddy went into the hospital, and he was really nice to me after Daddy died. I loved my grandparents very much, but I didn't really want to live with them. Papaw was very strict and treated me like a little girl. I was more comfortable talking to Bea. She understood that I was used to being responsible for Daddy and myself. So I was more mature than most girls my age. I loved my grandparents, but I missed Mommie, and I missed the fun I had living in our home with Daddy.

＊＊＊＊＊＊＊＊＊＊＊

For the next three years, I only stayed with Mommie twice a year. We were together in Mommie's house the week leading into Christmas, and we vacationed together away from Parkersville for about a month during the summer. We traveled to locations where Mommie was performing. We spent time in Idlewild, Michigan, with my godmother

Josie and her niece and nephew. Mommie told me she didn't want to spend a lot of time in our house in Parkersville because she missed Daddy. But I heard enough of the "discussions" she had with Papaw to know that she had a difficult relationship with her father, and poor Bea was caught in the middle. Mommie and I were happier together away from them. We had so much fun. Then she would leave and be gone for half a year, and I would miss her terribly.

Once I settled in, life was okay for me with Bea and Papaw in their home. I knew that they loved me, and we had fun together doing some of the same things that I had done with Mommie and Daddy. We played Monopoly, Backgammon, Scrabble, Go to the Head of the Class, and Bea's favorite card game, Gin Rummy. Bea and I cooked and sewed together; I always preferred cooking to sewing. In fact, I loved cooking. It was almost like playing because it was so much fun. That's why I wanted such a spacious kitchen in this house. However, sewing was more like work than fun, and I wasn't very good at it. That's why I never bought a sewing machine. (*She and I both laughed as I mentioned that she doesn't even have a sewing kit. She sends clothes to a tailor for the simplest repairs, like replacing a button or hemming.*)

I was a straight-A student, but I hated junior high school. I had been skipped—double promoted—enough times to have me in grades and classes where the other students were two years older than I was. That was one reason I found it challenging to make friends. The kids my age were still attending the elementary school. The kids at my school made fun of my clothes and my lack of social savvy. The dresses I wore to school were beautifully made by Bea, who perfectly copied clothes in the children's departments at Saks Fifth Avenue and J. L. Hudson Co. However, Papaw was very insistent that I dress appropriately for my age. Bea tried to tell him that I was getting too old for dresses with full skirts and sashes, but he did not want me to wear straight skirts and sweaters or other teen styles. The problem was that the other girls at school were twelve to fifteen, and they dressed more like they were fourteen to seventeen. I was ten, dressing more like I was eight. I was teased constantly about looking like a baby. My classmates were into boys and parties where they danced in dark basements, preferably ones with one or more poles in the rooms. I wasn't allowed to go to house parties with boys. But that was okay with me because I would rather be at home, setting my three-foot-tall doll's hair with water and rollers. The girls in my classes were *Growing Up and Liking It*, just like that paperback guide to female puberty said, and I didn't even know what that meant or what a "monthly visitor" was. Once, I naïvely said in a group that my aunt June was a monthly visitor at my grandparents' home. The other girls laughed and said I had "book smarts" but no "life smarts." They called me Childie or Superbaby, referring to the fact that Papaw was the school superintendent. That was what they said to my face. Behind my back, they said meaner things about me and my mother. I knew that they were just echoing what their mothers were saying in their homes. They supposed that Mommie never really loved my father or me. They said that's why she ran off the first chance she got. They also said that she had to give me to Bea and Papaw because Papaw was going to have the courts declare her unfit for abandoning me. They assumed she was living fast and loose, traveling all over the world with her "man"-ager who had probably been her lover since before Daddy died.

Nobody ever said these things aloud when I was around, but they whispered and sneered when I walked through the halls. Bea told me that a lot of people were jealous of Papaw's influence in the town, Mommie's success, and my academic achievements. So they were looking for ways to tear down our reputations. I held my head high and stared back at them but said nothing. They thought I kept to myself because I was stuck-up and thought I was better than they were. The truth was that I didn't trust any of them. I was afraid that they only wanted to get close to me to get "dirt" on my family that they could use for gossip. I knew that they were wrong about Mommie. I knew that that she loved Daddy. I heard her tell Godmother Josie that her manager, T. Bone, asked her many times to give him a chance with her but she always turned him down. She didn't want to be with any other man because she loved Daddy, and I knew she loved me, too. She made long-distance calls to me from every town. She wrote long letters to me at least once a week and sent me lots of presents and money to buy whatever I wanted. Still, I would rather have had her with me all the time. I prayed that God would let me grow up and marry a man who loved me as much as Daddy loved Mommy. I promised God that if he granted me that, then I would love my husband back just as much and I would choose a career that would allow me to always stay close to him and our children.

I tried to hide my negative feelings about the kids at school from Bea and Papaw. The only one I told was Moody. After Daddy died,

Moody said that he was going to be my big brother, since I didn't have one. Before Mommie left, he came by the house as often as he could to see if he could help us with anything around the house. He helped us pack when Mommie left and I moved in with Bea and Papaw. I started talking to him about my feelings about school and people. He liked Mommie, and he didn't judge her. He thought her records were really cool and that she looked superhot on television and on her album cover. I knew that he must have talked to some of the kids at my school because they started being nicer to me. They still weren't my friends, but they stopped making fun of me and laughing at my naïveté. Moody stopped being our paper boy in the summer of 1958 when he turned sixteen and got his driver's license and a used car. But he still came by weekly to help Bea and Papaw with heavy work around the house. He mowed the lawns and raked the leaves at their house and at Mommie's. He helped Bea take down all the curtains to wash them twice a year and hung them up for her again when they were clean. He went with Papaw to buy the Christmas trees and set them up in the living rooms of both houses. And he did other jobs throughout the year. We always talked when he came to the house, and I helped him when he worked outside at Mommie's house. He really was like the big brother I wished I had. He had become my friend, my confidant, and my protector.

I was twelve when I started high school in 1959. Moody was a senior, and he told everybody that I was his little sister by choice, not by chance. So he said that he would consider it a huge favor if they looked out for me when he wasn't around. He was very popular because he was a big-time football player. All the boys in town looked up to him, and the girls all had crushes on him. So they were nice to me to score points with him. I knew they didn't necessarily like me, and I didn't trust them, but I did relay messages to Moody when they asked me. I teased him about his groupies who were using me to get invited to parties with him and his three friends who were collectively known as the Fabulous Four. They were the stars on the Parkersville High School Panthers Varsity Football Team from 1957 to 1960.

The Fab Four consisted of Oliver Horne (Ollie), the precision-throwing quarterback; Leonard Mills (Lenny), the big and powerful noseguard who served as defensive captain; Robert Baker (Bobby), the fullback on the most protective line in the league; and Moody, the sure-footed and sticky-fingered wide receiver. In the fall of 1959, their senior year, they carried the Panthers all the way to the state finals. It was the first time such a small high school from such a small town played for the state championship. And it was the last time that the Fab Four would be playing together on the same team. All of them had clenched football scholarships. Bobby and Moody were scheduled to be Tigers at Grambling University, while Lenny was looking forward to being a Nittany Lion at Penn State, and Ollie was heading to Michigan State, hoping to follow in the footsteps of former MSU Spartan, Willie Thrower, the first African American to quarterback a Big Ten college team and the first to play as an NFL quarterback when he threw for the Chicago Bears in 1953.

Busloads of fans traveled from Parkersville to East Lansing to see the game that December. With only one and a half minutes left to play, the Panthers were trailing 17-21 points. But they had the ball and enough time left to score another touchdown. Ollie threw a thirty-yard pass to Moody, who was running along the edge of the field a little past the fifteen-yard line. The pass was high, but Moody jumped almost two feet into the air and caught it. Before he landed in bounds, he was hit from behind by the first of four of the biggest defensive players any of us had ever seen. As he did a complete flip and tumbled to the ground bottom down and legs up, the other three caught up and piled on top of him in quick succession, coming from different angles. But Moody held on to the ball. Flags were thrown by the referees, but Parkersville declined the penalty, accepting the completed pass and great field position. We were so excited because we just knew that the Panthers were going to bring the championship trophy home to Parkersville. We all cheered wildly for Moody until we realized that he was not getting up. Then the mood changed quickly. His mother was standing, gasping, and crying. I started crying too. Everyone went from thrilled to somber as he was carried off the field. He was waving and even trying to smile, but it was obvious that he was really hurt. The Panthers scored the touchdown, but with only a minute left to play, the Grizzlies managed to counter with another touchdown to win 28-24. We were all still proud of our team though. It was the first time our town could celebrate having the number-two-ranked team in the state with a perfect record going into that championship game. We were much less upset about losing the championship than we were to learn that Moody's football days were over. He had fractures in his pelvic bone and coccyx vertebra, and his right tibia was broken in two places.

Moody and the rest of the Fab Four received trophies at the awards dinner for the Parkersville High Class of 1960. It was hard for him, knowing that he was not going on to play in college like the others. But he was genuinely happy for them, and they all stayed close through the years. After graduation, Papaw interceded on Moody's behalf with Mr. Parker, who owned most of the businesses in the town started by and named for his family. Mr. Parker offered to pay Moody's tuition at Wayne State University in Detroit. But Moody was not excited about going to college. He had been excited about continuing to play football with hopes of maybe going professional. He was willing to keep up his grades to stay eligible to play. He wasn't enthusiastic or motivated about studying just for the sake of learning or pursuing a different profession. So Moody thanked Papaw and Mr. Parker but decided to go to work instead. Mr. Parker gave him a job as assistant manager for coordinated custodial services at his plant and company-owned stores in town. Even after Moody started working full time in September, he continued to help out at our house and Mommie's. He came by Saturday mornings to drive Bea and me to a farmers' market in Detroit. Papaw said he didn't like to drive in the city because there were too many bad drivers there, but that wasn't the real reason.

The day before Thanksgiving 1960, a student messenger brought a note to my biology teacher from the principal, summoning me to his office. When I arrived there, a policewoman told me that my grandparents had been in an automobile accident, and she was there to take me to the hospital to see them. Moody called Mommie at the hotel where she was staying while she was performing in Chicago. She flew home on the next flight available, leaving T. Bone to cancel her scheduled appearances for the weekend. The policewoman was careful not to tell me how my grandparents were doing. She said only that they were alive. When we arrived at the hospital, Papaw was in the emergency room being treated for minor cuts and bruises. He had been given an oral pain killer and was waiting for results of tests and X-rays. Bea was not there. I was afraid of the worst, but Papaw told me that she was in surgery. A drunk driver ran a red light and hit the passenger side of their car as they proceeded through an intersection. Bea had been pinned in her seat by the mangled door and had remained unconscious since the impact. She had a concussion and had sustained serious cuts and internal injuries. Papaw and I held each other while we waited for the surgeon to complete his work and come to speak with us. They told us that the surgery would probably last at least two hours, but we didn't want to leave the waiting area, so we sat there quietly praying. Less than an hour later, the surgeon came. They were able to stop the bleeding from the cuts, but he was sorry that they could not repair the damage to her internal organs. Unfortunately, she was not going to recover and probably had only hours to live. We were devastated. Papaw and I were holding each other tightly. He held back his tears, but mine were flowing.

The surgeon gave us a moment to process the tragic news. Then he told us that during the surgery, they discovered that she had cancer throughout her digestive tract. They could not reach her organs because the cancer was blocking them from view. He explained that the cancer had not shown up on the X-rays because the cells were not in the form of tumors but rather had manifested as fine interlocking hair-like strings that resembled the roots of a young tree. The surgeons could not remove the cancer cells because they were tangled around every organ from her esophagus to her large intestine, squeezing them and keeping them from functioning properly. He told us that the cancer must have been growing in her body for years to have spread so extensively and that she had to have been experiencing great physical pain for months. If there had been no accident, she would likely have been unable to handle the pain much longer and would have died within a couple of months at best. The injuries she sustained in the accident probably saved her from prolonged suffering. Papaw and I were both in shock. Bea had never let on that she was in pain. She appeared to be in perfect health. We asked if she would regain consciousness. He said that she would wake up from the anesthesia soon and be alert for a while but that she would be sedated when the pain became too much for her to bear.

Moody met Mommie at the airport and brought her to the hospital. She was crying when I first saw her. She talked with the doctors and nurses but said nothing to Papaw as she sat at Bea's bedside across from him. They were both watching Bea as she regained consciousness. I was waiting outside the room with Moody, who was trying in vain to comfort me. Mommie came out to tell us that Bea was awake and wanted to speak with Papaw alone. In just a few minutes, Papaw came to say that

Bea wanted to speak to Mommie. Finally, Bea asked Mommie to bring me to her so that she could speak to me alone. Bea was the strongest woman I have ever known. She spoke with authority, and regardless of what she was saying, her voice commanded attention and respect. Even as I saw her lying in her deathbed and heard her soft whispery voice, I felt that each of her requests was a mandate that I had to follow.

She asked me to always remember that she loved me and that she would always be near me, watching over me. She told me that my grandfather and my mother also loved me and that they loved each other but they were both stubborn and angry with each other a lot. She told me she had tried to shield me from their anger, which was based on things that happened long before I was born. She had tried not to take sides, and she implored me to try not to do so either. They had both made mistakes as she had and as I was bound to do. But their biggest mistake was failing to forgive each other. She wanted me to try to help them use their shared grief and their love for me to find a way to forgive each other and move on together in peace. Finally, she asked me to always be true to God and to myself, to love deeply and unconditionally as Jesus loves us, to forgive myself and others as Jesus taught us to do, and to be happy for that is how God wants us to be. She said that she was not afraid to die because she knew that it was not the end but rather the beginning of eternal life, free from the constraints of an ailing body and of time and space. Then she stopped and looked past me as though someone else had entered the room. I turned around but saw no one. Then she smiled and spoke to her visitor who was invisible to me. "Oh, Bus, I knew you'd come." Then she looked at me once again, still smiling, and reached for my hand. She held it tightly, and looking at the ceiling, she said, "God, have mercy on my soul." She closed her eyes and exhaled as her head dropped into the pillow. Her life on earth was over, and she was on her way home to God. I called Mommie and Papaw, and the doctor came when he heard Mommie scream.

Moody drove us all home from the hospital. Nobody spoke at first. Papaw sat in the front next to Moody. He stared out of the window humming "Just a Closer Walk with Thee." In the backseat, Mommie was crying and hugging me tightly. I finally asked if they knew who Bus was. Papaw told me that he was Bea's elder brother who had died as a young man more than forty-five years earlier. When I told them what had happened in Bea's room, Mommie said that Bea believed that God sent an angel from heaven to guide the soul of a believer on its journey from its body on earth to its place in God's kingdom. Sometimes the angel came days before the scheduled departure; other times, the angel might not come until moments before. Bea believed that the angel would be a loved one: a parent, a sibling, a spouse, or a dear friend, someone who would assuage fear and bring peace and joy to the traveling spirit. Papaw and Mommie agreed that Bus would be the perfect angel to come for Bea because they were so very close growing up and she had been devastated and terrified when he died in front of her when she was a teen. For the rest of Bea's life, she had spoken of him with love. Whenever she felt overwhelmed with sadness, fear, or anger, she longed for Bus to calm and comfort her. Mommie smiled when she was telling me about Bea and Bus, but then she began to cry again. She was so sad. But once we came home, her mood changed. She wasn't sad; she was mad. She told me to pack an overnight bag because we were going home. I begged her to stay at her parents' home for the night so that the three of us could be together. I didn't want any of us to be alone, not that night. Reluctantly, she agreed to stay there just for one night, but she said that we would go to our home the next day.

Mommie put me to bed, but I couldn't go to sleep. I was thinking about all Bea said to me just before she died. And besides that, it was too noisy for me to sleep. Even with my door closed, I could hear Mommie arguing with Papaw in the living room. I got up and listened intently at the door, hoping to learn why Mommie and Papaw needed to forgive each other. I thought that would help me figure out how to reach them and bring them together like Bea told me to do. Much of what they said to each other didn't make sense to me. Mommie said Papaw murdered Bea, and I knew he wouldn't do that. Papaw called Mommie a liar. They yelled a lot and spoke about things I didn't understand, some things that happened before I was born. Mommie said she couldn't stay under the same roof with him and she was taking me home with her the next day. They argued about me. Papaw said Mommie gave me to him and Bea. Mommie said she wanted me back.

They said more, but I stopped listening after that. I had heard enough to know that my mother loved me and wanted me with her. Bea had always told me that Mommie wanted to be with me all the time but she couldn't because her work kept her traveling. But everyone else, including Papaw, had insinuated that she left me with them because her work was more important to her than I was. I remember crying myself to sleep that night filled with emotions: profound sadness at losing Bea, overwhelming concern about helping Mommie and Papaw find the love Bea said was buried beneath their anger, and exceeding joy at the prospect of living with my mother again soon.

When we woke up in the morning, it was Thanksgiving Day. I was surprised to see Mommie and Papaw both smiling and acting so cooperatively. Mommie told me that they were amused by the fact that, true to form, Bea made sure to leave them a complete meal before she left. The Thanksgiving turkey was already stuffed and ready to go into the oven, along with the macaroni and cheese and sweet potato pudding. The collard greens were cleaned and cut in seasoned water with chunks of salt pork. The deviled eggs, crackers, and tuna salad were already on the hors d'oeuvres trays in the refrigerator. Bea's perfect pound cake was on the cake platter covered with aluminum foil, and her delicious homemade vanilla ice cream was in the freezer. My aunt June (actually Mom's first cousin) was already on her way to the house. They knew that she would handle the baking of Bea's dishes and she was bringing whole cloves to finish preparing the ham. June arrived as we were finishing breakfast, which Mommie prepared. Moody came by later and agreed to drive us to Stinson Funeral Home and Allen AME the next morning to make all of the arrangements. Other people brought food to the house for the next several days, but Mommie, Papaw, and I preferred eating Bea's great cooking for the last time.

Mommie and Papaw continued to act in one accord as they planned the activities surrounding Bea's burial. They were both determined to give Bea the very best funeral because they agreed that she was deserving of a home-going celebration befitting such a wonderful Christian woman. Mommie said it was the last event she would be able to plan for her mother, so it had to be perfect, and Papaw felt the same way about planning a perfect memorial for his wife. It made me so happy to see them working together, and I knew that Bea was pleased looking down from her new enlightened vantage point. Papaw left the choice of Bea's outfit and the floral arrangements to Mommie, and they agreed on all of the other decisions regarding the casket, burial plot, cement vault, and the program for the service. Mommie chose Bea's peach-colored lace dress and fitted jacket with pearl and rhinestone beads on the lapels and a large pearl fastener at the waist. Bea had just made it for the mayoral inaugural ball scheduled for January when Papaw's protégé, Kenneth Tanner, would be celebrating the beginning of his term as the sixth mayor of Parkersville. Papaw would be honored at the ball for his service as the town's first mayor. Mommie ordered a white orchid to be placed on the left side of Bea's jacket just above her heart. She also ordered a blanket of white roses to be placed on the casket. Papaw selected two of Bea's favorite hymns for the choir to sing at the funeral service, "Since I Met Jesus" and "Peace in the Valley." He and Mommie agreed to accept a request from a soloist from Mt. Zion Church in Battle Creek, Michigan, to sing "I've Done My Work." And my voice teacher, Bettye Wright, sang "The Angels Keep Watching over Me." They decided that the scripture selections should be Psalm 23 and 1 Corinthians 13:1–13.

Bea's funeral, the Monday after Thanksgiving, was the largest one ever seen in Parkersville, as well as one of the most moving. She was an inspiration, role model, and mentor to so many people in the community. She had taught about half the women in town to sew between classes in the high school and smaller ones in her home. She had cooked or baked for so many people when they were sick or shut-in and had made bridal gowns and outfits for women in Parkersville and all around Southern Michigan. The family hour and wake were held at the town hall because Papaw knew that Allen AME, our church, would not accommodate all of the members of the Michigan Conference AME Lay Organization, who traveled from around the state to support Papaw, and Bea's large family from Mississippi and Chicago. So many people wanted to give tributes to her that Reverend Hardeman had to limit everyone to two minutes. Of course, nobody paid any attention to that, and at least a dozen people were disappointed because we ran out of time before they got to speak. Reverend Hardeman allowed three of them to be added to the program of the funeral service. He could only allow three more speakers because Mommie did not want the service to last longer than an hour and there were already six people scheduled to bring "expressions," including two presiding elders and the bishop of the Fourth District. The others who wanted to speak were advised to address the family privately at the repast served at the town hall after their return from the cemetery.

After the service, the caravan to the cemetery was so long that two pairs of motorcycle police escorts were required, along with police stationed at key intersections along the route to keep other cars from interrupting the procession. Bea was buried in Detroit Memorial Park, the first black-owned and operated cemetery in Michigan. Papaw purchased two adjacent plots so that he could be buried next to Bea when his time came. Mommie had done the same when Daddy died. Bea and Papaw's plots were in the same section of the cemetery, so I used to put flowers on all four graves when I visited there many times as an adult. I always put flowers on Grannie's grave as well. Her body had been buried in a different section of the cemetery about three-quarters of a mile away from the others.

Mommie and Papaw had remained cordial for the five days from Thanksgiving until the last guest left the house Monday night. Then I felt the warmth they had shared begin to cool. Mommie told me to go upstairs to gather whatever I needed to take home that night. I heard Papaw ask how soon Mommie would be leaving and she said the next day. He asked if she'd be back for Christmas, and she said she would return by December 15 and stay through Christmas Day. Then he said that he really loved Bea and Mommie and that he was truly sorry if he had said or done things that made either of them feel that he didn't. He added that he believed that Bea understood him but conceded that he had not effectively communicated his genuine affection to Mommie. She said that she believed he loved them both and said that she loved him too. She was sorry that he did not understand her or approve of her. Perhaps, she reasoned, it was because she was more like him than like Bea. She said he would probably have been proud of her if she had been his son instead of his daughter. He didn't deny that but responded that he was proud of her success, even if he disagreed with some of the choices she had made along the way. He really hoped that she got a local television show so that they could work on mending their relationship. She reminded him that if she did get a show, she would challenge their custody agreement in court. He said that if she got a long-term contract for a show, then he would support her right to regain custody of me. I was happy that they were coming together without me having to intervene, and I was ecstatic looking forward to living with Mommie full time.

Mommie took me back to our house that night, but I returned to Papaw's after she left the next day. I never told Mommie or Papaw that I had overheard their conversations. The only one I ever told was Moody. I told him what Bea said to me before she died and how I hadn't understood what she meant until we came home from the hospital and I heard Papaw and Mommie going at each other. I wasn't sure how long the peace between them would last, but I hoped it would be forever. I even wished they would find it in their hearts to live under the same roof. I didn't want Papaw to live alone. He needed someone with him once Bea was gone. But as much as I loved him, I so wanted to be with Mommie all the time. Yet I knew that he wouldn't move to live with Mommie, and I knew that she wouldn't move into his house. Moody cautioned me not to get too excited until Mommie actually had a contract for her own show. That could take a while, and then if Papaw wasn't satisfied with the length of the contract, they could be tied up in court, even after she got a show.

Moody was my "big brother" and almost like family to Mommie and Papaw as well. When Mommie returned two weeks later, he helped her and Papaw pack Bea's clothes to donate to charity before he helped them with holiday decorations, which were more subdued at both houses that year. Each of them kept one of Bea's outfits to hang in their closets to keep a part of her near them and to make her spirit feel welcome in their homes. Mommie kept the mother-of-the-bride ensemble Bea wore in Mommie's wedding in 1943. Papaw chose the dress she made for their fortieth wedding anniversary party in 1955. Bea kept both of those outfits in a cedar chest in the guest room, so they were like new. Moody kept the hat Bea wore when he drove her to the farmers' market each week. He delivered the rest of her clothing to Goodwill Industries.

Bea's death hit me really hard. I was sad and missed her so much. I was also beginning to feel angry and resentful. It seemed that my childhood was suddenly yanked away from me. I was thirteen years old, and I needed to grow up quickly. I had just lost the only adult who was a constant caregiver to me. Most of the kids at my high school had two parents living with them and at least one grandparent who sometimes helped take care of them. I had taken care of my father before he died, and my mother was away most of the time. Papaw worked late at the school and in his law office. He also spent a lot of time traveling as president of the state lay organization. So I had to assume a lot of responsibility for my everyday life. With Bea gone, I had to learn to cook by myself and to see to the other chores involved in running the house. Since Papaw didn't want to leave me at home alone when he traveled, I also had to learn to pack and iron his clothes and mine and how to interact with lay and clergy in business and social settings. The one responsibility I was actually glad to assume was shopping for my clothes with less interference from Papaw. I made sure that they were tasteful and ladylike but more appropriate for a teen than a little kid.

****

As things turned out, Moody had advised me correctly not to think that Mom would be moving back home anytime soon. T. Bone spent two years trying to get Mommic a fifteen-minute show on a Detroit station. WXYZ-TV, channel 7, showed some interest in the summer of 1962 but said that there was difficulty in finding enough sponsorship. This would be the first time a black woman would be hosting a show in that area, and Mommie wasn't as popular an R & B star as she had been before. She hadn't had a hit record since 1959. Most of the black female artists who were in Billboard's Top 100 in 1961 and 1962 were in their teens and twenties, and they sang in groups or with backup singers. The Shirelles, the Marvelettes, the Crystals, the Ikettes and Gladys Knight and the Pips were heard on radio and seen on TV dance shows way more than she was. Big-hit songs about dances like the Mashed Potato, Loco-Motion, Watusi, and especially the Twist were more upbeat than Mommie's blues. And the simple content of songs about young love and heartbreak were more relatable to the young people buying records than her songs about complicated adult relationships. She was still a big draw in clubs and hotel showrooms that catered to middle-aged and older crowds. But without demonstrated star power, the station and sponsors were reluctant to gamble on her potential for a hit show. T. Bone had similar experiences in his negotiations with WWJ-TV, channel 4, and WJBK-TV, channel 2. The Canadian-based CKLW-TV, channel 9 in Detroit, was more interested in former movie stars or popular newspaper critics to host televised showings of old and B-rated movies.

So I continued to live with Papaw throughout 1961 and 1962. There was a parade of older women trying to impress Papaw with their cooking skills. They brought us food and baked goods at least twice a week, usually Friday and Sunday, if Papaw was in town. Still, Moody took me grocery shopping every Saturday. I made breakfast every day before I went to school and prepared dinner during the week, ordering Chinese or barbeque on Fridays if none of Papaw's lady friends stopped by. Papaw was not so much a playboy but a serial monogamist. He would keep a steady lady dangling on his hook for a few months until she figured out that he had no intention of remarrying. Still, a new candidate, confident that she could change his mind, would emerge shortly after the previous one gave up on him. They all tried to get my stamp of approval, not realizing that my opinion mattered far less than they knew. Papaw had me on his arm as he traveled to various parts of Michigan on business for the lay organization. He enjoyed bragging about my intelligence, musical talent, and cooking, which reminded him of Bea's unmatchable culinary skills. When he wasn't traveling, he found me a worthy opponent in Scrabble and Monopoly and a challenging debater on current events. I was at home almost all the time. I wasn't sixteen yet, so I wasn't allowed to date or wear makeup. I also wasn't allowed to go to house parties unless Papaw knew the parents were churchgoing people whom he trusted would properly chaperone coed socials in their homes. As long as I was happy to work and play with him at home, as Bea did, and to travel with him, as Bea rarely did, he didn't need or want another wife. Besides, he didn't believe in remarrying anyway.

In July 1962, Mommie and I were on our annual vacation with my godmother, Josie, and her family in Idlewild, Michigan. Mommie told us that she and T. Bone were becoming increasingly annoyed with each other and she was thinking about dropping him as her manager. She was losing confidence in his management, since he had not been able to get her a show on Detroit television. He told her that she was being difficult, turning down engagements because she wanted to spend more time at home with me. I didn't realize how much money she was losing and how much she was damaging her professional image by thumbing her nose at major opportunities on my account. T. Bone told her that with no recent hit record, she needed to keep her name on people's lips if she wanted to attract sponsors for a television show.

Godmother Josie asked Mommie if she would be interested in radio. She told her that her brother, Larry, the doctor who delivered me, was a close friend of Dr. Wendell Cox, a co-owner of Detroit-area radio station WCHB. Larry and Wendell were classmates at Meharry Medical College, and they were active together in the NAACP and Omega Psi Phi Fraternity, Inc. She explained that Dr. Cox and his father-in-law, Dr. Haley Bell, had launched the first radio station in the United

States to be built from the ground by black owners. Its call letters were their initials, and the Inkster-based Bell Broadcasting station broadcast daily from 6:00 a.m. until 5:30 p.m. at 1440 on the AM dial. Josie was sure that if Larry introduced Mommie to Dr. Cox, he could find a spot for her within the R & B, gospel music, and jazz programming or maybe let her introduce something new to the station. There was a tweeny time show which targeted two to six-year-olds. With Mommie's junior and senior high school teaching background, she might interest them in having her develop a teen talk show where she could talk with teens about music and the music business. Mommie was excited by the possibilities and asked Josie to get Larry to set up a meeting for her with Dr. Cox.

Christmas 1962 was my happiest one in a long while. Both the people I loved most were with me, and we were all happy. I was so excited when Mommie told me that her meeting with Dr. Cox went well and that she would officially hit the airways on January 2, 1963. I couldn't wait for all the kids and teachers at school to hear Mommie daily on her own show on the most popular radio station in town. But the best part of her declaration was that she was going to stay permanently in Parkersville. She said she planned to keep appearing at local clubs but that her New Year's Eve engagement in New York would officially be her last out-of-town gig. I begged her to let me go with her to New York. I wanted to see the Rockettes at the Radio City Music Hall Christmas show and ride in a horse-drawn carriage through Central Park. But Mommie insisted that I should spend my last New Year's Eve in Papaw's house with him. She knew that he was going to miss me when I moved back home with her, even though I'd just be living two blocks away and I would see him every day at school and on Sundays at church. I was surprised that Mommie cared about Papaw's feelings. I guess whatever Bea said to each of them before she died must have finally sunk in because they were both trying hard to get along. I was really happy about that because I loved them both so much and I wasn't feeling pressured "to keep the peace" between them.

Mommie pulled out all the stops for Christmas dinner. She took two days to cook and bake. I learned so much by helping her. We made Spritz cookies and homemade ice cream to leave for Santa on Christmas Eve. I didn't believe in Santa any longer, of course, but I liked the tradition anyway. Papaw ate the ice cream and cookies after I went to bed, like Daddy used to do when he was alive. The centerpiece of the Christmas meal was Bea's favorite, roast suckling pig with prunes in the eye sockets and a bright red apple in its mouth. Bea's recipe for roast suckling pig was simply the best, but Mommie's was really good too. I didn't help her make that, but I helped with the stuffed turkey, leg of lamb, and all the usual sides. Mommie and I baked Papaw's favorite dessert, pecan pie, and Bea's perfect pound cake. Aunt June came with her family, and she brought a red velvet cake and apple cobbler that she had baked. All of the desserts were served with the homemade vanilla ice cream left from Christmas Eve. There were enough leftovers to last the week so that Mommie would not need to cook another meal for the rest of the year. Mommie and I got a break from the leftovers the Saturday after Christmas when we went to my godmother Josie's for our annual spaghetti feast with Mommie's friends and their kids.

As much as I enjoyed the food, I was also thrilled with my presents that year. I got stylish clothes from Mommie and cash to do more shopping. But the best present was the promissory note she gave me in a decorated envelope. I had completed Drivers' Education at school, and I had my driving permit. So Mommie promised to buy me a car for my sixteenth birthday if I got my license. I could tell Papaw didn't agree with that decision, but he didn't say anything about it. Getting a license on your sixteenth birthday was a rite of passage for Parkersville teens. It was expected that one would be late to school that day because he or she would be taking the road test at 9:00 a.m. and not get to school until afterward. Most parents let their kids drive the family car to school that special day so that they could flash their new status. For everyone else, this occurred in the spring of their sophomore year or fall of their junior year. But I wouldn't be sixteen until after I graduated, and I couldn't take my road test until the day after my July 4 birthday, since it fell on a national holiday. I didn't care, though, because I would be getting my own car, even if I couldn't take it with me in September as a freshman at Howard University. I told Moody about getting the car the next July when we took Mommie to the airport December 30. He told Mommie that there would be no convincing me that I wasn't grown once I had my own wheels. She said not to worry. She would make sure I kept my head on straight. We all laughed.

New Year's Day 1963 was such a messy day. It was snowing and cold, so the roads were icy. It took twice as long to get to the airport as it had when Mommie left just forty-eight hours earlier. Moody didn't want Mommie or me to have to walk too far to the car so he dropped me off at baggage claim and then went to park the car. I checked the monitor and was surprised that Mommie's plane had not landed. Due to traffic and bad roads, we didn't get there until half an hour after her scheduled arrival. I figured the bad weather had slowed her flight as well, so I went to the gate that was posted next to her flight number on the monitor. When I arrived at the gate, there were no other people waiting, but a ground stewardess was behind the counter to answer questions. She said that because of the bad weather conditions in Detroit, all flights to Detroit Metropolitan Airport had been cancelled. Mommie's plane was already in the air when that decision was made, so the pilot had been told to reroute to Cleveland, Ohio. Passengers on the flight were given the chance to spend the night in a hotel near the airport at the airline's expense and then fly out to Detroit in the morning. They said we could call the airline in the morning or wait for a call from Mommie to tell us when her rescheduled flight would arrive.

So Moody drove me home to spend another night at Papaw's. I answered a phone call a little past 6:00 a.m. from the Ohio State Police. Mommie was driving a car she rented at the airport and had apparently lost control of it on an icy patch of road near Toledo. The car had skidded off the road and hit a tree sometime around 1:00 a.m. but had only been discovered after daybreak. Mommie was still in the car when the police and ambulance arrived, but unfortunately, she was pronounced at the scene. "Pronounced?" I asked. I didn't understand what that meant, but the stricken look on Papaw's face when he heard me say the word explained it before I got the policeman's response.

Moody drove us to Toledo to identify Mommie's body. T. Bone was there when we arrived. He told us that he was on the plane with Mommie and thought he had convinced her to accept the overnight hotel stay as he had done. He said that she was anxious to get home to prepare for her first day at WCHB. He also told us then that Mommie had been diagnosed with asthma more than a year earlier. She had demanded that T. Bone keep it a secret because she was afraid that if people knew about her condition that it might adversely affect her bookings. There was an inhaler found on the floor of the car she was driving. It was among all of the items that had spilled from her open purse and were scattered around the car's interior. Apparently, she had suffered an attack while she was driving, and she lost control of the car before she could get to her inhaler or pull off on to the shoulder of the road. I heard what was said, but I didn't really believe that Mommie was dead until I saw her lifeless body in the morgue. She looked beautiful, but she wasn't breathing, and she felt cold and stiff.

I can't describe how awful we all felt on the long ride home. Moody was more quiet than I'd ever seen him, and I could tell he was holding back tears as he drove. Papaw was devastated, feeling almost as much guilt as grief. He and Mommie were starting to become closer, but they had not fully resolved their issues from the past. He wanted more time to do that, but there was no more time. He had not wanted me to move out of his house, and it seemed that he had gotten what he wanted, but he didn't want it that way. I didn't feel any guilt, but my grief was immeasurable, and so was my anger. How cruel was God? He let me believe that I was on the verge of getting what I wanted most—to live with Mommie all the time—but instead, I had lost her forever. I had lost too many people I loved in the past few years. There was only Papaw left in my life. I was so afraid of losing him too. He was older than Bea and my dad and way older than Mommie. But there was no time for me to dwell on my grief, my fears, or my anger. I had to focus on ensuring that everything about Mommie's funeral was beautiful, tasteful, and uplifting, the way I knew that she would want it to be. I had watched her plan her mother's funeral and her husband's, so I knew how she liked these things done. I planned to help Papaw attend to every detail.

Mommie had so many exquisite gowns that she had worn for performances, but Papaw and I chose to have her dressed in a beautiful white silk suit with red piping on the edges of the collar, cuffs, and hem of her jacket. I put a string of pearls around her neck, and Papaw put a small white leather-bound Bible in her right hand, just like the one he had put in Bea's hand two years earlier. At the wake, one of her sorority sisters put a violet corsage on her bosom during the beautiful Omega Omega service that is the rite of passage for deceased Deltas. Papaw and I were moved by that service and by the support given to us by her sorors in Detroit Alumnae Chapter during those difficult days. That is when I began to understand why the sisterhood had meant so much to Mommie.

Mommie's funeral was beautiful and the biggest one I had attended. Everyone in Parkersville came to bid farewell to their most famous homegirl. You would have thought they never gossiped about her in life, the way they carried on after she died. Once again, Papaw's constituents and friends from the lay organization had come to support him, and Mommie's friends and her colleagues from Central High School were there. The church choir sang "Blessed Assurance" and "When We All Get to Heaven." My voice teacher sang a solo at Mommie's funeral as she had at Bea's. For Mommie, she sang "His Eye Is on the Sparrow," Mommie's favorite. One of Mommie's former students at Central High School in Detroit had become a music teacher. She sang "If I Can Help Somebody" and spoke about Mommie as her most inspiring and best loved teacher. Some of her other former students came and echoed those sentiments later at the repast. The church was filled to capacity with overflow in the basement, where speakers had been mounted so that people down there could hear the service. Once again, we needed police escorts and officers strategically placed at key intersections for the trail of cars that went to the cemetery.

An impromptu concert erupted at the town hall during the repast after we left the cemetery. T. Bone and some of the artists and executives from Atlantic and their subsidiary, Atco Records, were there: Ruth Brown, Laverne Baker, and others, including Ben E. King, who was really popular then with big hits like "Spanish Harlem," "Stand by Me," and "Don't Play That Song." He was almost twenty years younger than my mother, but he said that she had offered him good advice when he decided to leave the Drifters to become a solo performer. Ebony Hues, the jazz combo that Mommie helped form while at Howard University, played Mommie's signature song with them, "Jumpin' into Love." Other artists present sang some of Mommie's songs and their own hits. Some of my classmates asked me if it would be tacky for them to ask for autographs. I didn't answer. I just looked at them in contempt and disbelief. Truthfully, I didn't care about their groupie behavior. It was trivial to me, but what seemed really tacky was the fact that they were bothering me with questions about fan etiquette on the day that I buried my mother.

****

In the months following Mommie's death, Godmother Josie and Aunt June both spent as much time with me as possible, trying to be there for me as they knew my mother would have wanted them to be.

I loved them both and appreciated all they did for me, but I missed Mommie so much. Moody understood. He came by every day and listened to me talk and cry for hours. He held me, encouraged me, and cared for me like a real big brother. In the fall before Mommie died, she and Aunt Josie had arranged for me to be presented at the Thirteenth Annual Cotillion Debutante Ball in May. Papaw had not supported the idea. He felt that those kinds of events were pretentious attempts by well-to-do Negroes to emulate Southern white aristocracy. Papaw did not like what he called elitist bourgeois behavior that separated black people instead of bringing them together. However, Mommie wanted me to enjoy feeling like a princess and sharing culturally enriching experiences with teens outside of Parkersville. She thought I should sample elegance and sophistication before I left for Howard University, where I would meet people from all social classes and cultures of the world.

Godmother Josie had asked her brother, Larry, to sponsor me as a debutante, since he was an active member in the Cotillion Club, along with Drs. Haley Bell and Wendell Cox and other prominent black men in Detroit, who pooled their influence and resources for social action. The annual Cotillion Debutante Ball, planned primarily by the Cotillion Wives Auxiliary, was a posh affair that served as the coming-out ball for the daughters of well-to-do black families and other young ladies chosen for their academic achievements and potential for future prominence. They made their debut in front of over five hundred of Michigan's social elite. The governor of the state, the mayor of Detroit, and other white politicians and businessmen were among the guests each year, daring not to snub some of the most influential blacks in the state. Everything about the debutante ball was different from anything I had ever experienced. The selection process required me to be sponsored by a Cotillion member, to submit a detailed application, and to be interviewed by the Cotillion Wives Auxiliary. The vetting process was almost as thorough as what presidential candidates do to possible vice presidential running mates. The Cotillion Wives reviewed the formal applications and used informal means of assessing character and reputation, including asking their teenage sons. The debutantes selected were expected to exhibit the finest qualities of young ladies who were ready to begin dating. As one of the wives expressed it, "It is a coming-out event. We are not interested in girls who have already

been out and would have to go back *in* to *come out* at the ball." Once
the debutantes were selected, we began a six-month process of education
and training that was like a charm school. We learned how to sit, stoop,
stand, and walk like ladies with our backs straight and our heads held
high. We perfected formal dining and table setting protocol, as well as
polite conversational techniques. We also learned to curtsy, and with
our escorts, we learned to waltz.

About a month before the ball, we demonstrated what we had
learned at a mother-daughter tea held the afternoon of Palm Sunday
in the mansion home of one of the Cotillions. The tea was covered by
local papers, including the *Detroit News*, the *Detroit Free Press*, and the
black-owned *Michigan Chronicle*. I was selected by the other debs and
the Cotillion Wives to chair the tea. It was a big honor, kind of like an
informal recognition as the "deb of the year". Godmother Josie stood in
for my mother at the tea. She was so proud of me, and we both wished
that Mommie was alive to see me shine as the mistress of ceremonies.
I missed her so much. After she died, I hadn't really cared about being
a debutante or about much of anything else. But I continued because
I knew she wanted me to do it. Moody reminded me of that when he
drove me to the meetings and classes every Saturday.

Papaw stopped badmouthing the debutante experience after
Mommie died. He didn't say anything about it at all until he read the
articles in all three newspapers about the mother-daughter tea. Then he
said that he was proud of me too. It gave him a reason to smile amid the
generally somber days he was experiencing in the hospital. Mommie's
death had taken a great toll on him. He never seemed genuinely happy
and rarely smiled. He didn't have as much energy as he used to have,
so he came home tired and went to bed early most evenings. Before
Mommie died, he had been considering a run for national office in
the lay organization, but after her death, he didn't even travel to many
events in the state. For the first time, he missed the lay organization's
statewide oratorical contest for high school graduating seniors, which he
had judged every year since he had helped organize it. He announced
that he would be retiring as superintendent of schools in June, right after
my high school graduation. However, on March 15, he was rushed from
his office on the ground floor of the high school to the hospital with
severe abdominal pain that appeared to be food poisoning. He thought
it might be from the over-the-counter cold and flu medicine he had been

using to treat his persistent congestion and coughing. But the battery of tests he was given revealed that he actually had advanced hepatitis.

The doctor told me and Aunt June on Easter Sunday that he had acute liver failure and would probably not last any longer than two weeks. I found that hard to believe because Papaw, despite the pain killers he was being given, was quite lucid and in control. Because the doctor chose to tell us on Easter Sunday that Papaw was going to die, I asked him if he was a Christian. "No, miss," he had responded, "I am Jewish." I confidently told him that if he could not do anything for Papaw, then he should leave him alone and bear witness to the healing power of Jesus. I firmly believed that Papaw was as faithful to Jesus as anyone could be. So I had faith that Jesus would heal him just as He had done so many times in the Bible. He had made the lame to walk, the blind to see, and even raised Lazarus from the dead. Healing Papaw's liver, I thought, would be much easier, and surely Jesus would do that for His faithful disciple. God knew how much Papaw was needed by me, the church, and so many other people who depended on him. He would not take him from us yet. Also, it would be a chance to show a nonbeliever the power of the true Messiah. Everyone, except me, accepted what the doctor said, even Papaw. As word of his prognosis spread throughout the church, community, and state, he was bombarded with visitors. At his request, Reverend Hardeman, our pastor, came every day. They prayed together and discussed church business. He also summoned board members of the groups he headed, Allen AME Trustee Board and the Michigan Conference Lay Organization Executive Board, to discuss what should happen after his imminent departure.

Papaw died nine days after Easter on Tuesday, April 23, 1963. During his last two days, he was in a lot of pain, and the morphine he was given caused him to sleep a lot and to be confused when he was awake. He sometimes thought that I was Mommie or Bea. He told everyone he thought I was, including me, when he recognized me, that he loved us. He thanked me as Bea for standing by him and forgiving him when he went astray. He said that she deserved better because she was such a good woman with true inner and outer beauty. He said that he truly loved her and would love her always to eternity. When he thought I was Mommie, he fussed at me for trying to drive home in all that snow and ice. She was just so stubborn, he said. He admitted that she got that trait from him, and that was probably why they were always butting heads. He told me as her that he was proud of her when she was on television. He always made sure to call the biggest gossips so that they could spread the word and have everybody watching her. He said that he had always loved her but knew that he didn't always know how to show it. She was just different from the way he was raised to think women should be. He understood that she thought that there shouldn't be any difference between men and women. He just didn't agree. Maybe he was wrong, he admitted, but it was what he believed.

When he recognized me as myself in his final hours, he talked continuously, telling me to go to college and keep going to get a doctorate in whatever field I found interesting. He said that, eventually, the doors of opportunity would open up for Negroes, but only the educated ones would be prepared to walk through those doors. He told me to guard my reputation and to be faithful and forgiving to my husband when I was old enough to marry. The Bible says how blessed is a man who has a virtuous woman as his wife. I should be virtuous. I should expect my husband's love and respect and return them to him in kind. He advised me to marry someone who could grow with me and not try to hold me down. He said that if I didn't, I would feel trapped and look for ways to escape. I remember wondering if that is how he thought Mommie felt. Marriage vows are sacred, he said, and couples should live together under one roof until death separates them temporarily. Finally, he told me that he was tired of his ailing body and he knew that soon he would be free of it because God was calling him home. Just before he closed his eyes, he smiled, looked up toward the ceiling, and said, "I see you, Bea, and I'll be with you soon."

He slept about an hour as I held his hand and rested my head on his chest. When I felt his heart stop beating, I knew he was gone, and it was time to plan yet another funeral. I knew his would have the most dramatic impact on my life. At five, I had been the only child in my family with five adults from three generations responding to my every need and desire. But in just ten years, they had all died, and I was officially orphaned at fifteen in my last semester of high school. I wondered what I had ever done to deserve this fate. I had grown up believing that God would always take care of me. But at that moment, I felt that God had forsaken me, and I didn't know why. I was heartbroken and furious. I was angry that my prayers seemed to have gone unanswered and even angrier that Jesus had seemingly turned His back on a faithful follower like Papaw. Moody was the only person who truly understood that I felt God had abandoned and betrayed me. I shared with him how hurt and angry I had become with God since Mommie's death. And when Papaw died, so did my faith and trust in God.

However, once again, I had to lay my feelings aside temporarily to execute the perfect home-going for Papaw. This was my fifth funeral in ten years. Each funeral had more people in attendance and more testimonials than the one before it. And I knew that this would be the biggest of them all, given Papaw's standing in the church and community. But I was prepared. I had been increasingly more involved in planning the other funerals, and I knew Papaw's wishes. Nonetheless, I got so much help, sometimes too much help. So many people thought they should be in charge, since they believed that this was too much for me to handle at my age. AME Church laymen and clergy from around the state called to be sure that the right people were included in the service. There was even controversy about who should officiate at the funeral. The bishop would do it, but he was in Africa and would not be back for a week. I was not going to wait that long. My family had taught me that the real process of grieving would not begin until after the funeral was over, so it was best to have the funeral in three to five days. I knew that Papaw would not want me to wait. Another suggestion was to have the presiding elder do it. But I took charge, backed by Aunt June and Papaw's youngest half brother, JT. I wanted Reverend Hardeman to officiate. He was the pastor of Papaw's home church. They worked together closely since Papaw was still serving as superintendent of Sunday School and head trustee there. Papaw was important to a lot of people, but he was humble enough not to see himself as more special than any other member of Allen AME. He would want his pastor to officiate and let any other dignitaries offer tributes if they felt inclined to do so. I also wanted the wake and funeral services to be done as quickly as possible. I agreed to wait four days to accommodate church folk coming from around the state and Papaw's siblings and in-laws traveling from Mississippi and elsewhere.

I also asked Reverend Hardeman to hold those who wanted to speak to a maximum of three minutes because I didn't want to offend anyone but I did not want the services to last for hours. Reverend Hardeman did the best he could. The service and tributes at the wake lasted less than two hours, and the funeral took less than an hour and a half. The choir sang Papaw's favorite hymns, "Just a Closer Walk with Thee," "The Old Rugged Cross," and "It Is Well with My Soul." Soloists sang "The Lord's Prayer," "In the Garden," and "Swing Low, Sweet Chariot." Reverend Hardeman's eulogy was drawn from the scripture found in Luke 10:25–37, the parable of the Good Samaritan, which Jesus uses to answer a lawyer who asked Him what he must do to inherit eternal life. Reverend Hardeman said that Papaw was a lawyer who truly loved the Lord, and he showed compassion and generosity to all men, women, and children as his neighbors. He used his education, experience, time, and resources to give the best help that he could to others, whether they could pay or not. There were so many testimonies from those who acknowledged that they had been recipients of his wise counsel, advocacy, and mentorship. Reverend Hardeman also spoke about his conversations with Papaw in the hospital. He said that Papaw was prepared for the end of his mortal life because he knew that his sins were forgiven and that he would join his Savior in paradise as Jesus promised the repentant malefactor who was crucified on the cross next to Him in Luke 23:43. Those who had thought I was making a mistake choosing Reverend Hardeman to officiate Papaw's funeral had to admit that his eulogy was uplifting and that it fittingly memorialized my grandfather. I didn't need their affirmations. I knew it was the funeral that Papaw would have planned for himself. He was buried next to Bea, not far from Mommie and Daddy. It would be a year before I could stand to return to the cemetery, but I visited all their graves and Grannie's often after that.

****

My aunt June had come to stay with me in Papaw's house while he was in the hospital. We met with Papaw's lawyer on April 30. He explained that I was the sole heir to all of Papaw's and my mother's estates. As executor of Mommie's estate until I was an adult, Papaw had sold her house when she died. Papaw had put her furnishings in storage, and he kept her 1962 Rangoon Red Thunderbird Convertible in his garage to give to me when I passed my road test. While there was not much cash left in Mommie's estate, her home sold for $22,500 and there was over $7,000 left from her life insurance policy after her funeral expenses were paid. Royalty checks for her recorded and written songs were added occasionally to that amount. Papaw and Bea owned the largest house in Parkersville. It was one of only two four-bedroom houses in the town, the other being the parsonage made available to the pastor of Allen AME Church. The mortgage on it had been paid off years earlier, so the only expenses on it were taxes and maintenance. He left his house, all its furnishings, the contents of his law office, and what he had in cash assets and life insurance policies to me as well. His life insurance policy just covered his funeral expenses. Cash in his checking account handled outstanding medical bills. I was surprised that he had over $20,000 in savings because he had done so much legal work pro bono and he had not accepted a salary as superintendent for schools in well over a decade. He added the money allocated for his salary to the town's limited funds for education in order to pay teachers competitive salaries and keep the schools well-equipped. In case I was a minor when he died, he wanted to ensure that I followed the "right" path. So he had arranged to have his and Mommie's assets put into a trust fund which would give me an annual allowance of $5,000 to cover living expenses and provide additional funds of up to $2,500 per year specifically earmarked for tuition, room and board, books and other expenses at Howard University or any other college until I graduated or reached the age of twenty-one, whichever occurred first. At that time, I would have access to the balance of the funds available and would be free to sell his house and keep the money from that sale. However, for all his thoroughness, he had not named anyone to assume custody of me until my eighteenth birthday. So I would have to be under the guardianship of a relative or go into the child foster care system. I know Papaw never wanted me in foster care. I am sure he intended for Aunt June to assume custody of me.

Aunt June agreed to stay with me in Papaw's home for the next two months until my high school graduation. She planned to go home to her husband then and expected me to move in with them. However, Josie welcomed the opportunity to fulfill her sworn duty as my godmother and take care of me in her home after commencement. Aunt June and Godmother Josie left it to me to decide between those options. I didn't want to hurt either of them, certainly not both, but I didn't like either of those alternatives. So I thanked them both politely and promised to decide by graduation. But I had already decided that I didn't want to leave my home in Parkersville. So I needed to come up with a plan that would allow me to stay there. I did not want to move to Ferndale with Aunt June and Uncle James because their house was so much smaller than Papaw's. So I would have to put the piano and many other things, including my bedroom furniture, into storage. My godmother Josie had a big house on Edison Avenue with room for my piano and all of my furniture. However, I knew that she had her hands full with her change-of-life babies, both under two. Josie was forty-five years old and had been married fourteen years when she went to her doctor (and brother), Larry, complaining of heartburn, nausea, insomnia, and periodic low back pain. She had noticed what felt like a mass in her abdominal area. She was sure it was cancer and that she was going to die. When she wanted to know how much longer she had, Larry had to hold back his smile when he answered that she had about three and a half months. He told her that her "tumor" had arms, legs, a heart, and a head with a brain and would probably be born in about fourteen weeks. Josie gave birth to Chelsea on Valentine's Day 1962, a month after her forty-sixth birthday. When Chelsea was just twelve weeks old, Josie was shocked to learn that she was about six weeks into her second pregnancy. Jocelyn was born on Christmas Eve 1962, three weeks before her forty-seventh birthday and nine days before Mommie died. Josie had been a really good godmother to me, especially after Mommie's death. However, I did not want to add to the stress in her life, and I didn't want to become a live-in babysitter.

I soon thought of a third option. I could move in with my only real aunt, daddy's sister, Sadie. That seemed preposterous. She lived far away in Alabama. I hadn't seen her since Daddy's funeral, and she had never been close to me or Mommie. What I really wanted was to stay in Bea and Papaw's home, my home. I needed to think of a way to make that an option for me. Once again, I only shared my true feelings with Moody. He told me not to worry so much about where I would live after June that I couldn't enjoy the exciting things that were on my schedule for the rest of my senior year. I stayed busy in May, completing my classes and preparing for the debutante ball and my prom. I was sad and disappointed that neither my parents nor my grandparents would see me go out on my first dates. Since I had not yet reached sixteen, I had never been allowed to date. When I was allowed to go to a house party, Papaw used to pick me up at 11:30 p.m., so I would always be the first to leave. I was teased for being worse off than Cinderella, who at least got to stay out until midnight. I only got to stay at school dances until they ended at midnight because Papaw was always one of the chaperones.

So I was excited about going out twice in May when I could stay out late. Although they wouldn't be real dates because my escorts were just friends, I still looked forward to feeling special in my beautiful gowns.

My escort for the Cotillion Debutante Ball was Josie's nephew, Larry Jr. He was almost a year younger than me. We were good friends, and I didn't have a boyfriend. For the ball, the debutantes wore the most exquisite white gowns appropriately modest for the occasion—not too low cut in front or back, not strapless, and not tightly fitted at the hips. When Mommie was in town before Christmas, she and Godmother Josie had taken me to several bridal boutiques to find my gown. It was a beautiful wedding dress made of silk chiffon with tiny white silk roses appliquéd around the scooped neckline. Clusters of pearls in embroidered floral designs decorated the front of the fitted bodice, which was fastened with twenty-two pearl buttons down the back. The full-layered skirt was supported by a hooped petticoat, and the train at the back was removed so that the hemline was even. A week after Papaw's funeral, I went with Josie and June to select the two-and-a-half-inch white peau de soie heels, matching bag, and required elbow-length white gloves. I was given the red rose nosegay to complete my ensemble at the ball. Larry Jr. and the other escorts wore tails and gloves with red bowties, handkerchiefs, and cummerbund ensembles.

I was happy that June came to the ball to see me look like a real princess, along with her husband James, son James Jr. and his fiancée. Of course, I wished that my parents and grandparents were there instead. I also wanted Moody there. I couldn't have been a deb without him taking me to all the meetings and practices. But only members of the debs' immediate families were added to the guest list of Cotillion members' friends and dignitaries. June's family substituted for my parents and grandparents. A reminder of my loss, like I needed one, was in the printed program. I fought back tears when I read the bio next to my picture. It began, "Sarah Ann Morgan is the daughter of the late Alvin and Mary Morgan." I remember thinking, *They're not late, they're dead. It's not like they'll be arriving in an hour or so. They're never coming back to me, and neither are Bea and Papaw.* I felt sad and angry, but I forced a smile and tried to enjoy the festivities. I knew that they would all want me to do that. I did have fun at the ball and afterward. That was the first time that I could stay out all night. I attended the private after-party and breakfast for the debs and escorts in the mansion of

Josie's brother Larry on East Boston Boulevard. Josie and her husband stayed over there as chaperones and drove me home around 10:00 a.m. the next day. That had been Mommie's condition for me to attend the overnight party, and Godmother Josie kept the promise she made to Mommie before she died.

Mom stopped and went to retrieve some things from the bottom right drawer of her dresser. She shared two items with me then. The first was a newspaper article about the Thirteenth Annual Cotillion Debutante Ball with group pictures of the twenty-two debutantes and members of the Cotillion Club and Cotillion Wives Auxiliary. The second item was the program from the ball, which featured individual headshots and biographical statements for Mom and the other debutantes. I couldn't believe that she had kept those mementoes for over forty years and had never shared them with me. But then I realized that she had not told any of her children much about her life before she married Dad. As close as I was to my mother and as much as I investigated other people's lives, I had never looked for more information about hers. I set aside the program as she continued.

I hated that Moody had to miss my cotillion, but at least he was with me for my prom. He agreed to be my prom date, knowing that he would be the oldest one in attendance, except for the chaperones. Aunt June let me stay out late because she trusted him to look out for me like a chaperone. He bought me an orchid corsage, much nicer than the carnation corsages most of the other girls had. He picked me up in his car, just like a real date, even though it was strictly platonic. I didn't mind going with my "big brother." I didn't like any of the boys at my school, anyway, and Larry Jr. was nice but a bit snobbish. I didn't think he would have a good time at a dance in my high school gym with a bunch of kids that he didn't know and with whom he probably would find little in common. Moody didn't mind spending time with the seniors at Parkersville who were impressionable freshmen when he and the legendary Fab Four played for the state championship. Everyone, seniors and chaperones alike, was surprised to see Moody as my date. They wondered if we were "an item," but nobody dared ask. We enjoyed watching them trying to figure it out as they stared at us all night. We skipped the after-parties. Moody took me for midnight supper at a nice restaurant in Detroit before bringing me home at 2:00 a.m. We laughed at supper, knowing that the rest of the seniors wondered where we went.

Three weeks later, Moody attended my graduation and cheered loudly for me with Aunt June and her family and Godmother Josie and her family. A copy of my valedictory address was printed in the *Parkersville Times*, the local newspaper, along with my picture. *(That was the other item she had taken from her dresser drawer and she gave it to me then.)* I knew that Papaw was watching and listening to me. He had been honing my oratorical skills since I was in elementary school, and he would have been even more proud of me than Mommie, Daddy, and Bea. I thanked all of them posthumously for the love, support, and guidance they gave me. There was a lump in my throat as I held back tears of sorrow and regret that none of them were there with me and that the time had come when I was going to have to leave the home and neighborhood I shared with them. Even as I spoke the words that they would all be with me always, I was feeling like leaving my home would somehow break my connection to them. So in that moment, I became determined to find a way that I could stay in that house forever.

After I told Godmother Josie that I had decided not to move into her home, Aunt June expected me to move in with her. However, I shocked her by asserting that I wanted to visit my aunt Sadie in Alabama first. You see, unbeknownst to June, I had spoken to Papaw's lawyer the morning after graduation. And I discovered that I had another option. I hatched a plan that would allow me to stay in Papaw's house. I discussed it with Moody because I needed his help and my aunt Sadie's to make it work. So when James and James Jr. came to get Aunt June on Sunday, June 30, they took me to the airport to board a flight to Birmingham, Alabama. They stayed with me until they saw me board the plane. They didn't see Moody waiting to board the same plane because he was at an adjacent gate, hiding behind an open newspaper until he saw them leave.

I had asked Moody to be my guardian and to move into Papaw's house with me. Moody had always protected me as his "little sister" and was willing to do whatever was necessary to take care of me when I needed him most. Of course, we both knew that as a single male just twenty-one years of age, he would not be allowed to adopt me or to serve as a foster parent. The only way that we could make the arrangement work was for us to get married. So I had packed the four death certificates of my parents and grandparent guardians, and I planned to ask my closest living relative, Aunt Sadie, for her permission to marry. If Sadie agreed, we could get a marriage license in Alabama on July 5, the day after my sixteenth birthday. I only planned to live platonically and to stay married until I turned eighteen. Then I could live on my own in Papaw's house and Moody would be free to marry for love. However, we knew that Sadie would never approve of such an arrangement, so we had to pretend that we were in love and wanted a real Christian marriage. I knew we could fool her and everyone else. We saw how the seniors and chaperones looked at us at the prom, speculating that we were more than "brother and sister." Even Aunt June had questioned me about our relationship when Moody showed up with the orchid corsage and asked to keep me out after the prom. That's when I first got the idea to capitalize on their musings. Under normal circumstances, I would not have perpetuated such a lie, but these were extraordinary circumstances. At that point, I had lost faith that God would take care of me, so I was taking the necessary steps to take care of myself. Of course, my reasoning was flawed. It was based on anger, hurt, sadness, and a misguided adolescent understanding of scripture. But it was what I believed in the days just before my sixteenth birthday.

****

Before Mom could tell me what happened when she and Moody saw her aunt Sadie, we both heard Cara's cheerful voice, saying, "Hi, everybody," as she came into the house. She must have been as surprised as I had been earlier that Mom was not downstairs and that she was not already preparing dinner. However, as Mom and I came down the stairs to greet her and her attractive male companion, she only asked, "What's for dinner? You know, we came hungry." I couldn't believe how easily Mom's mood seemed to transition from solemn and serious as she talked to me upstairs to her more typical buoyant and jovial demeanor with Cara and her guest downstairs. CJ arrived with his femme du jour shortly thereafter, and an impromptu evening of lively conversation lasted until my siblings and their dates left a few minutes ago. Mom seemed to welcome the interruption in our conversation. I am always happy to spend time with my brother and sister, but tonight I just wanted to get back to my alone time with Mom so that she could finish explaining why she questioned my paternity. That was so important to me that I didn't care much about anything else.

In a little more than an hour, we were dining on another feast Mom prepared in short order. The entrée was one of her signature dishes, crab-crusted salmon, and she served it with wild rice, fresh asparagus in hollandaise sauce, tossed salad, and sorbet with fresh fruit for dessert. After dinner, Cara and I helped Mom clear the table and load the dishwasher. I was never very good at hiding my emotions. So before we joined the others, Cara called me into the living room to ask if I was all right. She said that I seemed detached and solemn. She also asked why Jason hadn't come and if I planned to stay overnight because she didn't want me driving home alone so late in the dark. I couldn't tell her the real reason that I was upset, that I wanted all of them to leave so that I could hear the rest of Mom's story. So I told her about my discussion with Jason this morning and my ongoing distrust of Delia. As I said the words, I was astonished that Jason and I talked this morning. With all that I learned today, my conversation with Jason seemed to have occurred long ago. Cara offered the same advice to me as Mom did earlier, adding that we could hire someone to "kick Delia's ass." She was joking, of course, and we both laughed. That lightened my mood. I pulled myself together enough to feign interest in her love life and to enjoy guessing how long CJ's new girl would be in the picture. By the time we joined the others in the family room, I was feeling more upbeat, and I was able to join in the fireside family chitchat.

The house is quiet again. Mom and Dad are in bed. So I'll have to wait until morning to hear the rest of Mom's story. It's like being at a pivotal point in a novel and feeling an urgency to keep reading to the end, except this is more intense because it isn't fiction. It's the truth about who I am. Still, I guess it's a blessing that I have this time to write down everything Mom said so far. For the second consecutive night, I'm not getting to sleep until 6:00 a.m.

Sunday, November 28, 2004
9:30 p.m.

I only slept about four hours but felt rested when Mom called me downstairs to enjoy a typical Sunday morning breakfast of a vegetable cheese omelet with pancakes, turkey bacon, and juice. Dad was dressed when we ate, and he left alone for church around 10:35 a.m. Mom and I rarely miss Sunday services at Mercy Baptist, but we both knew that we had to finish what we started yesterday. I called Jason so he wouldn't worry when he didn't see me in church. After Dad left, Mom and I went up to the master bedroom, where Mom resumed her life story. To avoid further interruptions, she prepared a pitcher of iced herbal tea and a tray of healthy snacks.

The Oral History Recounted by My Mother Sarah Anne Morgan Reynolds (June 1963–July 1974)

Aunt Sadie was expecting me, but she was surprised to see Moody. I reminded her that they had met before at Daddy's funeral and that he had been close to our family for many years. She said that she remembered him but wondered why he had come with me to see her. I told her that we had come together to ask for her permission to be married. She was not happy to hear that. She looked at Moody and said, "I seen you sniffin' after her at my bruh's funeral. You's a grown man, and she jus' a chile. Why you wanna marry her? You wanna git yo' han's on all that money she jus' got."

Moody told her that she was wrong and that he loved me and wanted to take care of me. She said, "Hmph! I don' believe that for one minute." I told her that I loved him too and that there was no money. I explained that Papaw had most of what money there was tied up in a trust fund that I couldn't touch for another four to five years.

She shook her head and said, "Fattenin' frogs for snakes! My bruh' and yo' ma spent all kinds o' money on all them fancy lessons so you git yosef a docta or somebody wit' money, and you th'ow yosef at a bum wit' no edication. You marry him and you ain't gon' get none either."

Moody told her that he had a good job. He said he would take care of me and see to it that I got a college education. He might not be educated or rich, but he was a decent man, and he would give me a decent life with everything I ever wanted.

I asked her to take the next four days to look him over and try to get to know him. I would be sixteen on Thursday, but since it was a holiday, we couldn't get a license until Friday anyway. By then, I was sure that she would be convinced that he was a good man just like her brother, who was without a college degree. And she would see that Moody loves me like her brother loved my mother, who was twenty-five years younger than he. If she wasn't convinced, then she wouldn't sign for us to get the license. But if she saw the good in Moody that I saw in him, she should allow me to marry him. She agreed reluctantly. She said he would have to sleep on the couch. We weren't married yet, and no matter what we might have already done, we weren't going to do "married things" with each other in her Christian house. Moody and I assured her that we had not done "married things" and would not want to do them before we were married. Of course, I didn't tell her that we had never even kissed, that I wasn't planning to have sex even after we were married, and that I loved Moody like a big brother.

Friday, July 5, Sadie signed papers giving her written consent for us to marry. I presented the death certificates for my mother and father, and we were issued an Alabama license to wed. We went to a justice of the peace for a civil ceremony, which Sadie did not like, so she didn't want to be a part of it. She said it might be legal, but she did not think it was right. Marriage vows are sacred and should be handled by a man of God in God's house. But I didn't want that, in part because I knew that it was an arrangement, not a sacred commitment, and in part because I still had feelings of anger toward God for leaving me alone and making this arrangement necessary in the first place. Sadie waited in the car while we had the ceremony.

Moody paid the necessary fees and bought a thin gold wedding band for me, which he placed on my finger during the ceremony. Afterward, the justice of the peace signed the marriage certificate, and his secretary signed it as the witness. He told us that once we signed it and gave it to his secretary, she would file it, and then our marriage would be legal. The justice motioned for us to go back to the secretary's desk in the anteroom, and he started to perform another ceremony. His secretary left her desk to stand as the witness for the next ceremony, leaving us alone in the anteroom while we signed our certificate on her desk. Moody signed the certificate right away, but I hesitated for a minute. I had an epiphany. I told Moody that as long as we had the signed certificate, people in Michigan would believe we were legally married. That's all that mattered. If we took the certificate, it couldn't be filed and our marriage would not be legal. Without being legally married, we wouldn't have to go through a divorce later, saying ugly things we didn't mean about each other and paying a lawyer a lot of money. Besides, I didn't believe in divorce, and neither did Moody. So I put our signed certificate in my purse, and we left. Moody and I took an unsuspecting Sadie back to her house. We packed our things and flew home. That's when I got Moody to go along with living my lie.

"Mom," I interrupted, "how can you call it your lie? Moody agreed to a marriage in name only so it was his lie as much as it was yours. Obviously, you didn't coerce him into anything."

You see, the whole thing was my idea. The fact that it was not supposed to be a real marriage was one lie. Then the fact that we never filed to make even the fake marriage a legal one just compounded the lie. We were living in sin, not because we were having sex, because we weren't, but because we were pretending about both the legality and the sincerity of our marriage. We were convincing, and everyone believed us. We were the hot topic of gossips in Parkersville and Detroit. I knew that I had disappointed June and Josie, who both thought I should have allowed them to take care of me until I was eighteen or until I finished my bachelor's degree. Josie was also embarrassed, although she never said it to me. She had pushed Larry to sponsor me as a debutante, and getting married at sixteen, especially to a man without a college degree, fell far short of the expectations for a Cotillion Deb. I felt bad about any hurt or embarrassment I caused June and Josie because I knew that they both loved me. I didn't care about all the other gossips because I knew they didn't care about me any more than they had cared about my mother. I gave them even more grist for the rumor mill because I stopped going to church. Mom's friend, Gladys, was still directing the choir and asked me to sing or work with the children, but I couldn't commit to that either. I remember that Moody and I went the Sunday after Thanksgiving that year because Allen AME had purchased chimes for the pipe organ in the sanctuary. At a special ceremony after the service, they were played for the first time and dedicated as the "SC and Beatrice Mann Memorial Chimes" in honor of my grandparents.

I was still working through my adolescent anger issues with God. Fortunately, God loves us and is patient with us when we stray. He understood that even when I was angry with Him, I never really stopped believing in Him. I knew that He existed and believed that He could do all things, but I was angry because He didn't choose to do what I wanted Him to do. I know now that God doesn't always give us what we want, but He always gives us all we need. But I didn't understand that then.

****

Moody and I were happy living together in Papaw's house. I wanted to go through with my plans to attend Howard University on full scholarship in the fall of 1963, but I knew that was no longer practical. So I enrolled at Wayne State University in Detroit. I got my driver's license as soon as Moody and I returned from Alabama so I could drive Mommie's T-Bird back and forth to campus. Moody's salary as assistant manager of custodial services for Parker Industries, Inc. and the allowance from my trust fund gave us the resources for a good lifestyle, especially since we had no mortgage to pay on the house.

Moody loved my cooking. After all, the two best cooks in the world had been my teachers, and I had grown up apprenticing in their kitchens. Moody helped me with the dishes, laundry, and housekeeping in general. We were playing house. We weren't married, but we had to make everyone think that we were. We had to appear to love each other as wives and husbands do, not like brothers and sisters do. That was not as easy as I had thought it would be when I concocted that plan. I just thought about beating the system, outsmarting all the grown-ups who wanted to control my life. I never thought about how difficult it was going to be to pretend. I also never considered what a toll this arrangement could take on Moody or on me. We were not actors, and we were both basically honest people. Yet we would have to lie and pretend constantly and deny any possible feelings we might develop for other people. I was just sixteen. I had never had a boyfriend or felt anything close to romantic love. Moody was twenty-one and had been a normal sexually active young man. I wondered if I was expecting too much of him to trade his healthy relationships with women for a game of pretend with a precocious yet naïve teenage girl. That was the question I asked myself only after we had gone too far to back out. Yet Moody seemed fine with our arrangement, and if he was unhappy, he didn't show it.

Things got complicated in the summer of 1964. The rest of the Fab Four from Parkersville High School Class of 1960 returned in June to be recognized at graduation. Noseguard Lenny had just graduated from

Penn State after completing four years as a starter with the Nittany Lions. He was on his way to Buffalo after receiving a hefty signing bonus to play in the AFL for the Bills. Bobby, the full back, had just graduated from Grambling and was moving to Cleveland to play in the NFL on the Browns. Quarterback Ollie graduated from Michigan State, but due to an injury to his throwing arm during the first game of his senior year, he was not going to play professionally. He was going to move a few miles from campus to Lansing, where he would be serving as a high school physical education teacher and football coach. Moody was also recognized when the four were presented with Spirit Awards for taking the Parkersville High School Panthers all the way to the state finals in football. They were touted for being not only good athletes but also good role models for the good character they demonstrated in high school and in the years that followed their graduation. Moody was used to being the high school hero, loved and respected by everyone in our small town. But even as he accepted his medallion with his friends, he was aware that he was viewed by many in the town as an opportunistic cradle robber and, by a few, as a statutory rapist. Of course, none of those labels were justified. Moody and I were not having sex. I couldn't admit to that, but I still wanted to defend him, to tell everyone that it was my idea, but he said that we should stick to our story that we fell in love and made a commitment to each other in the most appropriate way. We admitted that Papaw's death affected the timing of our marriage, but we insisted that the marriage itself was inevitable.

Moody was aware that Ollie, Lenny, and his best friend, Bobby, found it strange that he would marry the girl he always swore was his kid sister. They were close enough to him to ask him what happened. I knew that he wanted to tell them the truth, but he stuck to the script. It was hard for him to hang out with them. Our age difference made it awkward when we went out with them together. Ollie was married to a coed he met at MSU, and Bobby was engaged, but they were adult couples who could go out to clubs. Of course, I could not do that. When he took me with him to house parties or gatherings with the guys and their ladies, the women treated me like a child who was annoying the grown-ups in the room. I encouraged Moody to go without me, but when he did, he said he felt uncomfortable. Moody was a groomsman in Bobby's wedding. He, of course, went to the bachelor party alone, and we attended the rehearsal dinner and the wedding together. A few people stared at me, but nobody said anything rude at those events. They were two of the rare occasions when neither Moody nor I was counting the minutes until we could leave.

By August, Ollie, Lenny, and Bobby had left Parkersville and Moody to move on with their careers. They called him often, especially Bobby, but they were not around to want to hang out with him constantly. After they left, at least once or twice a month, Moody would go out on Saturday night "to blow off some steam," as he put it. I never asked where he went or what he did. He was always home by 2:00 a.m. If he was seeing other women, he acted with discretion. Anyone from Parkersville who saw him messing around would have made sure that I found out, whether they wanted to help me or to hurt me.

When I turned eighteen on July 4, 1965, we decided not to end our arrangement. I was halfway through my degree program in psychology and had received merit scholarship incentives based on my near perfect average. Moody didn't want me living alone yet, and he couldn't continue to live there with me unless we continued to be "married." We loved each other, even if we weren't in love. Neither of us was in love with anyone else, and whomever Moody was seeing on the outside accepted his terms and his living arrangements. However, by my nineteenth birthday in 1966, our relationship was changing in ways that were not good. We were being tested, and we would have to make some tough decisions if we were to survive independently and together.

Trouble came into our lives in all caps, and that TROUBLE was spelled L-E-N-N-Y. Lenny had opted out of the third year of his initial contract with the Buffalo Bills. He said it was because he hated living in Buffalo and hated playing for a second-rate team with second-rate racist coaches. But that did not ring true to me or to most people, considering the Bills had won back-to-back AFL Championships in both years that he had played with them. We always watched the Bills and the Browns, hoping to cheer on Lenny and Bobby from our living room sofa. We knew that Lenny had barely played the first year and played only a little more in the second year but still managed to sustain serious knee injuries both years. He was being moved to the first string defensive team for the 1966 season, and Moody confessed to me that he thought Lenny was scared. The professional players were bigger, stronger, faster, and meaner on the field than Lenny and most of the college players he had faced at Penn State. Like Lenny, all of the pros had been the best of the best in college, and some were among the best in the professional league. If Lenny moved to the starting defensive lineup, he would be facing these players every week throughout the season. Coming off the injuries he had sustained playing only occasionally, he probably did not want to imagine what could happen to his knees or to the rest of his body if he played on a regular basis. However, he could not confess such fears to his boys or even to himself. He was a member of the Fab Four, and they were men of heart and courage. He could not, would not, dare not think he had "punked" out.

Because the Bills had not fired him and he had walked away from his three-year commitment to them, he had violated the terms of his bonus. He thought that when he left, they would have to give him two-thirds of his $100,000 bonus because he had played two of the three years in the contract. That would be enough to pay off his bills in Buffalo and secure a nice home in Parkersville or Detroit with a big garage where he could park his 1965 silver El Dorado. The problem was that Lenny had not read his contract with the Bills. If he failed to play for all three of the years tied to the bonus, he forfeited the entire bonus. So since he was refusing to play the third year, the Bills owed him nothing. Lenny swore that this was racism, but the Bills and his lawyer said it was just business. The Bills ultimately settled with him by paying off his Cadillac and paying the two months of rent left to complete his obligation on the lease on his apartment in Buffalo. They also generously agreed to pay off another $5,000 in credit card debt for him. The grand total came to $30,000, less than one-third of the bonus. However, it was $30,000 more than he was entitled to get according to the terms of the agreement. Moody agreed with Lenny's lawyer that the Bills were generous, but he couldn't tell Lenny that because Lenny was too angry to hear the truth when he came home to Parkersville.

There were other hard truths Lenny was not ready to face. Lenny had big ideas about becoming a defensive coach for the Detroit Lions or for a major college team like University of Michigan or Michigan State. His other option was to use his celebrity status as a former AFL professional player to secure a position as a television commentator or sportscaster. However, although everyone in our small town of Parkersville was impressed that he had played in the pros, his two years spent mostly on the bench had not garnered him celebrity status outside of Parkersville. He was insulted by offers to join a team of commentators on a local radio station or to coach high school football. If he accepted the coaching job, he would have to take some education courses to meet state certification guidelines, since his degree was in sociology. He could have worked as a case worker based on his academic credentials, but his professional football experience would not provide him with any advantages in that venue. Lenny was an angry young man. And Bobby's success with the Cleveland Browns made him envious and angrier. But he couldn't face those feelings either. Bobby was his boy, his bro, part of his family, and he should be celebrating his success. But I think Lenny wanted Bobby to fail so that he would feel like less of a failure. Bobby was clueless about Lenny's feelings. Unlike Moody, he and Ollie were not around Lenny every day. Bobby had taken Lenny at his word that he just didn't want to play football in Buffalo any longer because he didn't like the organization or the city. Lenny also asserted that because of his three-year contract with them, he couldn't play anywhere else for at least a year. Lenny didn't want Bobby and Ollie to know that he didn't ever want to play professional football again.

Hanging with Moody and visiting Ollie and his family in Lansing were good for Lenny's ego. Neither of them made it to the pros. But Lenny had difficulty handling Bobby's success with the Cleveland Browns. The Fab Four were reunited at Bobby's home that June to celebrate Bobby's twenty-fourth birthday. Moody and I rode with Lenny and his date, Jacqueline Phipps, known as Phippsie, in Lenny's Cadillac. Phippsie was just a year ahead of me at Parkersville High School, so although she was three years older than me, she talked to me like an equal. She was considered to be a real fox in high school, and she was the most popular girl in her class: cheerleading captain, prom queen, secretary of the senior class. She stood five feet eight inches tall and had flawless mahogany-colored skin and long thick wavy black hair that she pinned behind one ear and let fall freely in her face on the other side. It often covered her eye, so she looked like a silhouette of the old movie star, Veronica Lake. She tried to look sexy by pouting her lips and tilting her head as she combed the hair away from her face with her fingers. I thought she looked phony and silly doing that, but it had her desired effect on most of the men in town. Lenny was proud to have a gorgeous date to the party, and Phippsie was proud to be going to the party as Lenny's date and an old friend of the host. She thought Lenny had money, and she wanted to be more than a casual date to him.

We were all laughing and talking during the three-hour ride to Bobby's. Bobby and his pregnant wife, Diane, lavishly entertained us and about eighty other guests at their spacious home in Shaker Heights, Ohio, a picturesque suburb of Cleveland. The wide streets were lined with beautiful trees and perfectly manicured lawns. All of the homes were huge and beautiful, each one with lots of windows, exquisite doors, long driveways, and unique walkways. Bobby's house was on a corner and six-foot evergreen hedges encircled the property to provide privacy. Bobby could not have been a more gracious host. He was so happy to greet us and instructed the servers to make sure that we had all we wanted to eat and drink. When he gathered everyone together so that he and Diane could formally address their guests, he began by saying that he was so blessed to have played on three teams where players supported one another and gave their best for the good of the team. He introduced Moody, Lenny, and Ollie to everyone as his main dudes in high school and told everyone how the Fab Four brought Parkersville its only appearance in the state finals. The two other Grambling players in attendance lifted their glasses to toast him as he spoke about their prowess and unselfishness on his college team. Most of the guests were his current teammates on the Browns, and he spoke of the camaraderie within the organization. He said how blessed he had been in his first year of pro ball to have blocked for the legendary Jim Brown in practice and occasionally in actual pro games. Jim Brown smiled as Bobby reiterated things that Jim had taught him through word and example about playing successfully in the pros. Finally, he spoke with love and admiration about how God had blessed him with such a beautiful, loving, and supportive wife and how He was blessing their union with a child. Diane and all of the guests were moved as Bobby shed tears of joy as he spoke of how important his family and all of the invited guests were to him. Bobby always showed humility, and he never failed to give thanks to others for their support and praise to God for everything good in his life. That's why we all loved Bobby.

As usual, the men and the women hung out in different areas of the home and the grounds. Diane and Phippsie didn't tell the other wives and dates how old I was, so they didn't talk down to me or treat me like a child. I had a really good time all afternoon and evening. When the party ended, Moody and I stayed overnight at the house, along with Lenny, Phippsie, Ollie, and his wife, Gail. Diane and Bobby took us on a tour of their home. Bobby acted like it was no big deal, but it was the most fantastic house any of us had ever seen. It was a Georgian-style brick home with five huge bedrooms and four full bathrooms, plus two powder rooms. None of us had seen houses with a library, sitting room, and exercise room, and the knotty pine-paneled recreation room in the basement was much larger than any we had ever seen. The three fireplaces, three-car garage, beautifully manicured lawn, and large swimming pool area impressed us as well. All of the designer furniture and exquisite furnishings added to the luxurious surroundings.

After the breathtaking tour of their home, Bobby and Diane retired as did the rest of us. That was the first time Moody and I slept in the same bed. Phippsie had not asked for a room separate from Lenny, and they weren't married. It would have certainly been strange for me to ask for a room separate from my "husband." I felt awkward changing into my nightgown in front of Moody, so I changed in the bathroom next to our room and turned the light off when I came into the bedroom. A shirtless Moody was standing by the bed in his pajama bottoms. The moonlight shining through the window was bright enough for me to see the silhouette of his muscular body. I stared at him for a few seconds, long enough to realize what a handsome man he was. I looked into his eyes and realized that he was looking at me differently also. I knew that he was seeing me as a woman. He was pulling back the covers on the side of the bed where he was standing. He asked if I wanted him to sleep on the floor beside the bed. I said of course not. He walked to the other side of the bed to turn back the covers for me. It was a sweet gesture, like pulling out a chair for a lady to be seated or opening a door for a lady, both of which he had always done for me. He stood upright and looked into my eyes. He cupped his hands around my face and leaned in to kiss my lips. I panicked and turned my face to the side, forcing his lips to land on my cheek. He walked silently back to the other side of the bed and lay down. I entered the bed from my side, and we were lying with our backs next to each other in the queen-sized bed. I usually fell asleep imagining myself as the heroine in a scene from a romance novel or movie. That night, I fell asleep imagining Moody as the hero in the scene with me.

The Fab Four joined the two Grambling players at their hotel the next morning for a champagne buffet brunch. Nobody asked me for identification, but Moody had fake ID made for me after I turned eighteen, and I had it with me just in case. Afterward, we left for home, promising to get together again soon. The mood in the car on the way back home was very different from the lighthearted one on our way to Ohio. We were all saying how much we enjoyed ourselves, and Phippsie was talking about Bobby's fabulous house and how cool it was to meet Jim Brown. As we crossed the state line into Michigan, Lenny went into an angry rage and yelled at her, saying that the house was ostentatious, Bobby was burying himself in debt to keep Diane happy and she was a gold digger, just with him for the money. He said Bobby had bought into the white man's game, and he was crazy if he thought the Browns organization cared anything about him as a person. He said that management thought of their players like slaves on a plantation. To them, he was just another black buck, and they would trade him or replace him in an instant if they found someone who would play well for less money. And all those players he thought were his friends were competing against him for bigger crumbs from the white man's plate. He told Phippsie that he wasn't like Bobby. He wasn't going to be anybody's sugar daddy, so if she was with him for the money, she might as well get to stepping.

Moody and I were shocked, and Phippsie was crying. Moody tried to calm Lenny and asked him to pull off at the next exit, four miles ahead of us. Lenny pulled into the parking lot of a diner. Moody got him to leave the car with him. I tried to comfort Phippsie. I knew that she was embarrassed as well as hurt and scared. Lenny had acted like a madman, and none of us knew what he would do next. I assured her that she need not be embarrassed or scared. Moody would not let Lenny harm her, and neither of us thought that she had done anything to warrant his behavior. I also assured her that Moody and I would never talk about what had happened in the car to anyone else. She thanked me and stopped crying. Moody brought a calmer Lenny back to the car about ten minutes later. Lenny apologized to Phippsie and to me for his outburst. He also apologized to Phippsie for what he said about her. Once again, I looked at Moody as a hero. For the remainder of the trip, the car was quiet until Lenny said goodbye to Moody and me when he dropped us off. I was afraid to leave Phippsie alone with Lenny in the car, but Moody said that they needed time alone to talk. I don't know what he said to Phippsie after we got out of the car, but it must have been really good because she continued to date him. She was gorgeous, and a lot of guys wanted to be with her. She had her pick, but for whatever reason, she picked Lenny.

Lenny continued to act out, and Moody continued to be the one who could calm him down. They went out drinking almost every Thursday and Friday night. I was pretty sure that Lenny was smoking weed, and I suspected that Moody was too. Moody swore to me that he wasn't getting high on anything but liquor. He never said one way or the other about Lenny. Lenny got mean and abusive when he was high, but Moody was usually able to keep him from getting into trouble. Moody and I went to double feature movies at theaters or drive-ins most Saturdays, usually with Lenny and Phippsie. We all liked action movies, but Moody and Lenny would sit through one romantic comedy if there was an action flick playing with it. Actually, Lenny slept through most of the romantic comedies. When he was awake, he made random, nonsensical comments about the movie and munched continuously on candy, popcorn, hot dogs and soda. He said it was because he was bored but I knew he was stoned.

Lenny still didn't have a steady job, but he managed on money he made from local commercials and endorsements at car dealerships and small stores in Detroit, Parkersville, and other nearby suburbs. I knew that Lenny was headed for serious trouble, and I begged Moody to distance himself from him. Moody said that Lenny had problems, and true friends don't abandon each other in times of need. I tried to get Moody to see that he was an enabler. He allowed Lenny the security of knowing that if he got high and lost control, Moody would take care of him. Moody would try to calm Lenny and the people he offended so that he would not get involved in fights. While Lenny became paranoid and argumentative after mixing reefer and booze, Moody became more nurturing and protective when he drank.

I was afraid that Moody was becoming dependent on alcohol, but he insisted that he wasn't. He insisted that he just drank when he was with Lenny and sometimes to take the edge off when he was feeling stressed. He wouldn't tell me what was stressing him, but I sensed that his feelings toward me had changed, and he was feeling the pain of what he thought was unrequited love. I wanted to tell Moody that my feelings had also changed, but I didn't know what to tell him. If he had tried to kiss me again, I would have kissed him back. I was ready to share love and passion with him. He was the closest thing I knew to the heroes

I read about and saw in movies. He took care of me when I felt alone or in trouble. He was certainly my hero, and I loved him for that. He had been so patient with me, and I was finally ready to respond to him as a woman, not as a little sister. But since that night I turned away, he had not reached out to me, and I didn't know how to reach out to him.

Moody lost his job in August. Mr. Parker said that he had been drunk on the job too often. Moody said that it was because the Parker businesses were losing money and he couldn't afford as many managers. Then on Friday night, August 19, Lenny was driving drunk at sixty-five miles per hour, weaving back and forth as he barreled down the southbound side of Woodward Avenue in Detroit. Moody was in the passenger seat, passed out and not wearing a seat belt. Shortly past midnight, Lenny ran a red light and hit a pedestrian crossing the avenue. He kept his foot on the gas pedal and then crashed into a Buick Electra 225, what we used to call a deuce and a quarter, parked on the north side of Woodward. On impact, Lenny's car stopped, standing crosswise in the right and middle lanes. An approaching city bus tried to stop but could not avoid hitting Lenny's car on the passenger side. The El Dorado turned over, resting on the driver's side, and Moody went through the windshield and landed on the sidewalk. The bus driver and his passengers were shaken but all right. A few suffered minor bruises. The pedestrian was DOA at the hospital. I got a call from the police around 1:00 a.m. and made it to the hospital as Moody was being taken into surgery. I was beside myself. I hated calls from police. I hated having them tell me someone close to me had been in a car accident. My mother and grandmother died after car accidents. I hated hospitals. I last saw Daddy, Bea, and Papaw as they lay dying in hospitals. Moody could not leave me. He had helped me hold myself together after I lost each of my loved ones. Who would help me keep myself together if I lost him? I was so angry at Lenny. Lenny caused the accident by driving impaired, but he was fine, with only minor cuts and bruises, while his passenger was in surgery. Yet I was also angry with Moody for getting into the car with Lenny high behind the wheel.

Lenny was still inebriated when he was taken to the hospital. He was charged with DUI (driving under the influence of alcohol) at the scene of the accident, and since the pedestrian died, he was charged at the hospital with vehicular manslaughter. Luckily for him, the police did not find any marijuana on him or in the car, so he avoided additional charges for drug possession. He was taken from the hospital in handcuffs while I waited for word on Moody. Phippsie was there and sat with me after she was told she would not be allowed to talk to Lenny and that she could not post bail until Monday morning. A doctor finally came to tell me that Moody would be fine, but he would need time to heal. Miraculously, Moody's most serious injuries were two broken ribs, one of which punctured his right lung. In addition, he had minor cuts and scrapes on his face and arms and a hairline fracture in his right tibia, the same one he had broken during the state championship game six years earlier. The doctor also said he would probably sleep through the morning. They said I should go home and return around noon. Phippsie and I left the hospital a little before dawn and went across the street to the Rx Diner for an early breakfast. We talked for a couple of hours before we went home.

When I returned to the hospital around 11:30 a.m., Moody was awake and talking to a woman I didn't know. She was short, slim, and cinnamon-colored with a short curly hairstyle and heavy makeup. She was wearing white shorts, showing off her shapely legs and full hips. She was running her fingers through Moody's hair and kissing him on his forehead between words she whispered in his ear. I was furious. I had told Moody and myself that I expected him to find female companionship as long as he was discrete. But I wasn't just furious because she came to the hospital so scantily clad and kissing him in full view of others. I was jealous to learn that there was another woman in his life. I knew that he didn't know how I felt about him, but I didn't want him to care about anyone else. I forced a smile and walked cheerily in his room.

"You look better," I said, "not well but better."

He smiled at me and then introduced me to the other woman. "Lanie, meet Samm. Samm, this is Lanie." I was seething that he did not say that I was his wife. I wondered who he wanted her to think I was.

She smiled and extended her hand for me to shake. "Is Sam short for Samantha?" she asked.

"No," I answered. "It's the name formed by my initials: Sarah Ann Morgan–Moody. Moody gave me that nickname years ago, long before we were married." If she was surprised that he was married, she didn't show it. She said it was a pleasure to meet me and that she had to leave to get to work. I wondered what kind of work she did in shorts.

As soon as she left, I asked Moody who she was and why he hadn't told her I was his wife. He could tell I was upset with him, but he laughed. He said, "She's just a friend, but why are you acting like you're jealous?"

"Why do you think?" I asked sarcastically.

"I don't know, Samm," he responded. "I need you to tell me how you feel. I need you to explain what you want from me."

"I want you to act like my husband and not go out with other women," I replied.

"You know that I would never disrespect our arrangement," he said, adding, "I'm always discrete. So why else do you want me to stop seeing other women?"

Uncomfortably, I admitted, "All right, I love you, and I want you to love me back."

Moody wasn't satisfied. "Are you saying you love me like a *wife?*" he asked.

"I'm saying that I want you to kiss me again, and when you do, I won't turn away."

Moody shook his head and smiled. "You are a tough one, Samm. I guess that's good enough for now. I can't do much more than kiss you now anyway."

I laughed and said, "That's for sure."

Then he wondered aloud, "And when I'm able to do more than kiss, will you turn away then?"

I told him that I would be ready for more but only if he promised to quit drinking and doing anything else to get high. I wasn't going to give myself to a man who loved alcohol or anything else more than he loved me. I was too afraid of losing someone else I loved. I couldn't risk my heart on him if he continued to risk his health and safety by drinking and hanging out with self-destructive people like Lenny. He said again that he wasn't getting high on anything except alcohol, and he could stop drinking if he wanted to. If that's what it would take to keep my love, then he wanted to stop. I knew that it was not going to be that simple. But I was prepared to be patient and supportive if he was trying his best and willing to get the help he needed.

We kissed each other a lot while he was in the hospital and when he first came home. I liked kissing him, and I fell asleep at night in his arms, dreaming of making love to him. It took a few months, but as soon as he got clearance from his doctor, we were both anxious to consummate our "marriage." I was excited, anticipating that I would feel such passion and pleasure that I would feel my heart beating hard and fast, and I would be panting, trying to catch my breath. At the same time, I was nervous, afraid that I wouldn't know what to do and that I wouldn't satisfy him. Moody was gentle and soothing, patient and considerate as he always was with me. When it was over, I didn't feel at all like I had expected I would. I didn't feel anything particularly good or satisfying. It was disappointing, but it wasn't horrible. Moody realized that I wasn't as pleased as he was. He assured me that it would get better as we discovered each other's desires and likes. He was right. I lowered my expectations and found a modicum of enjoyment in sex. I never loved it, but it was all right, and I loved Moody enough to fake feeling the euphoria and enthusiasm he showed. I knew that some women like sex better than others do. I knew I wasn't frigid but I just wasn't as turned on by sex as some others seemed to be. I did like the intimacy Moody and I shared when we cuddled afterward. So I did enjoyed being his *wife* better than being his *little sister*.

****

After Lenny and Moody's accident, I rediscovered my faith in God. I had stopped praying after Papaw died, but when I got the call about the accident, I prayed that God would spare Moody. When He did, I believed that He had not forsaken me, even though I had turned away from Him. There was no earthly reason that Moody had survived the accident. Clearly, God had protected him that night, and I bore witness to more of His blessings. Moody thought he could just quit drinking but found it was not that easy. When he was released from the hospital, Lenny was not around because he was incarcerated. The judge said that he was moved by Lenny's lawyer's plea for leniency and by the pleas of his mother, high school football coach, principal, and, of course, the rest of the Fab Four. However, a good man had died because of Lenny's reckless driving, and the judge said that he could not ignore that or the pleas of the man's family for justice. He sentenced Lenny to serve three to five years in the state prison of Southern Michigan, located in Jackson.

I thought that Lenny's absence and my declaration of love for Moody would inspire him to clean up his act. However, Moody was drinking during his recuperation at home. I prayed that God would help me help him turn away from alcohol. I took a semester off from school to stay home and take care of him. I also started going to church regularly again at Allen AME and got Moody to go with me. He wouldn't go to Alcoholics Anonymous, but he did agree to talk about his problems in weekly private meetings with Reverend Hardeman. Fellowshipping with others at Allen AME, Moody rekindled friendships and made new friends with churchgoing men, and I began to develop close relationships with some of the young women, including Phippsie. Through these relationships, we developed a positive social life together that didn't involve alcohol consumption. We enrolled in Bible study classes and became active in church activities. I helped Gladys with the children's choir and joined the women's club and the young adult usher board. Moody worked with other former high school jocks coaching youth in church-sponsored athletic activities throughout the year. He also joined the men's club, which provided services for elderly and disabled members of the congregation, such as transporting them to and from church and delivering meals and groceries to them in baskets that were prepared by the women's club. We became a happy couple who stayed together by praying together and playing together with other Christian couples.

I hated to interrupt her but I had to know if she really loved Moody, so I asked her if she did.

Moody was my friend, my lover, and my husband in every way that mattered to me. For years, I thought that we would be together for life. But life is complicated, and so is love. There are many different kinds of love between men and women. Furthermore, love and relationships evolve as men and women grow and change over time. I didn't understand that then. I thought that what I felt for him was the only kind of love and I thought that it would last.

Once again, Mom went to her dresser drawer. This time she took out a picture album filled with candid shots of her and Moody taken at various locations and on various occasions between 1963 and 1973. I couldn't stop myself from laughing at a picture of them taken in 1968. Mom was wearing a floor-length dashiki, and Moody was wearing a hip-length one made from the same brightly colored fabric. Both had big smiles and huge Afro hairstyles. Mom was wearing big hoop earrings, a wide bangle bracelet, and a necklace made of cowrie shells. She looked very different from the way she looked in the debutante pictures taken five years earlier. She had blossomed into a beautiful young woman with a style that exuded sophistication, confidence, and pride in her African American heritage. She said that picture was taken during a significant year in her life and her relationship with Moody.

As 1968 began, my relationship with Moody began to change again. We seemed to be drifting apart, pulled in different directions by our reactions to changes in our community and the world. Following the riots in Detroit during the summer of 1967, I became actively involved in protesting economic, political, and social inequities in our area and across the nation. I marched in demonstrations and attended rallies to voice my opposition to the Viet Nam War, my demands for equal rights for black people and for women, and my call for the worldwide elimination of biological and nuclear weapons. While Moody said he agreed with my positions, he was not involved in protests. So I often attended them with Phippsie and some friends I made in the movement. Moody told me that his leg injuries from football and the accident bothered him when he stood a long time or walked too far. But I knew he had other reasons for not being more involved. I had stayed out of school in the fall of 1966 so that I could take care of Moody when he came home from the hospital. I hadn't returned to finish my degree, but I was educating myself and exploring my identity by reading every book I could find about African and African American history and politics, as well as history and politics throughout the African Diaspora. I attended a number of lectures and discussions on Wayne State's campus and community forums on race relations in Detroit and surrounding suburbs. I read newspapers and news magazines and watched television news programs. I analyzed biases and different perspectives expressed in reporting current events. I became knowledgeable about the issues of the movement and relatively conversant on our history, government, and politics. Moody is intelligent, but he had no desire to study like he was back in school. He was happier watching television westerns and action dramas than news and documentaries. He would rather do almost anything other than go to lectures or engage in informal discourses with other activists. So we were apart a lot, even when we were both at home. I thought back to what Papaw had said to me when he was dying about finding a man who could grow with me. I felt like I was learning and growing, while Moody was content to stand still.

In the spring of 1968, I was looking forward to turning twenty-one in July and, for the first time in my life, casting my vote for the president of the United States of America. I volunteered to work for Robert F. Kennedy's campaign, stuffing envelopes, making phone calls, and distributing flyers at community events. My resolve to get him elected was fueled by the assassination of Martin Luther King on April 4 and the fiery responses on the streets of Chicago and other urban areas across the country. I mourned the death of Dr. King. He was a truly great man, and when he spoke, I thought about my dear Papaw, who was quite an orator himself and who wanted equality and justice for black people. I watched as "Bobby" supported Coretta Scott King and the immediate King family members. I truly believed that getting him elected as president would be the best revenge against violent racists, organized crime, and the war mongers. That's why his assassination on June 5 was so devastating to me. Moody comforted me then as he had on April 4 and after the deaths of of my parents and my grandparents. The distance I felt was growing between us disappeared as, once again, Moody rescued me from despair. He went with me to vote for Hubert H. Humphrey in November. However, the excitement that I should have felt when I pulled the lever in the voting booth for the first time was gone. I kept thinking about June 5, when I lost the man I really wanted to vote for. Moody tried to make the day special for me with a celebratory dinner to mark the occasion. I was almost happy until I got news of two disappointing occurrences. First, Richard Nixon beat Humphrey. Second, and even more disconcerting, Lenny had been paroled and would be home in two days.

I was worried because I didn't know what would happen to Moody under Lenny's influence. I cared about Lenny but not as much as I cared about Moody. Moody had visited Lenny in prison a couple of times each month, often traveling the hour and a quarter from Parkersville to Jackson with Lenny's mother and Phippsie. Only Ollie visited Lenny more often than that. Living in Lansing, he was even closer to Jackson. He made the forty-minute trip from there almost every week. Ollie had become an assistant principal and talked to Lenny about using his education and experiences to counsel teens after he was released. He asked him to speak at his school and said that he might be able to find a job for him in Lansing. Bobby, the other member of Parkersville High's Fab Four, was still living and playing professional football in Cleveland. Despite the fact that the trip from there was over three hours, he visited Lenny at least once a month during the off-season and wrote to him every week during the training and playing seasons. Lenny was not a hardened criminal, and he had experienced a much easier life before prison than most of his fellow inmates. He developed a strong relationship with the chaplain and attended services every Sunday. He learned to count his blessings and to see how good God had been to him. He helped some of the younger inmates improve their reading and writing skills so they could read and respond to letters they received and communicate more effectively regarding appeals and at parole hearings.

I had not visited Lenny in prison, so I was pleased to see that he had changed for the better while serving his time. Indeed, it was because he had been a model prisoner that he was paroled after two years. Once he was released, he was determined never to return. He joined Allen AME and worked with Moody in the men's club and in the church's youth athletic programs. He volunteered as the announcer for the Parkersville High School Panthers football games and eventually landed a job as a sportscaster on a local radio station. He started taking social work courses at Wayne State to earn a master's degree. He was grateful that Phippsie had stood by him, considering how badly he had treated her when he was drinking and smoking. He was finally ready to give and receive her love. He promised to be the man that she deserved him to be, and they were married by Reverend Hardeman at Allen AME in June 1969. Moody and I stood by them at the altar as best man and matron of honor. Most of the time, I didn't think about the fact that Moody and I were not really married, but that day, it bothered me a lot. I felt like a liar, assuming a married woman's role in a sacred ceremony in the house of the Lord.

Moody and I had talked about getting married legally after we consummated our union in 1966. I was trying to figure out how to do it without admitting to everyone that we had been living a lie for such a long time. Whenever we thought about admitting the truth, we decided that in our hearts and in our minds, we were already married. We were living by the vows we had spoken in Alabama in 1963, even if we had never filed the paperwork. I didn't want to have another civil ceremony. When we did get married, I wanted the ceremony performed by a minister in a church. By the time of Lenny and Phippsie's wedding, we had been living together as a couple for almost six years. A year later, on July 5, 1970, we would meet the requirements to establish common law marriage status. So that is what we finally decided to do. We didn't have to tell anyone that we were lying, and in July 1970, our lie would become the truth. When that day came, we invited friends over to celebrate our seventh anniversary, which we secretly acknowledged as our "lawful wedding day." I suggested to Moody that we have a church wedding without raising suspicions by asking Reverend Hardeman to officiate in renewing our vows in July 1973 after we had been together ten years. Moody said he liked that plan.

Moody had taken a big pay cut when he went to work on the assembly line at Mr. Parker's plant. After he recovered from the accident, he went to Mr. Parker to try to return to his managerial job, but Mr. Parker said that he had eliminated that position and didn't have anything comparable available for Moody at that time. I was legally in charge of the balance of my inheritance on my twenty-first birthday, July 4, 1968. However, Moody refused to live off the money that Papaw had left me. I told him that the money belonged to both of us because we were a couple, and we didn't have to use all of it, just enough to make our lives easier. But he didn't want me to use any of it, and I didn't want to hurt his pride.

Moody was the only one of the Fab Four who didn't have a college degree, and he was the only one without professional status. He felt bad about that but not bad enough to stay in school. We both took a couple of classes in the winter quarter of 1968 when Lenny started work on his master's. Moody was smart, and he got good grades, but he didn't like all the homework, and he didn't type. When he had to write papers, he had to rely on me for help. I didn't mind typing and editing his papers, but he hated asking me to do that on top of my own studies. I encouraged him to stay in school, but I didn't want to pressure him. I wanted him to know that I would be with him whether he got a degree or not. So when he chose not to return for the spring quarter, I stopped attending as well. I went to work at Parker's plant. I wanted to finish my degree and go to graduate school. Papaw had instilled in me that I should get a doctorate in something, and I was feeling the urge to get back on track to do that. Even though Moody never told me I had to drop out when he did, I sensed his insecurities about my leaving him if I got too much more education than he did. I wanted to respect his feelings about school and about the money I inherited. So I lived within the means that we had from our salaries, and I kept the rest of my trust in savings for a rainy day.

****

On Thursday, July 1, 1971, all of the workers at the Parker plant were called to the cafeteria at 8:00 a.m. to meet the new plant manager, a hot-shot efficiency expert who was going to get the plant operating at a profit again. So Moody and I were together when we met the dashing and dynamic Mr. Claude Reynolds. A native of Chicago and a Viet Nam veteran, he was armed with a bachelor's degree from Kentucky State and an MBA from University of Illinois. He was actually employed by National Amusement Rides and Equipment Corporation (NAREC), the company that had bought controlling interest in Mr. Parker's manufacturing business. They ordered Mr. Parker to put him in charge of the plant or risk losing it altogether. Of course, I was like all the other women assembled in noticing that Mr. Reynolds was tall, dark and quite handsome. As he spoke, he personified the title of Nina Simone's hit song, "To Be Young, Gifted, and Black." He was articulate and intelligent. I guessed him to be about twenty-nine, the same age as Moody, but he seemed to have the maturity of one much older. There was an air about him that reminded me of how I used to feel in the presence of Papaw and the elite black men in the Cotillion Club. However, most of them were older when I was around them. Similarly, my cousin James Jr. had some high position at Ford Motor Company, but he was thirty-six and I had never seen him at his workplace. Claude Reynolds was standing in front of me, explaining his plans for moving the plant in a new direction, and everyone, including Mr. Parker, was paying attention. I couldn't help but stare at this fine young brother, who was polished and professional, cool and confident, large and in charge. At least, that's the way I saw him. Moody said he was arrogant and aloof. He called him an Oreo, black on the outside and white on the inside. Moody said the new boss showed up thinking he knew everything and feeling superior to the workers. Many of the assembly linemen were geared up to give him a hard time and show him that he couldn't push them around. I urged them to give him a chance and try to work with him. It was the first time that a black man was the boss at the plant. I said that we should try to help him. At least, we should give him the same respect that we had given the white bosses before him. Moody and the others said that they would see if he was really a black man or just the white man's puppet, a black overseer like those on the plantations of the Old South, "one step up from field slaves and scared of slipping back down." I agreed that we would have to see what kind of a man he was, but I didn't think we should rush to judgment after one brief meeting.

Mr. Reynolds ended his address by saying that he hoped he wouldn't have to let go of any of the employees but he was instituting a hiring freeze for the time being. So he announced that he was looking within the ranks of the clerical staff for an executive secretary. The position would involve general clerical and organizational duties, as well as conducting research, preparing reports and interacting with vendors and contractors. He instructed all who were interested in the position to submit a letter of application by the end of the day, stating their qualifications, experiences, and reasons for their interest. Most of the women at the plant wanted the higher salary and stated that in their letters. Of course, I wanted the salary increase. However, I wrote that I wanted the chance to expand my clerical skills, apply my knowledge of psychology and learn effective business strategies by observing and working with him. It might have sounded a little over the top, but I knew that working with him would be more intellectually stimulating than maintaining records and distributing checks in the payroll department.

He stated that applicants would be evaluated on the basis of clerical and organizational skills, as well as professional attributes and experiences related to the other duties of the position. Almost all of the office employees applied. None of us had experience conducting research and writing reports for the plant. Phippsie had completed a six-month training program at a business institute, where she learned shorthand and other secretarial skills, and she was working as a secretary in the personnel office. She thought that gave her an advantage over the rest of us in clerical positions at the plant. I thought writing about my excellent grades on research papers and reports I had done for college classes might work in my favor, as well as my A in statistics. Interviews were the next day. He only interviewed four of us. I'm sure that the others were not considered, at least in part, because of the poor grammar and punctuation in their letters. The interviews were different than we expected. He didn't ask about our skills and experience. Instead, he tested our skills by dictating a letter and a memorandum for us to type. He also gave us a set of reports to file. We had to design our own system and explain it to him. He said that he rated our typing on accuracy and speed and our filing on its logic and simplicity. My grammar and punctuation skills were excellent, and I was a good typist. Papaw made me take typing in high school, so I would be ready to prepare my papers in college. I did have three years of college, and I was an A student. So I knew how to take notes. I had an excellent memory, and although I didn't copy everything word for word, I recorded the important points and details of what was being said. I developed a two-tier system for filing the set of documents, which made it easy to retrieve and insert letters, reports, regulatory forms, purchase orders and invoices, labor issues, etc.

Your dad was impressed. He called me out for making changes in his wording on the letter and the memo I prepared for him. However, I pointed out that the changes that I made affected the tone of the communications, not their content. I thought it was important for him to explain the new procedures without making them sound like mandates ordered by a dictator. I thought that he could get greater cooperation and compliance with a softer tone. Everyone knew that he had the power, "the big stick" so to speak, so he could afford to "walk softly." As Bea had taught me, I thought he "could attract more flies with sugar than with vinegar." He laughed and asked if I was applying to be his psychologist or his secretary. I responded that I had over ninety credits toward a degree in psychology and that if I was hired as his executive secretary, I hoped that he would want me to use my brain as well as my hands to help him. I told him that I had no trouble knowing that he was my boss and doing whatever he wanted me to do. However, I wouldn't be a robot. I would offer suggestions which he could decide to use or not. He said that I was bolder than the other candidates. He said that they "knew their places," but I seemed to think that I could define my own place in his office. I apologized if I had come across as rude or disrespectful. He said that he liked my style. He thought we would make a good team as long as I didn't get upset if he didn't accept every suggestion I made. Then he told me that I had the job. It was 4:30 p.m. on Friday. So before I left, he had me complete the personnel forms and type the announcement of my appointment to post on the bulletin board. I started my new job on Monday, July 5, the eighth anniversary of my "marriage" to Moody.

From the beginning, there were whispers about Mr. Reynolds's intentions toward me. Phippsie said that I didn't know shorthand and didn't type as many words per minute as she did. In truth, I typed almost as many words per minute as she did and I took notes efficiently with my version of speedwriting. Apparently, she ignored the other duties that went with the position where my experiences and qualifications surpassed hers: conducting research and writing reports. She thought she should have been his choice, so she surmised that he had made his selection on the basis of something else, perhaps his obvious attraction to me. She said that she and others saw the way he looked at me and took a special interest in me. She was my friend and did not accuse me of encouraging him, but she didn't trust the new boss. Nobody did. Moody wondered if Phippsie was correct and told me to tell him if Reynolds ever got fresh with me. I knew that people were watching us, but I didn't care. There was nothing inappropriate for them to see. In the office and in public, we referred to each other as Mr. Reynolds and Mrs. Moody. In private, he told me to call him by his first name, and I agreed he could do the same with me. Everyone else called me Samm, as Moody did. However, Claude called me by my given name, Sarah. He liked the fact that he was the only one, aside from older people at my church, who did.

We developed a good working relationship and a solid friendship over the next twelve months. I became really good at my job, and he kept assigning more duties to me. I was drafting reports he edited for the regional and national headquarters of NAREC. I was preparing letters and memoranda for his signature based on anecdotal comments rather than formal dictation. I was organizing data and assisting him in designing graphs and flowcharts for presentations that he made at conferences. We discussed everything that needed to be done and became so mentally in tune that we each knew before we spoke exactly how the other would tackle any problem or challenge that arose. I also helped him organize his active personal life. He was a player. He was dating several women. I kept files on the three main ones that included their favorite colors, flowers, candy, foods, and fragrances. I entered their birthdays and special occasions on his calendar. When I reminded Claude of upcoming holidays and their birthdays, he gave me his credit card to order candy and flowers to be delivered to their offices, and he asked me to make reservations for him to take them dining and dancing. So I was well aware that he was a smooth operator with multiple romantic liaisons just as he was aware that I was a married woman. Even if I wasn't married, I could never see myself with a man like that. I could not trust him as a lover. However, we were friends, really close friends. In fact, by the end of my first year working with him, we were best friends. We trusted each other, shared confidences, and solicited each other's advice on personal matters.

****

On Wednesday, July 5, 1972, I celebrated two anniversaries. It was my first one working with Claude and my ninth one "married" to Moody. I awoke that morning to Moody's amorous advances. He said that he had planned a special way for us to spend our anniversary. He just needed me to call in sick as he had already done. Then we could spend the morning making love. He would order barbeque for lunch, and after an afternoon of more lovemaking, he would pick up fried chicken for dinner. Before I could respond, he gave me a small gift-wrapped box. He urged me to open it immediately so that I could see his gift to me and know what he was hoping to get in return. I complied and found a heart-shaped fourteen-karat gold locket on a thin gold chain. It was engraved with the letters M-O-M. Inside, there was a picture of the two of us on one side and the other side was empty. I looked at him and saw that he was dangling my packet of birth control pills, preparing to drop them in the waste basket by the bed. He was beside himself with pride over the very romantic scene he thought he had created. I thanked him for the locket as I gently retrieved my birth control pills. I told him I had to go to work that day, and we could have a nice evening when I returned home. I quickly got out of bed and prepared to take a shower. He seemed genuinely stunned at my reaction and stuttered as he asked me what was wrong. I replied that I had a really busy day at work and couldn't stay home. Truthfully, I just needed to get out of there. Moody got up with an apologetic smile and arms reaching to hug me. I lowered his arms and kissed him on the cheek. I faked a smile and promised, "Later."

Moody had been trying for months to convince me to have a baby, ever since we learned that Phippsie was expecting her second baby with Lenny. Ollie and Gail had three children, and Bobby and Diane had four. So Moody was the only one of the Fab Four to have no offspring, and he was the one who had been "married" for the longest amount of time. I understood why he wanted to have a child like his friends, but I couldn't live my life based on others' timetables. I told him that I wanted to go back to finish my degree before we started a family. I just turned twenty-five the day before, and I realized that if I had stayed in school, I could have completed my doctorate already. I didn't regret stopping out of school to take care of him in 1966, but I felt that I had been foolish not to go back when he was better. I had my own dreams, and I had abandoned them, losing a part of myself as I tried to be the kind of wife I thought Moody wanted. I wanted a professional career and a family. And I knew that I could have both of them if he supported me the way that I always tried to support him. I wasn't ready to be a mother yet, and I thought he knew that. I had certainly been clear and direct in communicating it to him. He had told me that he understood. So I wondered how he could possibly think that it was romantic to pressure me with his gift of a "Mom" locket and his suggestion that we spend a day trying to make a baby. I was not turned on by the whole scenario. In fact, it turned me off.

At the office, Claude acknowledged our first anniversary working together by presenting me with two gifts that showed how much he valued me and understood me. First, he promoted me from executive secretary to executive administrative assistant, recognizing that I assumed many more responsibilities than a secretary. The new title came with a new salary, twenty percent higher than I made when I left work the day before. It also came with travel benefits. From then on, NAREC would pay my expenses to attend the quarterly corporate conferences and workshops for executives and their assistants. The second gift was special, and I appreciated it even more. NAREC was going to pay my tuition for one or two classes a quarter, up to six per year. Claude explained that he had argued that my work performance could be enhanced if I gained knowledge of business management and marketing. Claude pointed out that if I took the psychology courses I needed in my major and used the business classes as electives, I could earn my degree within two years. He said he could justify the psychology classes as being relevant to marketing. We both laughed at that. As the day went on, I reflected on the contrast between the ways the two men chose to honor our anniversaries. Moody gave me a gift that he hoped would encourage me to do something he wanted me to do, while Claude gave me a gift to encourage me to do something he knew I wanted to do.

Word spread through the plant about my new position and salary, not from me or Claude but from the gossips in personnel and payroll, including Phippsie. Once again, rumors and speculations about our supposed affair were refueled. They were false. We were not lovers. However, my feelings for Claude had deepened and changed. I trusted him more than I ever trusted anyone outside of Moody and my family. I could tell him anything about myself, and he never judged me. He trusted me the same way. I respected him and had genuine affection for him. I knew he genuinely cared for me as well. However, we were both linked romantically with others, and we maintained appropriate boundaries in our interactions. Nonetheless, I felt more for him than just admiration and adoration as my mentor and my best friend. I recognized that my feelings for Claude were unique to me, different from any I had ever experienced before. I was excited to come to work each day to be near him. Instead of dreading Mondays and loving Fridays, I felt the opposite. I hated the 5:00 p.m. bell on Friday and began to miss him before I even made it home. I listened to him more intently than I had ever listened to anyone and remembered every word he uttered in my presence. My heart fluttered when he entered the room and skipped a beat when he left. I had never before analyzed how different individuals walked. Yet I knew how every muscle of his body moved when he strode down the hall. I enjoyed watching the way his lips moved when he talked, and I liked how brightly his teeth glistened and how his cheeks ballooned when he smiled and laughed. I didn't want to be aware of all those things. I didn't want to notice everything about him, but I did. I couldn't seem to stop those feelings from growing stronger inside me, overtaking my whole emotional being. I wanted to protect myself and Moody from hurt. So I tried to bury and deny my feelings. I pretended that nothing unusual was happening to me, and I worked hard at appearing normal.

****

As Claude and I grew closer, Moody and I grew more distant. I still loved him, but we wanted different lifestyles and different things from our relationship. He had come to think it was okay for me to use my trust fund so that I could stop working and stay home to raise a family. He wanted me to be more like my grandma Bea. But I was my mother's daughter, and I needed him to understand that I wanted to use my brain and talents to build a professional career that served God by serving others. I didn't think less of Moody for not wanting that for himself. So I didn't think he should think less of me for not wanting to be a stay-at-home mother, at least not yet. He resented the time I was devoting to studies in the evenings. He wanted me to play whist with Lenny and Phippsie or watch television with him from the time I finished cleaning up after dinner to the time we went to bed. We didn't even like to watch the same programs on our new twenty-five-inch console television. I wanted to watch the news, documentaries, public television programs, and historical or political dramas. He preferred westerns, police and action dramas, variety shows, and comedies. He said the purpose of television was to entertain and help people relax after a hard day's work. He couldn't relax watching all of the horrible stories about the war, poverty, and crime. However, our differences were not the real reasons that I became irritated with Moody or ignored him altogether.

I finally faced the truth. I had fallen in love with someone else. I felt so guilty, and I hated myself for that. Moody was a good man, and he loved me. He had been there for me since I was a child. He had gone along with my crazy plan to get married then not to legalize it. He had lived with me platonically for over three years, even after he fell in love with me, until I was of age and told him that I loved him. He had done everything I asked him to do for me throughout more than a decade before asking me to do anything for him, even if it was something I really didn't want to do. We had a powerful history together, and we should be able to build a solid future on that. Moody wasn't perfect, but he was a good, decent man who loved only me and was faithful to me.

But I was in love with Claude, a man who was a player. In romantic relationships, he was not committed to anyone but himself. He had at least three women who seemed to love him and want to be with him exclusively, but he made them share his time and affection. He wasn't in love with any of them. They believed that he was thoughtful and attentive because I kept him aware of their special days and made sure to order what they thought were symbols of his affection. I fantasized about being with Claude, sometimes during intimate moments with Moody. I felt like I should have a scarlet letter A on my forehead to show my shame. I knew that if Moody found out that another man was in control of my heart and my soul, it would hurt him much more than if he thought that the man only had access to my body. But it was all moot. I would never leave Moody. I took our marriage vows seriously. Whether they were legal or not, I said them aloud, and I knew God heard me do so. Papaw had taught me not to believe in divorce. There had been no divorce on my mother's side of the family in the four generations since slavery. Papaw taught me that when God blesses you with a good life partner, it is an affront to Him to leave that partner without due cause. Moody had never abused me physically or emotionally, and he had never cheated on me. The disagreements we had were hardly irreconcilable. I wasn't in love with Moody as I was with Claude. However, I loved him and was bound to him by honor for the rest of my life. Therefore, I would have to find some way to get over my feelings for Claude. I knew that was not going to be easy to do, but I knew that I had to try.

I did try to stop myself from falling deeper in love with Claude, but I didn't succeed. Yet I never acted on those feelings, and I didn't share them with anyone. Indeed, neither Claude nor Moody was aware of them. Almost two years later, in April 1974, I was happily looking forward to graduating with my bachelor's degree in June. I had already been accepted to graduate programs at Wayne State and University of Michigan. The first part of my plan for getting over Claude was to get away from him. I planned to leave my job right after graduation and attend graduate school as a full-time student. That would allow me to finish my master's degree in a year and move on to pursue my doctorate. The other part of my plan was to have a baby with Moody. I stopped taking birth control pills and asked Moody to use condoms through June, as my doctor advised, before I started trying to conceive. As always, I had a plan.

At the same time, Claude was making plans. I was surprised when he told me that he decided to settle down. After a couple of years of dating several women, I knew that one of his girlfriends had risen from the pack. Her name was Angela, and he had been dating her exclusively for almost nine months. I met her on a few occasions when she came by the office to meet him for a dinner date. She was a pharmacist and she was smart, attractive and pleasant during our brief encounters. He said that she was pressing him to make a commitment, and he believed that he might be ready to do that. Claude and I had discussed her a few times before. She seemed to be in love with him, and I knew he cared about her. However, he had not indicated to me that he was in love with her or that he was contemplating a change in their relationship. I asked him if there was a specific reason for what seemed to be a sudden change in his attitude toward marriage. He admitted that he was being considered for the Northeast Regional Vice President of NAREC. He said that one of the strikes against him for the position was his marital status. That seemed to be a bigger obstacle to his promotion than his race. Being black had not hurt him in climbing the ladder of success so far. He was the highest-ranking black man in NAREC, but there were others in the pipeline, including one who would probably replace him at Parker's if he got the promotion. But all of the VPs at that time were married men. The president, CEO, and members of the board of directors were very conservative. They preferred their executives to be happily married, preferably with children, because they saw that as a sign of stability. Of course, they could not state that as a criterion for the position, but it was generally understood among the managers and executives that single men only moved up so far in the company.

I knew that image was important in the corporate world, but such a policy, stated or not, went against the principles of civil rights and affirmative action. I told him that he should fight that prejudice and go after the position on his merit and his record with the company. He had brought the Parker plant from the red into the black and then to the most profitable factory in the Midwest region of NAREC. He always received the highest ratings for workshops he led at conferences. He deserved the promotion, and he should stand up to those "tight asses" and tell them straight out that they all knew that he was the best man for the job and they should give it to him because of that. If they didn't, he should leave and take his talent and experience to a company that would appreciate him and treat him fairly. He laughed and told me that he loved my fiery passion for what I believed in and my take-no-prisoners determination to win. He reminded me that it was that bold attitude that made him hire me in the first place. We thought how funny it would be if we both left the plant that summer. We wondered what the gossip mongers would make of that.

Claude was interviewed in New York two weeks later, a few days before we went to the spring quarter conference in Chicago. After the opening session and reception at the conference, we went to have a night cap in the hotel lounge. We had been so busy preparing reports and materials for the conference that this was the first time we got to talk seriously about his round of interviews in New York. He said that he had met separately with the president, CEO, and several members of the board, as well as with two other regional vice presidents. He shared his portfolio and thought he had presented a convincing argument for his appointment. They did not discuss his bachelor status; it was the "elephant in the room." However, he had thought a lot about it and decided that regardless of whether he was appointed or not, he was going to propose to Angela. She was a good woman and he could see himself happy with her as his wife. He said that he wasn't going to get married right away, but he did plan on getting engaged soon. He asked me what I thought about his plans, and I responded by asking him why my opinion mattered. He said that we were friends and he valued my opinion. I said I thought he was getting engaged too quickly. He seemed to be rushing to act because it was what Angela wanted and because he thought that it would help his career. He didn't respond to that. He asked me if I would go with him to shop for an engagement ring. I couldn't tell him that given my feelings for him, it would be too painful to try on rings that he was buying for a woman other than me. I simply said, "I can't help you with that."

"You can't, or you won't?" he asked.

I repeated, "I can't." When he continued to press me as to why not, I blurted out, "Because I love you!"

As soon as the words came out, I threw my right hand over my mouth, wishing I could push them back in. I bolted from the lounge and took an elevator to the floor where our rooms were located. Claude caught up to me as I was opening the door to my room. He followed me inside and put his hands on my shoulders as the door closed behind us. He turned me around to talk to me, but I couldn't look at him. My head was down, and I was crying as I said, "I'm sorry. I'm so sorry. I didn't mean to say that. I'm sorry. I'm so—"

"Okay. It's okay," Claude assured me, holding me in his arms. "But was that the truth? Did you mean what you said?"

It was so difficult for me, but I finally admitted it. "Yes, it is true. I do love you."

Claude held me tighter and confessed that he had been in love with me for a long time but had no idea that I felt the same way. He lifted my head with his hands and kissed me fervently. We unleashed all the passion that we had been feeling for each other for so long. Years later, I understood the lyrics to Madonna's "Like a Virgin," because although I had been having sex with Moody since 1966, I felt "touched for the very first time" on Friday, April 26, 1974. I finally understood what all the fuss was about. When we made love that night and all through Saturday, I "felt the earth move under my feet," I heard the bells ringing and the whistles blowing, I saw the fireworks and felt them exploding inside me.

Mom stopped abruptly. She was surprised and embarrassed that she got carried away and forgot she was telling me, her daughter, intimate details about my parents. I was so engrossed in her story that I had almost forgotten those lovers were my parents. Her abrupt silence and embarrassment made me remember she was talking about her and Dad. I did feel a little weird about that, but I assured her that I was okay and wanted her to continue.

As we ate breakfast together on Sunday morning, Claude asked me if I wanted him to go home with me to talk to Moody. I told him that wasn't necessary. He just wanted to be sure that Moody wouldn't hurt me when I told him that I was leaving him. I told Claude that Moody would never hurt me, and besides, I didn't plan to leave Moody. I could never do that. I loved him too much to hurt him. Claude said that I told him many times that weekend that I loved him but I was apparently okay with hurting him. I told him that I loved Moody and had made a commitment to him eleven years earlier that I could not break. But as much as I loved Moody, I was in love with Claude. I had never felt about anyone the way I felt about him. I loved him from the depths of my soul to every corner of my mind and with all of my heart. I told Claude that I would love him and cherish that weekend for as long as I lived. I said that when I married Moody, I spoke vows and made promises to him. I would stay with Moody for life. Of course, Claude pointed out that I had broken my vow of fidelity many times that weekend. I said I knew that and I would undoubtedly pay for those sins, surely every time I remembered with longing the way I felt when he touched me. But we could never speak of the things that we did and the love we shared in our rooms in Chicago. As impossible as it seemed, we had to go on with our lives as though none of that happened.

Claude was hurt, angry, and confused. He accused me of being the ultimate tease. He said that he knew that women played games at being "hard to get." They flirted and teased but stopped short of "going all the way" to see how much a chump would do and spend to get their goodies. But this was so much worse, he said. I had let him sample the goods just enough to get him addicted. Then I told him that he couldn't have them anymore. I was giving all that was left in the world to another addict just because I let him sample them first. I cried. I tried to make him understand that I had been on the same "high" that he was on all weekend. But we had to face the reality that we could never get that high again. I told him that I wished things could be different. I wished that we could be together forever. I wished that my wishing could make it so, but unfortunately, it could not. I didn't know how I would find the strength to do it, but I had to go back to my life as it was before. I told him that I would never be sorry for what happened, but I was sorry that it hurt him. Claude stared at me coldly and didn't speak to me at all on the flight to Detroit or on the drive to Parkersville.

When Claude dropped me off that evening, Moody was so happy to see me. I didn't know why because I had been treating him so badly for weeks. He had prepared dinner for me, and while I ate it, he prepared a warm bubble bath for me. After I finished my bath, he brought a cup of hot Vernor's Ginger Ale to our bedroom and placed it on the nightstand on my side of the bed. Then he turned off the light and pulled the door just far enough to leave a bit of light from the hallway so that I could see my cup and saucer. I fell asleep before I finished the Vernor's and slept soundly through the night. As I lay on my back in that last twilight sleep that comes just before one awakens naturally, I was dreaming about making love with Claude. Or maybe I was just remembering. In either case, it was so vivid that I could actually feel it. But somehow it didn't feel right. I opened my eyes to see Moody looking down at me as he moved in and out. I realized that the fantasy was over and this was my reality. I started to push him away, but I didn't. I felt guilty about betraying him, and I didn't want him to sense a change in my feelings toward him. So I pulled him closer and responded passionately as I closed my eyes and imagined being with Claude.

****

For the first time in almost three years, I dreaded going to work on Monday morning. I knew that Claude was going to be angry at me, and I didn't know how he was going to show it. I also felt guilty about being with Moody so soon after I left him. I felt like I had cheated on Claude with Moody instead of the other way around. When I arrived at the office, I was bombarded with emotions, some of which I couldn't discern. Claude wasn't there yet, so angst was one of them. When he finally came in, an hour later than usual, he walked past me to his inner office without looking at me or saying a word. Half an hour went by before he summoned me by intercom into his office to "take dictation." He hadn't used that phrase since we met. He knew I didn't know shorthand, and he usually had me take notes and draft a letter or memo from them. When I finished the letter, typewritten verbatim as he said it, he signed it and told me to put it in the outgoing mail. For the rest of the day, he spoke to me only when necessary, by intercom rather than in person if possible.

When the 5:00 p.m. bell rang, I started to leave but went into his office instead, closing the door behind me. I told him that I couldn't work like that. He was being cold and indifferent toward me and that was too hard for me to bear, given how close we had been, even before the past few days.

He looked at me in amazement and spoke sarcastically in a raised voice. "Do you mean the weekend? You need to get over the events of the weekend. Pretend they never happened. What we did in Chicago meant nothing, and it doesn't change anything. You're married, and I'm about to become engaged. So I suggest you get your act together, Mrs. Moody. This is a place of business, and that is all we have to talk about from now on."

I went back to the outer office, holding back my tears, and pulled some tissues from my desk. I was blowing my nose when I saw Phippsie at the door. She asked if I was all right, and I told her that my sinuses were filling up again. I probably had a cold or hay fever. She said that the pollen count was high, and she hoped I felt better soon. She asked if I wanted to stop to get a soda or a drink on the way home. Monday was the day Moody and Lenny hung out, so they would both be coming home late. I asked for a rain check because I was tired and just wanted to lie down for a while.

Moody didn't come home that night, and he didn't show up at work the next morning. I discretely checked the time cards and saw that Moody's had been stamped "sick." That meant that he had called from wherever he was to say that he would be out sick for the day. Since I knew that he was alive and well enough to call in, I wondered why he never came home the previous night. I also wanted to know where he was and what he was doing that prevented him from coming to work. Claude was acting more decently toward me that day. We weren't back to normal, but I felt like we might be headed in that direction. I knew that it would take time for us both to figure out how to deal with what happened and to regain our friendship. When 5:00 p.m. came, I drove straight home to hear what Moody had to say about his absence at home and at work. I was surprised to see him sitting on the sofa not watching television. He looked up at me with a poker face when I walked through the door. I had no clue as to what he was about to say. He asked me how I was doing, and I said, "Fine, but I wasn't the one who called in sick today." He smiled weakly. Then he began to tell me that he was sorry if I had been worried about him. He just needed some time to think about things. He said that he had been trying to think of a way to say some things to me without hurting me or making me hate him. I told him that I could never hate him, no matter what he did.

He said that he had been seeing a woman at the Riverfront Diner, where he usually hung out with Lenny and his guy friends on Mondays. I wondered what he meant by seeing her, and he said that they had been talking for a while as friends but that it had recently become more than a friendship. He said that they had so much in common. They liked the same things and wanted the same kind of life. He said that there was no easy way to say what he had to say so he would just "cut to the chase and get to the bottom line." He wanted out of our arrangement because she was going to end things if he didn't leave me to be with her all the time.

Arrangement? I thought. He did not call our life together an arrangement. He was the one who called it a marriage right from the beginning, even in the years before we consummated it. After all those years and the evolution of our relationship to what I finally considered a marriage, he was calling it an arrangement. Moody continued to say that she refused to sneak around with him any longer and he couldn't stand to lose her. He had packed a few things and was leaving right away. He said that he would come by to get the rest of his things while I was in class. I was dumbfounded. The whole thing was surreal. I heard his voice, but I couldn't process what he was saying. Had I been so wrapped up in my studies and my fantasies about Claude that I had missed signs that Moody was pulling away from me toward someone else? As he picked up his Parkersville Panthers duffel bag, which I had not noticed lying on the floor next to the sofa, I asked him why he made love to me the day before. He said that he was trying to find out if he could be faithful to me again and let her go. He knew afterward that he could not, and he felt terrible about that. He pointed out that since we had never filed our marriage license in Alabama and never petitioned for common law status in Michigan, we didn't have to go through with a divorce. But he told me that he knew I could plan a way to do this so that people would not figure out that our marriage was never real. He said he would go along with whatever plan I made. Then he left.

I had tried my best not to interrupt Mom, but I couldn't help but ask, "Are you kidding me? What a colossal jerk! I know for certain that he is not my biological father, and I don't understand why you still care about him after that." Mom begged me to calm down and listen. She said that there was more to the story, and she didn't want me to judge anyone until she finished. I found that hard to do, but I tried to keep an open mind.

If there had been no strain in my relationship with Claude, I would have told him the next morning about what Moody did and how I was feeling. I was confused because this was so different from anything Moody had ever said or done before. In the nineteen years since I met him, he had always made me feel like he was my personal hero. No matter what I did, what plan I concocted, he stood by me and loved me. It was inconceivable to me that he was not going to be there for me any longer. I felt such a sense of loss because our relationship was dying. I felt angry and betrayed because he cheated on me. I knew that I had cheated also, but I wasn't leaving him for the man I truly loved. I felt angry at myself and stupid because I had put Moody's feelings above my own and he had not reciprocated. At the same time, I felt relieved that I could be with Claude without feeling guilty about hurting Moody. But I was afraid that I had ruined my chances with Claude by walking away from him with what he perceived as indifference to his feelings. I felt sick at the thought that Claude might have already proposed to Angela when I knew that he belonged with me. I felt frustrated because I needed to talk to my best friend, Claude, about all I was feeling, but I had messed up that relationship as well. I needed to figure out how to end a marriage that was never real without exposing the truth. I wished I could have a do-over, but I was not going to get one. So I prayed. I prayed for God's forgiveness and for His help in getting through the maze I had made of my life.

Claude and I were far less tense by Wednesday, but we weren't talking like we did the week before. He asked if I was okay, and I said that I wasn't yet but that I would be soon. We went about our work until the end of the day. Then I asked if he had a few minutes to talk. When he affirmed that he did, I went into the inner office and told him that Moody had moved out of the house. He asked if it was because of what we did, and I told him that Moody didn't know about us. He had left to be with someone else. Claude asked how I felt about that. I admitted that I had mixed feelings: anger and hurt but also relief and fear. Claude said that he understood all of those feelings, except fear. He said that he thought I was fearless, so he couldn't imagine what could make me afraid. I told him that I was afraid that I had lost my best friend when I needed him the most. Claude said that he missed his friend also. We both laughed to break the tension. I was still afraid to ask about any other feelings he had toward me or whether he had proposed to Angela yet. I turned to leave, and he asked if he still had to pretend that he had forgotten the things we said to each other in Chicago. I said that I remembered everything that happened there, but I would pretend not to if that would make him more comfortable with his fiancée. He gently pulled me away from the door, looked me in my eyes, and said, "How can I marry Angela feeling the way I do about you?" We kissed, and he asked if I would like to go to dinner with him some place far from Parkersville with great food and good ambiance. I happily accepted. We drove separately to the garage on Main Street, where I parked my car. Then I rode with Claude to Joe Muer's Restaurant on Gratiot Avenue in Detroit.

We had a wonderful dinner and even more wonderful conversation. When the restaurant closed, we went to a small bar a few blocks away to continue talking before driving back to Parkersville around 1:00 a.m. We decided to try to have a normal courtship. We would go out dining, dancing, and to movies and concerts. We were already friends. We knew we had passion. We just needed to see if we were as compatible socially as we both thought we were. Thursday morning, I tendered my resignation effective Friday at 5:00 p.m. Claude asked Phippsie to assume duties as his acting executive secretary Monday morning, making it clear that she could apply for the permanent position once it was properly posted. Once I was no longer a plant employee, Claude and I began dating, mostly outside of Parkersville. We were relatively discrete, not flaunting our relationship but not hiding it either. That drove the gossips crazy. Everyone knew that Moody and I were separated and that he was living with Mavis Johnson. So, Claude and I weren't doing anything behind his back, and we were not breaching corporate policy. Moody refused to say anything bad about me or my relationship with Claude, and I acted accordingly about him and Mavis. So there was nothing to provide grist for the rumor mill.

Claude and I went together to the Parkersville Memorial Day barbeque in the park. I graduated from Wayne State University with honors the first week in June, and Claude was there to cheer for me. That night, we went out to Baker's Keyboard Lounge, one of the venues where my mother sang shortly before she died. Claude went back to New York the following weekend. He and the other two finalists were invited to spend two days in meetings with other vice presidents and the president of NAREC. The other two finalists were told to come with their wives. The wives spent most of their time with the wives of the vice presidents and president, but they all joined the men for meals and a reception on Saturday night. Claude came by to see me as soon as he returned from New York. He said that he thought the assistant vice president from New Jersey seemed to be the frontrunner. Claude said that candidate knew the Northeast because he was already working within the region. Claude also said that he and his wife seemed to gel the best with the executive couples. We agreed that we would be all right no matter how things turned out. I knew that God was not finished with him yet. If that door of opportunity closed, it was only because God planned to open a better one for him. Claude invited me to attend his church with him. I enjoyed the service at First Baptist, and it didn't seem very different from the ones at my church, Allen AME. We worshipped the same God. We were compatible, very happy, and very much in love.

Flag Day, Friday, June 14, was a red flag day for me. It was the third consecutive day that I awoke nauseated and had to hurry to the toilet to puke. I knew what that meant, but I hoped that I was wrong. I made an appointment at a clinic in Detroit. They gave me a pregnancy test and a pelvic exam that confirmed what I already knew: I was about six and a half weeks into my pregnancy with you. That's how long it had been since Claude and I spent a passionate weekend in Chicago. I had been off the pill for almost a month, and our spontaneous encounters were unprotected. I hadn't planned on getting pregnant, but I was overjoyed to be carrying Claude's baby. Then I remembered having my last passionate encounter with Moody that Monday morning, and I recalled that he wasn't wearing a condom then. I was really mad at him for doing that the day before he left me. I wanted you to be Claude's baby, but I couldn't be positive that you were. I knew I should tell them both about my condition. It was the honest thing to do. I had lied for so long to so many people that I just didn't want to lie anymore, especially not to Claude. I called him at the office to say that the doctor's appointment went well and that I was feeling better. I asked if he would come to my house that evening at eight. He asked why I wanted him to come so late. I told him that there were some things I had to do before he came by. I didn't need to call Moody. I knew that he'd be at the diner after work. So I decided to go there first to talk to him.

Moody seemed pleasantly surprised to see me when I walked into the Riverfront Diner a little before 6:00 p.m. He stood up and met me halfway between the door and the bar. He asked what brought me there, and I said that I wanted to talk to him. He said that it was fine with him, and he escorted me to a booth on the right wall. A waitress came to the booth while we were walking. Her stare told me that she must be Mavis Johnson. Moody confirmed that when he introduced us. She smiled but looked at me with suspicion as she asked if I wanted to order anything. I said that I just wanted a bowl of chicken soup and a glass of lemonade. Moody said that he wanted his usual Friday night fried fish platter. He started our conversation, telling me that I was looking really good and asking me how things were going with Claude. I told him that they were fine and we were happy. I, in turn, asked about his relationship with Mavis, and he said that they were happy also. Neither of us elaborated.

After Mavis brought us our orders, I felt confident that we wouldn't be interrupted, so I became more serious. I asked Moody why he thought we didn't make it. He said he didn't know. He said that we were young when we almost got married. We both grew up, and we grew differently. He said that I wanted to get a doctorate and change the world, while he just wanted to have fun and change a few babies' diapers. I was still growing, and he was settled. He said that we were both good people, just not good for each other. I asked if he thought we could have made it if we had a baby. He said that a baby would have only complicated things. In the end, we would still have wanted different things, but we would have felt obliged to stay together because of the child. He said that he had wanted me to have a baby to keep me at home, but that was a selfish reason to bring a life into the world. He was glad that I insisted that we wait. I said it was odd that he decided to leave when I was ready to start trying to have a baby and that he seemed to be trying to make a baby right up to the day before he left. He told me the timing of his move was based on Mavis's threat to leave him. That was why he left suddenly that day. Before then, he wasn't planning to leave. He asked if I had a plan yet for how we would end our "marriage." I said that I was thinking about going to Reno, Nevada, to pretend to get a quickie divorce, but that I hadn't worked out the details yet. He said that he'd go along with whatever I decided and there was no rush unless I was thinking about getting married. I didn't react, except to thank him. I didn't tell him I was pregnant. I wouldn't allow a man who saw you as a complication or an obligation to claim you as his child.

It was almost 7:30 p.m. when I left the diner. I had to hurry to get home before Claude arrived. When I answered his knock on the door, he kissed me passionately before either of us said, "Hello." He said he had news that he couldn't wait to share with me. He showed me a letter that had come by express mail to the office that afternoon. It congratulated him on being selected as NAREC's new Vice President of Northeastern Sales and Distribution. A contract was enclosed for him to sign and return within forty-eight hours. Claude said that he was really surprised by the offer because he had followed my suggestion and insisted that he would not get married until he was ready to do so. He said that he told them that if his work was not appreciated, he would gladly try to use his skills and experience to advance his career in another company. They had not seemed to respond favorably to what they saw as a threat, but then the offer arrived five days later. He knelt in front of me and pulled a jewelry box from his pocket. He said that he wanted me to go with him to New York as his wife. He said that he had been planning to ask me to marry him for a while, but he didn't want me to think that his proposal was motivated by his desire for the vice presidency. Now that he had it, he knew that I could be certain that his only motivation for proposing was his unconditional love for me. I started to cry. I told him that I wanted to say yes because I loved him unconditionally as well. But I needed him to rise and sit down first because I had things to tell him that might change his mind about wanting to marry me.

I told him that I was pregnant, and before I could say anything else, he was on his feet, lifting me off the ground. He was even more excited than he had been about getting the promotion. He chuckled, put me down, kissed me, and began rubbing my stomach. He laughed at the thought that he might not want to marry me because I was with child. "How blessed I am," he said, "to become a husband and a father to a woman and child that I'll love and cherish forever." Tears of joy fell from my eyes, and I knew that he was the only man who deserved to be your father. He wiped the tears from my cheeks and asked me again to marry him.

I said, "Of course. I will be honored and happy to be your wife always and forever." He declared that he wanted us to be married as soon as possible. He wanted us to be married when we went to New York two and a half weeks later if I didn't mind getting a quick divorce and eloping. I told him that I was fine with that, but I had something else to tell him first. I was so deeply ashamed that I wished I could avoid admitting it, but I had to be honest with him if I wanted our marriage to be based on trust. I told him about my fake marriage to Moody and why I did it. I confessed to living a lie for more than a decade and for wanting to cover it up even then, after it was over.

Claude was shocked but not angry. He was happy that nothing stood in the way of our getting married, and he suggested that we could still fly to Reno and elope there. He was so wonderful to me. I said I wanted to be truly married for my first and only time by a minister in a church. I knew an old friend of Papaw's who had a church in Toledo, Ohio. I wanted him to marry us. We could still fly to Reno for a quick honeymoon to cover my supposed divorce. I felt awful about getting him involved in my lies and schemes. I should have come clean and told everyone the truth, since I was leaving town anyway. But it was not my reputation alone that would be tarnished. My Papaw and Bea valued their reputations, and I didn't want to smear the Mann legacy in Parkersville because of my actions and lies. Claude said that I was a child who felt alone and desperate when I started down the path of deception. I said that while that was true, I kept lying long after I became an adult. I told him that I didn't want him to compromise his morality to become part of my lies. So Moody and I would be the only ones to say anything about ending our marriage.

After we moved to New York City, we never told anyone about Moody or my previous "marriage." People there were a lot less interested in details of our lives, and that suited us just fine. Outside of the top executives at NAREC, nobody knew when we were married, and it wasn't discussed. After you were born, Claude and I decided that we would annually celebrate the anniversary of the night we declared our love for each other and probably made you. We thought it would be easier for you when you were old enough to question if we got married because I was pregnant with you. We didn't, of course. Claude asked because he loved me before he knew you were inside me, and I accepted because I loved him. We both loved you so very much because you were made from our love. So we let you and everyone else assume that the anniversary we celebrate on April 26 is our wedding anniversary, which is actually June 21. We deliberately withheld information, so I know that means we lied to you. What a hypocrite I am! I've raised you children to always tell the truth, and I've led you to believe that Dad and I always told you the truth. But the truth is that I'm no paragon of virtue. I've lied to you . . . a lot. I thought that the lies I told wouldn't hurt you, but now I'm not so sure. I know that I hurt Moody, and I hope that he can forgive me. I hope that you can too.

****

At last, Mom had finished her story. I rose and gave her a bear hug. "Mom," I said, "I'm not judging you. Dad was right. You did what you thought you had to do, first to protect yourself and then to protect me. How could I blame you? I love you. But I still don't get why you think you hurt Moody. He didn't want me or you. I'm glad you didn't tell him anything about me then. And no matter what we find out about my paternity, you shouldn't tell him anything now."

"That's because you don't know the whole story," she responded. "You don't know what I just learned two nights ago. When you know what else happened back then, you will change your mind about him."

I was about to ask what she learned that could change my opinion of Moody when we heard Dad come in from church. We went downstairs to greet him. He asked how our talk was going.

Mom answered, "I told her all that happened in 1974, except what you told me Friday evening."

"Do you want me to tell her about that?" Dad asked.

"You should," she replied, "because you can give her a firsthand account of your meeting with Moody. If I tell her, I'll be repeating what you told me, and I might not remember it exactly."

Dad spoke with less emotion than Mom. He sounded like some of the detectives with whom I've collaborated on past investigations. He told me the facts with some speculations but little commentary. He began by reiterating how coldly he treated Mom at work the day after they returned from Chicago. This is how he described what happened in his office later that night.

Dad's Account of Events of April 29, 1974

I was very hurt and angry that your mom had chosen to return to Moody and expected me to pretend to forget what we said and did in Chicago. So when she came to speak to me in my office after work, I was sarcastic and mocked her by throwing her words back at her. Someone, probably Phippsie, must have been listening in the outer office. She heard me tell her to get over what happened between us that weekend. I told her that what we did meant nothing to me. I only said that because I thought that it meant nothing to her. But Phippsie, or whoever was listening, didn't know that. She took my words at face value. She must have told Moody what she heard me say. I was working late that night, going through papers on my desk. Moody burst into my office around 9:00 p.m. He was drunk, and he was pointing a gun directly at me. The gun was shaking because his hand was trembling. My first thought when I saw him was that he knew about Chicago and was enraged. I was afraid for your mom. I didn't know if he was going to harm her or if he already had. I wanted to call and warn her, but he was too close and the gun was loaded. But when he finally spoke, I knew that Sarah was not in danger.

Moody showed all the physical signs of drunken instability, but he spoke with the clarity of sobriety. He said that he was going to kill me for what I did to your mom. He said that he had warned her that I was no good but she wouldn't listen. She gave herself to me, and I treated her like a whore. He said that he loved her more than his own life and he wasn't going to let me break her heart and live to tell about it. She was too good to be treated like that. She was better than me, better than both of us.

I probably could have wrestled the gun from him. He wasn't steady on his feet. But I believed I could talk him down. I told him that if he wanted to kill me, I couldn't stop him. However, I said that he was wrong about me. I loved Sarah, and I wanted her to be my wife. I didn't toss her aside. She tossed me aside. I told him that he won. She was going to stay with him. I said that he would be a fool to lose her by killing me and going to jail. He stared at me for a minute, probably trying to discern if I was telling the truth. Then he asked if I really loved Sarah. I told him that I did and that I had told her so. He said that she would not have been with me like that unless she loved me. I told him that she said she did love me, but for reasons I did not understand, she said she could not be with me and she was going to stay with him.

He said that he understood her reasons very well. She would never break promises she made to him long ago. But he didn't want her to stay with him out of gratitude or a sense of honor. He had been looking out for Sarah since she was a child. She had faced so much sadness then, and all he ever wanted to do was to make her happy. He said he knew that she couldn't be happy staying with him if she'd rather be with someone else. He asked me if I thought I could make her happy. I said I believed that I could. I would spend my life trying to always keep a smile on her face and joy in her heart. He seemed convinced. Then he said he loved her and he was used to protecting her. He would find a way to protect her from her herself. He finally lowered the gun to his side and told me not to give up on her. He said I should be patient and wait for her to come to me.

He left my office and the plant. He didn't go home that night, and he called in sick the next day. He told your mom that he was leaving her for Mavis less than twenty-four hours after he threatened to kill me for wronging her. That didn't make sense. He loved Sarah enough to want her to be happy. So I figured he was leaving her so she would be free to come to me. I couldn't be sure of that, but it made sense based on our discussion the night before. When your mother came to me, I didn't tell her what happened between me and Moody. I didn't tell her because I was afraid she wouldn't leave him if she knew how much he loved her. I planned to tell her one day, but I never did, not until two days ago when Mavis came to see her. She said she was surprised that after thirty years, I had not told my wife about my encounter with Moody that night. She told her that she and Moody were pretending to be a couple then and did not become one until after we moved to New York.

Mom was quick to defend Dad. "I was surprised too, but I understand why neither you nor Moody wanted me to know about that night. Mavis kept quiet too. She only shared her part in the deception now because Moody has cancer and is refusing the recommended treatment. She hopes that I can get him to change his mind if I visit him. I didn't understand why she thought I could influence him, since he left me years ago for her. That's when she told me the truth."

I asked, "Why did Mavis go along with Moody's story if they weren't together?"

Mom answered, "Mavis said she went along with staging an affair because she really liked Moody. He was in a bad way, and she wanted to help him. She admitted that she had flirted with Moody since he started coming to the diner years before. He never flirted back and was quick to show his wedding band. That made her like him more. He was nice and good-looking. He was a good tipper. He never got drunk. He never even bought a drink before that night."

"She lied to everyone because she had a crush on Moody?" I said. "There must have been more to it than that."

Mom shared the rest of what Mavis told her Friday. "Moody was sitting with Lenny in the diner that Monday when Phippsie rushed in and told him something that upset him. He started drinking and saying that he was 'going to fix that son of a bitch.' He was pretty drunk when he left the diner around 7:00 p.m. He came back around 10:30 p.m. and continued drinking until he nearly passed out. The owner was going to put him out on the street. Mavis knew Moody must be hurting pretty bad. She felt sorry for him. So she took him to her place across the street from the diner, where he passed out on the couch and slept through the night."

Dad interjected, "I checked on Moody the next morning and learned that he called in sick. I wanted to have a sober conversation with him, but I changed my mind by the time he returned the next day. By then, I was hearing rumors about his breakup with Sarah. I decided to wait to talk to her."

Mom continued. "Mavis said she shook Moody to wake him for work, but he had a terrible hangover. "She was furious when the gun fell out of his pants pocket. She told him to leave because she did not allow guns in her apartment. He told her that he had just bought it the night before. He didn't use it, and he was going to return it that day. Over coffee, he told her what had happened in Claude's office and his plan to leave me. He thanked Mavis for being a friend and asked her to pretend to be more than that for little while. She said she agreed because she hoped that with me out of his life, he might just learn to love her for real."

"Is that what happened?" I asked.

"Yes," Mom answered. "She and Moody eventually became a couple. They married, and he adopted her son, George, who was nine when all this happened. She wanted me to know that he's been sober since he fell off the wagon that night over thirty years ago."

I was confused. "If things are good between them now, why does she want you to talk to Moody?"

Mom looked at Dad, and he nodded before she spoke. "Mavis wants me to tell Moody that he is your father. She thinks he is, or she thought he was when she came to see me Friday. She said she suspected I was pregnant when she met me at the diner after Moody and I broke up. She knew I talked to him about a baby but didn't say I was pregnant. When news got back to Parkersville about Claude's and my baby, she did the math and knew that Moody might be your father. He was clueless, and she never told him."

"Good!" I exclaimed. "He isn't my father!"

"Now, Claudia," Mom said calmly, "we don't know yet if he is or isn't. I told Mavis that Moody is not your father. But after she left, I knew that I needed to tell you, your dad, and Moody that he might be. Mavis said she tried to have a child with him, but she couldn't. She told me that he watches your show every week and is your biggest fan. He always says how beautiful and intelligent you are and how much you remind him of me. She thinks that if he knew that he was your father, he would want to get to know you, and that would give him a reason to fight to live."

Dad said, "Now that we are going to learn the truth in a few days, your mother will wait for the test results before she goes to Detroit to speak with him."

"Once we know that he's not my biological father, you won't need to go to see him," I held.

Mom explained, "Regardless of the test results, I have to apologize to Moody for the way I treated him. He was so good to me, and I had no regard for his feelings. I always did what I wanted, when I wanted, and the way I wanted. I asked him to marry me for my convenience then not file the papers and live a lie because I didn't want to be really married. I didn't become his lover until I was ready and only agreed to have his child after I felt guilty for falling in love with someone else."

"You're not being fair to yourself. You weren't scheming to hurt Moody. You were a child trying to take charge of your life when you felt alone and abandoned," I reasoned. "You loved Moody in the way you understood love to be. By the time you understood love better, you cared enough about him to have stayed with him and tried to please him."

"Maybe I was too naïve at first to realize how much he loved me and that he hoped I would come to love him the same way. Yet as I matured into womanhood, I understood the depths of his love for me, even if my feelings for him were not reciprocal. I hurt him and betrayed him. Still, he loved me enough to not want me to feel trapped in our 'marriage' when he knew that I loved Claude. So he pretended to leave me. He is a good man, and he deserved better from me."

"You didn't know that Moody was pretending," I reminded her.

Mom was not going to be excused for her actions that easily. "I knew Moody. I knew he still loved me right before he left me. I should have known that he was pretending about loving Mavis and about having been with her for a while. He was lying about their relationship the same way I got him to lie about ours for so long. I should have seen through Moody's scam, but I didn't mind him leaving because I wanted so much to be with your dad."

Tears ran down Mom's cheeks. Dad put his arms around her to console her, but she shook her head and said, "I have been so selfish. I did what I wanted without regard for anyone else's rights. I came to New York and worked hard to put my past behind me. I tried to be a better person. But if Moody is your father, I have kept him from his only child for thirty years. He deserved to know you, and you deserved to know him. I know that Jesus paid for my sins and God has forgiven me. I'm even sure that you, your dad, and Moody will forgive me. But I'm not sure that I can forgive myself."

Mom was beside herself with remorse. Dad and I both tried to console her. We spoke of all the good she has done for so many children and adults through her school and through her years of dedicated service in the church and in other organizations. Dad told her that she is the most loving and wonderful wife, and I said she is the best mother. But she was too filled with guilt and self-deprecation to hear us. I have never seen her so sad.

She recalled, "I thought God had forsaken me when Papaw died. I was angry and arrogant enough to think I could take charge of my life with my plans. I should have had faith and trusted God's plans for me. I believe He planned for me to be with your dad. But He didn't want me to use and hurt Moody. I wronged him, and I pray that it is not too late to make it right."

Finally, I spoke up. "Mom, you are assuming that Moody is my father. You have no reason to feel guilty for not telling him anything if he isn't. I'll discretely arrange for a DNA test tomorrow. We'll know for certain in a few days that Claude Reynolds is my father. If I'm wrong and the test says otherwise, we'll still be fine. We love each other, and we love you. Nothing will ever change that."

Mom was physically and emotionally exhausted. She apologized to Dad and me again for involving us in the mess she made. Again, we assured her that her apologies weren't necessary. We were all hungry. Mom wouldn't let me help with dinner. She said she was just broiling steaks and serving them with the last of the vegetables and side dishes left from Thanksgiving. I gathered what was needed for the DNA testing while she was in the kitchen. I clipped Dad's nails and put two of the cut pieces into an envelope. I also put in hair from his comb before sealing it. I put some of my hair with some toenail clippings in another envelope and sealed it.

During dinner, we enjoyed a relaxing conversation about Dad's day at church. He shared that he sat with Jason and let him know that I was all right. When Mom and Dad adjourned to the family room to watch television together, I came upstairs to call Jason and to get some sleep. But of course, I could not sleep until I wrote down all that Mom and Dad shared with me today. Even now, as I'm finishing, I'm not sure that I can sleep. I am too wired, wondering what the DNA tests are going to reveal about my paternity. It appears that Moody and Dad are both good men who loved Mom when I was conceived. But Claude Reynolds will always be my Dad, and I want him to be my father too. I want my baby to be his first grandchild. I love him so much, and I love our relationship. I know we said that it won't change if he's not my biological father, but I can't help but think that it will somehow. I don't want to be his stepdaughter. I don't want to be CJ's and Cara's half sister. So I'm not going to consider those possibilities unless the test results I get force me to do so. For now, I'm going to remain positive and get my first decent night's sleep since Thursday.

Monday, November 29, 2004
12:45 p.m.

I awoke this morning to the sweet smells of the hearty breakfast Mom prepared. Dad was about to leave for a round of golf with his Monday morning foursome by the time I made it downstairs to the kitchen. He kissed Mom and me before he left, toting the bacon-and-egg sandwich and thermos of black coffee Mom packed for him. Over breakfast, I told Mom how much the weekend meant to me. I feel closer to her than I did before because she has allowed me to really know her as a whole person, not just my mother. I am beginning to understand how her beliefs and values are rooted in incidents and teachings from her past.

I was curious to know what and how she came to understand the tension between her mother and grandfather. When she talked about what she heard from Bea, she indicated that she didn't understand it until much later. Who explained it to her then? She chuckled as she said that Mary and Bea explained it to her after they died. I was baffled. She took my hand and led me upstairs to her bedroom. Once again, she pulled things out of the bottom drawer of her dresser. This time she showed me a dozen old journals. Some were clothbound and frayed.

Others had covers of worn leather and vinyl. The pages in all of them had yellowed with age. She reminded me that we came from a long line of educated, literate women. She was raised by two of them: my grandmother Mary and my great-grandmother Bea. They taught her the values and beliefs passed down from those who raised them. She also learned from her Papaw, my great-grandfather, Solomon C. Mann, principles and faith which he had learned, in part, from his mother, my great-great-grandmother Juliette.

I was surprised to discover that, like me, all of these women kept journals. Mom told me that she first found the journals of her mother, Mary, when she was cleaning out her house after it was sold. They were in a locked drawer of the cabinet where my grandmother kept lyrics and melodies that she wrote, some of which she didn't live to record. Mom found Juliette's journals in the safe in Papaw's law office after he died. She found Bea's journals a year later when she was looking for a place to hide a Christmas gift she bought for Moody. When she opened the cedar trunk in Bea's sewing room, she found Bea's journals among her treasured fabrics and fine table linen. Mom read all of the journals. That is how her mother, grandmother, and great-grandmother helped her understand more about her family after they died. From her ancestors' accounts of their experiences and feelings, she discovered how they developed the attitudes and values that were instilled in her as a child. Mom encouraged me to let these women tell me their stories in their written words as she told me her story aloud. I asked why Mom never kept a journal. Her response was that she supposes it's because she didn't want to admit, even to herself, how guilty and unhappy she felt about the choices she made and their consequences. She said that she made me her "journal" over the past two days. She affirmed that she didn't mind my recording her words herein as accurately as I could remember them.

Mom gave me the journals of Juliette Mann, Bea Mann, and Mary Mann–Morgan. I brought them to work with me, along with the samples for the DNA testing, in a locked valise I borrowed from her. We hugged tightly and silently for a long time before I left the house. She drove across the field to the PEACE Academy, and I drove to New Rochelle, where I took the Metro North to Grand Central Station. As soon as I arrived at the office, I contacted Dr. Victoria Williams, a geneticist who often helps me in investigations. I sent the samples across town to her lab via courier. She promised to get the results to me on Thursday.

I called Jason and told him that I love him. I said I miss him and I'll be so happy to finally come home on Friday. But first, I really need some solitary time to immerse myself in tons of research for an important story. I let him know that I plan to spend the next few days in our condo in the city, close to the resources I need. He doesn't need to worry, I said, because I will take care of myself and Baby BUMP, eating nutritious food and getting enough rest. I promised to call him every night when I'm about to go to bed so he can be sure that I'm not staying up too late. He agreed to get my car home from the train station in New Rochelle tonight and to pick me up Friday.

Of course, the important story I'm researching is the one of my heritage. I am finding it hard to concentrate on any other work. I want to immerse myself in reading the journals I got from Mom. Focusing on the history of my maternal line, of which I am certain, will keep me from dwelling on the uncertainty of my paternity while I wait for the results of the DNA test. Three days seems like an eternity to wait to find out if my sense of being is a lie or not. I can't just go about business as usual until I know.

I spent barely two hours at my office, working feverishly to approve the final edits for Thursday night's show, tape the promos for next week's show, and return phone calls related to another story I am researching. I left the office at noon. I told my assistant I will be working out of the office for the next three days and she can contact me on my mobile phone. I stopped by Au Bon Pain to pick up a cup of wild mushroom soup and a vegetarian sandwich. I headed here to the condo. Now I'm about to plunge into research, reading primary resources provided by my ancestors. My mother's recollections of her childhood whetted my appetite to learn more about her mother (my grandmother), Mary, and her grandmother (my great-grandmother), Bea. Mom spoke a lot about Papaw, her grandfather Solomon, and his influence on her development and on the development of the whole town of Parkersville, where she grew up. So I am excited that I may have the opportunity to learn about his upbringing when I read the journals kept by his mother, Juliette, Mom's great-grandmother (my great-great-grandmother and Bea's mother-in-law). I'm going to begin my reading with Juliette's first journal, dating back to 1885. I'll continue chronologically through her journals and Bea's, finishing with the final entry in Grandmother Mary's last journal, dated December 19, 1962, two weeks before she died.

Claudia's Maternal Ancestry

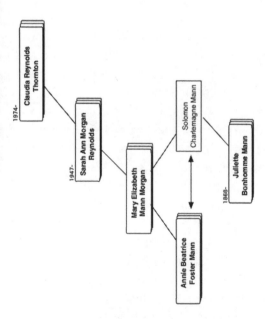

1974- Claudia Reynolds Thornton

1947- Sarah Ann Morgan Reynolds

Mary Elizabeth Mann Morgan

Solomon Charlemagne Mann

Annie Beatrice Foster Mann

1868- Juliette Bonhomme Mann

Mother (left), Father(right)

Wife ←→ Husband

Part 2

EXCERPTS FROM THE JOURNALS OF JULIETTE BONHOMME MANN

24 April 1885

Owing to a surprising chain of events today, I have been seized by excitement and anticipation. For the first time since I moved from New Orleans to Mississippi, I enjoyed being engaged in lengthy social intercourse with a gentleman caller. Until today, I had all but relinquished my once cherished dreams of becoming a wife and mother. Finding no men of interest to me and none who showed interest in me, I have contented myself with teaching the children of others. Yet now it seems quite possible that love and matrimony may not be beyond my grasp. For though I met Mr. J. R. Mann just today, I feel him less a stranger and more an intimate acquaintance than many whom I have known far longer. His delicate flattery and forthright statement of his intentions toward me have shattered the shield protecting my heart. After months of melancholy, I am prepared to embrace pleasure.

As is my custom on Fridays, I sojourned across town this afternoon to the general store to procure provisions for my students, Grand'mère Lizzie, and myself. The manager, George Williams, introduced me to

Mr. Mann with whom he was conducting business upon my arrival. Mr. Williams suspended his dealings with Mr. Mann to assist me, extending his usual cordiality and generosity as he helped me gather all I needed and forthwith load them onto my carriage. Mr. Mann stood silently until we finished, saying simply "Good day" when I left. Though his intonations were pleasant enough, he did not appear to look upon me with favour. That is why I found it surprising to see him just two hours hence, standing on the porch and knocking on Grand'mère Lizzie's front door.

I watched and listened from the kitchen as Grand'mère Lizzie greeted Mr. Mann. He has a commanding presence. His physique, though more diminutive than most men I know and at least a quarter of a foot shorter than my own, looms much larger because he stands erect and exudes more confidence and pride than is often seen in white men and rarely in Negro men. His skin is like ebony, dark and rugged from labour in the sun. His African ancestry appears to be pure, undiluted by the forced European intrusion of masters and overseers into the wombs of female slaves. When he introduced himself to Grand'mère, I took note of his voice, so deep and melodic. Mr. Mann made his intentions clear at the onset. He asked Grand'mère Lizzie for her permission to court me. He revealed that he had made inquiries to Mr. Williams and had learned particular facts about me, one being that I am her granddaughter. I found a certain irony in his discovery of that fact on the day he met me when I had only learned it myself six months ago, a quarter of a year before my seventeenth birthday.

Grand'mère Lizzie moved outside and sat on the porch with Mr. Mann to listen to him express how he comes to believe himself to be a worthy suitor. I moved closer to watch and listen. In plain and direct discourse, he offered a condensed description of himself, his heritage and holdings. He purports to be a good Christian man of sufficient fortune to support a wife and family. He owns four hundred acres of land that his father, the senior Mr. Mann, purchased after slavery ended with money he had been saving to free him and his mother. The slave master freed his father a few years before the war between the North and South began. The master's decision to free the senior Mr. Mann, whom he called Thomas, was one of convenience rather than conscience. It was so the master would not bring trouble on himself by teaching Thomas to read and figure enough to help him with his trading business. The master's grown sons cared more about spending their father's fortune than helping him earn it. So they found it pleasing to have Thomas learn to do what their father wanted them to do. To keep Thomas from leaving the plantation once he was freed, the master kept Thomas's family enslaved. He told Thomas that he could buy the freedom of his woman and their son with his earnings. Thomas learned to figure well enough to know that with the wages he was paid and the price the slave master set, he would be required to work the rest of his life to pay for their freedom. Still, Thomas kept working and saving.

During the war, the master's sons joined the Confederate Army. Thomas helped the master get food and supplies to the soldiers fighting in Mississippi and Alabama. The master's sons both died on battlefields, one in Vicksburg, the other in Mobile Bay. Thomas and the master returned home afterward. The master died in his sleep the day after Mississippi and Alabama surrendered. A few weeks later, Thomas's family was freed like the rest of the former slaves. The master's widow wanted to get money quickly to move to Virginia with her cousins "before the damned Yankees stole or ruined what little was left" of the antebellum treasures she once held dear. Thomas used the money he had saved to buy from her four hundred acres of land, the house, wagon, horses, and equipment. The property is located outside of Newton, Mississippi. The Okatibbee Creek runs through it. Thomas continued the trading business he had run for his former master. The white people with whom the former master traded remembered Thomas kindly and maintained good relationships with him when he took charge as a freeman. As a freeman and land owner, Thomas changed his name to Mister Mann.

J. R. Mann grew up traveling with his father along his route from Newton to Meridian, Jackson, and Vicksburg, stopping in Yazoo City and Philadelphia on the return trip to Newton. He also farmed the four hundred acres with his parents and a dozen sharecropper families who still live on the property. His parents have now both gone to heaven, his mother four years ago and his father last year. As their only child and heir, he now runs the trading business and supervises the farming of the land. He lives alone in the antebellum mansion he and his father restored. The mansion sits by the creek atop a high hill that overlooks most of the property. That is where he says that I will live if I agree to be his wife. Presently, he spends a day in the Vicksburg area every two months. That is when he visits Davis Bend. However, he will come more frequently and stay longer if Grand'mère Lizzie grants him permission to court me.

His manner of discourse is more terse, vigorous, and genuine than that of the educated gentry I knew in Louisiana. Yet it reveals intelligence commensurate with any I have known. His education seems to have been gleaned less from formal schooling and more from absorbing experiences in business and travel. Grand'mère Lizzie's demeanor and subtle smile evidenced her positive disposition to grant his request. Perhaps it was because he seemed neither arrogant nor pretentious about his fortune. Perhaps it was because his background is reminiscent of that of Isaiah Montgomery for whom Grand'mère Lizzie holds great esteem and deep affection. Isaiah is the former manager of Davis Bend and beloved son of Grand'mère Lizzie's dear departed friends, Benjamin and Mary Montgomery, whom she had known since 1867 when she moved to Davis Bend. Benjamin Montgomery and his wife were both of pure African descent, so their son, Isaiah, is an African thoroughbred. Also, akin to Mr. J. R. Mann, Isaiah Montgomery inherited ownership of land bought by his father after the war. Davis Bend was built on the four thousand acres of land that included Hurricane and other plantations sold to Benjamin Montgomery by Joseph Davis, elder brother of Jefferson Davis, president of the Confederacy. Grand'mère Lizzie was one of the first residents of this community. Like the other former enslaved Negroes who settled in Davis Bend, she came here seeking equality, justice, and pride in a town owned and governed by her own kind. Although she is half white, she rejects the label of mulatto and prefers to be acknowledged as a Negro and to live among other Negroes. She has a fondness for those whom she calls pure African Negroes like Isaiah Montgomery and J. R. Mann because they have no white blood which she believes to be tainted with evil.

Even after Davis Bend was beset by agricultural and economic problems that led most residents to leave, including Isaiah Montgomery and his family, she is one of the few who has remained. Ownership of the town was reclaimed by the Davis family four years ago, but they do not generally intrude in the affairs of the last stalwarts like Grand'mère. Mr. J. R. Mann inherited only a tenth as much land as Isaiah Montgomery and his siblings. However, J.R. is still in possession of his land and business, and he seems well positioned to maintain

ownership for years to come. The four-hundred-acre property owned by
J. R. Mann is more than enough to sustain one family in comfort and
style. If I become his wife, we will live in a mansion with ample space
for us and as many babies as I bear. Grand'mère Lizzie knows that it
is much more than she and Ma Mère have between them. Of greater
importance to me than his fortune is the respect he affords me. He
wants to marry me and that makes me very happy indeed. I want to be
a Christian bride and exchange vows for life in accordance with the laws
of God and man. An offer of matrimony is something else Grand'mère
acknowledges that neither she nor Ma Mère ever had.

Grand'mère saw me staring hopefully as she rose from her chair.
She granted her approval for J. R. Mann to inquire as to my interest
in accepting his ingratiating attention toward me with a view to
establishing a matrimonial union. I demurely acquiesced. J. R. Mann
is an intriguing man. Without much formal education, he is versed in
social graces. He brought a book of poetry for me and an embroidered
handkerchief for Grand'mère. He demonstrated proper table manners
when he joined us for dinner. For more than two hours afterward, under
the watchful eyes of Grand'mère, we engaged in social intercourse that
was highly stimulating and quite pleasurable. He enjoys poetry and
asked me to read some poems of my choosing. I find him to be equally
engaged by the works of Keats, Poe, Longfellow, Elizabeth Barrett
Browning, and Phillis Wheatley. His interpretations have merit, and
his convictions are not lacking in strength and consistency. Yet he
seems respectful of my divergent views and is willing to consider them
without prejudice.

At nine o'clock, he bid me adieu and asked Grand'mère if he could
return in a fortnight. She responded that it was my choice. Though my
heart was filled with unbridled excitement, I resolved to control my
effusions. "Yes," I said calmly. "It would be pleasing to see you then."
When he was a safe distance from the house, I hugged Grand'mère
and confessed to her how much I adore him. My imagination is racing
toward love and marriage, though I have known him but a day. How
shall I find the patience to wait for his next visit?

8 May 1885

I spent last night in restless slumber, eagerly anticipating my visit this evening with J. R. Mann. All through the day, my joyful effusions were such that everyone surely took note of my euphoria. This morning, my students were not too absorbed in the tasks that occupied them to observe that I seemed less critical of their work, offering them more praise for correct responses and less chastisement for what I deemed to be careless mistakes. George Williams, always gracious and prone to appropriately measured flattery, took favourable notice this afternoon of my jubilant manner. Though ignorant of the reason for my elevated pleasure with life, he did not inquire about it nor about the reason I requested more than double the quantity of lemons, eggs, and sugar habitually on my list of required provisions.

J.R. arrived promptly at six o'clock. Once again, he brought gifts for me and Grand'mère Lizzie. On this occasion, he gave me a beautiful knitted shawl trimmed in the most delicate lace, and for Grand'mère, he brought a bag of pecans and half a bushel of peaches from Georgia. He said that he had been told that Grand'mère Lizzie prepares the most delicious peach cobbler and also pickled peaches. He did not say but must be aware that Grand'mère has a fondness for nuts and that pecans are her absolute favourite ones. When we three sat on the porch, I served sweet tea and I donned my new shawl.

Our interchange was amusing at first as we conversed about our first impressions of one another. J.R. confessed that he was put off by what seemed to him to be the slave-like servitude George Williams showed to me, whom he thought to be a white woman. He said he came across mixed Negroes before, but none of them had hazel eyes like mine or light brown hair so long and straight. He noted with disdain that George called me Miss Juliette and attended to me smiling enthusiastically while making every effort to fulfill all of my requests. J.R. wondered if I noticed his scowl as he heard George say that he looked forward to seeing me the next week and saw him seem to all but bow to me as I departed. I responded that I looked upon J.R.'s facial expression not as a scowl but certainly less than cordial. He continued, commenting that after I left, he asked George why I came all the way to Davis Bend to shop instead of shopping at a white store in Vicksburg. George explained that I live in Davis Bend, and because of the work I do, providing education to everyone who wants to learn, he gives me what he can to help me. Most of my students are unable to pay me because they have very little themselves, but they bestow gifts of food they grow or prepare as tokens of their gratitude.

J.R. said that his desire to court me did not spring from his attraction to my façade. With sincerity, he confided that he had not studied my features when first he encountered me. Having neither trust nor affection for white women, he was cautious about regarding me at all. Indeed, even after discovering my Negro heritage, he had no interest in knowing me. Given his bias toward mixed Negroes, he assumed me to be haughty and condescending. Yet George defended my character, insisting that J.R. could not be more wrong. It was the high esteem which George places upon me that captured the attention of J.R. and ignited his interest in me. George described me as humble, kind, and charitable. He spoke of my concern for others and described my munificence in sharing what I learned through privileged schooling. He further depicted me as a Christian woman of faith and purity. J.R. said it was as though George somehow knew and was listing all the traits J.R. wanted in a wife. He questioned George about my suitors, and upon learning that I had none presently, he sought directions to find me. That is what led him to come to Grand'mère's home.

I was blushing, embarrassed by such kind words about my character. Overtaken by modesty, I lowered my head to avoid gazing directly at J.R. Then he lifted my chin with his hand but withdrew it quickly when Grand'mère cast a disapproving stare at him. He quickly apologized for touching me. He explained that he meant no disrespect. He only wanted me to observe his countenance to discern the truthfulness of his words as he expressed his adoration of both my outward and inner beauty. He says he is captivated by my face and form, my sweet voice, and my graceful movements. He finds pleasure in the way I read poetry and converse knowledgably about many things familiar and unfamiliar to him. He said that as we face life together, he will seize opportunities to be my student and my teacher. I smiled upon hearing these declarations. They were unexpected but welcomed. I have always been taught that a woman should well conceal her intelligence in the presence of men. I have not done this well, and that is perhaps why no man has sought my company following our first conversation. Yet J.R.

Mann is neither intimidated nor repulsed by my erudition. Rather, he appreciates it. *Quel homme!* What a special man he is indeed!

Following his confessions of sincere affection for me, J.R. sought to learn more about me and my feelings. He made an inquiry regarding my childhood and how I came to be so well educated. It was a natural question but one which pained me to answer. I contemplated exercising brevity and restraint in my response, ignoring information that I had acquired only recently. Yet I am wont to be truthful in most situations and feel I should be so to one who is seeking my hand in marriage. Still, I found it difficult to take such an emotional sojourn into my past without revealing the anger and bitterness I would suffer along the way. Grand'mère knows my feelings and has sincere pathos of her own with regard to these matters. She said naught, but the sudden rigidity that overtook her entire form evidenced her tension.

I recounted growing up with Ma Mère Amanda, Grand'mère Lizzie's quadroon daughter, and Mon Père, M. Pierre Bonhomme, a wealthy man of French parentage. We lived in a well-appointed home in the quadroon quarter of New Orleans, a section of the Vieux Carre below Orleans Street near the Ramparts. My father spent most Friday and Saturday nights with my mother and me but habitually departed Sunday noon to "do business" during the week. (I did not reveal to J.R. that I discovered of late that my father maintained two homes. When I thought he was away "doing business," he was actually with his wife and sons in his primary residence, a mansion on St. Charles Avenue.) I informed J.R. that I attended a Catholic school for girls a short walk from our home until two years ago when my father enrolled me in Miss Granville's Academy, a boarding school for young ladies of fine lineage. It was common practice for girls my age from Vieux Carre to complete their studies at boarding schools in Paris, but Ma Mère did not want me to go so far away from her. J.R. seemed satisfied with my disclosures. He did comment that he has met many mixed Negroes not nearly as fair-skinned as I who try to pass for white or who only mingle with other mixed Negroes. He is surprised that I left the quadroon society in New Orleans to come to Davis Bend. He is pleased that I am here but curious about why I didn't choose to go North, where I could surely pass. I explained that as a Christian, I am predisposed to speak and live truthfully and I would be ashamed to lie about who and what I am. I am a Negro by law and in my heart as well. I have spent every summer since

I was three years old here in Davis Bend with my Grand'mère Lizzie. That is why when I concluded my studies, I returned here to teach in the town that is my second home. J.R. smiled contentedly.

I surprised J.R. with a lemon pie I baked before he arrived. It so pleased his palate that he requested a second slice. He expressed gratitude and astonishment that a woman of my beauty and charm is also an excellent cook. I blushed, unable to conceal the embarrassing pleasure I derived from his fawning. He was flabbergasted by the sudden rosiness of my cheeks and concerned that I might be ill. Grand'mère Lizzie laughed as I tried to explain that it was a positive reaction to his gracious remarks. He found the phenomenon to be endearing and vowed to give me reason to blush every time we are together. He said he will return again in a fortnight and that he will come early enough to take Grand'mère and me for a ride in his carriage if Grand'mère will allow him to do that. Grand'mère accepted his invitation on behalf of us both. I promised to exhibit my skill with a needle and thread by wearing something special I will make for the occasion. He beamed. So once again, he left me excited about the events of today and impatiently anticipating our next encounter.

Reflecting now on how I responded to his inquiry about my background, I am comforted that I spoke no actual falsehoods. I confess that I did omit unpleasant facts regarding my familial relationships and the circumstances surrounding my abrupt departure from boarding school. Barely six months ago did I become aware that my beloved Miss Lizzie is actually my grand'mère. I knew that Miss Lizzie had raised Ma Mère but thought she did so in servitude to Ma Mère's parents. I surmised this because Ma Mère never used terms of maternal endearment in reference to her but always called her Miss Lizzie. I addressed her likewise and was not corrected. Yet that is but one of many beliefs about relationships in my family that I held in error until recently. I might never have learned the truth had it not been for a chance encounter with my half brothers. When the young ladies from Miss Granville's were invited to the neighboring military academy for a social, I was introduced to Charles Bonhomme. It did not take long to discover that we had the same father. While I was perplexed and stunned by his existence, Charles knew exactly who I was. He told one of my classmates that his mother often spoke about his father's "Negro whore and their bastard." Before the social ended, word had spread to most everyone.

I pretended not to observe the metamorphosis of once smiling faces into frigid stares on those who looked upon me. I feigned ignorance to the fact that those who formerly engaged me in vibrant intercourse turned away and became involved in whispered conversations about me. Upon our return to the academy, I was humiliated and taunted. Miss Granville sent a telegram to Mon Père, summoning him to fetch me immediately. She had me pack my belongings and stay in the maid's room until his arrival. Only after this occurred did Mon Père and, later, Ma Mère finally entrust me with the truth about my lineage.

Mon Père exuded sympathy for me, following Miss Granville's disclosure to him of what she knew about the names the other girls called my mother and me and the things they told me about his real family. He said he wanted to correct misconceptions I must have formed. He declared that Ma Mère is not a whore and he does not consider me to be a bastard. Beset with misery and fume, I spoke not but listened intently to his disclosures of events which occurred ere I was born.

Ma Mère, Amanda, was a waif of thirteen years when she arrived in New Orleans in the spring of 1866. She had run away from her mother in Mississippi, leaving behind the scorn she felt there from resentful whites and Negroes. She had come seeking acceptance and affection in the nice community she had heard was a haven for mixed Negroes like her. She began her harsh journey walking alone but intermittently found transportation in others' wagons. She was bumped, bruised, and cut by nails and splinters as she rode in the back amid boxes and tools. By the time she reached her destination, she was worn, weary, filthy, and hungry. Penniless and illiterate, she was directed to the boarding house of Mme. LaTourette, a quadroon who offered shelter and employment to destitute quadroon girls.

Mme. LaTourette took pity on *la jeune fille* Amanda. She tended to her cuts and bruises, gave her a bath and clean clothing to replace her tattered ones, and fed her a good, hot meal. She agreed to allow Amanda to stay in her boarding house in exchange for Amanda cleaning the house and assisting with the cooking. Mme. LaTourette said that she was too young to perform any other duties yet. The other tenants at the boarding house earned their keep by pleasuring the rich men who frequented Mme. LaTourette's at night. Amanda changed their linen and prepared their baths. She longed to one day wear clothes as fine as theirs. She hoped to find love with a man who would pay her debts to

Mme. LaTourette and marry her. However, she would have to wait until Mme. LaTourette deemed her old enough and properly prepared to comport herself in a genteel manner consistent with quadroon society. To that end, Mme. LaTourette and her other residents tutored her in hygiene, beauty, social graces, and polite, proper conversation.

Mon Père said he first took notice of Amanda a few months after she came to live at Mme. LaTourette's. He saw her cleaning the chamber adjacent to the one he was about to occupy. He said that he was immediately stunned by her natural beauty. Her wavy reddish-brown hair was swept up into two braids that crossed each other to form a crown atop her regal face the color of spun gold. Without cosmetic enhancements, her aquiline nose was colorfully encircled by her big brown eyes and long eyelashes, her prominent rosy cheeks, and her heart-shaped bronze lips. When she smiled at him demurely, he was captivated. He was unaware of her young age and innocence until he made inquiries about her on his next visit. He exacted Mme. LaTourette's promise to be the first to lay with Amanda when she was deemed ready. In the meantime, she agreed to let Amanda serve him refreshments when he was gambling or lounging downstairs in the parlor.

Over the next several months, he engaged Amanda in conversation on each visit before ascending to a chamber to engage the favours of an available companion. He learned that she embarked on her hazardous journey because she feared for her safety in Mississippi. She said that although slavery was over, the plight of Negro girls and women there had not changed much. Unprotected women, like she and her mother, were subject to assault or even death at the hands of white men infuriated that the Confederacy lost the war and former slaves were free. She had observed the way white men in Mississippi leered at her. She knew the time was nigh when she would be violated in freedom as her mother and grandmother were in slavery. Amanda said she was willing to risk death to avoid that fate. She fled with only the clothes she wore to a place she only knew by name and its reputed community of mixed Negroes. She traveled without money or clear directions for getting there. Yet with God's mercy and grace, she encountered a series of benevolent strangers who helped her reach New Orleans safely.

Mon Père said that he admired the young Amanda's bravery and her determination to improve her lot. When she implored him to teach her to read and write, he agreed and brought books to her at Mme. LaTourette's. He spent an hour or more tutoring her every Friday and Saturday evening when he frequented the bordello. Sometimes he spent all evening dining, drinking, and tutoring Amanda, never venturing to a chamber upstairs. He found more pleasure in conversations with her than he enjoyed in intimate encounters with others. Yet he did not tell that to anyone because it made him uncomfortable to admit that he was falling in love with her.

I broke my silence to ask Mon Père, "Why did loving Ma Mère cause you discomfort?"

"Ma *chérie* Amanda was a child to me then," he said. "She was mature, fearless, and smart but still barely fourteen years old, and I was a grown man of twenty-two. I also knew she was anxious to read, write, and learn proper etiquette in hopes of finding a husband, and I knew I could not marry her."

I wanted to know why he couldn't marry her. "Were you already married then?"

"No," he responded. "But I was betrothed. I told my father that I loved Amanda, but he ordered me to proceed with the wedding. My fiancée was the only child of one of the richest, most prominent men in New Orleans. My father had invested great effort and considerable resources to arrange for me to marry into that family. Even if I did not keep to my scheduled marriage, I would not have been allowed to marry ma *chérie* Amanda."

I knew why not but sought his confirmation when I inquired, "Because of her Negro ancestry?"

Mon Père explained, "Yes. Quadroons married each other or other mixed Negroes, and white men married white women. It was accepted practice for rich white men, married or not, to support Negro courtesans or *placées*. More than a few lived in the Vieux Carre amidst well-to-do quadroon families. My father-in-law had such an arrangement at one time, and he did not object to my doing the same so long as I did not use money from his estate to lavish on any woman other than his daughter. He never questioned me about my affections. He expected me to sire a male heir to inherit his fortune and demanded that I treat his daughter with respect."

When Amanda was fourteen and a half, Mme. LaTourette deemed her old enough and prepared enough to attend a quadroon ball. If she found a mixed Negro man who wished to marry her or a white man who agreed to support her, he would pay her debt to Mme. LaTourette, and she would be free to depart. If no man offered to pay her debt, she would continue to live at the boarding house and be offered for full services to the male customers. As the date of the ball approached, Amanda was excited and hopeful that she would find love and never have her body sold by the hour. She said she had not left Mississippi and worked so hard to improve her manners to succumb to what amounted to her to be solicited rape in a clean bed. She wanted her first intimacy and every one after that to be with a man of her own choosing. That was when Mon Père proclaimed his feelings. He asked Amanda if she would forego the ball and choose him. She said she already had chosen him. So he paid her debt to Mme. LaTourette and moved her into what later became our home in the Vieux Carre.

One day, perhaps, I will tell J.R. all I discovered about my family. Presently, I still find some things too upsetting to contemplate or discuss. I cannot bear the pain I feel knowing that I was sent to Mississippi every summer because Mon Père, whom I loved so much, didn't want me around. It is a fact that he never wanted me at all. He never wanted Ma Mère, his *chérie* Amanda, to have a child. He told her that he had children at home with his wife. When he was with his *chérie*, he had no desire to share her time and affection with anyone else. Ma Mère told me that when she conceived the first time, Mon Père took her to a shanty outside of the city. He instructed the woman there to "eliminate the problem," and she did. However, when Ma Mère conceived me soon afterward, she beseeched him to permit her the joy of birthing and raising just one child, whom she promised would not be an inconvenience to him. He allowed her one child only. After giving birth to me, Ma Mère undertook measures to avoid another conception. Despite her most diligent efforts, she had to eliminate two more "problems" before they were detected by Mon Père. Ma Mère is generously compensated for her obedience. She owns her home in the Vieux Carre, and Mon Père gives her whatever she needs for us to live there stylishly and comfortably. He even gives her money to send to her mother, my Grand'mère Lizzie, each month. He doubles the amount of Grand'mère's allowance during the three months annually when she keeps me with her in Davis Bend, away from him and his *chérie* in New Orleans.

I wallowed in desolation when I discovered that Mon Père attends to me to appease Ma Mère. He acknowledges me as his daughter and has given me his name. He provides me a modicum of affection and a fair allowance. I am beset with despair when I think of the restrictions on Ma Mère as his mistress. She cannot be seen on his arm outside of the Vieux Carre. His wife is the one whom he escorts to the grand affairs around New Orleans and elsewhere. She sits beside him in church. Everyone knows she is his wife, and she is respected. Ma Mère can only look forward to being seated by his side and dancing with him at quadroon balls. Ma Mère is called vile names, though she has known intimacy with only one man in her life. However, that man is not hers by law. He is the husband of another.

Six months ago, I was consumed with anger at both of my parents. Their failure to be truthful to me left me vulnerable to the cruelty I endured at Miss Granville's. It is what compelled me to flee New Orleans, bringing my broken spirit to heal with Grand'mère Lizzie and the children in Davis Bend. I still harbour enormous resentment toward Ma Mère and Mon Père. Yet I am not devoid of affection for them, and I feel compassion for Ma Mère. When she ran away from Grand'mère, she was naïve and did not foresee what her life would become. That is what Mon Père explained to me during our ride home after he fetched me from Miss Granville's Academy.

Mon Père says that he has always loved Ma Mère and considers us part of his real family. Yet that declaration does not resonate with truth to me. He has never introduced us to the rest of his family and we have never been invited to family celebrations. Mon Père believes he satisfied his father-in-law's demands. He provided two grandsons as heirs to their family's fortune, which has grown owing to his good management. He has made improvements to the family mansion, and his wife is lavished with all of the finest accoutrements of wealth. His support of Ma Mère and me has come from the money he brought into the marriage and the salary he awards himself for operating the sugar plantation. Still, his wife resents that he gives Ma Mère much of his time and affection and that he claims and supports me as his child. And though he told me he loves Ma Mère, she has not told me that she loves him. She says she is content with their arrangement. Yet I sense some melancholy within her. She will not disclose to me her true feelings for Mon Père and her feelings about being the mistress of an adulterous married man. I know she confesses something every week to the priest and does penance as instructed. I know she desires better for me. Yet we are in disagreement as to what is better. With God's blessing, I will have a better life with J.R.

22 May 1885

In the silence of the night, I look back on today with kind eyes and I look forward with anticipation of blissful dreams to come to my charmed sight in slumber. For this day has wrought a most romantic proposal of marriage from J. R. Mann, whom I love most dearly. My acceptance was appropriately demure, concealing my unbridled eagerness and euphoria as I responded affirmatively. Although I had reason to expect an eventual proposal, it was surprising to me that it came today during what is only his third visit. To some, our expediency might seem rash and impulsive, but disposition, not time, determine the intimacy of relationships. For his part, he made his intentions known from the beginning, before our first stimulating conversation. Each subsequent encounter has been prolonged enough to augment our mutual understanding, admiration, and affection. My heart is open to him, ready to welcome ecstatic experiences as his wife and mother of his children.

As he had promised a fortnight ago, J.R. arrived earlier today than has been his custom. It was nigh half past one when he arrived in his carriage. Grand'mère Lizzie and I greeted him together at the door. He did not enter the house but bade us to come forthwith to ride in his carriage. He had planned a pleasant ride that took us through Davis Bend and Vicksburg to the edge of the Mississippi River. It was there that he stopped and extended an invitation for us to take a short walk with him along the river. As we strolled in the sunlight, he gazed upon me and smiled. He inquired about my dress, wondering if I had made it. When I affirmed it as my handiwork, he stopped walking and stood erect, silently scrutinizing my entire façade. Finally, he spoke.

"Dear Miss Juliette Bonhomme, you are truly an accomplished woman and a beautiful one. You are a fine cook and seamstress. Your voice is pleasing to my ear. You are good-natured and a virtuous

Christian woman. I love you. I will always provide for you and protect you. I want you to be my wife. Will you marry me?"

When I accepted, he admitted that he was a man of passion but not patience. He wants to marry me in a fortnight when he will return to Davis Bend. Grand'mère Lizzie and I agreed that we could make the necessary preparations to have the ceremony then. Then J.R. presented us with the gifts he brought for us. It was his practice to present them upon his arrival, but he indicated that these gifts were more appropriate to present after my acceptance of his proposal. Indeed, he was correct. For me, he brought the finest white silk for making my wedding dress, and he brought a beautiful pink-and-white hat for Grand'mère to wear to the ceremony and to church afterward. We were most delighted with our presents and with all that transpired on the banks of the Mississippi River this wonderful day.

There was one more surprise today. Ma Mère was waiting on the porch when we returned home from our carriage ride. This is the first time she has visited Davis Bend since my return here more than six months ago. I wondered why she had traveled from New Orleans after all this time. Whatever her purpose, I was not pleased to see her. The sight of her brought to the surface the anger I harbour within me. I have learned not to show it, and I pray not to feel it. However, it is difficult for me to regard her without reproach and complaint. Yet I remained steadfast in my desire to forbid any querulous manifestations to be observable to J.R. I have not yet shared the reasons for the melancholy and resentment that overtake me in the presence of my parents. I was equally determined not to allow anything to detract from the unmitigated joy J.R. has brought to me this day.

Channeling the remnants of love I still feel for Ma Mère, I managed to appear cordial as I introduced her as my mother to J.R., my fiancé. Ma Mère's polite words evidenced a warm acceptance of him that was rendered counterfeit by her frosty, disapproving glares throughout dinner and the intonation of finality in her goodbye upon his departure. Yet Grand'mère and I reaffirmed our expectations and preparations for a wedding to take place at half past four in the afternoon on the fifth of June. Grand'mère will call on our minister tomorrow to make the arrangements to have the ceremony and reception at the church. J.R. left smiling, apparently undaunted by Ma Mère's transparent objections.

Before JR's carriage disappeared from view, Ma Mère vocalized her refusal to sanction my marriage. She was furious. She said she had come from New Orleans as soon as Grand'mère informed her of the courtship and his plans to visit today. She arrived expecting to make J.R.'s acquaintance but had no idea that a proposal would be offered and accepted ere she had even approved of him as an appropriate suitor for her daughter. She forbade me to move forward with plans to enter into a union that she believes would be such a terrible mistake. She ranted,

> *He is short, black, and ignorant. You have nothing in common with him because he is common and you are not. You were raised for better. Three generations of Negro women had to lay up under white men to make you able to move North and pass for white. Don't you know that if you marry a white man, your children will be white? All signs of their Negro blood will disappear forever. Their nipples, private parts, and every dark part will all be pink. Your parts are such a light brown that nobody would notice. But your children's will be pink for sure. But if you marry this man black as night, you'll put your children back three generations. And you will be withered and worn in a few years' time. I see the lust in his eyes when he looks at you. He'll destroy your body inside and out, forcing himself into you like a wild beast and making you his broodmare. You'll be pregnant all the time and wind up birthing a dozen ugly babies, if you live long enough. Is that what you want for yourself?*

I looked darkly on her tirade. She knew nothing about J.R. She made no effort to converse with him this evening. Her depressing depiction of my future was not her assessment of J.R. It was a concoction of her prejudice and ignorance about Negro men. The fury within me caused a rise in my temperature and in the volume of my voice as I countered,

> *What I don't want is to have the father of my children married to someone else! And I don't want to have to move far away and pretend to be something I'm not. I don't want to live in fear of being humiliated and run out of town if someone from my past arrives and tells everyone who I really*

am. I don't want my children to hate me for lying to them about their family. I want to be a Christian wife, accepted and respected as what I am. I don't want to be a—

I refrained from saying anything more hurtful and disrespectful to Ma Mère, but she pressed me to continue. She inquired,

You don't wanna be a what? What do you think I am? I'm a mother who did the best I could for my child. I'm a woman that white people see as a nigger, even though three-fourths of my blood is white. But I'm hated by a lot of black people because they mistakenly think I have it easier. The truth is no Negroes, if they be light or dark, have a fair chance in this world. I wanted better for you, and you had it. You lived in a fine home, ate good food, and had a good education.

I was not without compassion for her, but I defended my right to make my own decisions about my life. I acknowledged,

Yes, I had all of that, but I paid a high price for it. All of my supposed friends at Miss Granville's Academy turned mean and nasty once they learned that I was not white. They called me a nigger bastard and called you a nigger whore. What hurt even worse was that I didn't know that my life was a lie. I didn't know that Mon Père was married to someone else. He didn't love either one of us enough or respect us enough to ever marry you. I thought I was his princess, but I was just his dirty bastard. I was never good enough to play with his clean white children or to go with him for beignets outside of Vieux Carre. I want to be regarded and respected as a Christian wife. I want a white wedding, and I want to sit in the front pew of the church every Sunday with my husband and our children. Mr. Mann loves me and respects me enough to want me for his wife. I'll never be hidden away. Everyone will know I am Mrs. Mann. My children will know the truth about who they are, and the truth will set us all free.

Ma Mère was relentless in trying to dissuade me from my decision while justifying her actions.

I never lied to you. I just didn't tell you everything. I'm sorry that your half brothers were at that social and told everyone about us. I didn't think you'd ever meet them. I thought that if I stayed away from the academy, Miss Granville and the other girls would never find out that you weren't white. They only found out that you were part black because Camille Bonhomme is an evil witch. She spread her jealous hatred of us to her sons when she learned that your daddy paid to put you in that fancy school. But before all that ugly mess happened, you had been there long enough to get the education you need to talk and act as proper as any white lady. You learned enough to live well, and you can escape the labels people want to put on you. You don't have to be dishonest if you move away. You just don't have to volunteer information. I guarantee that if you go North, nobody will even ask. They'll just look at you and listen to how you talk. They'll assume you are a pretty white woman, and you'll enjoy all the respect and privileges that pretty white women get just 'cause they're white.

I was amazed that she thought it appropriate to blame Mon Père's wife for hating us for what we represent—her husband's betrayal.

I'm sorry, Ma Mère. I derive no pleasure in hurting and disappointing you. I am appreciative of all that you did for me. Yet I have compassion for a wife who resents her faithless husband's mistress and the child of that relationship. I understand how much the slave master's wife hated looking at Grand'mère Lizzie and her momma working in her house. Grand'mère's momma was a slave with no choice in the matter, and the master harboured no feelings of love for her. You chose to be with Mon Père, and he obviously has earnest affection for you. That must cause his wife considerably more misery than the wife of Grand'mère Lizzie's master father.

Ma Mère showed no regard for the melancholy of the wives of philandering white men.

I know more about Miss Lizzie's life than you do. I know that my mother was gang-raped by her half brothers and their friends when she was only eleven years old then sold away like it was her fault. The master's wife didn't care that her sons had raped a child, just that it was incest. She blamed Lizzie for tempting them, just like she blamed Lizzie's momma for having her husband's child, even though he raped her when she was just a child herself. The master's wife always hated Lizzie and her momma, so she used what happened to Lizzie as a way to punish them both. She wanted Lizzie gone, and the master gave her what she wanted. That just proves what I am telling you. Three generations of women in this family have suffered at the hands of white men and women. Now you have the chance to cross over and end the suffering in this family. Go North and live your life as a white woman. Marry a rich white man and get whatever you want from him.

Grand'mère finally broke her silence to address her daughter, Ma Mère. Though she is not learned through formal education, she has wisdom that arises from years of observations and experience, and she has good intuition which she attributes to God communicating directly with her soul.

Since y'all talkin' 'bout my life, I get to tell y'all what I think. I 'mit I hate white folk. Bible says it's wrong to hate, and I'm tryin' to stop. I ain't there yet, but I ask God e'ry day to hep me. The master that was my daddy call hisself protec'in' me by sellin' me to a ol' widow man. He was still mo'nin' his wife what died. He didn't wan' me to be no bed warmer. He jus' wan' me to cook an' clean an' mend his torn clothes. He didn't jump on me for more 'an a year. When he did, he felt so shame he cry. He won't so bad. He an' his wife ain't had no chilluns. You, my baby girl, was his only chile. He name you Amanda 'cause his wife always wanna have a girl name' Amanda. Even afta his wife died, he try to give her what she wan'. He love' you an' even me in his own way, I guess. But he ain't free me or you. He die' and we was bof still slaves til afta the war. I guess that's why I can't abide white folks. Even the ones who ain't bad, just ain't good neither. I'm glad my Juliette don't wanna be wit' a white man who gon' love her in his own way. 'Cause his way ain't gon' be her way. I think Mr. Mann love her real hard. He got lan' an' a business, so he can take good care o' her. An' he's offerin' her the respec' a wife gits. It's mo' 'n you or I got, Mandy. Let this chile make up her own mind. She the one who gotta live her life, just like you livin' yours. Your way won't what I wanted for you, but it's what you wanted for yosef. Anyway, God gon look afta her 'cause she right wit' him. I still here afta all I been thoo 'cause God made me strong an' kep' me goin'. He lookin' afta you too, Mandy. Even if you don't ax Him to stay in yo' life, He do anyway 'cause Juliette and me pray fo' you.

As it usually happens, Grand'mère Lizzie spoke the final words on the matter. Ma Mère and I seldom challenge or contradict her. Though her discourse is not polished, her message is always clear and logical. Some describe it as mother wit or common sense, but Grand'mère understands much more than she can put into proper English. This evening, her understanding guides her to support my plan to marry J. R. Mann and Ma Mère is wont to be silent rather than speak against it further.

8 June 1885

These are the first written reflections of one Mrs. Juliette Bonhomme Mann. Heretofore, my name and nom de plume was Miss Juliette Bonhomme. However, three days ago, Mr. J. R. Mann became my husband at First Baptist Church in Davis Bend, Mississippi. How excited and ecstatic I am whenever I say my new name or hear someone address me by it. It brings me such pleasure to use all forms of expressing my new status: Mrs. Juliette Mann, Mrs. J. R. Mann, or simply, Mrs. Mann. Even the less formal greeting of Mistress Juliette elicits a smile from me, as I realize that I have been elevated from the single status of Miss Juliette. So I plea for your indulgence as I digress from my recollection of recent events to express the pleasure and excitement I am deriving from writing the various forms of my new name in this paragraph. *Quel joie!*

I have been seized by euphoria for the past three days. Each day brought exciting experiences that I shall remember and cherish always. Friday was the wonderful day of my wedding to Mr. J. R. Mann. Grand'mère and her two closest friends, Violet and Minnie, toiled together for hours over several evenings to make a beautiful wedding dress from the white silk J.R. gave me. The ladies of First Baptist prepared a delightful repast of fried chicken, mashed potatoes, mixed greens, pickled cucumbers and tomatoes, corn, and fruity punch. It was served after the ceremony in the field behind the church. All of the residents of Davis Bend came to celebrate with us. Some of the former Davis Bend inhabitants now residing in Vicksburg joined in the festivities as well, among them Isaiah and Martha Montgomery. Ma Mère did not return to see me marry J.R.

J.R. and I left the repast a little past seven to spend our wedding night together in Grand'mère's house. Grand'mère stayed the night with Violet so that we could have privacy. Immediately upon our arrival at Grand'mère's, J.R. steered me toward the bedroom, anxious to consummate our union and lay undisputed claim to that which is his. Suddenly, I felt fear invade but not subdue my joy. I love my husband, and I wanted to experience intimacy with him. I had dreamed of submitting to him. Yet I had been kissed by a man for the first time only a few hours earlier during the wedding ceremony. I was apprehensive, wondering what would happen next. I recalled what Violet and Minnie told me when they were working on my wedding dress. They tried to prepare me for my first time. Violet recommended that I close my eyes, grit my teeth, and try to imagine something soothing while he flails on top of me until he is exhausted and discharges an explosion inside me. Minnie said that it would hurt tonight, but over time, I will grow to enjoy it almost as much as he does. She suggested I encourage him to be patient and gentle the first time. She said he probably won't do it, but it's worth a try. Violet didn't agree and said I should say nothing because men don't like to be told how to do it. They all like to think they know what to do, even if they don't.

J.R. sensed my trepidation and tried to be reassuring. He helped me with the buttons and bow on the back of my dress. Then he hurriedly undressed himself completely and waited for me to join him under the bed covers. I was embarrassed as he watched me disrobe slowly. I removed all garments but my drawers. I untied them and held them up in front with my arms crossed. Finally, I lay down next to him in the bed. He smiled then kissed me on the lips more passionately than he did during the ceremony at church. More kisses followed in quick succession, gentle pecks on my chin and down the front of my neck. I closed my eyes to savour the titillating sensations igniting pleasure and desire I had not previously experienced. He massaged my breasts briefly, alternately pinching and licking my nipples, which grew hard responding to his manipulations. He removed my drawers, stroking my inner thighs and legs as he pulled them down. As he mounted me, I noted that although I stand at least a quarter of a foot taller than he, our torsos fit perfectly when we lie. Once his fingers confirmed the abundant moisture in my private place, he guided his manhood inside. His initial entries were slow and forceful as he penetrated my virginal barrier. He continued thrusting with escalating speed and depth until I felt the explosion that Violet mentioned. I heard him moan ere his body relaxed on top of me. Afterward, I opened my eyes and saw him smiling broadly. That gave me confirmation that our first time brought him pleasure. He kissed me once more ere he moved to lie beside me. Slumber overcame him immediately, but I lay there conscious nigh half an hour longer, aching and sore yet strangely longing for another episode. I had only to wait until I awoke in the morning. J.R. wanted me again before we rose to pack for our journey to my new home. I found voracity in Minnie's assurances regarding my satisfaction with our romantic encounters. Indeed, though I was still sore, I derived more pleasure and experienced less pain the second time we coupled.

Grand'mère returned home in time to help me finish packing and to give me a big hug before we left. She hugged J.R. as well and implored him to be a good husband to me. She and I both felt assured by his declarations and promises. During the long carriage ride to what I have quickly come to call the Mann Estate, we enjoyed hours of conversation about our families and our hopes for our future. We affirmed our mutual expectations of trust. Not wanting to deceive my husband, I chose to disclose the veritable circumstances of my upbringing and my departure from the Miss Granville's Academy. J.R.'s response to my disclosure offered compassion and insight. He found nothing that I revealed to alter his perception of my virtuosity. He recognized me as the victim, not the perpetrator, of deception. He did not pass judgment upon me based on the sins of my parents. He further expressed his dismissal of any terminology white people use to castigate the offspring of any relationship.

It is his contention that any aspersions should be cast upon white men rather than their mixed descendants. Mulattoes born to slave women were conceived through rape by masters and overseers. The children and their mothers were powerless victims of relentless abuse and terror. So indeed, he opined, were their men who abhorred the violation of their women and suffered unspeakable humiliation for their inability to protect them. J.R. recounted stories Mister told him about man slaves who were beaten or killed for trying to save their women and daughters from being defiled. Mister told him how some slave parents tightly bound their daughters' breasts to conceal their maturing bodies and make them look too young to attract the unwanted attentions of the white men. He spoke of the woman the overseers called Crazy Coot, who deliberately burned one side of her face so white men would find her ugly and leave her be. She wasn't crazy, he alleged, but used a desperate act of defiance that succeeded. She was never again stolen away from the bed she shared with her man. He found beauty in her scarred façade and gave her four more babies. Mister explained that during slavery, his woman, J.R.'s mother, benefitted from his special relationship with his master. The master wanted to be sure that as a freeman, J.R.'s father would remain constant in his determination to free his family. Thus, the master did not sully J.R.'s mother and told the overseers to leave her alone as well. Even as a freeman, his father would not have been able to keep her safe without the protection of his master and, later, by the goodwill of influential white men he knew along his trading route.

J.R. confirms that he recognizes the importance of continuing to foster good relations with the white men in Newton and those around Mississippi with whom he trades. That has allowed him to preserve his business and to protect his property and the sharecroppers who dwell there. Nowadays, a full score after slavery ended, white men are no longer our masters, but they do not acknowledge us as equals. They continue to use violence to maintain dominance and power over Negroes. White men are permitted to harass and rape Negro women and girls and beat or kill Negro men in horrific fashion without fear of retribution. J.R. offers understanding of Ma Mère's decision to leave Mississippi, where her beauty would have rendered her vulnerable to white men's harassment or worse. She found security for herself and, later for me, living in Vieux Carre under the protection of Mon Père, a white man of wealth and influence. Ma Mère is not wrong in thinking that life for a white woman in the North would be easier than that of a Negro woman in Mississippi. However, J.R. declares that he loves me and will do all within his ability to ensure that I never bemoan my decision to marry him.

It was late Saturday night when we arrived in Newton County. Everyone on our estate had retired hours earlier. J.R. and I fell into deep slumber immediately after unloading the carriage and consummating our union for the first time in our bed. When we awoke yesterday morning, we prepared to attend church. J.R. was beaming, as was I, when he introduced me as his wife to everyone we met along the way, "Mrs. Juliette Mann, an octoroon from New Orleans and Davis Bend." I was bemused but well aware of the reason for the information he added to every introduction of me since we left Davis Bend. He and I observe the disapproving glares of white people and Negroes alike when they first observe us together, riding in the carriage or holding hands as we walk. An interracial union would be illegal and injurious for both of us, especially J.R. Negro men have been beaten, castrated, and hanged for suspected intentions of contact with white women. No matter how good his relationships are with white men in the area, they would sever business dealings and do much worse to him for such an egregious violation.

I was seized with ecstasy when J.R. led me to sit on the front pew on the left side of the little one-story white frame structure where the small devout congregation worships. I am a Christian wife, and I love sitting at the front of the church with my husband in front of God and everyone else. The preacher and all the people I meet are so respectful and friendly. I can hardly wait to repeat the euphoria of this experience next Sunday and every Sunday after that. In the meantime, I will occupy my days teaching the children of the families on the Mann Estate. There are about twenty children of schooling age. I became acquainted with most of them today. I shall initiate their instruction tomorrow in our home. The younger children will arrive in the morning, and the older ones will come later when they have completed their chores in the fields. Afterward, I shall find pleasure in delighting my husband with delicious food, stimulating conversation, and passionate lovemaking. Indeed, my life in Newton County has commenced in marvelous fashion, and I am overflowing with expectations of a joyous future.

5 July 1885

As is my custom on Sundays, I sojourned to church happily on the arm of my husband for the noonday service. We exchanged cordial smiles with everyone as we strolled down the aisle toward our habitual seats on the front pew, where we sang proverbial hymns and listened to the sermon. It was a typically pleasant Sunday afternoon ere we returned home for supper and lighthearted conversation. Yet J.R. exuded an uncommonly quiet pensiveness during supper.

J.R. broke his uncharacteristic silence by drawing my attention to a woman named Tessie who was seated with some of our sharecroppers in church. Tessie is a comely petite woman, about an inch shorter than J.R. Like him, she appears to be a pure African. Her smooth velvet like complexion is what the local residents call "fast black," meaning that the black of her skin is so permanent that "it don't fade, no matter how much she sweat or how hot her bath water be." I recall J.R. introducing me to Tessie my first Sunday in Newton. She appeared to be ill that day and left church before the conclusion of the service. Thus, she was not present afterward to engage in my initial conversations with the other women of the congregation. My subsequent encounters with her, limited to Sundays at church, have been extremely brief. We exchanged polite greetings, but that has been the extent of our communication. I found it curious that J.R. thought her important enough to warrant discussion and, even more surprisingly, that she was the subject of what his countenance signaled to be a serious dialogue.

Consistent with his commonly concise rhetoric, J.R. bluntly stated that she is carrying his child. He quickly added that he and Tessie were involved in a relationship that spanned two years but ended when he began courting me in April. He assured me that although he had some affection for Tessie, he did not love her and made no false utterances to her to the contrary. He emphatically declared that he loves me, and I am the only one he has ever asked to be his wife. He reminded me that he vowed before God and the witnesses at our wedding ceremony that he would love only me until we are parted by death and that he would take care of me and respect me until then. He affirmed his resolution to keep those promises. He never made such declarations to Tessie, never conversed with her regarding a possible future together. She is well aware of that, he alleged. When she informed him of her condition last week, she indicated that she had no expectations or hope that he would forsake me or that he would ever rekindle their relationship. He explained to her that he will assist her in providing for the child, but he will not disrespect me or violate his vows to me by having any other dealings with her.

J.R. feels an obligation to ensure the welfare of the child he sired. He implored me to understand that he cannot abandon a child that he created with Tessie ere we met. He believes that as much as I am concerned about educating and tending to the needs of children who are not my own, I must surely understand why he is compelled to assume responsibility for tending to the needs of his own child. He beseeched me to grant him my blessing to supply them with food, clothing, and shelter. He made known to me his desire to build a small house for them on the low ground near the southern border of the property, far away and outside the view from our mansion on the hill at the north end of the estate. However, he declared that he will only arrange for the construction of her house if I agree to sanction it.

Though seized by more than surprise at this set of circumstances, I was not overwhelmed with awe and disbelief. The confidence and skill which J.R. exposed when he took command of consummating our marriage evidenced his familiarity with passionate encounters. It seemed probable that in his twenty-seven years, he had known pleasures with other women. Yet I had not considered that he was entangled with another woman when he announced his intentions toward me. However, the revelation of this fact causes me neither bitterness nor jealousy. J.R. chose to bestow upon me the honor of becoming his Christian wife after he had spent two years with Tessie and never asked her.

I bear no anger toward Tessie. In fact, I am empathetic to her situation. She seems to be a decent woman who had the misfortune of caring too much for a man who did not care enough for her. After knowing him biblically for almost two years, she must have hoped that this honorable man would marry her when he learned of her condition. How awful it must have been for her to discover that ere she mustered the courage to enlighten him, he had married someone else. To make matters worse, she knew nothing of his involvement with this woman. J.R. never spoke about me to anyone in Newton until he brought me here as his wife. Recalling more about Tessie's reactions to me that first Sunday, I remember sensing her glances and greetings less welcoming than the others. I realize now that she must have been distraught, knowing that she was carrying J.R.'s child and hearing his declarations of love and joy as he introduced her to his blushing bride. Studying us smiling and holding hands as we sat together on the first pew in the church, Tessie frowned. At one point, she became nauseous and went outside to vomit, probably less as a result of the life inside her and more because of the death of her hopes and dreams of becoming Mrs. J. R. Mann. How hurt she must be and how embarrassed with everyone in Newton knowing her plight! It would be dishonorable for J.R. to abandon her and not make provisions for her and the child. I am not uncharitable and will not dissuade my husband from behaving honorably.

I acquiesced to J.R.'s proposed arrangements. He expressed relief and gratitude for my considerations ere he departed to share the news with Tessie. Thus, J.R. and I have been tested for the first time in our marriage, and relying on our mutual love and respect, we passed with excellence. There will be other tests, but I have no fear of them. Despite my limited experiences with the passionate impulses of human nature, my instincts and intuition leave me no doubt that Tessie will attempt to extract more than material necessities from J.R. I have been pleasured by him but a month, and I yearn for his fervent kisses and volcanic eruptions inside me every night. After two years of knowing that excitement, Tessie will not want to forever abstain from intimate knowledge of my husband. I trust J.R. and believe that he will resist her because he loves me and I am his wife. Yet she garners some attention and affection from him as the mother of his child. I impatiently long to ensure my supreme status in his heart and mind with children of my own. Tonight and forward, he will come to experience greater intensity in our lovemaking as my enthusiasm is ignited by purpose as well as pleasure.

26 October 1885

Yesterday J.R. returned from his first business trip since we wed. During the first four days of the week since we took leave of each other, I was besieged with melancholy in my solitude. It is my custom to bear whatever is unpleasant without yielding to the temptations of self-indulgence. However, on Wednesday, I succumbed to an uncharacteristic gluttony, devouring a supper of half of a chicken, rice, and vegetables, followed by a whole jar of pickled peaches and a full pound of peanuts which I soaked in a cascade of honey. Upon rising Thursday morning, I fell ill, violently expelling the contents of my stomach. Throughout the day, all that I consumed was similarly regurgitated within half an hour. When I awoke Friday, nausea and convulsions in my empty abdomen rendered me too weak to stand. The oldest of my morning pupils, ten-year-old Hattie, took charge of me and of the lessons of the day. She proved herself to be a worthy assistant. Following a morning of labour in the field, the older pupils were delighted to spend their afternoon relaxing their bodies outside in the cool creek instead of exercising their minds inside the warm house. As word of my malady reached the mothers, they sojourned to the house, bearing buttermilk biscuits and warm tea. They stayed with me until dusk, fanning me and applying cool rags to my forehead, amused by my failure to recognize the obvious symptoms that I am with child. Their confident assurances brought me unrestrained joy. When they departed, I felt better and was happier than when they arrived. Blissful dreams permeated my restful slumber that night, and I awoke with great expectations for a joyful reunion with J.R.

Given my success in digesting the biscuits and tea Friday evening, I anticipated the same result when I consumed the same fare for breakfast Saturday. My presumption proved to be wrong. Still, my attempt to digest a bowl of chicken soup at noon met with triumph as did my attempt with a second bowl two hours hence. My elated spirit willed my body to cooperate as I prepared supper for J.R. He returned about an hour before sunset, gifting me with an exquisite cameo brooch and greetings from Grand'mère whom he visited in Davis Bend. I did not conceal my jubilation but did not yet share with him all of the reasons for it.

As is our nightly custom after supper, J.R. settled in his favourite chair and bade me read to him a passage or poem of my choosing. He indicates that he derives great pleasure in the sight of my lips moving and the sound of my voice reciting those fancy words. It arouses him. I rarely finish reading ere he interrupts me with a kiss that is a prelude to passion. Last night, I exacted a promise from him to allow me to read a short poem in its entirety. I requested that he indulge me by giving honest, unvarnished criticism to alterations I made to my favourite poem, Elizabeth Barrett Browning's sonnet, "How Do I Love Thee?" I explained that I composed alternative verses to deliver a message that evoked in me feelings too special to convey through the prose of common discourse. I expressed my anxious anticipation of his reaction. Then, I read to him,

> How do I love thee? Let me count the ways.
> I love thee to the depth and breadth and height
> My soul can reach, when feeling out of sight
> For the ends of Being and ideal Grace.
> My love for thee fills my thoughts every day
> And my most beautiful dreams each night.
> I love thee freely with Joy and Delight;
> I love thee purely, and have not need for Praise.
> I love thee and what thy passion hath wrought,
> Planting a seed from which our child will grow.
> I love thee as I wait to feel it move
> And gather strength to leave its hidden place.
> From our love has sprung new life! And if God doth approve,
> In June, sunlight will shine upon its face.

J.R. smiled and requested that I read again the portion that was my original work. I thought at first that he had not understood my intent. However, his laughter as I concluded evidenced that he just wanted to revel in the repetition. "You one of a kind, my Juliette," he uttered. "I love the fancy way you speak a simple truth. Sweet, almost like singin'.

June, huh? Same month we got married. Seems like the best things in my life happen in June."

I had not thought it possible, but I was even happier than before, and J.R. continued to heighten my joy when we retired. His tender kisses and romantic caresses throughout our passionate lovemaking brought me to rapture ere I fell into euphoric slumber.

Today I found humour in J.R.'s insistence on communicating to everyone we greeted at church that I am with child, although I informed him that most people in Newton were aware of my condition ere he returned home from his travels. Throughout the service, I experienced a new pleasure as J.R. exuded love and pride through his constant massaging and patting of my belly.

7 January 1886

Tessie gave birth to J.R.'s son today. The news was delivered to us during supper by Lottie, the wife of the longest-serving and most trusted sharecropper on our estate. She apologized for the interruption and requested an audience with J.R. He told her that she should speak to him in the presence of his wife. She informed him that Tessie and her son were both fine and resting, but he could see them whenever he wanted. J.R. responded that she should tell Tessie that he would check on them in the morning on his way to the field. Lottie told J.R. that the baby boy was "kinda light-complected," but the black rims of his ear lobes and his black "man parts" proved he was "gon' darken up and be black as night like his momma."

Before Lottie's exit, J.R. asked who attended to Tessie during the delivery. Tessie's aunt Squirrel is the midwife who delivers most of the Negro babies in the area, and Tessie has been assisting her for ten years since she was just ten. J.R. wanted to know if anyone helped Squirrel with Tessie's delivery. Lottie replied that she was in the room to assist, but Tessie knew what she needed to do, and she did it. Squirrel didn't need any help.

After Lottie departed, I indicated that if J.R. wanted to see Tessie and the boy tonight, I would understand and be fine. He decided to pay his respects and left shortly after we finished supper. He wanted me to read a short poem or passage to him ere he left but was afraid that he would be too tired to make the visit if he waited any longer to depart. He implored me to retire soon as he is concerned about my health. I am still vomiting my first meal of the day regardless of its size or content. Yet I feel fit and famished the rest of the day, eating small portions of food almost hourly as I go about teaching a full day and cooking supper for J.R. and me. J.R. still worries about me and has Lottie assisting me all day in the house instead of working in the field.

I am successfully concealing my resentment that another woman birthed J.R.'s first son. Yet I am comforted by J.R.'s attentiveness to me and his sensitivity to my feelings. I am confident that Tessie's son is no more a threat to my child's position in J.R.'s heart than his mother is a threat to mine.

21 March 1886

J.R. failed to return home from Tessie's last night. I awoke to find he had not slept in our bed, and I realized that he had murdered my wifely bliss. I buried it alongside my naïveté in the pit of my aching stomach. Today I mourn their passing. My forced smile during the church service this morning concealed my pathos. Presently, I sit in solitude at my desk, my Bible opened to 1 Corinthians 13, which I have read more than a dozen times today. I pray for the fortitude to bear all things and endure all things with patience and kindness and without jealousy and unbecoming behavior.

Upon my request, J.R. has departed from our home, granting me a solitary period. Anger engulfs me. I cannot bear to gaze upon my husband less I yield to the temptation to unleash upon him the cruel utterances of reproach and condemnation swirling around my brain, frantically seeking to exit through my mouth. I would deem such offensive effusions unworthy of me as a Christian wife. Thus, I bade J.R. to take temporary leave of me while I seek a rational means of managing many conflicting emotions.

J.R. admits that he slept at Tessie's house last night. Yet he will neither confirm nor deny that he engaged in sexual congress with her. He maintains that whether he did or did not, it is of no significance because his actions with Tessie do not slight his love for me. J.R. purports not to understand my feelings of betrayal and deception. He argues that he spoke no falsehood when he proclaimed that I am the only woman he loves. Before we married, his sexual escapades with other women were not driven by love but by the lustful nature of men. His father, Mister, taught him that freemen satisfy that lust with many willing women, but they save their love and commitment for a single virtuous woman whom they marry for life. Since our first conversation in April, J.R. has shared with me his high regard for the words of wisdom he learned from Mister. Ere I accepted his proposal, J.R. informed me that Mister had inculcated in him the value of a virtuous woman and the sanctity of marriage, extending even beyond death. However, he never explained Mister's contention that a husband's sexual dalliances do not violate the sanctity of marriage. J.R. accepts this contention as a universal truth which Mister learned through years of observation and experience.

It occurs to me that Mister and other freed slaves received no formal education regarding the rights and responsibilities of freemen. They heard disconnected declarations of what freemen could do, such as learn to read and write, to marry, and to vote, as well as statements describing what freemen should not endure, such as being whipped or forced to work without compensation. However, their comprehension of the rights and common behaviors of freemen was gleaned, for the most part, from their earlier observations of freemen, particularly their former masters and overseers. The master freed Thomas, Mister's name as a slave, nearly a decade ere most slaves were freed after the war. During his years working as the master's freeman assistant in the trading business, J.R.'s father had experiences that shaped his attitudes about how freemen should regard and treat women.

On business sojourns around Mississippi, Thomas and the master often stopped to rest overnight at a plantation on their route. One of the courtesies offered to and accepted by the master was the service of a bed warmer, a slave woman ordered to "warm" his bed and satisfy his desires then sleep on the floor in case he wanted her again before his departure the next morning. In time, Thomas was liked well enough by a few of the plantation owners to be given a bed warmer to sleep with him on the hay in the barn or in the back of the wagon. The master also slept with slaves on his own plantation whenever he wanted. After the war, when all the slaves were freed, Thomas changed his name to Mister Mann but didn't change much about his attitudes toward women. He did recognize that free women should not be forced to be with a man. He impressed upon J.R. that he should only be with women who are willing. With this caveat, Mister pronounced that enjoying the sexual favours of willing women away from home is one of the rights of freemen. It is as much an allowance of freedom as legal marriages and ownership of land.

Mister further schooled J.R. that while it is fitting for him to enjoy the pleasure of many women, he must not become emotionally entangled with any woman willing to pleasure him outside of marriage. Such women do not warrant his respect and admiration, for they have pleasured or will pleasure others as well. During slavery, women were powerless against the advances of their captors, and slave men were often forced to share their women with others. However, free women can choose to be chaste or not, and freemen should be mindful of that when they choose their wives. Mister admonished J.R. to search for a virtuous woman who saves her favours to present them pure and undamaged to him after they are wed. Such a woman will be a faithful wife whom he can trust with his love. In the Bible, Proverbs 31 teaches that a man should value a virtuous woman above all else. When a man finds such a woman who stirs his soul, he should marry her and give her alone his love and respect. He should take care of her, protect her, and never turn away from her. If she precedes him in death, he should not marry again because in heaven, God reunites the souls of man and wife. It would not be proper or pleasing to God for him to spend eternity with more than one wife. If God blesses a man with one virtuous woman, he should cherish that blessing and not diminish it by greedily seeking another one.

I was stunned by J.R.'s audacity. His discourse was straightforward, reminiscent of the terse style of my geography instructor at Miss Granville's Academy. With an air of condescension and the expectation of my unquestioning acceptance, he imparted what he believes to be indisputable facts: The first fact is that he is committed to me and to our marriage. The second fact is that he loves only me and reveres me above all other women. The third fact is that whatever suspicions I may have about his conduct when we are apart, I must recognize that, as a man, he is naturally endowed with strong urges and needs that demand satisfaction. He responds to his urges and fulfills his needs with me, except when we are apart or I am incapacitated, as I am at present owing to my delicate condition. If he seeks temporary satisfaction with another, and he does not confirm that he has done so, his selection of her is a matter of convenience rather than affection and does not diminish his complete devotion to me.

Unfortunately, I understand all too well the beliefs of male entitlement and female acceptance that J.R. learned from Mister. They resonate with familiarity. Mister gleaned those beliefs from observing and interacting with men like Mon Père and the other white fathers of most of my schoolmates at the academy and my octoroon friends in Vieux Carre. They marry pious women whom they profess to love and admire. Yet they feel entitled to indulge themselves with other women, expecting their wives will remain faithful and grant them forgiveness, or at least acceptance, for their adulterous promiscuity. I knew this to be the common behavior of wealthy white men but did not realize that it is evidenced among Negro men as well. Thus, I find myself in the same position as Mme. Bonhomme and the wife of my great-grandfather, Grand'mère's master and father. I have the same resentment toward Tessie that Mme. Bonhomme must feel toward Ma Mère and that Great-Grandfather's wife must have felt toward Grand'mère's mother. And though I recognize the innocence of Tessie's son, the sight of him brings me unbearable pain because he is living proof of my husband's relationship with his mother. I know that relationship will never end. Hence, I know my pain will never end just as Mme. Bonhomme's pain never has.

Nonetheless, I prefer my status as the aggrieved wife to that of the mistress. Although women in both roles know the bitter taste of sadness, a mistress, such as Tessie or Ma Mère, must accept that she will never command the respect given to a wife. She will never experience the joys only a wife knows when her husband publically reveres her and takes pride in introducing her as his wife. Tessie will always occupy an inferior position in J.R.'s heart and in her seating proximity to him in church and in public. I am appalled by J.R.'s behavior and his arrogance. However, I love my husband, and I am not going to break the vows I made to stay with him through better and worse. Further, I will not ruin my marriage by harbouring constant feelings of anger and resentment. I believe that J.R. has greater affection for Tessie than he will admit to me and, possibly, to himself. Yet I believe he loves me only or, at the least, he loves me best. As for his adulterous behavior, I will express the anguish I feel because of it, but I will not denounce him for it. I leave it to God to judge him and to exact whatever punishment He deems worthy. I am not without sins of my own. We are all sinners, and God will judge us all.

14 June 1886

Yesterday I awoke alone in my bed with an unbearable and indescribable pain that permeated my lower torso. J.R. is away, owing to matters of business. He traveled earlier than is his custom in June so that he would return before I deliver our child. However, I surmised that the child was coming ere its anticipated date.

It was near ten o'clock when I tried to rise, but pain and fear rendered me temporarily paralyzed. I wanted to scream, but I knew that nobody would hear me. I just had to cope for about an hour when Lottie would be arriving to help me prepare for church. Yet God knew that I needed assistance sooner, and He sent Lottie to my house earlier than expected around half past ten. When Lottie saw my condition, she knew that I was in labour. She helped me sit, propping me up with pillows behind my back. She brought me bread and sweetened tea left from what I made to drink with supper Saturday night. Then she hurried to get the midwife, Squirrel.

To my shock and horror, Lottie returned with Tessie. Tessie was the last person I wanted to see. I know that she is experienced enough at delivering babies, but I did not want my husband's pregnant mistress to have my life and my baby's life in her hands, however capable they might be.

"No!" I protested and inquired, "Where is Squirrel?"

Tessie responded that Squirrel had taken ill midweek and was still bedridden. She could barely stand and would not be able to come to me or to deliver my baby, even if I were able to go to her. Tessie tried to reassure me, "You gon' be all right. You jes' scared, and you in a lot o' pain. I know how bad you feel. But I swear, once the baby come out and you hold it in yo' arms, you not gon' feel no mo' pain."

As much as I wanted to tell her to leave me be, she was correct about my fear. I was afraid to try to have my baby alone or with the assistance of someone unskilled in delivering babies. Tessie proved to be the right person to help me through. She kept me informed of everything that was happening to me in preparation for the delivery. She held my hand and allowed me to squeeze hers when I needed. She showed me how to breathe and kept cold compresses on my forehead. Of greater importance, in the nine hours we spent together, she spoke to me truthfully about her feelings toward J.R. and her insights about his feelings for her.

"I ain't gon' let nothin' happen to you or yo' baby. J.R. would turn away from me or do worse. I couldn't take that. God he'p me. I love that man. It don't matter how bad he hurt me marryin' you jus' like that, I can't he'p myself. I couldn't stand it if he lef' me or if he hated me."

If only Tessie had known what Mister had been teaching and preaching to J.R. for twenty-six years until he died, she might have been somewhat prepared for the inevitability of J.R. marrying someone else, someone he had not known biblically outside of marriage. I thought there to be no purpose, save cruelty, to share that information with her, so I did not say anything about that. I did share my feelings of love for J.R. and my hurt knowing that he still comes to her bed.

"You got no reason to hurt 'bout that. J.R. come to my bed cuz I know what he like an' I do it for him. Mister took J.R. to 'ho'es when he won't but twelve. Them 'ho'es taught him all 'bout what to do to make a woman crazy fo' him. An' they done stuff to him what made him crazy. He taught me to do what them 'ho'es did to him. I do them things, an' it still make him crazy."

At first, I thought Tessie cared less about causing me hurt me than I did about hurting her. I wondered how she could imagine that I would not find reason to be hurt by the suggestion that my husband found more pleasure in her bed than in mine. Yet when she observed my countenance, she elucidated her intention.

"J.R. like bein' in my bed, but he don't love me. I use' to think he did, e'en tho' he ain't say so. But I know now I 'as wrong. He say he love you from the day y'all met an' he gon' love you til he die. He use' to say he won't never gon' git married. He tell me that fo' two years. I hoped he change his min' when I give him a son. But he marry you real fas', an' you ain't had no baby fo' him. You an' me so dif'rent. You's white, an' I's black. You's edicated, I ain't. Maybe he jes' won't never gon' marry me cuz I won't pretty an' smart 'nuf fo' him to love me."

I wondered if she underestimated herself and J.R.'s feelings for her. I believe that Mon Père cares deeply for Ma Mère, maybe even loves her. Yet he may never have considered marrying her because she is part Negro, and he had been indoctrinated to believe that a Negro woman is not worthy of marriage. J.R. was indoctrinated to believe that an unclean woman is unworthy of marriage. Even if he loved Tessie, he would not have married her because she was not a virgin when he met her and she pleasured him outside of marriage. Still, J.R. does tell me I am virtuous and beautiful. He says that he loves to gaze upon my face and watch my eyes appear to change colors when I change the colors of my blouses and shawls. He says he loves the way I look and sound when I read to him. Yet I hope that his love for me is based on more than the superficiality of my white-looking appearance, my education, and my virginity, which he seized on our wedding night. I want to be loved for my character.

Yet I also want to please him in our bed. He has not made love to me for almost four months. He may find my swelling belly a challenge to his comfort or a deterrent to his desire. He purports to be protecting me and our child from his vigorous, passionate activity. It is too difficult for him to hold back, so he would rather avoid lovemaking until after the baby is born and I am healed. I take exception to his avoidance of lovemaking. He has only abstained from making love to me. He has certainly been with Tessie, since she is about four months pregnant. When J.R. and I reunite in our bed, I am going to ask him to show me the things that the whores taught him and he taught Tessie. I want to learn how to bring him to the same level of unbridled ecstasy that I have experienced when he pleasures me.

Tessie shared one more bit of information about J.R. that pleased me. While J.R. shows no signs of regret or remorse for his adultery, he has apparently acknowledged to Tessie his regret for hurting me. According to Tessie, Mister taught his son that part of a husband's responsibility to his wife was to spare her feelings by exercising discretion with his indiscretions. Mister taught him that it was inappropriate and disrespectful to his wife to exercise his adultery too close to home. In Mister's words, J.R. should never hurt his wife by "sashaying his misdemeanors" in her sight.

"J.R. say he don't like you seein' me ripe wit' his chile. It's like th'owing our deeds in yo' face. He feel real bad 'bout that. He say he s'pose to keep you from gittin' hurt from seein' sinful things. That be why God tol' Lot's wife not to look back at Sodom an' Gomorrah. J.R.

say he wish he found me a place to live far away from Newton. That be better fo' you an' him but not fo' me. I don' want him to sen' me 'way from my fam'ly an' e'rebody I know."

I told Tessie that there was no reason for J.R. to send her away now. It's too late to hide the truth from me, and he should be close to his children with her. Once again, I see the similarities in his thinking and that of the landed gentry in New Orleans. They thought they were being respectful to their wives by settling their quadroon mistresses in Vieux Carre, away from their mansions on St. Charles Avenue. Yet the way to shield their wives from hurt would be to abstain from adultery. Banishing Tessie from Newton would not keep me from knowing that somewhere along his trade route, she and her children were waiting to play house with him whenever he rested in their town.

"You's a beautiful lady, Miss Juliette. I wanna hate you, so I don't care 'bout tryin' to be wit' J.R. But you too kin' an' sweet. I know you prob'ly hate me, but I like you."

Somehow, her words did not ring true to me. I wish she liked me and respected me enough to stay clear of my husband. Still, I know from experience, when J.R. comes to you, it is difficult to resist him. I could not do it ere we shared passion and intimacy. It would be impossible for me to do it now. I love him, even when I hate what he does.

Tessie bade me push. I put all my strength and determination into bearing down to drive the baby out of me. The second push brought forth a head, and with the third one, I finally felt the rest of the body exiting my womb. Simultaneously, I heard my baby cry as Tessie excitedly proclaimed, "It's a boy! Miss Juliette, you got a son!" A moment later, she laid him on his stomach across my bosom. After she attended to the final matters associated with the delivery, she wrapped him in a blanket and placed him in my arms. He immediately began to foray for nourishment. I guided him to my nipple, and our bond was sealed. I am completely besotted with my son. After he completed his first meal, we both fell asleep, exhausted from hours of grueling labour.

Once again, J.R. returned a day after everyone in Newton knew what he should have known first. Yet I was pleased to surprise him by introducing him to our first son. J.R. seemed delighted to see me holding our son. He found him to be a handsome little guy with the complexion of a worn copper penny and a few wisps of hair the same color. J.R. showed concern for me and inquired about the birth. He was startled when I responded that Tessie had taken good care of me. I did not tell him about our conversation, but I expressed genuine gratitude for all she did for me. After an awkward moment of silence, he wanted my assurance that I was feeling all right. I was pleased to inform him that for the first time in almost eight months, I ate breakfast and didn't regurgitate it half an hour later. He expressed relief but suggested that Lottie should continue to come to me instead of to the field every day. I agreed.

J.R. wondered if I had considered what initials we should give the little fellow. I informed him that I named our son, John Augustus, subject to J.R.'s approval. John is for John the Baptist and Augustus is for the Roman Caesar who succeeded Julius Caesar. Thus, he will have powerful Biblical and historical names to strengthen him. J.R. did not subscribe to the necessity of formal names for boys. He is of the opinion that the initials his father gave him have served him well enough, so initials would be enough for his sons. He sought to compromise by conceding that our daughters could have spelled names like his mother, Miss Barbara.

I made a correction to his assertion that his father gave him initials for his name. That was not Mister's intention. As a freeman, Mister strategically selected names for his family to extract respectful greetings from white men. "Man" was his choice for a surname because he did not want white people to call him "boy" as was their customary way to address Negro men of all ages. His name was recorded with an additional letter n because that was the spelling of British and American whites with that surname. He chose "Mister" because that was the manner in which white men addressed each other, and he made no distinction between the title and the name. He just wanted to ensure that he would be known as Mister Mann. (Factually, he was Mr. Mister Mann, and his wife, whom he named Miss Barbara, was actually Mrs. Miss Barbara Mann.) He wanted his son to have the name that white men gave their eldest sons, Junior. Yet when he saw it spelled out, he didn't recognize it and thought the white man recording his names was trying to trick him. He insisted that it be recorded as Mister remembered seeing it on documents, abbreviated as Jr. His less than perfect memory led him to demand what he thought to be the correct spelling of Junior, "J period R period." I reminded J.R. that as he approached manhood, he felt that he had outgrown "Junior" and started referring to himself as J.R. He, not his father, promoted the use of initials as his name.

As Mister intended, I want to endow my children with proper names. J.R. opined that boys will have to sign their names often as men, and it would be easier for them to write initials rather than long names. He pointed out that it will be a long time before our baby has sufficient schooling to know the significance of what he described as a pompous name. Nonetheless, he said that as the mother, I can name my children whatever I like. Then it will be my responsibility to teach them to spell and write their names and to know their significance. I fully accept this duty and plan to teach my son all of that and so much more. I granted J.R. permission to call John Augustus by his initials, JA, sometimes. That could be his affectionate nickname for his son. I am aware that Tessie named her son RJ, his father's initials reversed, but I will not do that. Tessie was right about us being "so different." She may think initials sufficient in naming her son, but my son will have a proper Christian name.

31 July 1886

Last night, passion returned to my marriage when J.R. made love to me for the first time in four and a half months. He was tender and sweet, inquiring about my feelings at every turn. He kissed my lips fervently as his mouth commenced its journey down my torso. He suckled at each breast then declared, "My, my. No wonder John A. cries for your milk. It's delicious!" I was frenzied long before he plunged his manhood inside me. He proceeded slowly dare he hurt me, but my impatience and aggressive gyrations excited him. He continued with increasing zeal until we reached the summit of euphoria, evidenced by my scream and his sighs as his seed burst forth. When he collapsed atop me, our bodies were limp and engulfed in each other's perspiration. He kissed me softly, smiled, and rolled over to lie beside me. Our mutual satisfaction was so obvious that I startled him when I implored him to teach me how to pleasure him.

"How could you not know how much you please me?" he queried.

"You know things to do that arouse my deepest passion and bring me to ecstasy," I responded. "I know that you have been with women more experienced than I in the ways of pleasuring a man. I want you to teach me to do the things they do to excite you and bring you to ecstasy. I am your wife, and I can't bear the thought of another woman pleasing you more than I do."

J.R. was dumbfounded. Still, he reassured me with more words of wisdom he learned from Mister. "A husband loves his wife and reveres her for her purity. When he makes love to her, he is supposed to act sweetly out of love. Because he knows she is pure and clean, he will do things to please her that he will never do for any other woman. He finds pleasure in pleasuring her."

He added a personal reference. "You excite me with your excitement as you did tonight. That lets me know you appreciate what I do to pleasure you. If I lay with another woman, I don't love her. I don't pleasure her. She pleasures me and arouses my basest animal instincts. I can do crude things with her that I never want to do with my wife. You pleasure me with your purity. It sets you above all other women, and it arouses my finest passionate nature."

Once again, J.R. managed to convince me of his love and rendered me almost accepting of his infidelity. Whatever Tessie does that I don't know how to do is of no consequence to me. I enjoy the most passionate experiences with my husband, and he doesn't seem to want me to do anything differently. It is not in my nature to be crude, and I'm glad he doesn't want me to be. Still, I grow tired of his failure to be honest about his adultery. "If I lay with another woman" implies that he might do so. With Tessie's pregnant abdomen expanding daily, it is obvious that he is satisfying his animal instincts with at least one other woman, and I suspect that there are others. Yet I feel neither threatened nor jealous by them or Tessie's second baby. Now that she is "ripe," J.R. will soon cease to lay with her until after she is "back to normal." Having J.R. to myself for the next several months, I have no doubt that I'll soon have another child growing inside me. Given the unbridled passion we shared tonight, I might already have conceived one.

28 October 1895

My beloved grand'mère Lizzie died Wednesday, and J.R. took me and our children to Davis Bend to handle her affairs. Ma Mère arrived within an hour after we did Thursday evening. So much has happened in the decade since I last saw my mother. Thus, there was substantial content to provide for lengthy social intercourse. Yet our conversations were limited and less cordial than I hoped they would be. My children took delight in meeting their grandmother and offered her hugs and kisses. Although she did not dismiss them, her embraces lacked the warmth one would rightfully expect from a grandmother upon first encountering the children of her daughter. Indeed, her hugs lacked the enthusiasm that I and my children experienced when Grand'mère squeezed us, even during our last visit in August, when she was frail and weak. Yet I understood Ma Mère's initial chilliness toward my children. I sensed her dissatisfaction that they are not white. Their rich copper skin and wavy hair the same color clearly signal their Negro heritage. They are pleased with their appearances and unaware of the value Ma Mère and others like her place on passing for white. Ma Mère sensed their disappointment and my disapproval. She made an attempt to amend the impression of her detachment by forcing a smile and stating that she was simply overwhelmed by encountering so many of them at once. She queried them as to their names and ages, as well as their favourite things to do. They responded in chronological order.

"I am John Augustus Mann, nine years old, and best of all, I like to swim in our creek."

"I am Peter William Mann, eight years old, and I like to swim as well."

"My name is Rachel Joan Mann. I am six, but I'll be seven come January. I like to play with dolls."

"I am Solomon Charlemagne Mann, ma'am. I am four years and four months old. My favourite pastimes are reading, figuring and putting together puzzles."

Ma Mère regarded him curiously, taking notice of his precocity. Everyone laughed, and John took hold of Solomon's hand ere he spoke. "He always has his head in books, and he likes to use big words, but he has fun swimming with us too."

"Yes," Solomon affirmed. "I enjoy swimming also." He and the others looked to Esther. "Tell our grandmother your name, Esther," Solomon encouraged her, "and how old you are."

"EV," she responded and held up two fingers as she added, "I two."

Again, Solomon assisted his little sister. "Her name is Esther Victoria, but everyone, except Mother, calls her EV most of the time.

Her second birthday was last week. She likes to hear stories and play hide-and-seek. She is smart as can be, but she doesn't talk much to strangers." Exercising caution not to offend his grandmother, he added, "Oh, I'm sorry. I know you're not a stranger, but she doesn't know you yet. She'll have a lot to say when she warms up to you."

Once again, Ma Mère seemed surprised by Solomon's loquaciousness. Unsure of what Ma Mère was thinking, John jokingly remarked to her, "Little EV doesn't have to talk much because Solomon does her talking for her." The others laughed, and Solomon appeared uncomfortable.

I admonished the others and soothed Solomon's ruffled feathers. "Now you know that Solomon is just being a supportive big brother. He spends time with Esther, reading and listening to her, so he knows what she thinks and how she feels better than the rest of you."

For the first time since we exchanged greetings with Ma Mère, J.R. spoke. He had keenly observed the communication that had occurred. "Now, my dear, our boys meant no harm. The older ones tease the young 'uns, but they love 'em and look after 'em. SC needs to learn not to be bothered by 'em. Son, ignore 'em and laugh along or stand up to 'em and answer back. Either way, don't let what people say bother you. Just be yourself and be happy."

Ma Mère agreed with J.R. *Quel surpris!* She told Solomon that she found him to be a particularly charming and adorable child. Indeed, she smiled and told the children how charming and attractive they all are. She expressed her desire to become better acquainted with them over the next few days and to visit them afterward. Then she bade them to embrace her one at a time. They happily obeyed.

After J.R. and the children retired, Ma Mère and I conversed. Her initial statements were positive, commencing with her appreciation of my children's names and their apparent pride in them. I explained that the first names come from the Bible: John, Peter, Rachel, Solomon, and Esther. The second names are those of famous people: Caesar Augustus, William Shakespeare, Joan of Arc, Emperor Charlemagne, and Queen Victoria. Once they are of age to comprehend, I read or tell them the stories of the two people for whom they are named. When they become literate, they read the Bible and history books about their namesakes, and we discuss what lessons they can derive from those stories to guide them in life. At four and a half, Solomon knows that Solomon was a very wise king, the son of David and an ancestor of Jesus Christ.

He reads and studies to become wise like Solomon. He knows that Charlemagne was a great ruler and will learn more about him when he is a bit older. Ma Mère took notice of Solomon's vocabulary and interest in his studies, comparing his intelligence and personality to mine at his age. She appeared to actually take pride in acknowledging him as her grandson and in complimenting me as a mother and teacher. Reiterating that she found my children comely, she commented on their strong resemblance to Grand'mère. I see no particular likeness, except in their copper coloring. Yet I rejoice in my mother's glimpsing traits of her mother and me in my children. I believe it is a way for her to sense a connection with her grandchildren.

When I experienced momentary dizziness rising from my chair, Ma Mère stood quickly and held me lest I fell. She bade me to be seated again, and I complied. She commented that I appeared peaked. She conjectured that six pregnancies in ten years would take a toll on any woman. She declared her concern for my well-being. Unflatteringly, she asserted that although I am only twenty-seven, I have the countenance of one well into her thirties. She expressed hope that the child I am carrying will be my last so that my body can rest.

She reminded me, "I was afraid that if you married J.R., you would become his broodmare. I find no joy in bearing witness to the truth of my prediction."

I countered, "None of your predictions came true. I am no broodmare. I am a wife who loves having a big family. None of my children are ugly, and my husband is not ignorant. We enjoy stimulating intercourse on the Bible, literature, and contemporary occurrences. Thanks to his business acumen, we live quite comfortably on our estate. Further, without sharing details of our intimate relations, I declare he is no animal, and our passion brings me exceeding pleasure."

Ma Mère did not dispute me, though she commented that despite my effusions of joy and fulfillment, she senses melancholy buried beneath my blissful surface. She is aware that given our distance over more than a decade, I am not going to confide in her anything unpleasant. Yet she spent almost seventeen years caring for me and discerning my expressions. It is obvious to her that I love J.R. and our children and that I am generally pleased with my life. Yet she glimpses a tinge of discontent, although she knows not the cause.

Truly, I never shared with Grand'mère, and will not ever share with Ma Mère, my frustration with J.R.'s constant adultery and the resulting half siblings of my children. Tessie has birthed six children for him, maintaining her lead in childbearing. It is J.R.'s custom to avoid passionate engagements with either of us when we are "ripe." Thus, I solely occupy his passion during the last three months of Tessie's pregnancies and the first two months after the births of her babies. Yet he'll soon be spending almost every night with her for the next five months as I am due to deliver the end of January. Not surprisingly, our children are usually conceived about six months apart. Tessie gave him his first son, RJ, when I was pregnant with John. Since that time, she birthed his first daughter, May, US, TC, BK, and Baby April. Her house is now much larger than the other homes on the southern lowland of Mann Estate, though it is not nearly as large as mine. J.R. sets me above Tessie in every way but does not seem to show favour among the children. John and Peter work in the fields alongside their half brothers. The girls all do chores in the house under Lottie's supervision when they are not studying.

Strangely, Tessie and I have developed a bond that is akin to friendship, trusting each other enough to put our lives in each other's hands. Tessie has delivered all of my babies. After I apprenticed with Squirrel and then Tessie after Squirrel died, I began delivering Tessie's babies, starting with her fourth, TC. I teach all of our children once they reach the age of three to read, write and figure, and study the Bible. The girls and young boys spend most of the daylight hours, except on Sundays, studying in the big house. The older boys work in the fields early but join their siblings for schooling around two o'clock. Solomon is a sponge, soaking up everything he sees and hears. He stays closer to me than any of the other children. He loves to learn and keeps up with Rachel and US. He memorizes poetry and stories and recites them so well with the book open on his lap that all who hear him are flabbergasted, thinking he is actually reading at a much higher level than he is. All of the boys show aptitude for figures, but Solomon adds and subtracts handily at age four.

18 August 1899

J.R. departed on a sojourn to Jackson this morning with John Augustus and Peter William in tow. It is there that my first two sons will commence their initiation into "Mann-hood." Once again, J.R.'s actions, which I find reprehensible, are guided by the tutelage of his late father, Mister. In 1872, when J.R. was twelve years old, Mister took him to a brothel in Jackson so that he could learn from "professional" women how to enjoy being a man. Every fortnight for a period of two months, he and Mister returned to Jackson, where the prostitutes taught him well things that women could do to please him and how he could arouse a woman and bring her to ecstasy.

J.R. practiced his lessons regularly with women he met along his trading route, and he assumed the role of teacher with Tessie. She has confided to me that although he was the second man she pleasured, he is the only man she ever loved. She confesses that the mere sight of him approaching excites her and she is helpless to refuse him anything. She finds nothing too degrading if it ensures that he will return to her bed. J.R. seized control of her heart and soul sixteen years ago, and she loves him still despite the fact that he rejected her by marrying me two years hence.

I comprehend her apparent addiction to my husband, for I too love him and find him irresistible enough to endure his open adulterous relationship with her. I am captivated by his sensuality. From the moment he approaches our bed, I quiver with excitement. The animal-like way that he strides makes him seem like a black panther stalking his prey, ready to pounce in an instant. And I am eager for him to pounce upon me and devour me. Yet he postpones his attack, taking time to arouse me even more with kisses and massages that render me feverish and frenzied with desire. When at last he swoops down upon me, my soul climbs to euphoric heights. I ache with thoughts of him sharing the same experiences with other women, particularly Tessie. He swears that he does not bestow upon any other woman the romantic gestures he performs on me. That is how he attempts to justify the unjustifiable. I am not so much concerned about who does what to whom. I lament that he has intimate contact with Tessie and any woman other than me.

Alas, by now, my sons are no doubt taking pleasure in their instruction, developing skills that will enable them to break the hearts of women like Tessie and me. If they learn their lessons well, they will become smooth-talking lotharios who will charm and hurt many of the opposite gender, even the ones they will someday wed and proclaim to love. Though I am powerless to curtail their physical education, I will seize the power I exact in providing their mental and spiritual education. I will inculcate within them a fear of God, and I will help them realize that the best way to bring a woman to ecstasy is by massaging her spirit with love, kindness, faith, and fidelity.

7 June 1900

Quel dommage! The census taker arrived today. Bewilderment seized him in homes at both ends of the estate. In my home, he was puzzled regarding the color or race of my children. As in 1890, J.R. is designated as black or Negro in column 5, and I am designated as octoroon. The census taker in 1890 listed John Augustus, Peter William, and Rachel Joan as Negro, which I believe to be proper and which appears on their birth certificates issued retroactively that year. Yet today the census taker debated me on the subject, questioning whether or not it would be more accurate to cite mulatto as the color or race of Solomon Charlemagne, Esther Victoria, Naomi Phillis, Ruth Emily, and Zipporah Jane. His reasoning was that octoroons are mostly white so that the progeny of an octoroon and a Negro are almost half white. Regardless, I remained adamant that he was to list them as Negro because that is what we all are. I find the distinctions of octoroon, quadroon, and mulatto to be divisive. By law, we are all Negro, not white. Further, I do not want the birth certificates that will be issued retroactively to these five children to show a racial designation that differs from that of their three older siblings. I forced a civility in my countenance to conceal the offense I felt in his belief that having my children classified as mulattoes would be pleasing or beneficial to me or to them. Claiming some white ancestry might be important to Ma Mère but not to me.

After the census taker had visited the homes of the sharecroppers and Tessie, he returned to my home. He sought to confirm that J.R. and I are legally married, and he wondered if he should include all of Tessie's children with mine as a single family with J.R. as the head. I was consumed with embarrassment and anger, although the embarrassment should have rested on the shoulders or other body parts of J.R. and Tessie. Yet my countenance remained calm as I explained to him that J.R. and I legally wed on June 5, 1885, and have remained married the fifteen years and two days since. My husband acknowledges paternity of Tessie's children and has given them his name. However, they are not part of this household. Tessie Clark is single, the head of that household and mother to all of the children surnamed Mann who reside there. For several minutes, he erased and corrected data, shuffling forms and instructions. When he finished, he thanked me and bid me adieu.

I was still seething when my Rachel Joan and Tessie's daughter, May, were brought inside to me for discipline after an altercation outside during recess. First, I questioned the older girl, May, twelve years old to Rachel's eleven. May seemed eager to elucidate the circumstances. "She started it. She call my momma a bad name. I tol' her take it back, an' she didn't. I tol' her I hit her if she didn't. She didn't, so I hit her. She hit me back, an' we went back an' fo'th til they break us up an' bring us here."

When I turned my inquisition to Rachel Joan, she did not deny declaring that Tessie is a hoe. Startled that such a word had escaped from my daughter's lips, I admonished her and forced her to apologize to May. Afterward, I chastised both girls for conduct unbecoming young Christian ladies. I exacted promises from them not to engage in inappropriate intercourse regarding each other's relations and not to employ physical means of settling disputes. May was allowed to return outside, but Rachel Joan was detained for further discourse. Seized by awe and curiosity, I inquired as to what had precipitated her castigation of Tessie. Aware of my displeasure, Rachel Joan effused remorse. "May said our father doesn't love you. He married you so you got papers on him. He has to take care of you and your kids or you could get the law on him. She said our father loves her mother best. He takes care of her and her kids the same as he takes care of us. But Miss Tessie got no claims on him, so he ain't afraid of the law. He does everything he does for her jus' 'cause he loves her."

"So what was your retort?" I inquired, still wondering why she used a word I did not think she knew and did not believe she understood.

"I told her that our father loves you best. He married you to prove it. Our house is much bigger and nicer than theirs. He spends more time with us, and he always sits with us, not them, when we go places. He doesn't love Miss Tessie 'cause she's a—you know what I said."

"Where did you hear that word you called Miss Tessie?"

"That's what John and Peter told Solomon she is. I heard them when they were talking and didn't see me listening to them. They said Father loves you. He married you and treats you with respect. They said he doesn't respect Miss Tessie 'cause she's that thing."

"Do you know what a 'hoe' is?" I asked, still unsure of her comprehension of what she heard.

"I think it's that square thing they use in the field to turn over the dirt before they plant new seeds."

"You are correct," I affirmed, trying not to smile, relieved that she had not discerned the word they actually said and the meaning of it. "It is never acceptable to refer to people as objects or tools. That is rude and unacceptable behavior for one of my children. Your father will speak to your brothers about it."

I was furious, however, that nine-year-old Solomon had been apprised of such matters at his tender young age. The thought of my sweet little genius being brought into intercourse of such a nature was extremely vexing. His inquisitive and probing mind will lead him to pose questions that I am not prepared to have answered for him in his prepubescent years. I have no way of explaining to him what I cannot explain to myself, why his father behaves in a manner that is such an affront to the Almighty and why his mother remains at her husband's side in the face of his behavior.

Holding my peace through supper was challenging. I made no comments about the angry fire burning inside me, even when John Augustus and Peter William spoke words that fanned the flames. My two older sons made inquiries to J.R. about occurrences at baseball games when their Newton team played youth teams from Meridian, Jackson, and other cities that J.R. frequents on business. They both spoke of instances when a male chaperone or spectator would ask if they are related to J. R. Mann. Upon confirming that they are his sons, the man would point to a boy on the other team or sometimes introduce them to a boy and say, "That's yo' brother. His ma is Miss So-and-So, and J. R. Mann is his pa." When they consulted J.R. about the veracity of those allegations, he responded without looking away from the stew he continued to eat, "S'possible. Many things be possible. That's one of 'em."

When the children were finally in bed, I confronted J.R. There was no reading poetry to him. Instead, I told him about the frustration, embarrassment, and fury that had gnawed at me throughout the day. I was appalled that the census taker, observing my obviously pregnant condition, questioned the legality of my marriage and Tessie's status in our family. I was horrified that my children were being confronted with knowledge of his shenanigans and questioning his love and respect for me. Yet J.R. expressed his confidence that our children, like everyone else, are keenly aware that he loves me. They also know that he gives me his respect and demands that all others give me their respect as well.

He said, "JA and PW had no right to call Tessie out of her name, and I will deal with them about that and about talking to SC about man things when he's just a boy. But they said right that I love only you because I told them so."

He continued by reminding me that his love for me will be evidenced even after his death. His will stipulates that I will inherit all of his worldly possessions and that we are to be buried next to each other on the high ground beside our home. The burial space allotted for Tessie and her children is away from us on the low ground where the sharecroppers' families live and are buried.

I countered that while I believe that he told John Augustus and Peter William that I am above all other women in his heart and mind, I wonder what he has said to Tessie's teenage sons, RJ and US. May's utterances to Rachel Joan were repetitions of what she heard from her elder brothers. I am sure that J.R. did not discuss his feelings about Tessie to her sons in the same way he did to our sons. I know this because he would not give her children reason to show her disrespect or contempt. Yet as his children mature, they will come to know that this is an unusual arrangement, and each set of children will question the status of their mother in it. They will require explanations, just as the census taker did today. Moreover, their unavoidable rivalries will lead them to more confrontations like the one that occurred with May and Rachel Joan. They will note the inconsistencies and fallacies in his rhetoric about both women, and that may challenge their respect for him as well as for their mothers.

Uncharacteristically, J.R. allowed me to utter the final words of this interchange. He stood silent momentarily, appearing to contemplate the likelihood of the inevitable reckoning I predicted. He reached for me and attempted to quell my anger with a caress. However, uncharacteristically, I spurned his advances. My silent statement was sufficiently clear to dash all expectations and hopes he probably harboured for a passionate conclusion to the night.

28 July 1901

Through the years I have spent with J.R., I have come to believe that he is a silver-tongued scoundrel who can charm most any woman. Last evening, I witnessed him use his persuasive style with equal effectiveness on a man, literally saving one of his sons from harm. As we were finishing supper, Malachi Freeman, whose daughter, Dosia, is one of my students, banged on our door, brandishing a shotgun. His flared nostrils and heavy breathing evidenced his rage. J.R. stepped outside rather than admit him inside our home. Malachi stared at him coldly and stated his purpose succinctly. He was here to avenge the honor of his daughter who told him that the Mann boys had taken advantage of her. Yesterday was stifling. J.R.'s nine sons and eight daughters were enjoying the cool waters of the Okatibbee Creek that runs through our estate. We have always welcomed the children in the area to enjoy swimming and playing in the creek. However, J.R.'s pubescent sons (RJ, John Augustus, Peter William, and US) decided yesterday to establish a new rule that forbids girls from wearing any covering in the creek. When the girls complained that the Mann girls were not naked, they were told that those rules apply to all girls who are not part of the Mann family. Malachi stated that the Mann boys had shamed his daughter and that the oldest one, RJ, had his way with her.

J.R., who stands a scant five feet three inches, showed no fear of this irate, shotgun-toting father, who is over six feet tall. J.R. stood erect, looked up into his eyes, and calmly proclaimed, "Young men are s'posed to try to have their way with the ladies. It's in their nature to ask. But ladies are s'posed to say 'no' to 'em. Like the Bible says, ladies are s'posed to be virtuous. Did your Dosia say my boys held her down or that RJ forced himself on her?"

Malachi shook his head, indicating a negative response.

"So then," J.R. reasoned, "my boys did nothing wrong. In fact, they did what they are s'posed to do, but Dosia did not do what she was s'posed to do. You got cause and right to be angry but not at my boys.

You should be angry with Dosia and take a strap to her to teach her to do right and be a virtuous young lady."

I watched in disbelief as Malachi lowered his head and nodded affirmatively. He left for home to discipline his daughter. Our children, who watched and listened in nervous silence to the exchange, effused awe and relief upon Malachi's departure. I noted with particular interest Solomon Charlemagne's reactions. He is keenly observant and learns from every experience. J.R.'s words to Malachi will leave a lasting impression on him for two reasons: First, he admires his father and older brothers and absorbs their attitudes about girls and women. Thus, he will believe that there are differences in the expected and acceptable behaviors of men and women. Second, he will remember the adept strategy J.R. used to defuse a volatile situation by redirecting Malachi's anger away from the boys to his own daughter.

I watched Solomon radiate adoration and respect for his father's ability to calmly deliver a convincing argument. Already a skillful orator and debater barely ten years of age, Solomon found the events as instructive as any of his formal lessons in logic. I am certain he will want to analyze the reasoning J.R. used in his tutorial with me tomorrow.

Indeed, I love all of my children and find them to be intelligent. I attempt to teach them the value of reading and thinking so that they can learn whatever they want to learn, not just what others choose to teach them. By nine years of age, most can read and derive some understanding from the Bible, works by Shakespeare, and the romantic poets. They are proficient in all operations with figures by ten. When they reach the age of twelve, they become conversant on the Roman Empire and the major Greek philosophers. By then, most learn to solve equations in algebra, and some begin to formulate proofs in plane geometry. Most often, the girls demonstrate greater interest in literature and philosophy than their brothers, who prefer to study mathematics. Solomon is exceptional. He loves to learn everything. His natural intelligence and facility in all subjects is extraordinary.

Solomon is my best student and my closest companion. We are kindred souls in our love of learning and endless quest for knowledge. To my delight, J.R. granted my request that Solomon be freed from responsibilities in the fields so that he can devote more time to his lessons. He reads everything, deriving most pleasure from books about history. Well past school hours, he engages me in discussion and debates on history and social issues, as well as his personal concerns, such as whether he should have to do chores or go to bed at a prescribed time. He finds it amusing and instructive to question everything, even my responses to his questions. He is blessed with an excellent memory and demonstrates rare talent in elocution. He masterfully delivers monologues from Shakespeare's plays, Abraham Lincoln's "Gettysburg Address," and speeches by Negro senator Hiram Revels and Negro abolitionist Frederick Douglass. At ten, his understanding of what he reads and recites is superior to many of my peers at the academy who were fifteen to eighteen years old. His written command of the English language is equally impressive as are his mathematical skills. He studies algebra and geometry with his older brothers. Solomon is already inspired to pursue studies in a university. I pray that he will travel far beyond Newton County and Mississippi to become a learned and enlightened man.

13 September 1901

Quel jour! Le diable bat sa femme et marie sa fille! Indeed, what a day this is! The sun is shining brightly on this unseasonably hot Friday. Less than two weeks from my time, my extra weight causes me to feel the heat more intensely than the children at play. Yet in the midst of the sunshine, rain is falling. When this strange phenomenon occurs, people in New Orleans regard it as a bad sign. They say, "The devil is beating his wife and marrying his daughter." Of course, I find no more credence in this ridiculous myth than I find in other omens that could be applied to this day. I have no more fear of Friday when it falls on the thirteenth day of the month than when it falls on any other date. I know that God has command of my life as He commands the entire universe. Every day is controlled and blessed by Him. Nonetheless, I am struck by the uniqueness of the hottest day of 1901 occurring on Friday, the thirteenth of September, with simultaneous sunshine and rain. Such coincidences portend an important event is afoot.

Solomon Charlemagne and Rachel Joan are teaching the younger students today, and May is assisting Lottie in preparing lunch for them all. Exhaustion has seized me, and I lack the energy to rise from my bed. It is not my desire to rush my beloved ninth child in making its entrance into the world. However, my body yearns to return to normalcy. Resting in bed is not restful for me. I am agitated, impatient to teach my students, enjoy activities with my children, and renew nights of passion with my husband. He is spending most nights currently with Tessie. Yet he will soon return home to our bed once I am back to normal. Tessie's belly is growing bigger every day with her tenth child. Soon, she'll be too ripe for J.R. The time he is spending with her now has not bothered me nearly as much as before. My craving for him has been overshadowed by my fatigue and awkwardness. Indeed, my belly and my feet are more swollen than in previous pregnancies, and my ankles and knees ache from the burden of supporting so much extra weight. These days, I grow weary and even pass a bit of blood whenever I walk more than a few paces or stand for longer than a few minutes.

Oooh! I just felt a brief but intense pain in my stomach. It's not labour. This baby is not due to come until a fortnight from now. Painful cramping is yet another annoyance which I have experienced far more often carrying this baby than I did with my other babies. It is another reason I hope this baby arrives sooner rather than later. Yet not too soon! Oooh! This is the most intense pain yet, and my bed is suddenly soaked with liquid flowing uncontrollably from my body. It is an indisputable sign that I will meet my new baby within hours. It's time for me to summon Tessie to be my midwife once again. Indeed, the omens are correct. An important event is afoot.

Claudia's Maternal Ancestry

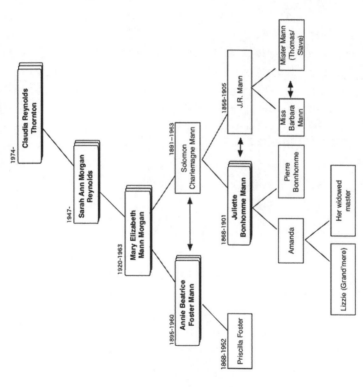

Claudia Reynolds Thornton
1974-

Sarah Ann Morgan Reynolds
1947-

Mary Elizabeth Mann Morgan
1920-1963

Solomon Charlemagne Mann
1891-1963

Annie Beatrice Foster Mann
1895-1960

Priscilla Foster
1868-1952

Juliette Bonhomme Mann
1868-1901

J.R. Mann
1858-1905

Amanda

Pierre Bonhomme

Miss Barbara Mann

Mister Mann (Thomas/Slave)

Lizzie (Grand'mere)

Her widowed master

Mother (left), Father (right)

Wife ←→ Husband

Part 3

EXCERPTS FROM THE JOURNALS OF ANNIE BEATRICE FOSTER MANN

Saturday, December 26, 1914

Dear Friend,

My eldest sister—Birdie—gave you to me yesterday for Christmas. She knows that I lost my best friend—my brother Bus—two years ago on Christmas Day. I never was as close to any of my other brothers and sisters. I am not as close to any of the friends I made in school. Birdie knows that I love to write. She says that I write good letters to her, but she knows I don't tell her everything like I used to tell Bus. Birdie says I might like writing letters to you. I can tell you my secrets and know that you will never tell them and never think badly of me. You will be like my best friend, and I can share everything with you.

I guess I should start by introducing myself to you. I am Annie Beatrice Foster of Meridian, Mississippi. I am nineteen years old. I have spent my entire life in Mississippi. This is my last year at Rust University in Holly Springs. I am the third of four children born to my mother Priscilla and the seventh of eight children sired by my father

Sebron Foster. Poppa Sebron was married before to Momma's elder sister—my aunt Abigail. They were in love. After Aunt Abigail died, Momma married Poppa because it was her duty. Duty is real important in Momma's family. Her mother—my grandma Lily—was a Choctaw Indian. Her father—my grandpa Nicodemus—was a free-born African. They passed on to her what their families taught them about honor and duty. As Aunt Abigail's oldest unmarried sister, it was Momma's duty to raise Aunt Abigail's motherless children as her own. She could not take them away from their father, since they had already lost their mother. Neither could she live with them and their father outside of marriage. So Momma and Poppa got married following the Sunday church service just five days after Aunt Abigail's funeral. Momma went from church to Poppa's house and became mother to his two sons—Sebron Jr. (called See) and Eugene (called Genie)—and his two daughters—Roberta (called Birdie) and Pearline (called Pearl).

Momma never considered refusing that responsibility. Duty was more important to her than her dreams of being loved the way Grandpa Nicodemus loved Grandma Lily and how Poppa loved Aunt Abigail. When Momma married Poppa, she was a good wife and mother. She did her wifely duty "in the dark under covers." She says no man, including Poppa, has ever seen her naked. Even so, she gave Poppa four more children. First came two sons—William (called Billy) and Stanley (called Bus)—and then two daughters—me and my little sister Othella (called Thella). My family never gave me a nickname. I am called by my given name—Annie. My parents are very strict, more on the girls than the boys. Still, we know they love us. They don't say it to us, but we feel it. They don't say they love each other either, but I feel that too. They weren't in love when they got married, but I think they grew to love each other after they did.

Christmas is my favorite holiday. All my brothers and sisters come home with their families. Momma spends the month from Thanksgiving to Christmas decorating the whole house, inside and out. My sisters and I help Momma prepare a huge dinner, and we all eat together until our stomachs ache. We sing carols and tell stories about growing up here in Meridian. It is the best day of the year. But I still worry until it's over because all the bad things in my life seem to happen between Thanksgiving and Christmas. When I was eight, I fell out of the red wagon Daddy made for us for Christmas. Bus was pulling me in it, and I begged him to run faster and faster up and down the road. When he tripped, I fell out and landed hard on the big rock with our family name painted on it. My knees were bleeding, and they hurt so bad that I was limping around the house for days. I still got the scars on both my knees. Poppa was mad at Bus and took a strap to him. That hurt me worse than my knees. It was my fault Bus was running too fast. He did it because I asked him to. When I was twelve, our barn caught fire on Christmas Eve. Poppa was sure that some crackers set it deliberately. The barn burned to the ground with all of our Christmas presents inside it. Most of my family dies around the holidays. My Grandpoppa Nicodemus died Thanksgiving Day when I was nine, and since then, I lost two uncles, an aunt, and a cousin in different Decembers. The worst day of my life was Christmas Day two years ago. That's when my beloved Bus died in front of the whole family while we were eating dinner.

We were sharing stories while we ate off the suckling pig and turkey Momma killed and prepared just like she does every year for Christmas dinner. A special treat that year was a giant catfish that Poppa caught on Christmas Eve. Momma fried it in cornmeal. I can't remember what story Bus found funny. He was laughing loud and waving his hands. He looked so funny that we all started laughing at him. We didn't notice when his laughter changed to choking. Suddenly, he was coughing up blood. So much blood! His eyes were rolling around. And the blood came faster and faster. Poppa and Billy snatched him up out of his chair. They grabbed his legs and turned him upside down. See hugged him around his waist and shook him. Then he reached in his mouth and tried to remove what was choking him. But there was too much blood for him to see or feel anything. Genie left to get the doctor, but by the time they got back, Bus was dead. Bus's blood was everywhere. Poppa, See, and Billy were covered in it. It was on the dinner table, and Bus's body was lying in it on the floor. It was the most gruesome sight I've ever seen. I've seen chickens and pigs killed, but this was a lot more blood than that. Worst of all, it was Bus's blood.

Momma, my sisters, and I just stared. We were shocked and so scared. None of us made a sound til Poppa finally laid Bus on the floor after he knew he was dead. That's when Momma screamed. We all started screaming and crying. We never did find out what Bus choked on. The doctor said it must have been something sharp that cut his throat from the inside. He said he would have to cut Bus open to see what was there. Poppa said nobody was going to put a knife to his son. Momma was sure it was a fishbone, and she hasn't eaten any fish since that night. Even when Poppa catches fish and fries it himself, she won't eat it. If anyone else eats it in front of her, she makes them pick it apart and mash up the meat to be sure there are no bones in it before they put it in their mouths. I understand Momma. I don't eat fish much anymore either, and when I do, I pick through it so much that it's cold by the time I start to eat it. I was closer to Bus than to anyone else in the world. My heart broke when he died. I loved him and trusted him with everything I thought. He stood up for me whenever anyone bothered me. My sisters used to tease me because I am the shortest one in the family. Bus said that is because the extra God gave them in their legs He gave to me in my brain. Bus told them that is why I'm the only one smart enough to go to college. I don't think that's true. I'm the only one who wanted to go. But nobody ever argued with Bus. Even though he was the youngest brother, he was the toughest one. They stopped teasing me because they didn't want to tangle with him.

Birdie was right about my needing to write things down. I haven't talked to anyone about the night Bus died or about how scared I am from Thanksgiving to Christmas every year. I can't tell Bus. He's gone. So I'll write to you all that I wish I could say to him. You can't stand up for me the way Bus did. That's all right. I've learned to stand up for myself since he died. That's something else I haven't said to anyone. I'm just telling you.

Yesterday was a happy Christmas. Thella came home for the first time since she got married and moved to Jackson. It was the first time Thella's husband came for Christmas dinner. So Momma used that as an excuse for telling her favorite story. But she tells the love story of her parents every Christmas and all year long, whether there is somebody new here or not. She tells it the exact same way every time. My sisters and brothers and I know it by heart. We could say it with her, but we don't. We sit still like we're hearing her tell it for the first time. She says,

> My momma, Miss Lily, was a pure breed Choctaw Injun.
> Huh gran'pappy fought under the great Pushmataha.
> He was one o' hunderds of Choctaw what helped
> Gen'al Andrew Jackson whoop the Creeks back in 1814.

Huh pappy refused to follow Mushulatubbee and the thousan's of Choctaw to the Injun Territory when the guv'ment move' 'em outta Mississippi in the thirties. He nevah got them 640 acres he was s'posed to get 'cause he stay' here and become a U.S. citizen. But he had a nice farm anyway.

Nicodemus was bo'n a freeman 'cause Masser Templeton done freed his momma and huh kids in his will 'bout a mont' 'fo' Nicodemus was bo'n. Nicodemus was a blacksmiff when he growed up. He met Miss Lily when he shoe' one o' huh pappy's ho'ses. Miss Lily and Nicodemus fell in love real deep. They got married and had three chilluns. One day, Nicodemus was out ridin' on his ho'se. Some slave catchas ax to see his freedom papers. They was three of 'em, and they had guns. They took his papers an' to'e 'em up. Then they tied him up an' took him outta Mississippi. They sol' 'im into slavery way up in No'th Carolina. This was 'roun' 'bout 1860, jus' befo' the war what ended slavery.

Miss Lily nevuh knew what happen' to Nicodemus. Afta 'while, she thought he mus' be dead. She marry a man name' Jessie. They had a chile. One hot day in 1867, Nicodemus show' up at they front do'. He had done walked on foot all the way from No'th Carolina back to Mississippi. It took him almost two yea's. He say he would'a walked ten yea's if he had to. He was dee-termined to find Miss Lily 'cause he love' huh so much. Jessie and Nicodemus went out back to talk while Miss Lily watch' the chillun. They say they bof' love' Miss Lily a 'hol' lot. They agree' to let huh decide who she wanna be wif'. Nicodemus say if she choose him, he raise Jessie's chile like it was his own. Jessie was already raisin' Nicodemus's chillun'. Miss Lily say they bof' good men, but huh heart belong' to Nicodemus. Jessie lef' 'em alone afta that. Nicodemus and Miss Lily got married again. And I was they firs' chile bo'n afta that.

Monday, February 1, 1915

Dear Friend,

I have been so happy all day. I got an A on my first test. Later, I had a friendly talk with my favorite professor—Solomon Mann. I took his math class for home economics majors last term. I had to pass it to graduate this May. I've always been good in math, but I never liked it. That's why I put off taking it as long as I could. But Professor Mann made the class interesting and fun. He is so smart and handsome. He is the youngest professor on campus, only four years older than me. His smooth skin and thick wavy hair are both the color of an old copper penny. And his big brown eyes seem to look right through me. He is much smaller than the men and women in my family. I don't think he's more than five feet four, and he probably weighs less than one hundred forty pounds. Poppa and my brothers are all about six feet tall. Momma and my sisters are all over five feet nine. They call me the runt of the family at five feet seven. I think that Bus was right. The big size that God gave to others in body, He gave to Professor Mann in brains. Professor Mann knows so much about so many things besides mathematics. He talked about philosophy and history in his lectures. His stories and jokes made me laugh and learn. That is why I like him and look up to him so much.

I saw him on campus today for the first time since I finished my class with him. I knew he liked me because he always smiled at me in class. He told me I was smart, and I got an A from him. We smiled when we saw each other this afternoon. He asked how I was doing. I told him that I'll be graduating in May and I hope to be teaching in Meridian next year. He wished me well. He asked if I had plans to marry in the near future. I told him that I was not interested in any men at school or at home. Still, I hope to someday find someone to my liking so I can marry and have many children. He asked how many children I hope to have, and I said at least seven. We passed a bench and sat down together. We learned that we have many things in common. We both come from large families, and we both want to have lots of children. We are both the first and only one in our families to go to college. The most important thing we share in common is our love and fear of the Lord. I grew up in the Holiness Church in Meridian. I worship in the

Methodist chapel on campus while I am here at school. Professor Mann took some theology courses when he studied in Atlanta and worships in the African Methodist Episcopal Church in town.

We talked awhile until the campus clock struck two. We were both due in classes and had to hurry. I enjoyed getting to know Professor Mann outside of class. That is why I am so excited that he wants me to meet him at the same bench after dinner on Friday. I can hardly wait. I wish he had said tomorrow.

Friday, February 5, 1915

Dear Friend,

Professor Mann met me at seven this evening, and we sat alone on what I now think of as our bench. We talked some more about our families. He told me about his mother who died when he was just ten. He said that she was so beautiful, kind, and gentle and, "She cultivated my unquenchable curiosity and thirst for learning." I love the fancy way he talks. He uses big words, but it doesn't seem put-on and hard to understand like some of the professors. It's just his natural way of talking, and I always know what he means. He said his mother was his first and best teacher, and he revered her so much. Then he said that I remind him of her. That is the best compliment he could give me. He went on to say that I'm like his mother because I love to read and I have a good, analytical mind. He likes that I am a devout Christian and preparing to be a teacher. He is impressed by my "gentility and conservative style," as well as my talent as a seamstress. He said that these things also remind him of his mother. I didn't tell him, but his words pleased me so much. The ladies at our church in Meridian told me and all the young ladies that a good man believes in God and loves his mother. If he doesn't love his mother and respect her, how can you expect that he'll care any better about you? If he doesn't believe in God and know He is greater than himself, he will be stuck-up and selfish. So I'm glad that Professor Mann believes in God and loved his mother. And I'm happy he says I'm like her.

I asked him about his schooling after his mother died. His father sent him and his siblings to a colored school in Newton. He hated it there. When he was only ten, he had probably read as much as his grown white teacher and he could do algebra and geometry. So he was bored by the work Miss Shirley was teaching the boys his age. His father made Miss Shirley teach him with the oldest students. Even so, by the time he was twelve, he convinced his father to take him to live with a business associate in Meridian so that he could attend the Meridian Academy. That's where my family went to school. He is the same age as my sister Birdie, but he was more advanced than she was. He probably took classes with See or Genie, but he doesn't remember them. He graduated in three years and moved to Georgia to study at Atlanta University. He liked Atlanta and stayed there long enough to get his bachelor's and master's degrees.

He even stayed in Atlanta a year after that and took classes at the Gammon School of Theology. He said it was founded in the tradition of the Methodist Episcopal Church. That is when he began to worship in an African Methodist Episcopal Church. Professor Mann is proud of his African heritage, and he believes that God is God all the time for everybody. White people and Negroes weren't seen as equal and didn't sit together in the Methodist churches he visited. So he was drawn to the independent AME denomination. Professor Mann said he considered becoming an AME minister. When he got the offer to teach here at Rust, he asked God for guidance. He says God led him back to Mississippi to "a ministry of teaching from a lectern instead of preaching from a pulpit." He believes he serves God and his people by preparing teachers to uplift our race. He also believes his work as an educator would make his mother proud. I never thought about teaching like that. I just thought it would be more fun than farming. I like to cook and sew. I'll enjoy teaching other young ladies how to do that.

I want to know how Professor Mann's mother died, and he promised to tell me next time we meet. He said it will take more time to explain than we had left to our evening. He wanted to speak to me about something else in the time left before my curfew. He said that he finds me beautiful in appearance and personality. I am about the same height as his late mother. I wear my hair in two braids crossed and pinned on top of my head. He likes that style, and he says it compliments my face. I was surprised when he complimented my figure and my carriage. I have always thought that my bosom is too large and my hips too broad. He doesn't think so. He says he thought I was pretty the first time I walked into his classroom. He became more attracted to me when he observed my intelligence and wit. I was his best student in all the time he's been here. He checked my record and knows that I will be graduating with high honors.

He realized that it would be improper to discuss his feelings with me when I was one of his students, even though his intentions were honorable. That is why he waited until I was no longer in his class to speak with me of such things. He wondered if I was embarrassed or put off by his admiration of me and his desire to spend more time getting to know me personally. My heart was racing as I told him that I was not embarrassed and that I also wanted to spend more time with him. On the way back to my dorm, he asked that when we are alone, I call him by his given name—Solomon. It was what his mother called him. The rest of his family calls him by his initials—SC. He wants me to feel that we are of equal status as we pursue a personal relationship. He expressed his hope that I will allow him to call me something less formal than the way he addressed me in class—Miss Foster. He asked my full name, and I told him—Annie Beatrice Foster. I told him that my family calls me Annie, but my favorite brother—Bus—used to call me Bea when he was alive. Professor Mann—Solomon likes Bea, and he will call me that in private. We made plans to meet after chapel Sunday morning and share a picnic lunch at a park nearby.

I am so very happy. I'm almost finished with school. I like my classes, and I have a distinguished gentleman courting me. Even though I am no longer a student in my Solomon's class, I am still a student. He is faculty. We're not hiding our feelings, but we will not talk about them to others until I graduate in May. So, dear friend, I'm only sharing this secret with you.

Friday, March 12, 1915

Dear Friend,

Solomon and I are closer than ever. Tonight he said he loves me, and I admitted to him that I feel the same. He decided that it is time to share with me the truth about his mother's life and death. He has told me so much about her but has never talked about how she died. He says that he has not spoken of the circumstances of her death to anyone since he left Newton when he was twelve. I was shocked by the story he told me.

My mother—Juliette—bore eight children for my father before she died, along with their ninth child, during the birthing process on Friday, the thirteenth day of September in 1901. I was ten years old at the time, her fourth child and youngest of her three sons. Tessie was serving as my mother's midwife during the fatal childbirth as she had for the other eight successful ones. Tessie said that she couldn't stop my mother from bleeding to death. After she died, Tessie took the baby boy out of her womb, but he had already died inside her. My two elder brothers and my elder sister voiced their suspicions that Tessie had done something to cause the deaths. Tessie had a relationship with my father before and throughout his marriage to my mother. When our mother died, Tessie was pregnant with her tenth child by him.

My father refused to believe their speculations for two reasons. First, he said that Tessie was a Christian woman. She would never harm our mother for fear of God. Second, he said that Tessie knew well his temper. She knew that if she ever did anything to harm his wife or any of his children, he would surely kill her without hesitation or remorse. So she would also not harm our mother and our baby brother for fear of my father. My elder brothers were not satisfied. They argued that Tessie had reasons and found an opportunity to get my mother out of her life, hoping finally to take her place as my father's wife. My father dismissed that idea because Mann men never marry more than once, and he believed that Tessie knew that. The relationship between my father and my elder brothers suffered because they never agreed about Tessie's part in my mother's death. The relationship between my elder brothers and my elder half brothers also suffered. My half brothers sided with my father, defending the honor of their mother—Tessie. While I was in Meridian, my two brothers left Mississippi and moved North. They never returned, not even for our father's funeral.

If Tessie did hope to replace my mother in my father's house, she was sorely disappointed. When my mother died, my father mourned her for more than a year. He was never the same without her. He was quiet and pensive, never seeming to laugh as loudly or smile as broadly as when she was alive. His love for her was stronger than anyone realized. When she was gone, he felt an almost constant ache in his heart. Tessie's tenth baby—another boy—was born six months later. Father rarely visited Tessie and that child, but he provided for them as he had always done before. I don't know if he had doubts about Tessie's story that he never admitted or if he was just grieving so hard for my mother. Either way, he didn't spend much time with Tessie after my mother died. I believe my father cared for Tessie, and he didn't tolerate any of us speaking ill of her. However, I don't believe he loved her as he did my mother.

Solomon saw that I was shocked and concerned about Tessie and her ten children by his father. He was quick to tell me that he is not like his father.

I love my father, but I came to be appalled by his infidelity. I know that it hurt my mother, though she never spoke to us about it. I am too ashamed of his behavior to have ever revealed before now the circumstances surrounding my mother's death and the resulting strains that tore my family apart. I never told the whole story to anyone in Meridian, Atlanta, or here in Holly Springs. I just said that my mother died in childbirth when I was ten. I love you and need you to know that I am a God-fearing man. I will not behave in such a manner as a husband.

Until tonight, I wasn't sure how Solomon felt. It surprised me that he spoke of loving me and of becoming a husband. We spend time together almost every day. However, we are still not openly courting. I know that students and faculty have seen us together enough to assume that we have a special friendship, but they cannot be sure that it is more than that. We have held hands when we were alone, but he hasn't tried to kiss me. But now I am happy and excited because I believe he plans to make me Mrs. Solomon Charlemagne Mann when I graduate. Momma is always telling me the stories about her marriage to Poppa and about Grandmomma Lily's marriage with Grandpoppa Nicodemus. Those stories taught me two things I want in a marriage, and Solomon will give me both of them. I want to be loved, and I want lots of children. I love Solomon, and it doesn't matter if I like how he kisses. I will do my wifely duty to keep his love and have his babies.

Tuesday, April 6, 1915

Dear Friend,

I am so excited that I can hardly keep from smiling constantly. Solomon told me two days ago—on Easter Sunday—that he will ask Poppa for my hand next month at the end of the commencement ceremony. But Solomon came to see me in the library today. He has never met me in such a public place. He asked me to meet him at our bench right after my last class. We meet there every evening after dinner anyway. I wondered what was so important that he couldn't wait to tell me then. I hardly paid attention in my afternoon class and left the second it ended to meet him.

He showed me a letter he got today. He has been offered the position of principal of the Newton County Training School. He is expected to start next week before the end of the term. He will receive wages and housing. As a single man, he will get a free room and meals with a family in their house near the school. But if he is married, he will get to live free in a private house with indoor plumbing and electricity. Few white folks and no Negroes in Mississippi have indoor plumbing and electricity. Solomon will not get the house free if he gets married later. He'll get just the room and have to rent a bigger space after we get married. Solomon knows he is asking a lot of me to leave Rust just five weeks before commencement. I have worked hard almost four years, and I want to graduate. But I want to be Solomon's wife even more. Once we are settled, I can finish my classes and get my degree.

Solomon will make arrangements to leave Friday. He has saved enough money to buy a horse and wagon. I cannot tell anyone my plans. The dean will call Poppa, and he will stop me. He is so proud that I will be the first college graduate in our family. He has worked hard to pay my tuition for four years. He would forbid me to leave so close to finishing my degree. And I would not be able to go against him. So I have to keep our plans secret until we leave Friday.

Monday, April 12, 1915

Dear Friend,

I'm settling into our home. We reached Newton yesterday at dusk. I am quite pleased with the house. As promised, we have electricity and indoor plumbing. The rooms are not as large as the ones in my parents' home in Meridian. Still, they are big enough and nicely furnished. The furniture is not new. But it is clean and looks nice. We want to start our family soon. So I am happy that there is enough room for us and our first two children. There is plenty of space outdoors for them to play and for me to make a nice garden. Solomon will not get much of a salary. But we can live comfortably, since the house is free.

Before I get too carried away dreaming about the future, let me tell you about the past few days. I went to classes and tried to act normal Wednesday and Thursday. I'm not showy about my feelings. But I was so excited that it was hard for me not to smile all the time. Solomon and I were married in the campus chapel Thursday evening by the Rust University chaplain. The chaplain's wife and chapel organist were our witnesses. I returned to the dorm and started packing. When my roommates saw that I was preparing to leave, they asked me why. They kept my secret until Solomon came to the dorm to pick me up Friday morning. We saw him arrive, and they helped me carry my bags downstairs. We heard the resident hall director—Miss Berry—sound disapproving when she asked what business he had with me. He didn't have a chance to answer her. My roommates and I were giggling when we came into the lobby with my bags. I told her that I was leaving with my husband—Prof. Solomon Mann. Married women are not allowed to reside in the dorm, so I had to leave there. I was going to reside with my husband. She was flabbergasted and shouted for me to stop. I didn't even slow down. Solomon took the bags from my roommates, and we put them in his wagon. I smiled and waved to everyone we saw on our way as we left the campus. But I never looked back. I am sure Miss Berry reported all she saw to the dean as soon as I left. He already knew that Solomon was moving to Newton. He didn't know I was going with him. He most likely sent a letter to Poppa right away. But Solomon and I planned to get to Poppa before he got the letter.

It took us two days to get to Newton from Holly Springs. We rested Friday night in Tupelo and Saturday night in Philadelphia. We stopped in Meridian on Sunday afternoon so Solomon could ask for Poppa's blessing on our marriage. I knew Poppa would be angry and disappointed about my leaving college before graduation. I hated disappointing him. He has worked hard all his life to provide for his children. He only completed high school, and Momma did not even do that. They worked our farm together. Poppa was in the field before dawn and worked there til noon. Then he went into town to work til dusk as a carpenter's apprentice. He finally became a carpenter the year I started at Rust. He wanted all his children to go to college and find easier work than farming. But none of my brothers went to college, and none of them are apprentices. They are satisfied running our family farm. Poppa wanted all of his daughters to go to college and come home to teach in Meridian. But all of my sisters married young and moved away. I am his only child out of eight to attend college. He has told everyone he knows that he'll be coming to my graduation next month and that I'll be coming home to be a teacher. I am overjoyed to be Mrs. Solomon Mann. But as we stopped in front of my parents' house, I was sorry that my joy was going to cause Poppa to be angry, disappointed and embarrassed.

With Solomon by my side, I was happy and excited when I knocked on the front door. Sebron Foster is a strapping man about six feet tall. As soon as he saw me, he rose stiff and straight to his full height. I smiled at him, but his thick handlebar mustache didn't hide his scowl when he looked at me. I began to introduce Solomon. But he stared at me and ignored Solomon. He cut me off to ask in his deep booming voice, "Why ain't you at the college? You ain't finished yet!"

I kept smiling, but I was uneasy when I answered him, "No, Poppa. I left with my husband—Professor Solomon Mann. He got a fine position not too far from here. He is principal of the Newton County Training School."

Poppa shouted at me, "Why you get married now? You pregnant?"

Poppa never even looked at Solomon. But Solomon answered him politely, "No, sir. We married because we love each other. We married now because I have to go to Newton now in order to secure a fine house provided for my family by Newton County while I serve in that position."

I was so proud of the way Solomon stood up to Poppa. He was respectful but not afraid. It made me confident. "That's right, Poppa. It's a real fine house with indoor plumbing and electricity."

Poppa was not moved. "Well, you didn't ask me for my permission, and I don't give it. If you ain't pregnant, I'll put an end to this thing right now."

"No, Poppa," I pleaded. "Please don't do that. I love him, and I want to be with him."

Poppa was surprised and furious that I challenged him. He surprised me with what he said next. "You want to be with this runt? I know all about the Manns of Newton County. They don't treat women right. They run around making babies wherever they go. I won't let you give up your college degree for the likes of him."

Solomon stayed calm and polite to Poppa. "With all due respect, sir, I am a Christian, and I believe in the vows of marriage. I love your daughter, and I will respect her always. She can complete her degree someday if she wants to. But she won't need it. I will always take care of her, and she will never have to work a day in her life unless she wants."

"I'm ending this marriage. She's heading back to Rust tomorrow. That's my final word."

I was so sad. "Please, Poppa. I beg you. Don't do that."

Poppa wasn't moved. He shouted at me, "Annie Beatrice Foster, get upstairs!"

I was crying, but I stood tall and corrected him, "My name is Annie Beatrice Foster Mann. And I'm leaving with my husband!"

Solomon was still calm. "Bea, do not be disrespectful to your father. Go upstairs as he asked."

I lowered my head and did as Solomon said. I have never disobeyed Poppa before. He must have been shocked and hurt that I defied him but not Solomon. Momma had been watching us silently since Poppa opened the door. She followed me upstairs. We were curious. I was afraid of what might happen. So we stood in the hallway and listened.

Solomon spoke first. "Mr. Foster, I have the greatest respect for you as I do for your daughter. Although Bea is old enough to consent to be married, I came here to ask for your blessing on our union. I know that she is a virtuous woman because she was a virgin when I married her. We have been married for two days now, and we have consummated our marriage. If you convince your daughter to go through with an annulment, then she will be an unmarried woman who is not a virgin, spoiled to any other Christian man. You asked if she is pregnant. Although she denied it, neither of us can know the answer to that for certain. She could possibly be carrying my child and not be aware of it for a while. If we remain married, I will love her and that child above all others, save God. If our marriage is annulled, she could become an unmarried mother. I just ask you to consider all of the facts before you decide to void our holy union."

Poppa said nothing. He knew Solomon was right. Momma and I have never seen him back down to any man before—no matter how big or even if he was white. But he stood there silenced by the words of my Solomon, a Negro man much smaller than he. Solomon seemed like the most powerful man in the world to me at that moment. I was so proud of him. But I felt sorry for hurting Poppa. He finally spoke to Solomon with a strong voice. "I'll give my blessing if you promise to be a good husband to my daughter." Solomon promised. Poppa called upstairs. "Annie, get your things and come down. You and your husband want to make it to Newton before dark." Poppa doesn't care that my husband calls me Bea. I am his daughter, and he'll always call me Annie.

Momma and I talked while she helped me collect things I had not taken to college. I told her I feel loved and chosen like Grandmomma Lily was. She was happy to hear that. She blushed, and we giggled when I told her I enjoy doing my wifely duty. My wedding night was better than I expected it to be. And the next night was even better. Momma hugged me. She said she is glad for me. I love Momma. I know she wants her daughters to be happier than she is. She feels sad that duty forced her into a loveless marriage. I think that's why she told us so often the story of her parents' love. She is happy to know all her daughters felt loved when they married. I think Poppa loves her now and she loves him. I don't know why they don't tell each other that. Maybe they think it is disloyal to Aunt Abigail. Lord knows she's been dead for almost thirty years. I just think they would both be happier if they admitted their true feelings.

Momma offered congratulations to Solomon before we left. Poppa wished us well and said he would pray for our safe journey to Newton. He invited us back to visit anytime. Momma said we should surely come for Christmas so Solomon can meet the whole family. Poppa's prayers were answered, and we arrived safely in Newton.

I hope Solomon will be as happy at work as I will be taking care of our home. I know we'll both be happy together at night.

Monday, December 27, 1915

Dear Friend,

Solomon and I just returned from a joyful Christmas visit to Meridian. All of my sisters and brothers came home to see Poppa and Momma. Their spouses and children came as well. Thella and I don't have children yet. But Solomon and I shared the news that I am expecting our first one in July. Everyone is happy for us. But Poppa is disappointed that I probably won't go back to finish my degree. I'm so excited about being a mother that the degree doesn't matter so much to me now. I don't want to leave my child to go to school or to work. Solomon doesn't want me to work either. So he says I don't really need a college degree.

I enjoyed watching Solomon impress all the menfolk. He's the only college graduate in the family, so they asked what he thought about almost everything. They asked about his work and what he does as a principal. Everyone understood how he has taken charge of everything at the school and is trying to make it better. Most of the books and supplies are used and old. So he makes a lot of materials for the teachers, and he teaches two of the math classes.

See asked Solomon if the white folks give him enough say-so and money to make the school any better. Solomon answered that he and his teachers are teaching more math and reading than they used to. He is teaching morality and courage by example. He told See and the others about his dealings with Mr. Wilson. Wilson's Ice Cream Parlor supplied the school with ice cream and frozen custard one day each week for many years. Solomon found out that Wilson's does not serve Negroes inside the parlor like white folks. Negroes make their orders and get served outside the back door next to the garbage. That's where white customers tie their horses and pet dogs while they're inside. So Solomon did not renew the school contract with Mr. Wilson for this year. He told Mr. Wilson that the students will not eat his ice cream in the school if they can't eat it in his parlor. He also told his students not to buy anything from Wilson's Ice Cream Parlor or any merchant who treats them badly. Solomon gets ice cream for the school from a dairy way off in Jasper County. They deliver ice cream every week in an ice truck. They keep it frozen with a huge block of ice that leaves a wet trail all the way to Newton as it travels in the hot Mississippi sun. Mr. Wilson is furious. So are the other folks Solomon has stopped buying from. Solomon ordered new books and refused to pay for any more of the used books the Board of Education tried to sell him. He tells his students and their parents to speak out against inferior treatment and services.

Poppa asked if Solomon thought it was safe for him to keep "messin' with them white folks." He was surprised that Solomon is still around. So-called uppity Negroes all over Mississippi and Alabama have been beaten and killed for doing far less than what he's been up to. He said that Solomon should "mind that they don't burn down that fancy house they let y'all live in." Solomon didn't think I was listening, but I heard him say they wouldn't burn down the house because white folks own it. He admitted that he has been told he is "an uppity nigger that's stirrin' up the good Negroes in Newton." Some "well-meaning" white folks have suggested that he ought to leave town. They say his "fancy talk and rebel ways" would work better up North.

Poppa reminded him he promised to take care of me, and he can't do that if he gets himself killed. Even if he's not afraid of dying, he shouldn't leave me a pregnant widow. It was the opposite of when they met in April. This time Poppa did the talking, and Solomon thought quietly about what he said. I am proud of my husband, but I worry about him. I try not to show how afraid I am. I couldn't bear it if

Solomon was lynched or burned to death for challenging white folks or acting too proud. I remember that Poppa thought white folks burned his barn to the ground years ago because they thought we lived better than Negroes were supposed to in Meridian. Few white folks and no Negroes in Newton County have electricity and indoor plumbing in their houses like we do. We live there free, and I'm sure those crackers think Solomon should be more grateful and make less trouble. I hope they don't burn down our barn or worse.

Saturday, March 25, 1916

Dear Friend,

My heart is broken. I lost my sweet baby boy yesterday morning. It was a horrible end to the most horrible month of my life. My son's tiny dead body came out of me four months before his time. I've been raised to be strong and have faith when bad things happen. But I can't stop crying, and it's hard for me not to scream out loud. Solomon is so sad. But he tries to comfort me. He says he loves me, and we will make many more children. I believe him, but I'm mourning this baby. And I'm angry at those hateful crackers responsible for his death.

The Ku Klux Klan started terrorizing us the first week in February. They came outside our house twice that month. The cowards were covered in those white hoods. They came at night when we were asleep in bed. We would wake up to the sounds of them whooping and hollering, shooting their rifles, and riding their horses around the house. We could see the light and hear the crackling sounds coming from a big fire burning on the grass. I always got out of bed shaking. I was scared they were going to burn down the house with us inside. Solomon would try to calm me down. He'd say they were just trying to scare us. They wouldn't burn down the house because a white man owns it. Every time they came, Solomon told me to lie down under the bed just in case a bullet came through the window. I was so afraid, and I begged him to stay there with me. But he would go and open the front door. He said he didn't want to give them any reason to come inside. He didn't even take his rifle. He didn't want them to get more riled up and shoot him. I'd be praying and crying the whole time I was under the bed. Those Mississippi crackers don't need a reason to shoot a Negro. So I was always terrified for Solomon. I would hear more gunshots and be afraid they had killed him. I'd be afraid they were coming after me when I heard footsteps coming toward the bed. I would be trembling and crying until I saw that it was Solomon lifting the quilt. He'd help me get out from under the bed and hold me close. He said they were shooting in the air and riding off by the time he got outside. I thanked God every night for looking after my husband.

I told him that I was scared to stay there. But Solomon said we would be fine. He cleared away the ashes and reseeded the lawn every time they came. But he couldn't do that once they started coming every night the first of March. They got bolder and even more terrifying than before. They started staying outside long enough to throw a bucket of some animals' blood on Solomon when he opened the door. I was shaking and crying the first time I saw Solomon covered in blood. He was upset but tried not to appear afraid. He washed himself and apologized for all the mess. He stopped going outside. He went downstairs and looked out the window at them. Then they'd use the blood to paint "LEAVE NIGGER" on the front door. The first week in March, I spent most of every day while Solomon was at the school cleaning up blood in Solomon's clothes and on the floor, or on the door and the porch. All the while, I was scared and I was mad. I've wondered my whole life how folks can be so hateful. They sent letters to the school and the house. They said they were going to kill Solomon if he stayed in Newton. He took the letters to the sheriff. But he was no help. He might be one of the cowards under those hoods for all we know. He said Solomon had no way of knowing who was coming by our house or who was writing the letters. Solomon was always certain that it was Mr. Wilson and some of his friends. He couldn't prove it because he never saw their faces. And they made so much noise that we couldn't make out any one voice in particular. The letters were always printed and not signed. They looked like a child wrote them. So we couldn't tell who sent them. The sheriff told Solomon he is a smart Negro with notions that won't work in Mississippi. He said Solomon would be better off somewhere up North. I agreed that we should leave Newton. But Solomon believed he was helping his students and their families. He thought things were going to change eventually if he didn't back down.

That's why I was shocked on Wednesday, March 8, when Solomon told me that it was time for us to leave. He said that Mr. Wilson and some other white men he didn't know came by the school in broad daylight. Mr. Wilson asked him once again to buy ice cream for the school from his ice cream parlor. Solomon said he wouldn't buy from Mr. Wilson until he allowed Negroes to eat ice cream inside his parlor. Mr. Wilson said it was a shame they couldn't work out a deal because Solomon was so unreasonable. Mr. Wilson and the other crackers started to leave. Before they got to the door, they stopped to say it was a shame about all the trouble they heard we were having at our house lately. Mr. Wilson congratulated Solomon on soon becoming a father. Another man said he hoped we didn't have worse trouble ahead. "It sho' would be a terrible thing if'n somethin' was to happen to yo' wife and that baby she's totin' inside her." That was the final straw for Solomon. He told me that risking his own life was one thing but he could not stay once they threatened me or the baby. So he resigned his position that very day. He told everyone we would leave on Sunday after church. He said he hoped they would leave us alone until then. It seemed that the Klan got word and they were satisfied. They didn't come to our house that night.

Solomon didn't trust the Klan. He thought they might do something to us over the weekend. Crackers get to drinking and acting crazy on Friday and Saturday nights. A mob of them will snatch a Negro off the road or right out of his very own house in front of his family. They drag him off and beat him or hang him and burn him alive or dead. Sometimes they snatch Negro women with their husbands or by themselves. They might rape them before they kill them, then hang them and burn them just like they do the men. Some lynchings turn into big parties for those godless crackers. They fetch their wives and children to watch the horrible murders. I heard tell that women and children were there last summer when they hung a pregnant woman named Mary by her feet. She was screaming when they poured gasoline all over her and set her on fire. One cracker sliced her belly open, and the baby fell out on the ground. They stomped on that poor little baby til his body was smashed and torn apart. They threw his parts to burn in the fire with his momma. They shot dozens of holes in their burning flesh. And the crowd was cheering all the while. How could that be fun to watch? I threw up when I just heard about it. And I wasn't pregnant then.

Just last month over in Scott County, a young pregnant girl named Alma was hung off a bridge. It happened on a Friday night. They strung her up along with her sister and their boyfriends who were brothers. The mob thought the brothers killed the white man who was the father of Alma's baby. But nobody knows for sure if that's true. Crackers came by the bridge all that Saturday. They took pictures of the bodies swinging in the wind. And they made postcards with the photographs. The sheriff finally sent folks to cut the bodies down and bury them Monday morning. The grave digger claimed Alma's baby was still alive and moving inside her when they buried her. One of the postcards showing them hanging off the bridge came to the house. It was the day before Wilson and his friends went to the school. There was no written message, and it wasn't signed. But there was a red circle drawn around Alma's pregnant belly. That's why Solomon wanted us to be long gone before Friday night. But he wanted the Klan to think we would be around on the weekend in case they were planning to do something bad to us before we left. We were really planning to leave in the dark around one o'clock Friday morning. We packed in secret to move away quickly for the second time in less than a year. I wasn't happy or excited about this move like I was about the first one. I wasn't leaving because I wanted to go. I was leaving because I was scared to stay.

We took back roads away from town. Solomon tried to keep the horse moving steady and quiet. We didn't want to wake the crackers to alert the Klan. My heart was beating hard and fast all that night. I nearly jumped out of my skin every time I heard an owl screech or a fox running through the woods. I was scared, and I was sad. Solomon didn't want to leave Mississippi, and neither did I. I didn't want to go so far away from my family. And Solomon told me many times that it was important not to go North like his elder brothers and so many others. He wanted to stay and make life better for Negroes in his birthplace. He said things will get worse for Negroes in the South if too many of us leave. So I knew Solomon was surely worried about me and our baby when he planned to move far away from Mississippi and the South.

Solomon and I have been reading Henry Ford's announcements since last year. They take up a whole page in the newspapers. Mr. Ford promises five dollars a day to any man—regardless of race—who comes to work in his automobile factory near Detroit, Michigan. That seems to be a place where Negroes are treated fairly. And that's where Solomon's elder brothers live. So that's where we were headed when we left Newton two weeks ago. Solomon hoped to find work as a teacher there. But he was willing to work for Mr. Ford til he could get a teaching position. We didn't make it to Michigan. God seems to have chosen for us to stay awhile in Ohio—one state short of where we planned to go. Our wagon broke down, and our horse was worn out. It took us twelve days to get here. And we traveled over some rough roads in all kinds of weather. We'll need to get a new wagon before we continue. But Solomon doesn't want to buy another wagon. He wants an automobile. He can't afford either one just yet. So we'll have to stay here til he can save up enough money to drive a Model T Ford to Detroit.

We got here Wednesday. I was weary from our journey. Solomon was even more tired, but mostly, he was relieved. Solomon tried not to let on, but I saw how worried he was all along the way. We prayed together every morning for God's protection. And we thanked Him every night for our safe travel. But Solomon looked down every time we passed two or more white men together. He stayed tense til they were out of sight. He was careful choosing where we slept at night. He looked for places where there were other Negroes. He figured we would be allowed to stay there. I slept, but he sat up all night. He kept watch over me and our wagon. Everything we own was in that wagon. Solomon calmed down some after we made it out of Mississippi. But he didn't start to act normal til after we got out of Tennessee and Kentucky and crossed over into Ohio.

Solomon was finally able to sleep through the night. We were happy and feeling safe in the North. We survived all we endured in Mississippi and on the way here. But our baby didn't. Solomon blames himself for the loss of our son. He says he should have known those crackers would come after him for trying to change things. I don't blame him. He was trying to make things better. He never raised his hands or his rifle against anyone. I blame those hateful Mississippi crackers for my son's death. They threatened to kill him if we stayed and forced us to leave on a long hard trip that killed him anyway. I know that Jesus wants me to forgive them. I might be able to one day but not today or anytime soon. I pray for my innocent baby's soul. And I pray that Solomon's dreams of equality won't get him into the kind of trouble here that made us have to steal away from Newton.

Tuesday, October 17, 1916

Dear Friend,

   We have settled in nicely here in Ohio. It is different in many ways from Mississippi. It's chilly here already, and folks are wearing coats most of the time. The leaves on the trees are colorful shades of orange, yellow, red, and brown. The houses here are closer together and taller than in the South. Some have apartments for two or more families. We are one of six families in this three-story house. Every family has a separate door to its apartment, and all of us have electricity and indoor plumbing. We live on the second floor. We have a bedroom, bathroom, kitchen, and a living room with a small balcony. The other families are friendly. Two are just couples like us, two have one child each, and the other one has two. The children are all too young to attend school. I like that because they will not be too old to play with our baby when it arrives in the spring. Solomon and I are both so happy and excited. But Solomon is anxious to earn more money. He is determined to provide a better home than this one for me and the baby. He has saved almost enough to buy an automobile. But he plans to use it to get a bigger apartment or maybe a small house for just us. I tell him I'm all right here and houses are so expensive in Ohio. But he says he wants our family to live in a house like we did in Mississippi.

   Solomon is still unhappy about his work situation. His college degrees and his experiences as a professor and school principal in Mississippi don't count here. Folks up North don't think highly of Negro schools and colleges in the South. He hasn't been able to get a job as a teacher anywhere in Ohio. We moved here to Youngstown so Solomon could get a job in a steel mill because the pay is good. But the owner is not hiring any Negroes. Instead, Solomon is working in a rubber factory in Akron that makes tires for bicycles, tractors, and automobiles. The wages are much lower than the ones in Mr. Ford's automobile factory in Detroit. And they are not the same for white workers and Negroes. The daily rate at the rubber plant is three dollars and fifty cents for white employees and only two fifty for colored ones. Solomon is fuming to find such unfairness this far North. But I'm pleading with him not to bring any trouble on himself. I don't want us to have to move again when I'm carrying a baby. Solomon is trying hard to hold his peace for my sake and the baby's. But he's looking for a way to change his situation.

Solomon is considering taking additional classes in theology to become a minister. We worship at St. Andrews AME. Solomon teaches a Sunday School class, and he assists the church treasurer. I sing in the choir, mend choir robes, and sew drapes and curtains. I enjoy volunteering in the church, but I don't want to be a minister's wife. I know all I would be expected to do, and it's more than I want to do. Solomon is a wonderful speaker and an excellent teacher. So I know he could be a really good preacher. But most of the ministers here work full-time jobs on top of the work they do for their congregations. Solomon would do that. We would live on the wages he earned from his job. And he would put into the church any money he might make as a minister. He would be working eight to ten hours a day at the plant and more hours doing the work to serve his congregation. That wouldn't leave much time for him to spend with me and our children. I cannot stand between Solomon and God. I'll be a good wife by his side if he decides to become a minister. But I have told him true that I hope he finds another way to serve God and help people.

Saturday, December 23, 1916

Dear Friend,

Again, I have a heavy heart going into Christmas. I lost our second baby Thursday afternoon. Solomon was at work when it happened. My upstairs neighbor—Leona—helped me and called the doctor. He came quickly, but the tiny baby boy had no chance. He was only about six inches long and weighed only half a pound. I knew it was already too late when I yelled for Leona. I knew as soon as I felt the pains and saw the blood running down my legs that I was losing another baby. I could feel his life was slipping away from him as his tiny body was slipping away from mine. Leona stayed after the doctor came and left. She cleaned up the mess and cooked dinner for me and Solomon so I could rest in bed. Solomon is so good. I know he's as sad as I am, but he tries to keep a positive attitude. He reminds me that God always knows best. And God has decided it is not yet time for us to be parents. He firmly believes that we will be someday, and he is making me believe it too. I'm just so miserable. I was sure I lost our first son because of those hateful crackers in Newton. Maybe God just doesn't find me fit to be a mother. Is it because I tried to talk Solomon out of being a preacher? I'm praying for God's guidance and comfort. I need to find the strength to keep trying and to be patient. Solomon and I both wanted a big family of seven children. Now I'll be glad to have even one child to call my own. Solomon told me today he has put his plans for the ministry on hold for now. He didn't tell me why he decided to do that. I know it's partly because he doesn't want to make me more unhappy than I already am.

You can't tell by looking at our apartment how low we both are. I decorated it so much before this happened. Solomon bought the biggest tree that would fit in our living room. I decorated it with edible ornaments. I made red, blue, green, and yellow popcorn balls with Karo syrup. I hung cookies shaped and frosted to look like Christmas stars, crosses, cradles, and presents with ribbons and bows. Solomon got a wreath that I decorated and put on our front door. I was so excited. I wanted our first Christmas up North to be a happy one. This is the first year that I won't be spending the holiday with my family in Meridian. I already wrote to Momma and Poppa. I sent messages in it to all of my siblings and their families. They understood that it was too far for me to travel in my delicate condition. And it would take more time to travel there and back than Solomon has off from work. I know Solomon misses his family too. We visited the Mann Estate near Newton a few times. There's still some friction between him and his half brothers. But his two sisters who live there adore him. And he likes to visit the graves of his mother and father. They lie side by side on top of the hill near the mansion. Their headstones are always clean, and flowers are always blooming there. Solomon thought we would be with his two elder brothers by now. But we haven't completed our journey to Detroit, and we don't know when we will. Neither of us has any family here in Ohio. But we do have good friends and neighbors. I am thankful and I praise God for them.

Wednesday, July 11, 1917

Dear Friend,

Another baby is growing inside me. I want to be happy, and I am. But I'm not telling Solomon just yet. He isn't with me now. I haven't seen him since the first of June when he joined the United States Army. I didn't want him to do that. I didn't understand why he would leave me here alone so far away from my family. What if he never comes back to me? Solomon tried to explain it to me. "Now that the Selective Service Act passed, it's only a matter of time before I'll be drafted. Besides, if Negroes want to be accepted as equals, then we must fulfill all of the responsibilities of citizenship. As an able-bodied man, it is my duty to fight for my country." I understand what Solomon said. But I think he joined the army because he's trying to get respect. White folks here don't respect him any more than they do any Negroes. With all his education, he can't teach or even get work in the steel plant. Solomon is disappointed. The North, at least Ohio, is not all we hoped it would be. Negroes here are still not treated the same as white folks. I think Solomon's hoping he'll get treated better in the army or better here after he serves. Folks here respect soldiers. So he thinks he might get a better job when he comes back. But I'm still afraid for him. I hear tell Negro soldiers get the worst jobs in the army—toting and cleaning heavy equipment, digging trenches, and picking up unexploded shells off battlefields. That's hard and dangerous work for big men. And my Solomon is not a big man. He has a good mind. That's what they should be using instead of straining or risking his body.

At first, the army officers didn't seem interested in Solomon's education. But my exceptional Solomon got their attention real quick. Few whites and no Negroes scored as high as he did on those army tests. When the officers saw his scores, they checked his education. And they told him he could train to become an officer. Imagine that—a Negro officer! I'm so proud of him. Solomon is now in Iowa in the Seventeenth Provisional Training Regiment at Fort Des Moines. He writes that there are about one thousand two hundred fifty cadets in that all-Negro officer training camp. He says some two hundred fifty of them came from Negro units in the army—Buffalo Soldiers from the Ninth and Tenth Cavalry and others from the Twenty-Fourth and

Twenty-Fifth Infantry. Around a thousand of the cadets are like him—
college graduates, doctors, lawyers, and professors. Most of them are
from Negro colleges like Howard, Tuskegee, and Hampton Institute.
But a few are graduates and faculty from white universities, including
Harvard and Yale. Solomon writes that he has never seen so many
brilliant Negro men together in one place.

He says, "I am blessed to be in the midst of this collection of
scholars, discussing politics and philosophy with some of the best and
brightest of my contemporaries from all over the country—the Talented
Tenth that my professor, Dr. W. E. B. DuBois, spoke about. We are
not just training and learning with each other, we are learning from
each other. We share our knowledge, experiences, and strategies for
improving the conditions of Negroes in America."

Cadets Frank Coleman and Edgar Love impressed Solomon talking
about the Negro fraternity they started with another student and a
faculty advisor at Howard University—Omega Psi Phi. Another cadet—
Elder Watson Diggs—talked about being one of the 10 founders of
Kappa Alpha Psi Fraternity at the University of Indiana, Bloomington.
Solomon says both these Negro fraternities and two others—Alpha
Phi Alpha and Phi Beta Sigma—have spread to other Negro and white
college campuses in the North and South. There weren't any fraternities
at Rust when I was there. I don't exactly understand what they are.
But Solomon heard about them from Professor DuBois. He is in the
Alpha Phi Alpha Fraternity. Solomon says the Negro fraternities are
"organizing large numbers of college-educated Negro men bonded in
brotherhoods to encourage Negro advancement through education and
achievement." Solomon says he doesn't plan on joining a fraternity. Yet
he has come to understand the importance of organizing Negroes to
"achieve together what they cannot achieve as individuals." On his own,
he hasn't been able to get a job in a steel mill in Youngstown or get paid
the same as white folks in the rubber plant. But he hopes to organize
the Negro workers here to change that when he comes home.

And Solomon plans to get even more education when he comes
home so he can become a lawyer. He looks up to one of the older
cadets—Attorney Samuel "Ron" Brown. Ron and his wife organized the
Des Moines branch of the National Association for the Advancement
of Colored People—NAACP. He was the president until he joined the
army. Solomon learned about the NAACP from Professor DuBois.

Ron has a lot in common with my Solomon. He's active in the AME Church, and he's a former school principal and a former professor at Bishop College in Texas. Solomon is very impressed by Ron's work as a lawyer. And my Solomon is not easy to impress. Solomon was shocked to find out that Ron has saved thirty Negroes in Iowa from the death penalty. He got ten of them off "scot free" so they didn't have to stay in jail. Solomon says, "We need Negro lawyers in the courts to fight for equal justice and equal rights." I'm happy that Solomon has so many plans for when he comes home. That means he'll do his best to get home. And I pray that he comes home all right. Maybe the war will be over by the time he finishes training. Then he won't have to go fight in some faraway land.

As much as Solomon likes being with the Negro cadets, he dislikes the white instructors in the training program. Solomon says they don't hide their low opinions of all those educated Negroes. Solomon says the instructors are West Point graduates and just as prejudiced as the crackers in Mississippi. He and the other cadets hear them tell each other that no amount of training will ever make Negro soldiers fit to lead. Solomon says the commander—Lieutenant Colonel Ballou— seems to be a decent man. At least Ballou says he believes the program will train the outstanding Negro cadets to be good officers. A lot of the cadets don't trust Ballou because he is white. They don't like that he was chosen to command the Negro officers' training over a higher ranking Negro officer—Col. Charles Young.

Solomon says he isn't surprised that Young got passed over. He writes, "Prejudice is just as much a fact of life in the North and in the military as it is in the South. But it is demonstrated with more civility and false courtesy in the North and more open hostility and violence in the South. The military shows it both ways. There are some high-ranking Negroes in the army. But Negro soldiers and officers get less respect than white ones regardless of rank, and white soldiers and officers are openly hostile toward them without reprimand."

The training program will last until October. Then they'll join the fighting over in Europe. I know that war is dangerous. And I want my Solomon to return home in one piece. I'm not going to write him about our baby. I don't want him to worry about me. I want him to concentrate on being safe. I'll surprise him with our baby when he returns. Til then, I'm going to be as careful with this baby's life as I want Solomon to be with his own. I can hardly wait for Solomon to hold me and our baby in his arms. I love them both so much. I pray they will both be all right. And I pray Solomon and I can enjoy making more children.

Monday, December 31, 1917

Dear Friend,

I spent yet another Christmas wallowing in pity and grief that I can't put into words. My womb is a tomb. Or maybe it's more like a dungeon where babies are sent to die. All I know for sure is my Solomon has given me three sons. And I have lost them all. This time was the worst. My son was born alive. But he lived for just a little while. Just long enough for me to hold him in my arms and fall in love with him, and long enough for me to memorize his face. I still see his face whenever I close my eyes. I ache for him so much.

Even before I lost my baby, I had to work hard at being happy during the holidays. I'm so lonely. I miss spending Christmas with my family in Meridian. And Solomon is away from me. I'm glad he's still in Iowa and not fighting in the war over in Europe. But I miss him so much. I'm proud my Solomon was among the six hundred thirty-eight cadets commissioned as officers in October. I'm really proud he is one of the few to be commissioned at the rank of captain. Solomon is ready to serve in an engineering regiment overseas. But I'm still praying the war will end before it is time for him to go. I'm sorry that he is so unhappy at Camp Dodge across town from Fort Des Moines. Solomon writes the Negro regiment there is so different from the men he trained with at Fort Des Moines. All of the soldiers at Camp Dodge enlisted in Alabama. Most have had little education and are barely literate. They're treated badly by the army and by the folks in Des Moines. Solomon says the Negro and white townspeople in Des Moines acted friendly toward the Negro cadets at Fort Des Moines. The white merchants welcomed them to spend some of the $75 in gold coin they got paid each month. But the army pays the soldiers at Camp Dodge in government script. And the white folks and merchants in town are openly prejudiced toward them. As an officer, Solomon is still paid in gold coin, and he's still treated well in town. He does what he can to help the soldiers deal with the merchants. But he doesn't think he's doing them much good. He's anxious to leave Iowa.

Leona and her husband made sure I had some holiday fun. They invited me upstairs for Thanksgiving dinner with them and some of their family from out of town. They took me to holiday parties with their friends. Other folks at St. Andrews AME kept me busy with socials and the church pageant. I was happy I felt good, and my baby was kicking strong inside me. Going into Christmas, I wasn't afraid anything terrible was going to happen. Solomon was safe, and I thought my baby and I were too. I was looking forward to meeting my baby near the end of February. But he was anxious to see the world. And my handsome son—Solomon Charlemagne Mann, Jr.—was born ten days ago on December 21. He was so tiny—a little over three and a half pounds and seventeen inches long. His silky brown hair clung to his head like the skin of an onion. When his big brown eyes opened, I was bursting with pride and joy. He had ten fingers and ten toes, and the cutest little button nose in the middle of his handsome face. I was so excited and happy. I didn't notice that his skin was a sickly yellow or that his breathing was shallow and strained. Leona and the doctor noticed everything.

I had called Leona and my doctor as soon as I felt the gush of water. It came from me and left a puddle on the floor. They both came in a hurry. They were there in time to see Master Mann make his way out of me. They heard him cry, and they stayed with me awhile after he stopped breathing and his tiny heart stopped beating. It didn't take long. His brief life lasted less than half an hour. The doctor said something about his lungs not being developed enough. I didn't really hear whatever else he said. I was shocked and grieving way too much to pay attention to anything besides my lifeless baby. Leona says that I didn't cry or say anything for a long time. She says I seemed like I was talking to myself when I said my womb was a tomb. She's right. I was just thinking out loud. Leona told me I shouldn't say bad things about myself. It wasn't my fault what happened. This baby wasn't meant to be. That's all. The doctor said I can have more. I didn't say anything else. I just cried. I was so sad. I wanted to die with my son.

I'm glad I never told Solomon about this baby. There's nothing he could do now, except grieve like I am. I'm grieving enough for both of us. I need Solomon to concentrate on staying safe and coming home to me. I've lost our third son. And I can't bear to lose my husband too. My pastor, friends, and neighbors are helpful. They're the reasons that I'm still in my right mind. They come by to see me and pray with me. They've been cooking for me and cleaning my apartment since Solomon Jr. died. And they helped me arrange a proper burial for him.

Monday, June 17, 1918

Dear Friend,

I got a letter from Solomon today. It's the first letter that came since he went overseas two and a half weeks ago. I used to get letters from him two or three times every week when he was in Iowa. Now he's in France fighting the Germans. He says I might not hear from him for a while, but he doesn't want me to worry. He's a captain in the engineering regiment of the Third Battalion, Ninety-Second Division of the American Expeditionary Force. I don't understand all the military words he uses. It seems like his assignment is important and dangerous. I can't promise him that I won't worry about him. I just promise to keep on loving him and keep on praying for him to be safe over there and to come home in one piece.

Solomon still plans to buy a car when he comes home. And he wants to save enough money to pay tuition for law school. I have a surprise for him that will make it easier for him to do all that. One of my friends in St. Andrews AME choir—Rose—introduced me to Mrs. English—the lady of the house she cleans. Rose told her I'm an excellent seamstress. Mrs. English paid me to make alterations on some of her dresses. She liked my work. And she asked me to make a dress for her to wear to church. I made a hat and lace gloves to go with it. She really liked that ensemble. So Mrs. English introduced me to some of her friends. Now I have six rich white ladies that keep me busy sewing for them. I like to sew. And they pay me good money for doing it. My dressmaking business helps me work through my grief. It keeps me too busy to wallow in my thoughts of the three sons I never got to raise. And it gives me a chance to earn money to help Solomon pay tuition for law school when he returns home. God is answering my prayers for comfort and peace. He is answering my prayer for Him to show me how to be a good wife and help my husband.

Thursday, December 26, 1918

Dear Friend,

This was my happiest Christmas since I left Mississippi. My faith and my joy are stronger than ever. I received a letter from Solomon the day before Thanksgiving. He is finally returning home. He sent me only two other letters since he went overseas in May. The letters he sent from France didn't say much. He wrote he missed me and he hoped the war would end soon. I prayed every day that he would return to me. I tried not to be afraid when months went by with no word from him. Everybody at St. Andrews is proud of him. They prayed for him with me. On November 11, the newspaper headline said the war was over! I thought Solomon would be home for Thanksgiving. But I only got a letter from him saying he was fine and hoped to be home soon. I miss my husband. I wanted him to come home the day after the war ended. I thank God that he survived the war. So I can be patient awhile longer.

I really wanted to go to Meridian. Momma sent me a letter and let me know our family is growing. My little sister—Thella—has a beautiful baby girl she named June. Momma says that June is the most beautiful baby she has ever seen. That doesn't surprise me. We all know Thella is the prettiest of the sisters with the handsomest of husbands. The last time I saw Thella was Christmas three years ago. I was pregnant for the first time. She told me then she didn't want any children. Momma says Thella wasn't happy about being pregnant. She never stopped going out dancing and having fun. She still goes out Friday and Saturday nights. She leaves little June with Momma every weekend. I don't understand why God blessed Thella with a baby when she didn't want one. But He hasn't seen fit to let me have a baby when I want one more than anything. I still have faith that God will bless me with a healthy child someday. When He does, I'll be so thankful. I'll love that child with all my heart and be the best mother I can be.

I kept busy here during the holidays. I spent Thanksgiving and Christmas with Leona's family. We went to friends' parties and gatherings at St. Andrews. But I spent most of my time at my sewing machine. My dressmaking business is bigger and better than ever. I made a lot of money the last couple of months. Mrs. English and her friends wanted a lot of fancy dresses and ball gowns for Christmas and New Year's parties. I've saved enough money for Solomon to buy a car when he returns. He's wanted a car since we first came to Ohio. I think he'll be happy to finally get one. And I may have another surprise for Solomon. Mrs. English is impressed that my Solomon is an officer overseas. She's married to the owner of a steel mill that refused to hire Negroes when we came here. I don't know how much she can influence her husband, but she promised to talk to him about Solomon. She said when Solomon returns home, I should let her know and then tell him to try again for a job at the mill.

My savings and a possible job at the steel plant are not the best surprises I wanted to give my husband when he returned. I'm sure that he would be happier to have our son. He doesn't know about him. So he won't be disappointed. I'm glad I never told him about being pregnant with our third son. Solomon Charlemagne Mann, Jr. was our only son to be born alive and given a Christian name before he died. I don't know if I ever will tell him. Why should he be as sad as I am, wishing things had turned out differently? And I don't want him to know I failed three times to take care of a baby he gave me.

Wednesday, February 19, 1919

Dear Friend,

My beloved Solomon returned home six days ago. I am so happy and so proud of him. Leona and I organized a welcome-home party for him Friday night. All the neighbors came and called him a hero. Reverend Carter at St. Andrews AME asked him to wear his uniform to church on Sunday. He had him come to the pulpit during the service. Everyone cheered and applauded for him. Solomon thanked the pastor and the congregation for their prayers. He thanked them for looking after me when he was away and promised to be more active at the church.

Few white folks and no Negroes any of us know have served in France as captains in the army. People keep asking him about his experiences overseas. He doesn't say much. He talks about how brave the Negro soldiers were and how warm and welcoming the French people were. He says he and his commander—General Ballou—got along okay. That's about all he says. But we know some bad things must have happened. Solomon has changed. He's angrier than ever about how Negroes are treated here. He doesn't show it to white folks. He acts calm around them. When he is alone with me or when only Negroes are around, he gets excited. He talks about Negroes working together to get equality. He says he used to think he would get it if he had a good education. But he didn't. He left the South and moved to the North to get it. But he didn't. He joined the army. But he didn't get it there either. He risked his life "to make the world safe for democracy." So he wants democracy here and now. He wants equality for himself and all Negroes. He says he and the other Negro soldiers in the war "earned" it for all of us.

Solomon isn't too angry to be proud of me. He's surprised at how much money I get paid for making clothes for white women. I'm giving it all to him so he can buy a Model T automobile. He's even more pleased that my first customer—Mrs. English—spoke to her husband about him serving as a captain overseas. Mr. English sent word through his wife to me that he wanted to meet Solomon. Mr. English refused to hire him at his steel mill two years ago, but he offered him a job today. Solomon starts Monday. The steel mill started hiring Negroes while Solomon was away. It pays better than the rubber factory where Solomon used to work. Solomon is happy about the job but not happy that white steel workers still make more than Negro workers. Solomon says he will find a way to change that. I worry about him stirring up trouble. The Klan isn't as bad in Ohio as it was in Mississippi, but it's bad enough for me not to want them coming after Solomon.

I know my Solomon is hurting about things that happened to him overseas. I can't help him because he won't talk about what happened. But I can avoid hurting him anymore. I'm not going to tell him that I lost another baby while he was gone. I won't tell him about the grave where our little Solomon is buried. I asked Reverend Carter and my friends not to mention the baby to Solomon either. I'm not asking them to lie. Solomon won't ask about the baby. He never knew I was expecting. He wants to try to have children now that he's home. I'm not telling him about Solomon Jr. until after I give him a healthy son or daughter. I pray that will happen. I hope it will happen soon.

Monday, May 12, 1919

Dear Friend,

Yesterday was so hard for me. I tried to hide the horrible sadness I felt. I didn't want to go to church. I couldn't tell Solomon why I didn't. So I went. It was Mother's Day, and the church service was dedicated to all of the mothers in the congregation. Every woman received a carnation when she entered the church. I got a red one because my momma is living. The women whose mothers have gone home to God took white ones. The Sunday School children sang "M-O-T-H-E-R." The sermon was based on the twenty-sixth and twenty-seventh verses in Chapter Nineteen of the Gospel of John. It was about taking care of our mothers who took care of us. There was a special Mother's Day dinner after the service and an afternoon program of poetry, song, and tributes to mothers in the congregation. Solomon and I stayed for all of the events of the day. It was so painful for me. I miss Momma so very much. I haven't seen her since I left Mississippi more than three years ago. I write to her often. I hear back from her sometimes. But I long to see her and Poppa and all of my family. Even more, I long to be a mother. I'm aching for the three sons I lost.

I was so sad in church imagining what yesterday would have been like for me if they had lived. My first son would be almost three now. He would surely be singing or reciting something with the other wee ones. Our second son would most likely be fidgeting next to me in the pew. And Solomon Jr. would be resting in my arms. I would be so happy. Sadly, that is just a wishful dream. The horrible truth is that none of my three sons is here. I only got to hold one of them. And he was taken from me less than an hour after he was born. I pray that God will one day bless me like he blessed Abraham's wife—Sarah. She was much older than my twenty-four years and well past her prime when she birthed Isaac. I have faith that my time will come sooner than hers.

Solomon seemed fine yesterday. I don't think he had any idea how bad I was feeling. This evening, he was feeling bad. He got so riled up that I quaked in my shoes. A letter came in today's mail from Lt. Jake Adams. Jake was in Solomon's regiment. He returned home to Georgia after the war, but sent the letter from his new home in Philadelphia, Pennsylvania. He wrote to tell Solomon why he had to leave Georgia. He said two other soldiers they knew were murdered there. Jim Grant was lynched, and Wilbur Little was beaten to death. Both of them were wearing their uniforms when the white mobs grabbed them. Jake said that he got beat up badly in his uniform and left for dead. He made it to his cousin's place after the crackers were gone. His cousin cleaned him up. And he gave him civilian clothes to wear when he stole out of town that night. He wrote he's heard tell of the same kind of thing happening to Negro veterans in Mississippi, Alabama, Florida, and Texas. Sometimes they're forced to remove their uniforms in public. They're beaten or killed if they refuse. Sometimes they're beaten or lynched wearing their uniforms. Jake says the military won't get involved because the victims are no longer active soldiers. The states are responsible for them as civilians. The sheriffs are no help. Jake says most of them are probably in the Ku Klux Klan that's responsible for many of the killings. The NAACP has tried to help in some of the cases. Still, no white men have been arrested or jailed.

Solomon was fuming when he finished the letter. He clenched his fist and hit the kitchen table so hard I thought it would surely break. He shouted, "Negro soldiers offered up their lives for this country, and all they got in return were betrayal, humiliation, and death on the battlefield or later back home!" I was shocked and scared. I never saw Solomon like this before. His eyes were staring at nothing I could see. His copper skin turned bright red. His body was stiff, and he was sweating hard. Solomon saw me trembling. He stood up and held me close. We both calmed down. He was finally ready to talk to me about his experiences overseas.

Solomon said he left the army angry and frustrated by all that happened. Solomon thought he had proven himself to the army. He scored high on every test, and they made him a captain. He quickly learned that Negro officers were not respected by white officers or even white soldiers. Negro officers didn't sleep in the officers' quarters in Iowa. "White soldiers weren't reprimanded or disciplined for daring not to salute Negro officers." Solomon hoped he would earn respect when he got to fight overseas. He was glad to be assigned to the all-Negro

Ninety-Second Division under the command of the newly promoted General Ballou—the same commander in charge of his officer's training at Fort Des Moines. Solomon trusted him to be fair.

The Ninety-Second did well in early campaigns in France. It was hard because the men didn't speak French, and they didn't know the lay of the land there. Solomon was one of the few who spoke some French. His half-French mother taught him before she died when he was ten. He said Ballou praised his Negro officers and soldiers. The other white officers—in and outside the division—spread lies through the army about the Ninety-Second. They downplayed its successes and exaggerated any mistakes. They constantly complained in front of Solomon and others about having to work with incompetent Negro officers and soldiers. They said the Negroes were inferior in intelligence and bravery. No matter how well the Ninety-Second did in battle, they had negative things to say about them. They said the Negroes could not be trusted around the white French women. So every Negro soldier of the Ninety-Second Infantry had strict curfews and had to be present at hourly checks from reveille to eleven o'clock at night. They were reported and disciplined if they missed a check-in. They had to stay within one mile of their base unless they were issued passes, and very few passes were granted. Negro officers and soldiers were transferred out of the division or court-martialed on bogus charges if they complained. Yet the Ninety-Second continued fighting through the final battle of the war. They lost over five hundred men on that last day. Solomon is still furious and bitter about the whole experience. He says, "Negro soldiers risked their lives for this country, and many of them died. Those who survived the war have returned home to find little gratitude for their service. In fact, some of them are being murdered, and the army doesn't care!"

Solomon said the Negro soldiers were treated better by the French than they were by their own countrymen. The American army loaned the other Negro combat division—the Ninety-Third—to serve under the command of the French Army. The French military and the French people were friendly and kind to them. Solomon said he heard that General Pershing sent a secret message to the French command, telling them that Negroes are inferior. He warned the French to keep a close eye on the Negro soldiers and keep them away from their women. But the French didn't seem to pay attention to the lies they heard from the

Americans. The French people—men and women—were grateful and gracious to the Negro soldiers, whom they found to be equal in bravery and honor to their own. The French military honored many of the Negroes under their command with medals. Some even got the highest French Army award—*Croix de Guerre.*

Solomon says he was outraged by the betrayal he felt in the U.S. military. He said it was nearly impossible for him to stomach the "disrespect, disregard, and distortions of the truth" he endured. My Solomon is a proud man. He's never been thought of as ignorant or incompetent. Even the crackers who ran him out of Mississippi called him a "smart nigra" who caused too much trouble. Solomon knew he was smarter than most of the white officers in France, even the ones with higher ranks than his. He was frustrated that he couldn't openly call them liars and speak the truth about the heroes of the Ninety-Second. Solomon says he didn't want to talk about his army experiences when he returned home. He's been trying to leave his bitterness and anger behind. He wants to move forward and fight for change. Solomon says his brief time with French people showed him how Negroes are treated by whites when they are respected as equals. It made him more impatient to get equal and fair treatment here in his home country. That's why he's more determined than ever to become a lawyer. He says that he still believes that education will help Negroes advance. But white people will never give us equal power. We will have to fight for it one way or the other. He wants to fight for it in the courts. It's going to take him years to become a lawyer. So he joined the NAACP and is trying to get everyone here to join it too.

Now I understand the changes I've seen in Solomon since he came home. In some ways, I know my husband better than he knows himself. Solomon thinks he has to be better and do better than everyone else. He finds power in his mental superiority. He's the youngest and smallest of his mother's sons. He pushed himself since he was a boy to outdo his elder brothers in school. He fought to get the highest marks in college. But he sees that folks in the North don't think much of Southern schools. His degrees from Atlanta University don't count here. It's a Southern university and a Negro one at that. So Solomon is determined to prove to himself and everyone else that he's smarter than these white Yankees. It hurt him to go from being a professor and a principal in Mississippi to being a factory worker here in Ohio, making less money than the white men working beside him, who have much less education than he has. He scored higher than most whites on the army tests and got the highest commission awarded when he finished officers' training at Fort Des Moines. Still, white officers and even backward white soldiers thought he was inferior to them. He is angry and frustrated. So he has his mind set on getting a law degree from a white school in the North. Then nobody can ever question his intelligence again. At least that's what Solomon believes. And it matters to him a lot that people recognize his superior mind. Maybe that matters to him as much as all the good he thinks he can do for other Negroes when he's a lawyer. I'm going to help him all I can. He wants me to quit sewing for my white customers. He says that he will provide for me, so I don't need to work. But I won't quit working until we've saved up enough to pay for him to go to law school. I pray that when he graduates, God will help him get the respect he wants for himself and all Negroes.

Sunday, November 2, 1919

Dear Friend,

I'm scared that Solomon is once again putting himself in danger when I'm pregnant. I'm happy but anxious too. I've lost three babies. I'm honestly afraid I'll lose my mind if I lose a fourth one. My doctor advised me to take things easy. He says I must get as much rest as possible, and avoid stress and being upset. But I'm too worried about Solomon to stay calm. The white steel workers are out on strike with their union. Negroes are not allowed in the union. So Solomon struck a deal with Mr. English on behalf of the Negro workers. They are still working. And they're getting paid more than before. The white workers are angry. They yell at the Negroes on their way into the mill. They call them strikebreakers and niggers. I'm afraid Youngstown could be headed for a deadly riot like the ones in Chicago and other cities this year. I can't bear to think my Solomon could be another Negro who made it out of the war alive, then got killed in his own hometown.

I wish Solomon would spend more time at home. I hardly see him much anymore. He's working almost twelve hours a day. He comes home hungry and eats dinner as soon as he gets in from work. He hardly has time to digest his food before he's off again to a meeting of the NAACP. He's keeping records of Negro deaths from lynchings, other killings, and riots. Solomon stays upset and angry these days. He says that he has documented seventy-four lynchings in the last six months. That's more than twice as many as in the whole of 1917. The Ku Klux Klan seems to be stronger than ever. It's spreading all across the South and even in some places in the North. Deadly riots have broken out in over thirty cities and towns in the North and South. Negroes are fighting back against white mobs. More Negroes than white folks die in these riots. Solomon says even more Negroes die after the riots are over. Even though most of the riots are started by white folks, Negroes are the ones convicted of crimes for their part in the riots. Solomon says it's not fair because most of them were just defending themselves or others. They get put to death for murder, while the white men are usually not even charged—let alone convicted—of anything they do in the riots. The riot in Chicago was the worst one. At least twenty-three Negroes died over the thirteen days it lasted. And hundreds of Negro homes and businesses were burned to the ground. Solomon wrote to the mayor of Chicago, the governor of Illinois, and Pres. Woodrow Wilson. He asked them to look into why only Negroes were on trial after the riot. None of them answered his letters.

Solomon tried to get the Negro workers to sign petitions to the governor of Ohio to demand that Negroes get the same wages as whites in the rubber plants and steel mills. Most of the Negro workers said they didn't want to sign their names. They were afraid of being labeled as troublemakers. They said they might lose their jobs or worse. All the white workers have joined unions—American Federation of Labor (AFL) and the Amalgamated Association of Iron, Steel, and Tin Workers (AA). The unions make deals with the mill owners to get their members more pay. Bad things happened to some whites who refused to join the unions. Now all of them are members. Negroes can't join the unions. Negroes knew bad things could happen to them if they went up against the unions. So they wouldn't sign Solomon's petitions. Solomon wrote to the governor on his own. And he got a letter back. It said the plants and mills are private businesses. So the owners can do as they please.

Solomon got the Negroes to support him when the unions went on strike in September. The strike shut down the steel mills here in Youngstown. So the Negroes were out of work while the mills were

closed. And they had nothing to gain. The unions were on strike til the
mill owners agreed to pay higher wages to their members—the white
workers. They didn't care if Negro pay stayed the same. So the Negro
workers got behind Solomon when he went to speak with Mr. English.
Solomon told Mr. English that he and the other Negro steel workers
would work as long and as hard as they needed to keep his mill going
with no drop in production. Solomon said he knew of workers in other
closed mills who would help. He said they would even train other
Negroes with no jobs. All Solomon asked in return was that Negroes
get the same day wages that the white workers got before the strike. He
asked that Negroes be paid for two days work if they worked a double
shift in a single day. Mr. English agreed. And he told other mill owners
in the area about the deal. Some of them did the same. Others waited
to see how things worked out at the English Mill.

Solomon and the rest of the Negro workers have done well in
keeping production at the same level as before. The mill owners are
in no hurry to end the strike. They brag to the unions that the Negro
workers are happy to work for the same wages that the white workers
were making all along. They'll lose money if they give big raises to the
white workers. The white workers are getting angrier every week that
they are out of work. They're angry at the unions. But the unions say
the Negroes are to blame. So they are angrier at the Negro workers.
Riots happen when white folks get angry at Negroes and Negroes fight
back. I'm really scared there'll be a riot here if the strike lasts much
longer. I don't think the white workers or the union leaders know yet
that Solomon is the one who made the deal with Mr. English. They'll
come after him if they find out. Solomon says I worry too much. Maybe
he's right. But I have a bad feeling about how this is going to turn out.

Thursday, December 11, 1919

Dear Friend,

It's two weeks til Christmas. I'm both happy and fearful once again.
I'm still pregnant. And I'm feeling good despite all I've been through the
past two weeks. My baby isn't due til March. That's still three months
to go before I know for sure if I'll have a healthy baby. I've been able to

relax and even sleep well the past few days. Maybe if I can remain calm, this baby will be all right. I pray for that every day.

The steel strike is still going on in some places, but the white steel workers in Youngstown went back to work a week before Thanksgiving. They had to. They needed to get paid something to keep eating. They needed money to buy Thanksgiving turkeys and Christmas presents for their families. They were out of work with no pay for two months. And after all that, they were angry about settling for just a fifty cent-a-day raise and some little changes to make things better for them at work. They were really angry about how well the Negro workers made out. The Negroes lost less than a week's pay and made back what they lost by working double shifts for a week. What's more, they now get a dollar a day more in pay than they did before the strike. Negroes still make less than the whites. But they only make fifty cents less each day than the white workers now instead of the dollar less they made before.

The union leaders were angry at the Negroes too. Their members wondered what good the union was doing for them. After the strike ended, some union officials praised the Negroes for how they bargained so well. They pretended that the union might consider letting the Negro workers join. They said they would have to add a Negro to the union leadership to handle the special problems of the Negro workers. They wanted to know who made the deal with Mr. English. The Negroes were excited by the possibility of getting into the union. That meant they would get the same pay and benefits as the white workers. They were happy to name Solomon as the genius who came up with the plan and worked it out with Mr. English. But the union had no intention of letting Negroes join. They just wanted someone to blame for the white workers not getting what they should have from the strike. The white workers and the union leaders were all angry at my Solomon.

Although Ohio is far north of Mississippi, the angry white folks in Youngstown got riled up and acted a lot like those crackers in Newton. Solomon got printed threats slipped into his lunch box at work with no signatures, of course. Solomon was afraid to eat his lunch because he thought they might have added poison to his food. They tied threatening notes to rocks and threw them through our windows when we were sleeping. "Friendly" white workers suggested that Solomon and I would be happier and safer somewhere else. Solomon said nothing would be gained by staying. He knew that the Negroes would try to protect us. That would surely lead to a fight or possibly a riot. Solomon said he might or might not get killed, but his friends would get hurt. They would lose their jobs and might go to jail or die. So Solomon and I packed as much as we could into our Model T and left Youngstown around three o'clock in the morning last Friday. We decided to complete the journey we started three and a half years ago. We headed to Detroit.

I love my husband very much. I'm proud of the way he stands up for himself and for Negro rights. I worry about him because of it. And I hate having to make sudden moves away from people and homes I like. The doctor says that I need to stay calm and get enough rest to give me a better chance of delivering a healthy baby. I don't want Solomon to think I blame him for my problems birthing babies. I don't. We lost our first son after our rough journey from Mississippi. I lost the second one and the third one—Solomon still doesn't know about him—when I didn't travel out of town at all. I asked Solomon on the way here to try to make it safe for us to stay put this time. I am determined to have this baby. And I want to raise it in a safe and peaceful place. Solomon promised me that we will make Detroit our home and stay here for good.

Solomon said I would like where we'll be staying in Detroit. His elder brothers—John Augustus and Peter William—both have houses here. They have their own business that is doing well. Peter lives in a big house where there is room for us and our baby until we can buy our own home. His house is in a beautiful community with mostly Negroes who own their own homes. It's called Conant Gardens. We made the trip from Youngstown to Detroit in a day and a half. We got to Peter's house Saturday afternoon around four. Peter and his wife—Agnes—were not expecting us but welcomed us. They invited us to stay with them as long as we like. Peter's house is a very large two-story home with two large bedrooms and two smaller ones. Peter and Agnes don't have children. Agnes uses one of the smaller bedrooms for sewing and crocheting. The other small bedroom is where Peter goes to read the newspaper and relax alone. The living room and kitchen on the first floor are bigger than the ones we had in Newton and Youngstown. They have a separate dining room and a basement with a furnace room and a laundry room. There is a storage bin for coal in the furnace room. The laundry room has two large sinks and an electric washing machine. Few white folks and no Negroes I know have a washing machine.

Agnes is taking really good care of me. She is excited about my baby and wants me to get the rest I need. Solomon told her that I am a really good cook. She says I should rest at least a week before I help with cooking or cleaning. This evening, I insisted that I have rested enough to at least do the dishes. I do like living here and don't want to be any trouble. Solomon likes it here too. It's a lovely community with many friendly people. We met many of them Sunday at Vernon Chapel AME Church. It's just three blocks away. Agnes and Peter are both members of the church. But Peter misses the service sometimes because he works all night Saturdays. He didn't get home this Sunday til we were leaving for church. He was asleep when we returned and slept all afternoon. He awoke in time to have dinner with us and talk with Solomon afterward.

Sunday, February 29, 1920

Dear Friend,

Solomon and I are settled and happy here in Detroit. Peter is happy to have his younger brother living with him. He and his elder brother—John—call my Solomon by his initials—SC, the way their father called all his sons. They are so proud to introduce him to everyone as SC—the "College Mann." Solomon is working at Ford Motor Company now. He's glad to get paid the same wages as the white folks. He's making enough to keep saving for law school. Agnes is happy to have a "sister" to spend time with and share household chores. She says that she wishes we would stay here permanently. She and I are so close, even though we didn't grow up together. We're both far away from our families, and we are a lot alike. We share our faith and our love for two brothers. We both like cooking and sewing. We make our own clothes and accessories. I make shawls, gloves, and fabric purses. Agnes makes fancy hats with flowers, feathers, and fur pieces to wear to church. I told her about the sewing and cooking classes I held in Youngstown. She wants us to start a sewing circle and cooking club here after the baby comes. She says she always wanted children but hasn't been blessed with any. So she is excited to welcome a baby in the house next month. She and I are making beautiful bedding for my "piece of Jesus." She volunteered to move her sewing room to the basement so we can make a proper nursery. But I want to keep the baby in the room with me and Solomon at least a year.

We don't spend much time with Peter. He's away from the house a lot during the day and every night til after Agnes and I are asleep. He's out all night on the weekends. He comes home Saturday mornings around ten. Then he sleeps all day. He wakes up for dinner and leaves right after that. We don't see him again til Sunday morning around the time the rest of us leave for church. Nobody talks about the business Peter and John have. But I'm pretty sure they're doing something against the law over at John's house. I smell liquor on Peter when he comes in on Saturday and Sunday mornings. It's been illegal for a month to buy or serve liquor in the U.S. Agnes told me it's been illegal in Michigan for about two years. So I know that Peter and John are breaking the law. I don't want Solomon tempted by their fancy cars and fine clothes. I don't want my husband going to jail because he gets involved in his brothers' shenanigans. Solomon says I don't need to trouble myself about what John and Peter are doing. He says they don't want him to work with them. They want him to go to law school. Peter also wants him to look after Agnes when he's not around. I don't think she knows exactly what her husband is up to. She doesn't talk to me about his business. I know she worries about him. She told me that and that she hated being left home alone so much before Solomon and I came.

Peter seems nice, but I don't like John, and I don't trust him. Solomon told me about him before we moved here. He lives alone in a two-story three-bedroom house off Hastings Street in the Black Bottom. He left his wife and their three children in Jackson fourteen years ago. He didn't say a word to them about it. He just left home one morning like he was going off to work for the day. Instead, he just up and went to Chicago. He spent eight years there drinking, gambling, and acting a fool with loose women. Then he showed up one day back at his home in Newton. His wife had a fourth child just a year old. He yelled she was an unfaithful slut. He beat her bad. Then he packed his things and left again. He didn't say where he was going or if he'd ever come back. That's when he moved to Detroit. Peter was already here, working at Ford Motor Company. John went to work there too. They bought a house for their business. John lives there. It's about half a mile from the house where Peter and Agnes were living at the time. Peter moved Agnes out of the Black Bottom to this nicer area of Conant

Gardens once they started making good money from their business. That's when they both quit working at Ford.

I told Solomon I figured out John and Peter are using John's house for illegal goings on. He didn't lie to me. He admitted they use the house for late-night carrying-on. He says the basement is set up like a small club. It's got a bar, a piano, and a small bandstand. They have a singer, a drummer, and a bass player all the time. They add a man to play saxophone on special occasions. There's space for about twenty couples to have drinks and slow dance really close. They use the living and dining rooms on the first floor like a restaurant. People pay to sit around card tables and eat fried chicken or chitterlings with potato salad, collard greens, and cornbread. A woman up the street cooks the food in their kitchen. Food service ends at one o'clock in the morning. Then people sit around the tables and play card games for money. John sleeps in one of the bedrooms upstairs. They rent the other two to couples by the hour from nine p.m. to four a.m. Monday to Thursday and nine p.m. to six a.m. Friday and Saturday. I was shocked by how they use the whole house for all kinds of sin and vice. I never imagined all that was going on at the same time. Solomon asked me not to tell any of this to Agnes. Peter doesn't want her to know anything about the business. I promised not to say anything to her. But I told Solomon she knows enough to be worried about Peter.

I asked Solomon how they get liquor for their bar. He says they use whatever they can get their hands on. Moonshine from illegal stills has seen them through bleak times. They much prefer to buy it in Canada whenever they can. They travel by car and take ferry boats across the Detroit River back and forth between Detroit and Windsor. Solomon says the liquor runs from Canada can be dangerous. Police are quick to arrest colored rumrunners. But John and Peter have never been caught. They don't keep the bottles hidden in the car or trunk. They wear them in special corsets with padded compartments. One of John's lady friends made them to hold two bottles in the front and one on each side. John and Peter wear suits two sizes bigger than what they need. So they look like two overweight friends coming home from Windsor. They look real enough to have avoided being searched. But they're not safe til they get back inside John's house.

One time, John didn't go right inside with Peter after they parked in front of the house. He went to a store around the corner. Members of the Purple Gang thought his "fat" looked funny. They followed him out of the store and searched him. They found the four bottles on him. He used the Mann talent for smooth talking. He convinced them that the liquor was for his wife's birthday party that night. They made him pay them ten dollars "tax" for bringing liquor into their territory. They took the bottles, and they made him buy them back at their price. Even after that, they beat him bad enough to give him bruises all over his body, two black eyes, and two broken ribs. They said it was to remind him and his friends to only buy liquor from them. They said they'd kill him if they caught him again with other folks' liquor. John and Peter still make their runs to Canada. It's cheaper to buy liquor there. When they return, they look to see that nobody's on the street and go straight inside John's house.

I didn't ask any more questions about John and Peter's business. The more I hear about it, the more I really want to move to our own house. Solomon begs me to be patient. He has been accepted by Detroit College of Law. He says God directed him there. It's a respected law school that has women and Negro alumni. Solomon is sure he'll be treated fairly there. He wants to stay here with Peter and Agnes. He hasn't saved enough money to pay his tuition and buy me the kind of house he says I deserve. He says he'll be away from me a lot. He'll be working a full shift at Ford and going to law school full time. He doesn't want me to be alone in a house when our baby comes. He says he'll worry less about me knowing that Agnes is helping me. She'll be good company, and she'll drive me anywhere I need to go.

I know how important it is to Solomon to do well in law school. I don't want him worried about me. So I won't bother him about moving into our own house til after he's graduated. He's determined to become a lawyer. He believes it's God's plan for him. I'm so proud of him like I always am. I'm happy to do all I can to help him. I don't hate it here. Agnes and I are good for each other, and we like being together. I'm not worried anymore about Solomon getting into business with John and Peter. He knows what they're doing is illegal and dangerous. He can't get mixed up in anything like that if he wants to become a lawyer.

Sunday, September 19, 1920

Dear Friend,

I'm so very happy tonight. All is well. My dear Mary Elizabeth is sleeping quietly in her crib beside our bed. And I will sleep better tonight than I have in a week. Solomon and I thanked God this morning at church. Reverend Evans and the congregation of Vernon Chapel AME rejoiced with us. Then my Solomon told everyone he is so proud of my faith and my devotion. Agnes touched my arm and said, "Amen." I wept. I looked at my healthy baby girl sleeping in my arms. And I was at peace. Mary didn't wake up til the service was ending. She seemed to smile at everyone who greeted her. It was almost like she understood them saying how beautiful she looked. The pink dress and bonnet I made for her perfectly matched the pink blanket her aunt Agnes crocheted. Mary wears matching ensembles every Sunday. She has one in every color. Agnes and I have so much fun sewing, embroidering, knitting, and crocheting for her.

Mary was wearing the most darling ensemble of all last Sunday for her Christening. It was a beautiful white gown I made entirely by hand—not a single machine stitch. I embroidered a flower-draped cross on the bodice and roses all the way around the bottom above the lace hem. I embroidered the same roses above the lace around the edge of her bonnet. Agnes crocheted the booties. And she finished knitting the white blanket I started right after Mary was born on April 10. We were all so proud when Solomon stood next to me at the front of Vernon Chapel. Mary slept through most of the ceremony. She woke with a startled cry when the water touched her face. She slept through most of the dinner at the house. I didn't notice how warm Mary felt til after the last guests left around six o'clock. I wiped her down with cool water. But by eight, her body had gone from warm to hot. And her breathing was shallow and strained. It reminded me of the way my little Solomon Jr. sounded when he struggled with every breath of his short life. I haven't spoken of him to anyone in Detroit, and Solomon still doesn't know. I was waiting to tell him when Mary turns six months old next month. So I couldn't tell Agnes and Solomon why I was so frightened when I heard those sounds coming from Mary.

Solomon called the doctor. He told us Mary had pneumonia in both lungs. He feared she might not survive given her weight and young age. He suggested ways to keep her comfortable. Solomon was so sad. But he accepted what the doctor said. He tried to comfort me. But I was determined to prove the doctor wrong. I didn't believe God finally blessed us with a healthy baby only to take her from us after five months. I raised my voice to Solomon for the first time in our marriage. I shouted, "Where is your faith?" He didn't answer me. I told him, "Jesus will show me what I must do for her. And I will gladly do whatever it takes to save her."

I spent nearly every minute of every day this week with Mary. Solomon couldn't be helpful. I understood. He's in law classes every day and works the night shift at Ford. So he wasn't here that much. And he was sleeping most of the time when he was home. When he was awake, he couldn't bear to see Mary so sick. I knew he wanted her to live. But he was afraid to expect her to live because he didn't want to wallow in despair if she didn't. He always says, "Blessed is he who expects nothing, for he will never be disappointed." It was all right for Solomon to feel like that. But I knew Mary would make it because I had enough faith for both of us.

I made his lunch every day and laid out his clothes for the next day. Those were the only times I left Mary's side. I fed her ice chips and gave her ice baths to try and break her fever. When she couldn't breathe, I covered her tiny nose and mouth with my mouth. And I sucked out the mucous and spit it into a bucket. I did it over and over til her passages were clear and she could breathe. I blew air into her mouth and massaged her chest when she got too tired to breathe deep enough. When Mary was too weak to breast feed, I squeezed my milk into a bowl and fed it to her with a spoon. I filled her mouth, held it closed, and massaged her throat to help her swallow. Agnes stayed with me as long as she could and slept only a few hours a day. She cooked and cleaned by herself so I could stay with Mary. Reverend Evans came by to pray with me and Agnes. Friends came to pray and offer help. I appreciated their kindness but didn't leave Mary to visit with them.

I hardly slept from Sunday to Friday night. I was taking a short nap when Mary woke me up with loud crying yesterday morning. She was hungry and strong enough to nurse at my bosom. She wasn't completely well. But she was surely on her way back. I was so happy that her temperature and breathing were back to normal. The color was back in her cheeks, and she smiled. All of our prayers for Mary were answered. Solomon, Agnes, and I were so happy and grateful. We rejoiced and praised God together. Solomon left for a little while. He returned with little gifts for Mary and me. He used to do that almost every day til last week after Mary took sick. Yesterday Solomon gave me a pearl bracelet. He made me cry when he said I was the best wife and mother in the world.

He said our little girl was living up to her name. Solomon and I chose her name according to the way his mother named him and all of her other children. Her first name is taken from the Bible, and her second name is taken from history. The Virgin Mary was Jesus's mother because God chose her for that most special blessing. Elizabeth was the daughter of Henry VIII and Anne Boleyn. She was a very strong woman. She survived a half brother, a cousin, and a half sister to become the queen of England. She ruled forty-four years and was known as the Virgin Queen. I think Solomon hopes that carrying the names of two virgins will encourage our daughter to be a virtuous woman. And he wants her to be strong and determined. She's just a baby, and she got through pneumonia. So I think she'll get through anything with faith in Christ to strengthen her.

Wednesday, May 16, 1923

Dear Friend,

My Mary has survived pneumonia for the fourth time in less than three years. This time was the worst. She was tired, hot with fever, and struggling to breathe longer than ever before. She was in bed for a month, from a few days after her third birthday til three days ago. I tended to her day and night. Agnes was by my side most of the time. I changed doctors after her second bout with pneumonia. The first doctor had no faith that she would survive. Every doctor we consult seems to believe it will be a miracle if she lives past age four. They say that even if she lives longer, she won't have a normal life. Her repeated struggles with pneumonia have left her frail and tiny. Her internal organs will always be small and weak. She'll be sickly throughout her life. She'll have problems getting pregnant and carrying a child long enough for it to survive. But I remain confident that God will continue to save Mary and me. He has not brought her this far to take her and leave me broken. My Mary has defied the predictions of her death four times already. I am certain she will prove the doctors wrong in their predictions about the rest of her life as well. I wish Solomon would be as confident as I am about Mary. He seems to have come to accept what the doctors say. He can't hide his fear that we're going to lose her. He seems to pull a little bit further away from Mary every time she gets sick. It's like he's afraid to love her too much because it'll be too painful for him if she dies. It's just the opposite for me. My love grows each time I battle to save her.

I feel like Solomon is pulling away from me too. We rarely make love. And he seems to be more in a hurry when we do. He's not as romantic before and after. We just do it. And he goes right to sleep. I miss the tenderness we used to share. And I'm really disappointed that I haven't become pregnant in the three years since Mary was born. I wonder if Solomon is holding back somehow. Maybe he doesn't want to have more children now. Is it because he thinks we can't afford another child while he's in law school? Is he afraid any other child I carry might die or be as sickly as Mary? I know she's going to be all right, and I long to have more children to love. I hope and pray that Solomon hasn't changed how he feels about me. Maybe he's just tired. He's in law school all day. He works at Ford til around midnight. Then he goes back to study in the law library for hours after that. Sometimes he's there all night. He's home just long enough to bathe and have breakfast. Then he's off to school and work again. I know he has a lot on his mind. He is studying hard for his last set of final exams before he graduates next month. And he has to take the bar exam over the summer. We haven't talked about his plans for the fall. We haven't really talked much at all. I've been giving so much time and care to Mary for the past month that I haven't been paying much attention to Solomon. He never seems to mind. He seems to appreciate my faith and devotion to our daughter. I hope I get pregnant again soon. Maybe we'll get back to making our family bigger when Solomon finally becomes a lawyer.

Friday, May 25, 1923

Dear Friend,

What a difference a day can make! Yesterday I was happier than I've been in a long time. Today I'm so deeply hurt and just plain mad. Mary has been well for almost two weeks. She is laughing and playing most of the day and proving to be so intelligent. I always read books to her at night and during the days when she was too ill to get out of bed. Mary likes to "read" the books to me and Agnes. Agnes tells everyone she's the most brilliant child ever. "That baby can read just like a grown up, even though she's not but three years old." I try to explain that Mary just memorizes the words of the stories and my way of reading them. She has a really good memory, but she's not really reading. Yesterday Mary showed me she knew more than I thought. Though it's been just seven weeks since her third birthday, my Mary is reading. She interrupted me when I was reading a story about a little boy who lost his dog. Mary pointed at a picture of a sign the boy made. It said, "LOST DOG." She smiled and pointed at the word—dog. "Mommy, look! That's God backward!"

I was shocked. "You're right, baby!" I picked her up and kissed her on the cheek. I was so proud. I got some of the books she's been "reading" to Agnes and me. She didn't know all the words. But she did know a lot of them. She knew the words that were used most often—*a, the, it, she, he, and, once, upon, time, up, down, in, out, end, go, ran, said, Jesus, God,* and *dog.*

Agnes watched the whole thing. She was nodding her face and twisting her tightly closed lips. She said, "Humph! I told you. She's smart as a whip. She can read as good as some grown-ups I know."

I was so excited. I don't know any white children or colored ones who figured out how to read like that at three. I couldn't wait to share the news with Solomon. I made his favorite dessert—pecan pie. I decided to surprise him at the law library. So instead of going to bed at eleven last night, I got all dressed up to go out. I planned it all so perfectly. I rode two buses down to Witherell Street. Agnes stayed up to listen out for Mary in case she woke up in the night. I knew Solomon would be leaving his shift at Ford at midnight. He would get to the library between twelve thirty and one in the morning. I couldn't wait to greet him with the pie I made. Then I'd find a comfortable chair to wait while he studied til we rode home together. I made it to the library around twelve fifteen. I waited and waited. But Solomon never showed up. I missed the last bus going north. So I had to wait for the first bus in the morning at five thirty. I made it home a little after seven. I put the pie on the counter next to the sink. I sat down at the kitchen table. Solomon came rushing in the house a few minutes later. He hurried upstairs to wash and change clothes. Then he came to eat breakfast in the kitchen. He planned to eat and leave in time to get to his nine o'clock class. He smiled at me, but didn't notice that I was all dressed up when I prepared his breakfast and packed his lunch.

I sat next to him at the kitchen table. I drank a cup of hot tea with a lemon wedge and three teaspoons of sugar. He gulped down his usual two eggs over hard, four strips of bacon, a cup of grits with enough butter to turn them yellow, and a slice of toast with more butter and strawberry preserves. I showed concern. "You've been up more than twenty-four hours. Are you okay to drive and work? I don't want you to have an accident. You could get hurt or even die."

He smiled and said, "I'll be okay. I'm just glad that I'll soon be done with this routine."

"Probably not as glad as I am," I said. "Did you get a lot done at the library last night?"

"Matter of fact, I did," he answered. "Actually, I finished my last paper. I have just three exams and a debate left to complete. Then I'll be studying for the bar most of the summer. I can do that during the day, since I'll be finished with school."

"So you won't have any more reasons not to come home before dawn."

"Bea, I know I haven't been here a lot for the past three years, even when I should have been here to help you with Mary. I thought you understood that I'm doing all of this for us and for Mary. I want to give us the kind of life we both want. I also want to make things better for our people. I'm almost ready to start doing that. Please don't lose faith in me now."

"I haven't lost faith in you, just trust."

Solomon finally began to sense that something was wrong. "Have I given you reason not to trust me?"

"Not til this morning." I spoke matter-of-factly, but I'm sure he could see anger in my eyes.

"I've stayed out studying all night before, and I thought you were fine with it. What's going on that I don't know about? Is it Mary? Did something happen to her?"

"Good questions! Mary's fine. I want to know what's going on that I don't know about."

"Bea, this isn't like you. Why are you turning my words around, acting coy, and playing some game of cat and mouse? Just tell me straight what's wrong."

"What's wrong is that Mary read yesterday, really read words in books. I was so happy that I baked your favorite—pecan pie. I couldn't wait to pack it in your lunch for today. So I got dressed up and took two buses in the middle of the night to bring you a piece still warm from the oven. I waited at the law library all night. But you never came. Now you're lying to me about where you were. I'm wondering how many other lies you've told me and for how long."

"Oh God, Bea! I was studying and writing at a friend's house near the library. It's more comfortable there."

"Solomon Charlemagne Mann, do not take me for a fool! Don't make whatever you were doing worse by lying. My trust is already broken. A lie now will destroy it completely."

Solomon knew I was angry when I called him by his full name. It was time for him to leave for school. He has never missed a class in three years. He looked at the clock but didn't stand up. He decided it was important to stay and straighten things out.

He tried to explain. "I was at the home of a friend whom I met at the law library. She's the only colored librarian there. And she has helped me a lot since I enrolled in law school. She finds books and reserves them or checks them out for me. She lives a few blocks from the library and has a table and chair where I can study and write comfortably."

"You've known her for three years? Why haven't you ever mentioned her before?"

"I don't know. Hers is one of the few colored faces I see around school. She's someone I can converse with from time to time."

"Have you had sex with her?"

I knew the answer before he spoke. He took too long to say something. "Yes, but..."

I didn't want to hear an explanation. I just wanted to know. "Do you love her?"

"I care about her, but I don't love her." He was quick to add, "I love you."

"I find that hard to believe. If you loved me, you wouldn't have laid with her."

"It just happened. It had nothing to do with love. She is still in love with her late husband. She knows how much I love you and that I'll never leave you for her or any other woman."

I was so angry hearing him say again that he loves me. It was a lie. If he loved me, he wouldn't have betrayed me. I threw my empty teacup at him. He ducked just in time. It would've hit him in the forehead. Instead, it shot through the hair on the back of his head. He looked shocked when he raised his head to look up at me. He looked so funny I almost laughed. His face was covered with the bits of eggs, grits, and strawberry preserves that were left in his plate when his face landed in it. I didn't laugh. I didn't even smile when I spoke. "I'm so disgusted with you. How dare you say you love me! I thought you were different from your father and brothers. I thought you understood that love is faithful. Your adultery is betrayal. You broke our marriage vows with your sinning."

"Aren't we all sinners? My flesh was weak, but my heart was always faithful to you."

"Don't be confused. I'm not your mother Juliette or your sister-in-law Agnes. I won't share my husband with other women. I won't accept disloyalty. My father never said he loved my mother. Yet he's remained faithful to her. You say you love me. You don't. You may *think* you love me. I think you love yourself more. I don't know if you've got it in you to really love me or anyone else."

"I do love you, Bea. Do you love me?" he asked. He was talking soft and sweet.

"I think I've answered that question in word and deed every day we've been married."

"If you love me, then you must forgive me." I couldn't believe his nerve.

"You have hurt me and betrayed me," I said. "I love you, but I can't trust you. I'll probably forgive you one day, but not today and not anytime soon."

"You will trust me again because I'm going to prove to you that you can. I've been working on something that is going to make you very happy. It's going to be good for us and for Mary. I know it's going to bring us closer together."

"It's going to take time for me to feel close to you again. There's nothing more you can say or do at this point to make me believe I can trust you. Get cleaned up and get out of here. You're close to graduating. It's important for you to attend the last classes before finals."

"This was more important," he claimed. "Bea, you are the most important thing to me. I can handle everything else as long as we're okay. But I can't handle anything else if we're not."

"Okay is too much to ask for right now. Right now, you need to go. It's almost time for Mary and Agnes to get up. I need some rest. I haven't slept all night."

That was not what Solomon wanted to hear. But he finally understood that there was nothing he could say to undo what his actions had done to damage our relationship. He said, "All right, I have to accept that for now. Over time, I'll earn your trust again. Then we'll be more than okay."

Solomon washed his face and changed his shirt. He tried to kiss me on the lips before he left. I turned my head. His lips caught the back of my cheek and part of my ear. I'm not ready to kiss him. I'm still furious that he has been with another woman. I want to make them both pay for hurting me so much. But vengeance is God's, not mine. I must forgive them eventually, after a lot of time and a lot of prayer.

Monday, June 18, 1923

Dear Friend,

This weekend was full of surprises. Agnes and I managed to surprise Solomon Saturday night. We gave a party celebrating his graduation from law school. We started preparing the food Friday evening while Solomon was at work, and we stored it in the ice box at Vernon Chapel overnight. We finished the cooking and did the decorating Saturday while Solomon was studying for the bar exam at the library. The house was filled with about fifty of his friends from church and the neighborhood when he came home around eight that night. Peter stayed home. His brother John came and so did his youngest half brother—JT.

JT moved to Detroit last month. Solomon helped him get a job at Ford. The rest of JT's siblings are still in Mississippi and don't want to leave. There are still bad feelings between the two sets of brothers about their mothers, even now that both women are long dead and buried. JT and Solomon are the only two half brothers who are close. They have stayed in contact since we left Mississippi seven years ago.

Solomon sat me down to talk after the party ended and before I started to help Agnes clean up. He said he had a nice surprise for me. He told me one of his law professors introduced to him to one of his friends—a rich white man named James Parker. Mr. Parker was the smallest and youngest of the original investors in the Ford Motor Company back in 1902. He built his own automobile factory in 1911. It was right in the middle of the 2,200 acres his family owned near the Rouge River outside of Dearborn. The car he built—his Parker J Sedan—didn't do well against the cars made by the other big motor car companies. So by 1915, Mr. Parker gave up on making his own cars and started making parts for Fords and Oldsmobiles. He lost a lot of money along the way. Now he figures he'll make it all back and then some. White men always seem to come up with ways to make money.

James Parker is developing the 2,200 acres around his factory into an affordable town for colored workers at his plant, Ford, and others along the Rouge River. It is not surprising that this town will be named to honor his family—Parkersville. Parkersville, Michigan will have nice homes, good schools, and all the best stores and services. You see, most colored workers in automobile factories can afford to buy houses in towns near the plants where they work like Dearborn and Highland Park. But colored families are not welcomed in those towns. Parkersville will be just as nice as any nearby town and will seek out decent, hard-working colored factory workers and their families. Through his various companies, Mr. Parker will hold the mortgages and own most of the stores and businesses in the town. That way, pretty much all of the money he pays in salaries to his workers will come right back to him when they pay their bills and shop for food and clothes. Mr. Parker wants an intelligent Negro to be in charge of running the town. His friend—Solomon's Professor Barnes—told him that my Solomon would be perfect to do that.

After his first meeting with Solomon, Mr. Parker was so impressed that he offered him the position of town supervisor to oversee everything involved in establishing and promoting the town. Mr. Parker is confident that Solomon's experiences as a professor and principal, and his law degree, make him the right man to handle the affairs of Parkersville. Solomon convinced Mr. Parker to change his title to interim mayor. Solomon doesn't want the town folk to see him as working more for the good of the company than for the good of the townspeople. He doesn't like the notion of overseeing the town. It sounds too much like the overseers on the plantations during slavery. Solomon genuinely cares that folks who come to live there will be happy. He is confident that he can win the support of the people and get them to elect him as mayor when the time comes. He knows he will need to gain "their goodwill, cooperation and trust to keep the town growing and flourishing in the years ahead." Of course, Mr. Parker knows the town's success will benefit him the most.

Solomon proudly announced to me that Mr. Parker agreed to his request. So I will be the first lady of the newly incorporated town of Parkersville. He says our two-story four-bedroom home is already being built. I can meet with the builders to make changes and choose colors to my liking. I have wanted my own home since we left Mississippi. I love Agnes and hope she will visit us often. But I've wanted to move out of this house since I learned how Peter makes his living. Solomon says our home and twenty others will be ready by October. We'll be among the first residents of the town. Another hundred families should be living there a year after that. October is when Solomon will be sworn in as an attorney if he passes the bar exam next month. He doesn't have to pass the bar exam to serve as mayor. He is determined to pass it so he can represent colored people in court. That's why he went to law school in the first place. He'll pass any exam they give him. He's the smartest person I know. He graduated from law school with top honors. Now he's studying harder than I've ever seen anyone study.

I'm happy and proud of my husband yet again. Few white people and no Negroes get homes built for them according to their likings. Even fewer white folks and no Negroes are mayors and first ladies. I can't wait to share the news with Poppa, Momma, and my sisters and brothers. It's taken seven years for Solomon to get a professional job in the North. This is so much better than anything he was hoping to get. Praise God! It's truly worth the wait. Solomon believes God has chosen and prepared him for this. He knows that making money is Mr. Parker's main concern. But my Solomon is more concerned about leading colored people in improving their lives. He'll be fair to everybody. He'll make the town a good place for colored and everyone to live. He told me he is proud that he can finally provide me with the kind of life he has always wanted for us.

We shared the news yesterday with the congregation at Vernon Chapel. My heart was filled with joy as I sang hymns of praise. Everyone is happy and excited for us but sorry we'll be leaving Conant Gardens. I'll miss our friends and neighbors, but I need this move. It's a fresh start for Solomon and me. Maybe I can leave behind the hurt and anger I still feel about his adultery and try to rebuild the trust in our marriage. Solomon is courting me like he did before we got married. He's trying to win back my loving with little gifts and romantic gestures. I'm beginning to forgive him. We're enjoying passion at night again. I'm happy and will be even happier when I feel another baby growing inside me. We both want more children. Now we're back to doing what it takes to make them.

Thursday, November 6, 1924

Dear Friend,

Tuesday was Election Day. The two hundred sixty-five registered voters in Parkersville voted unanimously to elect my dear Solomon as mayor. Nobody ran against him. Solomon has been an excellent interim mayor for the past year. He's managed to keep Mr. Parker happy. And the town folk are really pleased with him too. A hundred twenty-eight families are happily living here now. That's over twenty-five percent more than the hundred Mr. Parker thought would have come over the last thirteen months. Mr. Parker is making even more money than he expected he would be by now. He's collecting money on more mortgages. He has a lot more customers than he expected for the supermarket and department store he owns since people who don't even live here come to shop. Every home being built is sold before the construction is finished. There is a waiting list of families who want to buy homes when more become available.

Everybody in Parkersville respects Solomon. They appreciate him too. He offers legal services and advice they trust on personal matters that do not relate to the town. He doesn't charge as much as most other lawyers. But few white lawyers and no colored ones are as good as he is. Although there's no crime to speak of in Parkersville, town folks call on Solomon when they get into trouble in Detroit or other towns nearby. His town meetings every month give the people a chance to have their say in how the town is run. They talk about the budget. They tell what they want in the schools, parks, services, and special events. Right now the three hundred children going to school are all in one building with classes for kindergarten through twelfth grade. Solomon handpicked good teachers and the best equipment to see that children in Parkersville get as good of an education as you find in the best schools in the area. Solomon promises parents that their children will have "opportunities to develop their artistic and athletic talents as well as their academic skills." There are plans to build another school as the town grows to have the elementary school separate from the junior/senior high school. AME, Baptist, and Catholic congregations meet on Sundays in rooms at Town Hall. As new families move into town, they join the fund-raising efforts of their fellow worshippers to build churches. They will need a lot more money and a lot more people to get the churches built. Yet each congregation has started a building fund. Parkersville is a safe, clean, and attractive place to live. The families living here and Mr. Parker give Solomon the credit for all the good things that are happening here.

Solomon persuaded Mr. Parker to allow some shops and eateries--including an ice cream parlor—to be owned by town residents. This brought some colored business owners to live here. Solomon also helped the townspeople save on the money they spend for food. He wrote to Dr. George Washington Carver and invited him come to Parkersville. We paid his train fare. Dr. Carver stayed in our house for a week. He examined the soil around town and studied the weather patterns. He recommended specific vegetables and grains that were likely to grow well here. He met with groups of homeowners to discuss crop rotation and other ways to get higher yields. We followed his advice. Now vegetable gardens and fruit trees are growing next to flower beds in front yards and backyards all around town. We are growing more than twenty vegetables and fruits that we harvest in different seasons for trading. Many of us planted apple, peach, and plum trees that should bear fruit in a few years.

My life is better than ever. Mary has been healthy for a year and a half. She is beautiful and so precocious at four and a half. Nobody, except me, believed she would live and thrive this long. But our Mary is a blessing and a miracle. Now that Solomon finally believes that she will survive, he's allowing himself to love her like a father should love his daughter. He's so proud of her, and he dotes on her. Solomon secured second-grade books from the school for Mary. She reads them with ease. She is a whiz with numbers like her father. He teaches her by playing tricks on her. Then she tries to play those tricks on him. But Solomon always says, "Before you set out to fool with a fool, you must have a fool to fool with. You were my fool until you figured out the trick. I can't fool you with that trick any longer. However, you can't fool me with my own trick. You have to find one that I don't know to fool me." Mary never finds ways to fool her father. But she doesn't stop trying. It makes me glad to see them so happy together.

Solomon is being a wonderful husband. He's so attentive and sweet. We are working on expanding our family. We haven't made love so often and with so much passion since we first married. He is toeing the line where other women are concerned. He has ample opportunity to stray but doesn't show interest. There are plenty women who flirt with him. Some are downright shameful about it. A man with prestige and position draws women to him like moths to a flame. I know that firsthand. I fell in love with Solomon when he was a professor at Rust. I've fallen in love with him again watching him shine as the mayor. I am so blessed now. I want for nothing, except to have more children with him. I haven't conceived in over four years. Yet I'm sure our constant passion will soon bear fruit.

Saturday, December 26, 1925

Dear Friend,

I can't describe how deeply sad and empty I feel now. The fourth son Solomon gave me left my body after five months and died before he took his first breath. Then the doctors cut out all the baby-making parts inside me. They threw them away like garbage. All my hopes and dreams of a big family with Solomon were destroyed with them. I begged the doctors not to take away my chance to have more babies. They said I would die without an emergency hysterectomy. Solomon demanded that they do whatever they had to do to save my life. He persuaded me that I mean more to him than a house filled with children by anyone else. I was still crying like a starving wet baby when they put me to sleep for the surgery. My faith is strong. Still, I don't know why this happened. I did everything the doctors told me to do. Solomon and I knew in August that I was pregnant again. I got plenty of bed rest. Solomon was so happy and more attentive than ever. He hired a housekeeper—Mattie—to come every day. She cooked and cleaned and helped me with Mary. When I felt the first cramp the day before Thanksgiving, Solomon rushed me to the hospital. All the same, I lost my last baby.

Solomon and I always wanted a large family with six or seven children. We must now face the bitter truth that Mary will be our only child. I know that she will make us proud. She's remarkable. She is only five and a half and has already earned a reputation as a little genius. Thanks to early schooling at home, she skipped kindergarten and half of first grade. She is already in the second grade and at the top of her class. She is fun and creative and so caring. It's hard to be around her without having a good time. She's confident like her father and not afraid to speak her mind. She's had to fight just to stay alive. I know she'll knock out anything that blocks her future. All our hopes and dreams for six or seven children are now on her shoulders alone. I just hope we don't press her to make all our dreams come true. I pray we let her dream her own dreams and work to make them come true.

Once again, I am reminded of how my joy during the holidays is so often spoiled by tragedies. Poppa died the Sunday after Thanksgiving last year. I couldn't get to Mississippi to attend his funeral. Mary had taken sick on Thanksgiving Day. I couldn't leave her, and she was too weak to travel. This Christmas, while I was grieving my last son and the surgery that left me barren, I got more bad news. Momma's mother—Miss Lily—died Christmas Eve. She has been staying with Momma and Thella's daughter—June. Thella left her husband and took off right after Poppa died. She lives in Chicago. Her husband moved to Jackson. He said he couldn't take care of a six-year-old by himself. So he left June with Momma. Momma's glad not to be alone. She's been happy taking care of Grandmomma Lily and June since Poppa died. Mary and I stayed with them for a month after school let out in mid-June. I'm glad Mary got to know her great-grandmother. She was so sweet and loving, even though we could tell she wasn't well. We'll be on a train in the morning, going to say goodbye to my dear grandmomma. Solomon is going with us. He thinks I shouldn't go. It's only been a month since my operation. The doctors said I should take it easy for at least six weeks. But I didn't get to be with Momma when Poppa died, and I won't stay away from her now that she's lost her mother.

Monday, November 12, 1928

Dear Friend,

There were no surprises last week in the national or local elections. Republican Herbert Hoover won by a landslide for president. Solomon and I both voted for him. So did just about everybody in Parkersville. Solomon was the only candidate for mayor of Parkersville just like four years ago. So he won again by the unanimous vote of all nine hundred ninety-seven registered voters in our town. Everyone agrees he is the best mayor we could have. Life is good here. My Solomon runs a clean, safe, pretty town with good schools and friendly neighbors. Parkersville has grown bigger and better than the five-year projection model in the lobby of Town Hall. Almost all of the married workers at Parker's plant have moved here. A good number of workers from Ford and even some people not working in the auto factories live here too. Mr. Parker is pleased as punch. He pretty much gives Solomon whatever my husband says he needs to keep the town running smoothly and the residents happy.

What I thought about most on election night last week was how much my life has changed since Solomon's first election. We sat and talked while we waited for the votes to be counted back in 1924. This year, I was alone on election night after I put Mary to bed. Solomon stayed out until three in the morning. I was furious. I knew he was up to no good. It wasn't the first time he was out that late. I know he's catting around. It started after my hysterectomy. Solomon swore my being barren didn't change how he felt about me. He said he loved me the same as before, but I soon began to feel differences in our bed. He was so passionate before. It was like he was trying to get me pregnant every time. It hasn't been like that since the operation. It's like he knows no matter how much of his seed he puts into me, I'll never have another baby for him. So he doesn't work himself up into a frenzy anymore—at least not with me. Over the past couple of years, I've heard rumors that he's been with women, mostly when he travels on town or church business. I even heard one of the women had his child. He claims it's just false gossip. He doesn't acknowledge any other children. I still believe at least some of what I hear is true. I see the suspicious way some women look at him. He ignores them when I'm with him—even gives them angry looks. I'm sure he acts differently when I'm not around. I'm hurt that Solomon is cheating on me again. He promised he wouldn't ever do that again after we left Detroit. I'm so angry at his betrayal that sometimes I lose control. That's what happened on election night last week.

I met him at the door with my iron skillet in hand. He got it away from me. And he talked me down. He didn't admit to being with another woman, but he didn't deny it. He apologized for being out so late. He added, "Whatever you hear about me, just know that I love you. If ever my flesh is weak, my heart and mind remain faithful to you."

"I want all of you," I replied, "heart, mind, and body. That's what I give to you, and that's what I want in return."

"I know that, and I try to give it to you," he said. "But if I falter, do you really want to *kill* me? I know you're upset now, but do you want me gone forever?"

"Of course, I don't want you to die. I just want you to do better."

He promised to do better. I'm not sure whether that means that he'll stop his fooling around or just that he'll be more discrete about it. We went to bed. He held me close, but we didn't make love. We both wanted to go to sleep. He was tired. I was tired of his fooling around.

I know Solomon wants more children. So do I. I've tried to get him to adopt the son I know he's always wanted. He insists that any male who carries the Mann name has to be of Mann blood. He says he'd consider adopting a daughter, but we have Mary. I want to raise more children and give Mary a companion. I took in two foster children last year. Solomon put a stop to that. I got too upset when their parents convinced the state they were ready to get them back. Solomon admits he's disappointed that there is no son to carry on the legacy of Juliette's side of the Mann line. John abandoned his children years ago. His only son goes by his stepfather's last name. Peter has no children with Agnes. John and Peter cat around, but they haven't given their name to any children they might have sired outside of marriage. So the only Mann boys in Mary's generation are from Tessie's sons--Solomon's half brothers from his father's mistress. I'm sorry he's sad that Juliette has no grandsons, and I'm sorry I can't fix that. If he's catting around to try and make a grandson for his mama, then he should be honest about it. I'd still be furious, but at least I'd understand why he cheats on me. Maybe I am less desirable to him because I'm barren. Does he see me like a mule now instead of the fertile filly he married? Sadly, that is how I see myself.

I keep busy as much as possible. I don't want to have time to think too much about me being barren and Solomon being unfaithful. I keep my house clean and beautiful. I host a lot of dinners, teas, and parties for Solomon's political associates and his friends in the AME Connectional Lay College. I sing in the church choir, serve as secretary of the women's club, and teach in Sunday School. I never finished my college degree. So Solomon won't hire me as a high school teacher. I'm assisting the home economics teacher in sewing and cooking classes, even though she doesn't know half as much as I do. I go to town meetings and speak my mind. I encourage women to speak up and vote. I urge them to go to school and learn skills so they can work if they need or want to do so. I tell them about my dressmaking business in Ohio. I say they should be prepared to work if the plant closes or lays off their husbands. The men accuse me of "stirrin' up the women." They ask Solomon to "take me in hand." He knows better than to try to shut me up. Besides, he agrees with me anyway. Henry Ford is building small factories of his own to make parts for his automobiles. He won't need Parker's plant much longer. Solomon tells the men their wives should listen to me.

I love Solomon. He makes me happy more than he makes me angry and sad. Mary always makes me happy. She is so loving and so smart and talented. She's eight and already in fifth grade. Solomon has her reading Shakespeare and memorizing poems and speeches like his mother did with him. I'm teaching her to cook and sew. On Saturdays, Solomon drives us to Detroit for her piano lessons. She's great at everything!

Wednesday, August 7, 1929

Dear Friend,

I'm glad to be back in Parkersville after the month Mary and I spent in Meridian. I look forward to our annual visits to stay with Momma and June. I think it's good for Mary to see where her family comes from and spend time with her grandmother and cousin. Mary doesn't feel the ties to Mississippi that I do, and she hates the rules colored children live by there. She's used to speaking her mind and having people respond kindly to her. She is adored, admired and respected by most everyone here. A few adults find her to be cocky and spoiled. They say that because she's the mayor's daughter, she's full of herself and acts too grown for her age. Most everyone thinks that way about her in Mississippi. She makes colored folks there nervous and white folks mad.

Mary gets bored in Mississippi. She says there's not much to do except farming chores, which she hates. She gets tired of playing games of hide-and-seek, catch, and tag. She's used to spending her evenings practicing piano, playing checkers and games made up by Solomon to challenge her mind, and dancing with Solomon to music playing on the radio. Momma doesn't have a piano or a radio, and she doesn't allow dancing in her house. In fact, she doesn't allow dancing, period. Mary finds that strange because on Sundays at Momma's church, everyone seems to be dancing. Momma says those folks are not dancing. They are "being moved by the spirit." Mary says it seems like dancing to her.

Mary is used to spending all day every Sunday in church, where she is involved in lots of activities. She helps in Sunday School classes. She helps serve breakfast before the worship service and dinner afterward. During the worship service, she and her best friend—Gladys Renfroe—gather up all of the children four to ten years old. They take them to the church basement to rehearse the Allen AME Children's Choir. Mary and Gladys co-direct the choir. Gladys is eleven, just two years older than Mary. She plays the piano when the children rehearse and when they sing during service. Mary directs the children and sometimes plays piano when they sing in the service. The two girls are in charge of rehearsals without grown-ups watching them. Grown-ups are in the basement, setting up for the dinner following the main service. They don't pay much attention to the choir. They trust Mary and Gladys to do the right things because they are responsible. In Momma's church, children are not in charge of anything. They sit and listen quietly, except when they sing hymns or when the spirit moves them or leads them to "speak in tongues."

Momma and her friends believe that children should be seen and not heard. They also believe children should do what they're told and not question or correct grown-ups. They say Mary is willful. She acts like she's better than other colored folks, and thinks white people should treat her like she's white. That kind of thinking is dangerous in Mississippi and could get her hurt or worse. They think it's a waste of Solomon's money to pay for music lessons. They say we're just "fattening frogs for snakes." Mary will grow up "bein' all high and mighty." But she'll probably end up marrying some "slick-talkin' ne'er-do-well" who'll drag her down to his level. She won't think she's so special then. The truth is that Mary doesn't think she's special now. She's disgusted by how Negroes are treated in Mississippi and in Michigan. She thinks they should all be treated as equals by white folks. She doesn't think that she's better than anyone else, but she doesn't think that anyone—white or colored—is better than she is. Momma and everyone in Meridian has impressed upon her she's not to look directly at white folks and not to talk back to them, no matter what they say or do. "Just keep movin' and stay out their way." Mary says she tries to do that but finds it hard to ignore being called a "little nigger gal" or being told that she can't do what white girls do right in front of her.

Mary told me she had to say something when she and June went to buy candy. The owner of the store let white girls reach in the jar to get the candy they wanted, but told Mary she was not to put her hand in the jar. She was supposed to say what she wanted or point to it without touching the jar. Then he would get it for her. My Mary was not about to do either. She said politely, "No, thank you. I've changed my mind. I don't want any of that candy. Eating all that sugar would just cause cavities to develop in my teeth." She left the store and signaled for June to come with her without buying any candy. The white folks looked at Mary like she was from another planet, not just another state. They told June that her cousin talked funny and acted strange like she was "touched in the head." When June told Momma what happened, Momma yelled at Mary and told her that she could get herself and June both beat for talking like that to white folks. I tried to explain to Momma that Mary reacted the way she's seen her father act when he felt insulted. Solomon taught her not to give money to anyone who doesn't treat her with respect and courtesy. Mary didn't "sass" the man. She offered a good reason why she changed her mind about buying the candy. So she didn't get why Momma thought she was wrong.

I feel like a buffer between Momma and Mary. Mary doesn't understand that Momma loves her and just doesn't want her mouth to get her into trouble. Momma doesn't understand that Mary loves her and just wants to feel loved in return. Mary sees how Momma dotes on June and always comments on how pretty and tall she is. Momma takes June's side whenever she and Mary have a disagreement. Momma tells me that she gives so much love to June because June feels bad about both her parents leaving her. Momma wants her to know that she is loved. She says Mary has two parents who give her everything she wants. So she knows she is loved. She doesn't need special treatment from Momma. I understand Momma, but Mary doesn't. She feels her grandmomma doesn't like her. That hurts my baby and makes her sad. If we're going to keep going to Mississippi every summer, I have to get Momma to show more affection to Mary. I love spending time with my family, but I love seeing my daughter happy even more.

Monday, September 23, 1935

Dear Friend,

June visited us yesterday for the first time since she moved out in July. She wanted to share her exciting news in person with Momma and the rest of us. When Momma and June moved in with us a year ago, Momma was blind from glaucoma and June was starting her senior year in high school. June and Mary shared Mary's room, and Momma moved into the guest room. Neither Mary nor June had ever shared her bedroom. They both had to learn to live with a roommate. They had the same kind of arguments I used to have with my sisters when we were teenagers. June is almost two and a half years older than Mary. And she stands a whole foot taller at five feet nine inches. She called Mary Little Miss Four-by-Four—four feet high with a big ole butt that makes her four feet wide. June told her that she should get her head out of the books sometimes and learn to have fun. Mary said she knew how important it was to make good grades in her junior year. She knew she would need scholarships to go to college in this depression. June said she wasn't interested in college. She didn't plan to work. She wanted to get married and move to Detroit or Chicago. She knew she was pretty enough to find any number of young men willing to take care of her. Mary said she was going to college so she could take care of herself.

Mary saw how popular June was in school. Boys were always fussing over her. And they asked Mary to take her notes or "talk them up" to her. Mary wasn't interested in boys yet. Even so, she wondered if she was pretty enough for them to like her. June's teasing made Mary feel bad about her looks at first. Then she learned not to believe everything June said. She found ways to get back at June when she was mean to her. Whenever June and Mary argued loudly enough to be heard, Momma took June's side and Solomon took Mary's. I tried to be fair. That kept Momma and Solomon both upset with me. Even after June and Mary stopped bickering and became really close, Momma and Solomon stayed at odds over them. Momma had always shown more love and affection to June than to Mary. That didn't change when they moved here. Solomon and I were as loving and caring toward June as she allowed us to be. She talked and acted in ways to show she didn't need or want us to take much care of her. Solomon was stricter with her because she was older and because Momma favored her over Mary. He always showed how proud he was of her. He liked everyone knowing his niece and his daughter were the top students in the senior and junior classes at Parkersville High.

I believe June really wanted go to college but didn't believe Solomon and I would pay her tuition if she got in. She knew Mary would be ready for college a year after her and that Mary's education will be our first priority. Times are hard for everyone in this depression. Solomon has accepted a meager salary as superintendent of schools, since he chose not to run for mayor in 1932. He's not making much as a lawyer either. Most of his clients cannot afford to pay him cash. They give him baked goods, their homegrown vegetables, or IOUs. June knew we were already spending more money to feed and clothe two extra people—her and Momma. It would cost even more for us to pay for her to go to college now and for her and Mary to be in college at the same time starting next year. We told her we would find a way to do it. June didn't trust what we said. How could she trust someone else's parents to take care of her when she couldn't trust her own? She hasn't heard from her mother—Thella—since she left her. Her father hasn't written to her in over ten years. June doesn't understand how much Solomon and I wanted a big family. We think of her as more than a niece. She is like a second child sent to us from God. We would gladly find a way to provide tuition for both of our girls, even if it meant they would have to go to local colleges.

June once casually mentioned that she had thought about being a nurse. Solomon used his influence as superintendent of schools to get her a scholarship to attend the St. Joseph Mercy School of Nursing in Detroit. When he showed her the letter from the school in May, he expected her to be surprised and happy. He was disgusted to learn she was planning to get married a week after graduation. She said she would be moving to Detroit with her husband—James. She didn't want to go to nursing school. James is a good man and a handsome one too. He graduated from Parkersville High two years ago. He's working at Ford and has no plans to go to college. He said he loved June very much and would be a good husband to her. Solomon didn't approve of the marriage. He said June was too young, and she could do much better for herself with an education and an educated husband. Momma said it was up to June to do what made her happy. As June's guardian, she gave her permission to marry at seventeen.

Even since June's marriage three months ago, Solomon has been trying to persuade her to accept the scholarship and get a nursing degree. He tells her that will give them something to fall back on if Ford lays James off. Times are hard. More and more people are losing their jobs, and they can't afford to buy cars. Automobile plants are closing or cutting back. But June made it clear yesterday that she is not going to school anytime soon. She is pregnant, and she is moving to a new two-bedroom frame house that James bought in Ferndale near Eight Mile Road. Solomon and I had hoped June was coming by to tell us she was starting nursing school, not starting a family already. Solomon didn't hide his disappointment and disapproval. I think Momma was hoping June had decided to go to college. She didn't admit it. She just said she was very happy about the baby. Mary and I didn't say what we thought. We just wished June well.

When June left, I thought to myself, *She has no idea how hectic her life will soon become.* It won't be as hectic as mine is these days. I leave for school every morning with Solomon and Mary to assist the home economics teacher. I teach sewing lessons at home three nights a week. Of course, I handle the cooking and housekeeping here. Mary lends a hand with cooking and serving dinner, cleaning the kitchen, and doing other household chores. She would do the laundry and ironing, but I won't let her. I want her to have time to enjoy her senior year in high school. She has so much to do keeping up her A average, doing after-school activities, practicing for her Saturday piano lessons, and applying for scholarships to help with the cost of college. I should be helping her, but I use the time I have left from work and chores to take care of Momma. She is blind and can't do most things for herself. An older woman from the church—Mrs. Washington—spends time with her during the day when I'm at the high school. In the evening, Momma wants me to bathe and dress her for bed because she doesn't want a stranger to see her naked. She wants me to prepare all her meals because she is particular about the food she eats. She trusts only me to walk her up and down the stairs. So I get up early enough to prepare her food for the day, get her dressed, and walk her downstairs, all before I leave for work. I'm still acting as a referee between Momma and the rest of my family. Momma and Mary both think that I'm doing too much. They both worry that I'm too tired to take proper care of myself. Momma says she hears me breathing heavily on the stairs. She feels the tension in my hands when I bathe and dress her. She thinks I do too much for Mary. Momma says that Mary is old enough to do more around the house and that she should stop dragging me to Detroit on Saturdays for all those music lessons. Mary thinks Momma is too demanding of me and should let Mrs. Washington do more for her. Solomon knows better than to suggest I do less for Momma. He supports Mary's talents and drives us to and from Detroit every Saturday. He thinks I should stop giving sewing lessons altogether and cut back on the amount of time I spend working at the high school. He says he's "capable of supporting his family, even in these hard times." Solomon doesn't understand why I work and teach my classes. I do it for more than the money I make. Sewing relaxes me. It takes my mind off the tension between Momma and Mary. It keeps me calm when Solomon is "working" late at night or away on "church business." I do a lot for Momma, Mary, and Solomon. Teaching my sewing classes and working at the high school are things I do for myself.

Monday, June 15, 1936

Dear Friend,

Praise God! My cup is still running over with joy and pride. Mary is the Valedictorian of the Parkersville High School Class of 1936. After the graduation ceremony on Saturday, all of the parents worked together to give our children the best barbeque anyone could imagine. Few white teenagers and no Negro ones have ever had better festivities at graduation. Everyone had a wonderful time eating, playing, and dancing until dark. We hoped it would make up for all the special occasions our children missed celebrating this year. The graduation barbeque was the first time most of the folks in Parkersville have celebrated anything since New Year's. Mr. Parker's plant shut down January 6 and stayed closed til end of May. Ford and other automobile plants laid off a lot of their workers too, since auto sales are way down. Most of the men in town were out of work, and even the few families with nobody working at factories were suffering. Parker Credit Corp. sent letters saying that they would not foreclose on houses of people who could not afford to pay their mortgages temporarily. Solomon explained to me that interest would still be applied and when people could pay again, their monthly payments would go up to make up for the missed payments. Families still had to find ways to buy food and pay other bills. Even so, folks were relieved that they would not lose their homes while they were struggling.

Solomon had to give up his salary as school superintendent to avoid letting go of two more teachers. We had to live off the money we had saved for Mary's college education. Praise God, I found work making dresses for Mrs. Parker and a christening gown for her grandson. She loved my work. She introduced me to some of the few rich ladies in and around Detroit. I made dresses for one of the few big weddings this year and a honeymoon trousseau for one of Henry Ford's grandnieces. Even so, money was tight. There was no sweet sixteen party for Mary in April. I made a nice dinner and birthday cake. I gave her two dresses I made from material I had left over from clothes I made for customers. The only guests were June's family and Mary's best friend—Gladys Renfroe. Mary understood. There were no birthday parties or celebrations going on in Parkersville this year.

I tried to keep calm in my home. Solomon was miserable that I had to work. He believes a man should always be the one to support his family. Mary and Momma said I was working too hard with so much sewing on top of housework and taking care of Momma. Mary helped me as much as she could. She said, "Papa should spend less time helping his nonpaying clients and more time helping Mama around the house." Momma said when times are bad for everybody, they're always worse for Negroes, even the educated ones. She thought Mary should look for a job after graduation and wait to go to college til times get better. Solomon and I didn't agree. We were determined that Mary would be going to college this September. And I didn't mind sewing as much as I could to make that possible.

Thankfully, times are better now. Most of the townspeople are working again. They're paying their mortgages and catching up on their other bills. The businesses are making money now that they have paying customers. Solomon is getting some money from clients who owe him from before. Most of them give him a little something from each paycheck. And new clients are paying with money instead of sweets and vegetables.

The celebration after the high school graduation brought so much joy to everyone. We were happy to see our children achieving, thankful most of the town is working again, and grateful we could afford a celebration. Solomon and I may have been the happiest parents at the barbeque. We were surely blessed to see our Mary graduate as the valedictorian of the class. Momma went with us to hear Mary's speech. She was unusually kind to her granddaughter. She acknowledged her accomplishments and complimented her on her speech. June and James drove from Ferndale with James Jr. in tow. He's only six weeks old but already as handsome as he can be. How could he not be with his beautiful mother and handsome father? Solomon sat with me in the audience and stood from there when he was introduced as Superintendent of Schools. His most cherished title that morning was father of the valedictorian. He could have been the uncle of the valedictorian last year. June had the highest average in her class, but Solomon decided not to name her as valedictorian. He said it was because she had only been at Parkersville High for one year. I think it was because he knew June didn't plan to attend college. Solomon always has the valedictorian announce their plans for the future in their address. So he chose the next highest student because she was going to Wayne University.

Nobody was surprised when Mary announced her plans to major in music. She has a beautiful voice and perfect pitch. People describe her singing as angelic because she can hit the highest notes effortlessly and softly. But she belts out gospel tunes with a booming voice that seems like it should be coming from one much older and with a much larger frame than hers. People marvel that a four-feet nine-inch, ninety-eight-pound body can produce a voice that fills the church and the school auditorium with or without a microphone. She sings "The Star Spangled Banner" at assemblies and on the field at athletic competitions. She sings the solos in the school choir and in school programs. She is an accomplished pianist and a good dancer. Still, her passion is singing, and she wants to sing professionally. Solomon thinks "it's a phase" and says she'll realize what a better, happier life she would enjoy as a music teacher. I'm not so sure. Mary and all of Parkersville know Solomon expects her to graduate from college and return to teach music at Parkersville High School or in Detroit. I remind him that my father expected me to graduate from Rust and return to Meridian to be a teacher. There are no guarantees that daughters will follow fathers' plans for them. Mary will make her own decisions, starting with where she will go to college.

Solomon and I had different ideas about where Mary should get her college education. Since we did not agree, we left it to Mary to decide. She will be only sixteen years old most of her first year. So I wanted her to attend a college in Mississippi or Alabama. I have family there. They would look after her if she went to Rust, like I did, or to Talladega. Solomon wanted her to attend Spelman College in his favorite city of Atlanta, and stay there to get her master's degree at his alma mater—Atlanta University. Solomon has friends there through his AME lay connections. He could count on them to look out for Mary. Solomon says Atlanta is the most progressive city in the South. He wants Mary to "expand her cultural and social experiences connecting with the scholars among the faculty and the daughters of the well-to-do coloreds among her classmates." She chose to attend Howard University come September. That's her choice, not mine or Solomon's.

Howard has an excellent program for teachers and an independent conservatory of music. Mary said she didn't want to go to school in

the Deep South. She didn't enjoy the summers we spent in Meridian.
Mary got a scholarship from Howard. She also got one from the Detroit
Alumnae Chapter of Delta Sigma Theta Sorority, Inc. for having the
highest grade point average out of all the Negro women graduating
from high schools in the Detroit area this year. I don't know much
about sororities. There were none at Rust College when I was a student
there. I was impressed by the members we met at the scholarship
reception. They talked about public service activities they do in the
Detroit area and worldwide. I'm proud that they recognized my Mary's
achievements. The two scholarships Mary received added to our savings
will pay the costs for Mary to attend Howard and provide her with a
modest allowance while she's there.

Mary thanked Solomon and me at the end of her speech. She
promised to make us proud and to bring honor to her family and the
town of Parkersville in the future. Solomon beamed the whole time
she was at the microphone. Everyone commented on how wonderfully
she spoke. I wasn't surprised. Solomon has been honing her speaking
skills since she was in elementary school. She memorized countless
monologues, poems, and speeches he read and discussed with her.
He saw the fruits of his labor at the graduation ceremonies Saturday
morning. He told me that night how much Mary reminded him of
his beloved mother—Juliette. She was the one who taught him to love
reading and oration before she died when he was ten. He's certain she
was looking down on Mary with a huge smile.

Now that Solomon is making money, he wants me to stop sewing
for the white ladies. I enjoy sewing, and I want to be able to do more
for Mary. I've already made more than a dozen beautiful dresses for
her to take to Howard. I plan to continue making clothes for her over
the summer, and I'll give her fabric to make some for herself. She may
not have as much money as some of the coeds she'll meet at Howard.
But she'll surely have one of the finest wardrobes. Momma thinks I'm
spending too much time and money on Mary. She says that I'm still
"fattening frogs for snakes" with all these clothes. But I don't believe
her. And I don't care. Seeing Mary in pretty clothes makes me as happy
as it makes her to wear them.

Monday, August 31, 1936

Dear Friend,

I am so furious right now. I am praying God will give me strength to do what I know to be the right thing. It will surely hurt me to do it. But I will be hurt by my guilt if I don't. God knows how much I can bear. So He wouldn't bring me this burden without giving me whatever I'll need to handle it. I can't even describe all the feelings I have right now. I'm still trying to sort them out for myself.

Solomon and I had a wonderful trip this weekend to Washington DC. We left Friday afternoon. We were so happy and proud driving Mary to Howard University. We stayed overnight in Pennsylvania and made it to the campus a little before noon on Saturday. I enjoyed helping decorate her room in Truth Hall with items I made over the summer. Mary's roommate—Roberta Boyd of Valdosta, Georgia—is sixteen like Mary. She also got a scholarship from Howard and money from her church. The girls took to each other right away, and I think they are a good match. Solomon likes that Roberta is "a good Christian girl with a strong moral compass." He seems confident that they will keep each other out of trouble. Solomon took us all to dinner a little after four. After we dropped the girls off, we headed back to the hotel in Pennsylvania. Solomon had to pry me away from Mary when we said goodbye. This is the first time I've been separated from Mary, and I have mixed feelings about it. I want Mary to enjoy campus life as much as I did, but I began missing her as soon as we said our goodbyes. Solomon comforted me in the car on the way home. Last night, we consoled each other with the best lovemaking we've enjoyed in a while. Solomon slept with his head nestled between my breasts. I was smiling as I stroked his balding head til I fell asleep.

Momma complained this morning. "I'm blind, not deaf. Y'all kept me up with all that cavortin'." I apologized for disturbing her rest but not for enjoying myself "doing my wifely duty." I was too happy to let Momma bring me down. All morning, I had happy thoughts about last night and about how much fun Mary would have in college. I wondered if she'd fall in love like I did. Solomon called about half past noon. He asked me to meet him at his office. He said I should ask Mrs. Washington to stay with Momma later than usual. He wanted to take me out to dinner. I was excited about going to a romantic dinner with my husband after the passion we shared last night.

He looked uneasy when I met him at the office. He showed me two letters that came by special delivery from Dayton, Ohio. One was addressed to Solomon and the other to me. They were both from Dorothy Johnson. I remembered that name. She was the librarian Solomon slept with when he was in law school. I was livid.

"You swore to me you haven't been in contact with that woman since you graduated from law school."

"Bea," he pleaded, "I didn't lie to you. I swear I haven't heard from her in over thirteen years."

"Then why is she sending a letter to you? And why is she writing to me? I've never even met the woman."

"Bea, please just read your letter and read mine too. I have nothing to hide. Please believe I haven't been in contact with her and never expected to hear from her again."

Solomon had read his letter before he called me. But he didn't tell me what it said. The letter she sent to me was unopened. I read it first.

Gentle Beatrice,

Let me start by saying that I never expected to contact you or SC. I only write to you now because I find myself in the most desperate of circumstances. Based on our past, there is no reason for you to care what happens to me. However, though we have not met, I feel that I know you well enough to know that you are a very caring person and a good Christian woman.

I have breast cancer and have been told that I have only a few months to live. Before I die, there is information I have to share with you and a heartfelt request I must make of you. Please, I beg you, read this letter in its entirety. I am aware that it may seem outrageous of me to ask this, but I pray you will indulge me. I know that you do not know me, and based on what you know about me, you are not predisposed to like me. I am truly sorry for hurt my past actions may have caused you. I will not try to offer excuses for my behavior. Nevertheless, I hope in this correspondence to explain everything.

I have loved only one man in my life, my late husband
Charles Paul Johnson. We were childhood sweethearts
in Indiana. After high school, we attended Wilberforce
University together. We married when we graduated in
1910 and stayed in Ohio for the next six years. Then, we
moved to Michigan, where Charles joined the National
Guard. I found employment in the library of the Detroit
College of Law and moved into a small apartment a
few blocks from there. A year and a half later, Charles
was sent overseas to fight in the war. I thought about
returning to Indiana when he was killed in France in
1918. However, both my parents had died earlier and I
had no siblings. Without my beloved husband, I found
no reason to return to Indiana or Ohio.

During my first four years at the library, I rarely saw
Negro students. So I noticed SC the first time he came
there. I was happy to assist him because I wanted to
help him become a lawyer. I made sure the books he
needed were set aside for him. Over time, we became
friendly. I told him how much I still loved and mourned
my beloved Charles. He told me about you and little
Mary. Every time she fell ill, he shared how worried he
was about losing her and losing you as well if she didn't
survive. We bonded, in part, through our devotion to
our spouses.

I admired SC because he reminded me of Charles.
Physically, they could not be more different. My
Charles was tall, brawny, and very dark, the opposite
of SC. Nonetheless, both of them were intelligent and
confident Christian gentlemen driven by their desire
to help others. I often wondered what Charles would
have made of his life had he returned home from the
war. I thought maybe he would have become a lawyer
like SC was going to be. I wondered what our children
would have been like. Watching the children in my
building and hearing SC talk about Mary, I mourned
for the child Charles and I never made. I was angry

and resentful. The man I loved more than myself was gone, and I had no piece of him to hold close, to care for and love.

Approaching my 35th birthday, I desperately wanted a child, one I could raise as though it were Charles's and mine. So I decided to extend the limits of my friendship with SC. For over a year, I had been bringing the books SC needed to my apartment. I made a comfortable place for him to study and relax. We talked over coffee. He told me about combat to help me imagine what Charles's last months of life were like. SC shared his feelings of guilt for not being more supportive of you when Mary was sick. He never made advances. I seduced him. We did not express love for each other and had no expectations of entering into a lasting relationship. What we shared was an intimate friendship that we both knew would not last beyond his graduation.

I felt horrible about manipulating SC. He was a dear friend, and it hurt me to see him burdened by guilt because of our liaisons. He felt he was betraying you and using me, when I was, in fact, using him. When I learned that I was pregnant, I made plans to leave Michigan. The night you came to the library, I told SC that I was leaving three weeks later. I did not tell him that I was pregnant. I took a job as a librarian at Lincoln University in Pennsylvania. I told my son and everyone else that his father was my late husband, Charles, and that he died during my pregnancy. I never dated once I moved to Pennsylvania. I wasn't looking for a father for my son. He was a gift I did not want to share with anyone. I never intended to tell SC either. I didn't want my blessed treasure to be a complication or an obligation in his life.

Only now, because I am dying, I must share this information with you. It is not to ease my conscience but to seek a proper guardian for my dear son, Paul

DuBois Johnson. He is a charming, bright, sweet young man, who is looking forward to his thirteenth birthday on December 12. Regardless of how you feel about me, I know you recognize that Paul is innocent of any wrongdoing. I also know from all SC told me that you are the most loving and nurturing woman that God has created. That is why I hope that you will open your heart and home to Paul and help SC raise him after I am gone. Please consider this mother's plea not with your mind but with your heart. Mother to mother, I beg you to agree.

Most humbly and sincerely,

Dorothy Johnson

I could tell by Solomon's demeanor that he was shocked to learn about his son. The photograph of Paul that Dorothy enclosed in Solomon's letter left no doubts about the boy's paternity. His face was almost identical to Solomon's, except for the darker complexion. Solomon affirmed that Dorothy has ebony-colored skin. I stared at Paul's picture for a very long time. It brought back painful memories I've tried in vain to forget. It made me feel the rage and pain of imagining my husband in the arms of another woman. It reminded me of the profound sorrow I felt every time I lost one of my sons. It made me jealous that I'm not the woman who is giving Solomon the healthy son he's always wanted. But it left me with such compassion for the child about to lose the only parent he has ever known. I felt so many emotions I could not speak. I wept for a while, never letting go of the photograph. Solomon wisely let me be until I gained my composure and asked him for a tissue. He asked if I wanted to talk over dinner. I said I had no appetite. But I would accompany him to a restaurant if he wanted to eat. We talked briefly at the office before we left.

There was nothing much to be said. I knew Solomon wants Paul to come and live with us. He was too ashamed to ask me outright. He asked what I thought about the situation and how I thought we should respond. I said I needed time to think. He apologized for hurting me again. I reminded him that he promised me he would not be the kind of husband his father was to his mother. But I know that he has had numerous "liaisons" since Dorothy whether he admits it or not. I told him what he wanted to do was more hurtful than what his father had asked of his mother. "Even the notorious J.R. never expected Juliette to raise one of his mistress's children as her own."

Solomon was embarrassed by the comparison. He lowered his head and said quietly, "I know."

Seeing my husband squirm made me realize that I have power. Solomon will not bring Paul into our home over my objection. He is rightly ashamed and concerned about what I'm going to decide to do. My appetite returned. I said, "I've changed my mind. I'm actually very hungry."

I know that as a Christian woman, a wife, and a mother, I have no choice but to help Solomon raise Paul. He will be a constant reminder of Solomon's adultery and my failure to give him a healthy son. But I can't deny a motherless child the right to be with his father. And I can't deny my husband the opportunity to know his only living son. I won't tell Solomon what I've decided for a few days. I'll let him worry awhile. It's not revenge. Still, watching him squirm and do his best to please me every way possible will bring me some small measure of satisfaction.

Tuesday, September 7, 1937

Dear Friend,

I smiled watching Solomon and Paul leave together for the first day of school. As both my men kissed me, I thought my life is the best it's ever been. Mary is happy and doing well at Howard, where she is beginning her second year. Momma is getting along better with Solomon. She adores Paul to the point that she is practically flirting with him. Paul is the only one she wants to help her going up and down the staircase. Paul is the one she likes to tell and retell the story of Grandmomma Lily and how her Nicodemus loved her so. Paul is such a dear and listens to her every time as if it is his first hearing of the tale.

It is hard to believe Paul has only been a part of our lives for eleven months. It feels as though he's been here much longer. I love him truly as much as if I gave birth to him. I didn't think that would be possible before he came. I was afraid that being around him would remind me too much of how he came to be. But I rarely think about his origins when I'm with him now. His mother—Dorothy—had so many conditions on the living arrangements that I almost changed my mind about letting him come to live with us. Now I realize that all that she demanded was in the best interest of her son.

Dorothy insisted that we not tell Paul that Solomon is his real father. Paul grew up believing he was the natural-born son of Dorothy and her late husband—Charles Paul. We could not tell him the truth without exposing his mother as a liar and an adulterer along with his real father. Paul could be labeled a bastard. All of that would be hurtful to him and make him angry and bitter toward Dorothy and Solomon. Dorothy made Solomon Paul's legal father before she died by arranging for us to adopt him. We explained to Paul that we were the closest friends of his parents when we all lived in Detroit. We told the truth about Solomon and Dorothy meeting in the law library. We made it seem that the two couples became friendly. Dorothy shared her true feelings about admiring Solomon and seeing the many similarities between him and Charles. I knew it was best to make Momma believe that story as well. If she knew the truth, she would tell Paul "accidentally on purpose." And she would be furious with Solomon for what he did and me for staying with him once I learned the truth.

We all thought it best for Dorothy to move in with Paul as soon as possible after we agreed. We knew Dorothy would need care and help in her last weeks. Paul would need to know we cared about her to allow us to help him as he grieved her. She fought hard as her pain grew stronger and her body became weaker. She showed no fear and drew comfort through her faith. When she died in March, Paul found acceptance and comfort reading the Bible and talking with the priest at St. Ignatius Roman Catholic Church. Paul and Dorothy were active there til she became too weak to attend mass. Father Perham came weekly then to give Dorothy bedside mass and, finally, her last rites. He officiated at her funeral mass. Solomon still takes Paul and me to St. Ignatius every Sunday morning at eight so that Paul can serve as an altar boy at the first and second masses. My friend—Cora—picks us up at eleven so we can get to Allen AME in time for the service at eleven thirty. Paul enjoys Reverend Gibson's spirited sermons and the spirituals. We took him home right after service before Dorothy died. Now we stay for the afternoon dinner and programs so we can ride home with Solomon around six. Paul watches with pride as his dad takes charge of things at the church on Sunday and in school during the week.

Paul never lived with a father before he came here. So Solomon is the first consistent man in his life. Dorothy taught him manners and her thoughts about manhood, but Solomon is the one who is teaching him how to put those ideals into practice. Solomon knows how closely Paul is observing him. That is helping Solomon be a better man. Paul figured out that Solomon is the most influential man in town. He is a lawyer, Superintendent of Parkersville Schools, Senior Trustee and Superintendent of Sunday School at Allen AME--the town's largest church, and president of the local AME Connectional Lay College. Even though he has not been mayor of Parkersville the last five years, his portrait hangs in the auditorium of Town Hall because he will always be the town's first mayor. Almost everyone looks up to Solomon and owes him for something—handling legal matters for them, hiring them for teaching or local government jobs, or using his influence to get them jobs in Parker's or other plants. Even Reverend Gibson is beholding to him for leading the fund-raising efforts that paid for the parsonage he and his family live in next to the church. What I am happiest about is that Paul's close attention to Solomon has kept him toeing the line in our marriage. Even if Solomon is coming home early to spend time with his son, he is coming home every night as soon as he finishes work. His satisfaction has given him renewed energy and passion in our bed. I am enjoying that.

Paul has brought new joys to Mary and me as well. He is so smart, witty, and sweet. We have fun with him always. When Mary came home last Christmas, she and Paul bonded quickly as soon-to-be siblings. She had always wanted a big brother. And she got the next best thing—a little brother so much bigger than she is. He's taller than she is, and he picks her up easily. He is a good competitor in Scrabble, Monopoly, and Gin Rummy. So he is a welcomed addition to our family games. Even before the adoption was finalized, he started calling us Ma Bea, Dad, Grannie, and Sister Mary. Mary told him that she preferred that he just call her Sis. She said Sister Mary made her sound like a nun. She says she likes dancing and wearing makeup too much to consider that life, even if she was Catholic, which she isn't. She calls him Ba-Bro, short for baby brother. He adores her. They went with her friends to Belle Isle, Boblo Island, Edgewater Park, and Walled Lake Amusement Park when she was home for the summer. Paul and I were both sad when we left her at Howard last week. We hugged all evening when we got home. He kept reassuring me she's going to do fine, and he'll make sure I'm all right til she's home for Christmas. I was touched that he comforted me like I comforted him when his mother died.

Paul is wonderful. He can never replace Solomon Jr. and all the sons I lost. But he is everything I hoped they would be. He is good, kind, handsome, smart, polite, and confident. He's very popular at Parkersville High School. Between his friends visiting and my sewing assistants coming by to work, my home is filled with joy and laughter most afternoons and every Saturday. Solomon is almost always home by dinnertime, and we enjoy family evenings of lively conversations and challenging games. Praise God! I love my family! I love my life!

Friday, April 12, 1940

Dear Friend,

Monday was my twenty-fifth wedding anniversary. I didn't know what Solomon was planning. He only promised me a nice surprise. He told me to be sure that Mrs. Washington would spend the night at our home to take care of Momma and Paul. I guessed that we would enjoy a night of dining and maybe dancing that would end with an overnight stay in a nice hotel. But whatever Solomon had planned for us to do that evening didn't happen. We did go away together. We spent Monday and Tuesday nights in hotels. But we weren't celebrating, and our room wasn't filled with romance and joy.

The dean of women at Howard University called Monday afternoon a little before five o'clock. I answered the phone. She told me Mary has been suspended for the rest of the semester. We had to come for her immediately. She said a telegram with that information had been sent and should be delivered to our home Tuesday morning. Mary is due to graduate with honors in six weeks. The whole family—even Momma— is set to make the trip to Washington then. I asked what happened. The dean said, "This disciplinary action was taken because she broke a rule of safety and decorum." Before she said more, I asked her to speak with Mary's father. Solomon is an excellent lawyer. He's saved many clients in what seemed to be unwinnable cases. I hoped he could save Mary from suspension and keep her in school til she graduated.

Paul and I watched and listened to Solomon's side of the conversation. His manner went from defiant to accepting to angry and disgusted. He spoke matter-of-factly after he hung up. There was a bed check Saturday night. Mary was signed in at the dorm, but she was not there. The guard in the lobby watches the only door into the dorm from the outside. He was told to report to the dorm director if he saw Miss Mann leave or enter. Mary was not seen leaving the dorm for breakfast Sunday morning. But she was seen entering the dorm afterward. So it was obvious that she had been out all night. She admitted it when she was questioned. Solomon said he could not defend her. "There was nothing to discuss. The rules are clear and known by every dorm resident and their parents. Such a violation has only one possible disciplinary action—immediate suspension."

Solomon says we can meet with the dean of students to discuss the possibility of her returning to complete her degree in January. She will not be graduating next month because she cannot complete her classes this term. We will have to pay all costs for her fall term, since her four-year scholarship ended with her fees this term. Mary has an excellent academic record. The dean received a number of pleas from students and faculty at the conservatory. Still, he is adamant that he cannot show leniency. He says, "Such an action would send the wrong message and undermine the enforcement of rules of conduct."

Solomon is angry and disgusted by Mary's "shameless" behavior. He said the school has every right to be consistent in its discipline. "Mary has known the dormitory policies since before she moved in more than three and a half years ago. She showed disregard for the rules and for her own reputation." I tried to keep Solomon open-minded til he heard Mary's explanation. Paul said his sister must have had a good reason. Solomon said he had wanted to spare us. So he didn't tell us that Mary admitted to being out overnight with four male students. He felt there could be no excuse for such behavior on her part. I was shocked. Still, I insisted we shouldn't judge Mary til we heard her explanation. Paul nodded to show he agreed with me.

Solomon and I packed quickly and left around seven that evening. We said very little during the drive and not much at the hotel in Pennsylvania where we spent the night. Mary was packed and ready to go when we arrived at the dormitory Tuesday afternoon. The resident director met us and said that the dean would see us in his office. Solomon told her, "There is no need for us to meet with the dean. Mary won't be returning to Howard." That was news to me and Mary. We thought we would discuss it later. Solomon seemed to have made up his mind already. We spent less than half an hour on the campus—just time enough to sign the necessary paperwork to take our daughter home. Mary had said her goodbyes before we came. She wanted to leave as quickly and quietly as possible.

The drive home was different from the one to Washington. We talked a lot along the way. I asked Solomon why he said Mary couldn't return to Howard to finish her degree. He was angry and definite. He said, "She'll be transferring to complete her studies at Wayne University in Detroit. It is obvious that she cannot be trusted. Therefore, she will attend college living at home under our watchful and untrusting eyes."

I said I hadn't lost trust in my daughter. I wanted to hear what Mary had to say about why she stayed out Saturday night. Mary said for the past year, she's been singing and playing violin in a jazz group—Ebony Hues—with four male students at the conservatory. They made good money playing for parties on campus, receptions around the city, and at area dance clubs on the weekends. Mary always had to leave the clubs after the first set to make curfew at the dorm. The males in the group finished the other sets without a vocalist. Mary believes it's unfair that curfews for female students are so strict, while male students can do more or less as they please. She says she raised this issue at student meetings and she spoke to the dean of women about it.

Mary said Ebony Hues got the attention of an important musician in October. Fletcher Henderson is a black bandleader working as a pianist and arranger with Benny Goodman. He was attending his cousin's wedding when Ebony Hues was performing at the reception. He was impressed and spoke to the group about auditioning for one of his contacts at Decca Records. The Ebony Hues bass player—Gordon—said they could trust Mr. Henderson. His dad was his Alpha Phi Alpha Fraternity line brother at Atlanta University. Mr. Henderson remembered Gordon's dad. He was happy to learn that Gordon grew up listening to his music and that it had influenced his decision to play jazz.

Mr. Henderson followed through with his promise to introduce the group to a talent scout for Decca Records. Last Saturday, he arranged for a Decca representative to see Ebony Hues perform at their usual club date. He was supposed to be at the first set before Mary had to leave to make curfew, but he arrived as the first set was ending. So he stayed to hear the second one. Mary said singing professionally has always been her dream. We've taught her to go after her dreams. She just couldn't pass on this opportunity for herself and for the rest of Ebony Hues. So she stayed to perform. The Decca scout liked them. He offered them a chance to make a record and possibly sign contracts. Mary is under twenty-one and needs our permission to make any deals. She knew it was doubtful that her father would agree to let her travel around the country with four men singing what he called hoochie coochie music. She had hoped we might agree after she graduated. Once she knew she wouldn't be graduating next month, she knew Solomon wouldn't agree. He'd never give his permission for her to take a leave from college to record and tour.

Mary says she understands how much she has displeased and disappointed us. She isn't ashamed of what she did. Still, she is sorry for the outcome. She knows how bad it sounds that she was out all night with four men. She wants us to understand the males in the group are her friends. She did nothing wrong with them that night or any other time. By the time the second set ended, she had missed curfew. She knew she couldn't sneak into the dorm that late. She was up all night at a diner with the guys after the club closed. Mr. Henderson was with them like a chaperone until dawn. They celebrated their good fortune with country breakfast specials and toasted each other with glasses of orange juice. She returned to campus at nine in the morning. She tried to slip into the dorm unnoticed in the crowd returning from breakfast in the cafeteria.

Mary says she's been outspoken about her feelings that having different curfews for female students and male students is unfair. She understands that regardless of her feelings, she broke the rules. She asked for leniency given her clean record, her academic standing, and her proximity to graduation. Some of her sorority sisters in Delta Sigma Theta and her friends in the other sororities—Alpha Kappa Alpha, Zeta Phi Beta, and Sigma Gamma Rho—spoke to the dean on her behalf. Students and faculty at the conservatory also supported her request for leniency. However, the dean would not budge. He said that she broke the code of conduct and her suspension is mandatory. Mary says she's grateful for all the support she received at the campus. She hopes we will forgive and support her too.

Solomon is furious. He says her fate matters to him also. Her suspension will delay but not stop her from graduating and moving on with her life. He's determined for her to come home to teach music and earn her master's degree. He was already calling influential friends in Detroit before we learned of her suspension. He wanted to get her appointed to a school in a safe neighborhood. He said he thought she had abandoned the foolish notion of becoming a singer. She should use her God-given talent to do God's work—singing in the church choir and teaching God's children classical music. "Your foolish pipedream of singing the devil's music is what got you into trouble. You will finish your degree and teach music until you're old enough to throw your life away without my permission."

It was just past midnight—the start of Wednesday, April 10—when we were ready for bed at the hotel. I wished Mary a happy twentieth birthday. Solomon grudgingly did the same after I stared at him. Mary thanked us and apologized again for disappointing us. She promised to get her degree and to do whatever it takes to restore her father's faith in her. I requested the hotel cook write "Happy BD Mary" with whipped cream on top of Mary's pancakes at breakfast that morning. The waitress even put a candle in the center for her to make a wish. It made us all happy for a few minutes.

I finally told Mary how I felt once we were back in the car. I'm disappointed she never told us about being in Ebony Hues. I think she showed poor judgment breaking curfew so close to graduation. I understand her frustration about the curfew. But she can't just ignore rules she doesn't agree with. I understand how much she wanted to make a record and to get a contract. She knew she couldn't sign one yet. So she could have waited til after she graduated to audition. I haven't lost trust in her. I believe what she told me. I don't like or approve of what she did. I'm upset with her, but I love her. We'll get through this.

Solomon said he didn't care about her reasons. He told her that he's angry and embarrassed. "The fact that you were suspended and threw away your scholarships and our money by engaging in scandalous behavior will make us fodder for gossip in and around town. That can compromise my work in the church and my candidacy for state leadership in the lay organization." He says he's appalled by her selfishness and her deceit. "For over a year, you've been performing with a bunch of men in places where you shouldn't have been. How dare you sing in clubs where alcohol is served and who knows what else is going on!" Mary kept repeating that nothing sinful happened with her and the males in Ebony Hues. They are like big brothers to her. Solomon told her he has doubts about anything she says now because she betrayed his trust. It will take time for him to trust her again, and he may never trust her as completely as he did before.

Solomon said it doesn't matter what did or didn't happen with the young men. "Appearances and people's perceptions damage a young woman's reputation as much as what she actually does. You were out all night with four men. That's a fact. A young woman who would do that appears to be one with loose or at least questionable morality. There are only two kinds of women—virtuous or non-virtuous. Your actions make you appear to be the latter. No Christian man would want to marry such a woman. I can't believe I raised one."

Mary didn't take that without answering. "When did we start to care so much about what people think? I'm not sure I want to get married. If I do decide to marry, I want a Christian man who recognizes that he's not free of sin and shouldn't cast stones at me, especially when they're based on suspicion and appearances. I want a man who will love me unconditionally, one who will know me well enough to know the kind of woman I truly am and one who will appreciate me just like I am." At that moment, I knew Mary was saying what she wants from her father. I don't think Solomon realizes how much his love and approval matter to her. She won't admit to him—or to herself—how much she needs them now.

The car was quiet once again. Solomon surprised me letting Mary get the final word. I didn't know if he was thinking about what she said or just thought there was no point in continuing the discussion. His mind was made up. He didn't care what anyone said. I didn't say anything else in the car. But I had plenty to say later in our bedroom when we were finally alone. When we first got home, we explained everything to Momma and Paul.

Mary told her grandmother and brother what happened. She told them she'll be staying here to finish her degree at Wayne. It will take her a whole year instead of the semester she would need to finish at Howard. Paul loves his sister deeply. He's proud of her and wants to hear her sing the songs she performed with Ebony Hues. All Momma said to Mary was, "I understand." Momma spoke differently to me when we went upstairs. Mary and Paul were in bed, and I was helping Momma change into her nightgown. She said she always tried to tell me Mary is spoiled. "That gal think she can say and do whatever she want. She act out and 'speck to get away with it. Them folks at Howard were right to try to teach her a lesson. I jus' hope she learnt it. She don't seem to care 'bout wastin' yo' money and all them scholarships she got."

I told Momma Mary has apologized to Solomon and me several times since we left Washington. Momma says actions speak louder than words. Mary should get a job and pay her own college bills next year. I explained we don't need her money. I want her to concentrate on her studies. I'm caught in the middle again—respecting my mother and protecting my child.

When Solomon and I were alone in our bedroom, I spoke my mind. "Mary left school in April—weeks before she was due to graduate—just like I did twenty-five years ago. I remember how Poppa was upset then just like you are now."

Solomon was quick to say, "You left of your own free will. Mary was forced to leave."

"I just find it interesting that you are insisting that Mary graduate. You say you're keeping her at home to make sure of that. You never cared about me finishing my degree."

He said, "I didn't want you to have to work. I thought you wanted to be a full-time homemaker. But I would have supported you if you wanted to get your degree."

I said Mary is just like him. And we have to share some of the blame for her behavior. We raised her to be strong in her convictions. She defied a rule she believes to be unfair after she had asked more than once that it be changed. We encouraged her to pursue her dreams. Solomon was quick to voice his disapproval of her dream to be a professional singer. So she helped form a group without telling him. She did what she thought she had to do for a chance at a recording contract. I also reminded Solomon he has disappointed, hurt, and embarrassed me more than once. He always asked for my forgiveness, and I gave it to him. I even took the living proof of his betrayal into my home. I have grown to love him as if he were my own flesh and blood. Mary is our flesh and blood. We owe her our love and forgiveness. I don't care what anyone else thinks about her or us. Solomon insists he loves our daughter and forgives her. He says he will not soon forget what happened. So it will take time for her to earn his trust.

Solomon keeps saying he only wants what's best for his daughter. I tell him what he thinks is the best life for her might not be the life she wants for herself. I chose to marry him and not graduate. That's not what my father thought was best for me. The last twenty-five years haven't been perfect. Still, I think Solomon was the right choice for me. Solomon says he respects Mary's right to make her own choices. He worries about her getting a bad reputation. Men and women are seen differently by people. It may not be right or fair, but that's just the way it is. He doesn't want Mary to be seen as the kind of woman that men feel they can use or disrespect. I laughed. Our Mary will always demand respect. She is too strong and confident to be used by anyone.

Monday, June 23, 1941

Dear Friend,

Solomon and I stood tall as proud parents at church yesterday for the second week in a row. Reverend Gibson announced last Sunday during the service at Allen AME that Mary graduated with honors from Wayne University. Paul and the other graduates of Parkersville High School were recognized yesterday with their parents. We were busting out of our shirts when Reverend Gibson announced that Paul was accepted to all five colleges where he applied and chose to attend Tuskegee Institute in Alabama. Everyone applauded when Paul said he will major in biology to prepare for medical school. Paul hopes to find a cure for cancer because that's what took his mother from him. Solomon hopes Paul will change his mind. He wants Paul to become a lawyer so they can practice together.

Paul can surely do whatever he wants. He was captain of the Parkersville High School debate team and the baseball team. Some scouts tried to get him to play shortstop in the Negro National League. Solomon tried to run them out of town. He didn't need to. Paul was more interested in going straight to college. Mary worries about Paul living in the South. She has talked to him a lot about watching out for the crackers down there. We're all so proud of him. We just want him to be safe and have a good time in college. Momma wishes he would stay home to go to college. She loves him and depends on him. He is the only one in the house as tall as she is. So she loves to lean on his strong body for support going up and down the stairs and moving around in her sightless world.

Solomon paid for a huge graduation party for Paul Saturday night after they returned from a father-son outing in Detroit. They were gone from Thursday to Saturday afternoon. I'm not supposed to know about the specifics of their trip. But I know Solomon took Paul to a whorehouse for sexual instruction before he leaves for college. It's a disgusting tradition passed down from Solomon's grandfather Mister and continued by his father J.R. Paul didn't come into our lives til he was almost thirteen. So Solomon hadn't done it when Paul went through puberty. I don't think Paul was as thrilled about cavorting with whores as Solomon and his brothers were. Paul is a decent young man who respects women. I could tell that Solomon was disappointed when they returned home. I asked my husband what happened. He admitted Paul was hesitant at first. He did not plan to engage in sex before marriage. Solomon convinced him he should know how to pleasure his wife. So he accepted the opportunity to learn from professionals. On the way back home, Paul said he felt ashamed because of how much he enjoyed "his instruction." Solomon was surprised by Paul's attitude, but I was pleased. I love that Paul has morals. Maybe he'll break the pattern of adultery among the Mann men. Solomon swears that he didn't have sex in Detroit. I believe him. He wouldn't want Paul to see him as an adulterer. Solomon has cared about Paul's approval since he came to live here. It has made Solomon a better husband. He certainly never curbed his lustful habits because of my feelings.

I asked Solomon what he plans to do for Mary. She's spent the last fourteen months trying to earn his trust and his respect. She's been active in the church and community. And she's worked hard in college. She took two buses and a streetcar to and from campus the first term til she made friends with classmates from the area willing to drive her sometimes. She didn't try to start a singing career again, even after she turned twenty-one in April. She graduated with honors. She's going to teach in September and go for a master's degree at night. What more does Solomon want from her? He's doing so much for Paul but nothing for her. He told me he had a surprise for her. He didn't tell me what it was. I found out this evening the same time she did.

The doorbell rang during dinner. A man said he had a delivery for Mary. We were all excited to see a 1940 Plymouth Road King Coupe parked in front of the house with a big red bow tied around the hood. Mary was so happy. Solomon was beaming. Still, he wouldn't tell her he was proud of her. He said she needed suitable transportation to get her all the way to the east side of Detroit to teach music at the Trowbridge School. He didn't want her walking alone and waiting on buses coming home from Wayne at night. Mary and I knew it was more than that. He could have given her any car. But he chose the one he's heard her talking about to Paul and me. Solomon said he bought it because he got a good deal on a demonstrator from a friend of Mr. Parker. I don't know why he won't admit he's rewarding Mary for giving him what he wants by giving her what she wants. It's a stylish car with all the extras. "The Low-Priced Beauty with the Luxury Ride" is what they call it in the newspaper and magazine ads. Mary took Paul and me for a drive so we could see for ourselves how comfortable it is riding in it.

I think about how far God has brought us this past year. Tongues were wagging all over town when we returned home from Howard with Mary. May Ethel Carter is the worst hypocrite at church and in the whole town. She's always coming to me so worried about people having problems. What she really wants is to tell me about their problems. She isn't really hoping I can find a way to help them. She's just making sure that everyone knows their business. So I wasn't surprised to hear last April from my friends—Bessie, Cora, and Jean—and half of the Allen senior choir that May Ethel was trying to figure out how to help me after Mary got "kicked out of Howard for bad behavior." Mary and I told our friends what happened. They knew May Ethel was just fishing for "the dirty details" so she could spread her version of the truth. They didn't tell her anything. So she spread her guesses like they were facts to anyone who would listen. Bessie and Cora wanted me to "call her out." I knew nothing I said would matter to her. She and the folks listening to her were jealous of all the good attention Mary got most of her life. They wanted to be sure Mary got the bad attention she deserved for her "shameful" behavior. If I told them the truth, they would choose to believe "there was more to the story." I knew the gossip would eventually take a backseat to something new. Mary's trouble four hundred miles away was not as interesting as lots of things that have happened right here since then. Mary's life in Parkersville has given the gossips nothing bad to discuss in over a year. Now she's back in the spotlight again in a good way. She's got a teaching job. She's going to get her master's degree. Now she's got a fine car. Few white girls and no colored ones I know have much more than that going for them at twenty-one!

Thursday, November 5, 1942

Dear Friend,

I'm caught in the middle between Solomon and Mary again. Things have been going well with them for a long time. Solomon finally told her he is proud of her and trusts her again. The gossips—even May Ethel—have not mentioned her in quite a while. But Solomon found out last night that Mary is planning to date a man that he thinks is wrong for her. We know that May Ethel and others will soon be flapping their lips again about her.

Alvin Terrence Morgan is a good Christian man. He's treasurer in the lay organization at Allen AME. The problem is that Alvin is my age—forty-seven. That makes him twenty-five years older than Mary. Solomon says that he is too old to be chasing after our daughter. Alvin is old enough to be her father. That's true, and the two of them have a lot in common. They were both born and raised in the Deep South—Solomon in Mississippi and Alvin in Alabama. They are both Prince Hall Masons and World War I veterans. Alvin fought with the French Army in the Three Hundred Sixty-Ninth Regiment. He won the highest medal they give. The French treated him so good that he stayed in France for two years after the war was over. He settled in Detroit when he came back to the US, and he went to work at Ford's River Rouge plant. Like Solomon, he had problems related to a union. Alvin was caught up in violent attacks before Ford finally settled with the United Auto Workers (UAW) last year. Like Solomon, he owns one of the finest houses in Parkersville. He bought it four years ago.

Last night, Alvin asked for Solomon's permission to date Mary. It was right after the end of the Allen AME lay organization meeting. Solomon said he was shocked. He told Alvin, "Mary is grown and can date whomever she pleases. I have no objection if she desires to date you." He asked me if I had any inkling about the two of them. I spoke the truth when I said I didn't. Mary told me a few weeks ago that she was not interested in dating anyone. She likes going out on weekends with her girlfriends to parties and clubs in the city. She says most of the guys they meet are "trifling Jodies." They think they are "God's gift to women" because they're here while most young men are away in the war.

Mary says, "I am not looking for quick, meaningless romances with those jerks. I am also not willing to jump into a marriage with a man anxious to start a family in hopes of avoiding the draft. I do not want to commit to a soldier who will soon be going away, possibly not to return alive. Most of the men I meet are good for little more than a dance or two. Even the most attractive ones tend to be immature with limited experiences and conversation. They bore me."

I told Solomon if Mary had changed her mind, she didn't tell me. I also didn't know if she had seen Alvin outside of church. Mary came in from class at a quarter to ten. Solomon told her about his conversation with Alvin. He asked her if she would like to go out with Alvin. He acted surprised when she said, "Yes."

He asked, "Why do you want to date someone that old? Don't pressure yourself so much to get involved with someone that you settle for the best of the sorry lot available around here right now."

"I don't feel pressured, and I'm not settling for anything. I met plenty of men at Howard, in Detroit, and here before the war started. Alvin is the best of all of them. He's more interesting, more genteel, more fun, and more mature than any man I've ever met. Besides, I thought you'd be ecstatic! He is a good Christian man, and he thinks the world of both of you. He also thinks the world of me despite all the gossip spread around this town when I first returned home."

I asked, "Is that why you want to go out with him? Because you think it will please us?"

"No, Mama, I like being with him because it pleases *me*!"

Solomon's trust in her seemed shaken when he asked, "How well do you know Morgan?"

"Well enough to know that I like his company! And no, I don't know him biblically."

"I wasn't inferring that you two had been intimate," Solomon explained. "I merely wondered how and when you got to know each other. I've never seen you say anything to each other beyond polite greetings and simple acknowledgments."

"I ran into him a couple of times when I was with my friends in Detroit. He talked to us and looked out for us, even though we didn't need him to do that. He is a good conversationalist, and come on, Mama, you know he is handsome and dapper. By the way, do you know that he speaks French?"

Papa responded, "I know that he lived in France for a while after he served in World War I. It makes sense that he would have picked up some of the language there."

That was Solomon's way of reminding her how old Alvin is. I know Mary got his point, but she didn't say anything. Solomon waited for her to react. He continued when she didn't. "I don't object to you two seeing each other if that is what you want. I have nothing against him. I just would not have thought of you as a likely couple. I thought you would choose someone closer to your age and educational background. However, you are a grown woman, free to make your own decisions. Most of the time, you have made good ones. So I respect your decision to see Morgan socially."

"That's good, Papa, but try calling him Alvin. Use his first name. Forget about his age. He's dating your daughter. So do your father thing with him."

It was late. Mary had to drive to Detroit to teach this morning. We all chuckled and went upstairs to bed. Solomon still has concerns about Mary and Alvin. I urged him to keep them to himself. Alvin is a good man. Mary will figure out if he's intelligent enough to keep her interest. He is well read and keeps up with the news enough to have good conversations with Solomon. Solomon admitted he encouraged Alvin to find a good woman to wed. He didn't mean our daughter though. I reminded him they're only dating. He may be serious. Mary seems to be infatuated with him but has not said she's interested in getting married to him.

Saturday, January 2, 1943

Dear Friend,

    Solomon had a rough start to the New Year. He's frustrated and upset. Both our children have made decisions he feels are wrong. Mary is engaged to be married to a man Solomon finds unsuitable. Paul is planning to train as a pilot to fight in the war. Solomon thinks both of his children are throwing their lives away. He feels that Mary would be happier with a man "closer to her age and her educational background." He's afraid Paul could lose his life "before he realizes his potential and fulfills his dreams as a man." Solomon is certain his children are misguided. He's trying to remain calm as he tries to reason with them. He is frustrated that he hasn't been able to change their minds. He's listening to my warning to choose his words carefully, trying to show them he respects them as adults.

    Mary's fiancé—Alvin—is a wonderful Christian man. He's Solomon's friend and works with him in the Allen AME laymen's organization. Solomon likes him well enough, but he voiced his concerns to me. He thinks Alvin is too old for Mary and has told her that. Solomon admitted to me he wanted Mary to choose a professional man. Alvin works in the Ford foundry and makes good money. But Solomon expected Mary to be the wife of a doctor, lawyer, or at least a college graduate. He won't say that to her for fear of sounding like the snobs and hypocrites he's taught his children to despise. He raised Mary and Paul to value education and good manners. But he told them not to become uppity Negroes who look down on others with less. He taught them true class is based on one's kindness, goodness, and faith. He can't deny that Alvin has class based on those things. So he only talks about the twenty-five-year difference in his and Mary's ages.

    Momma is on Solomon's side. And she has not kept quiet about her feelings. "Why Mary wanna be with an old man? Old men are set in their ways. Like old dogs, you can't teach 'em nothin.' He gon' try to run her life like another daddy. She don't like minding one daddy. How she gon' like havin' two? Mary can't stand bein' told what to do. She need a young man she can boss around. She ain't ask me, but you oughta warn her, not that she'd listen to you either. She's stubborn like that. And it's gon' cost her. Mark my words."

Momma and Solomon also agree about Paul's decision to fight in the war. Paul wants to serve his country like both of his fathers did in the First World War. He says they both made it home safely and he will also. He doesn't know the man he believes fathered him didn't return home alive. Solomon wants to tell him that. But he can't without telling him the whole truth about how he came to be. Mary and I don't want Paul to go to war either. I shared with Paul how I worried every day Solomon was overseas. But he's determined to join the group of young airmen in Tuskegee. He headed back to Alabama this morning. He promised to try to stay safe. He says he'll finish college and medical school after the war. Solomon's fear and frustration lead him into my arms. Making love every night comforts us both. We don't think about our fears for Mary and Paul, at least for a little while. For awhile, we don't think at all. We just feel our passion. And it feels good.

Monday, May 3, 1943

Dear Friend,

I awoke this morning from the first full night's sleep I've had in months. I rested happily. All of my planning and hard work paid off. My dear Mary had a wedding like few white folks and no Negroes have seen in a long time. Mary looked beautiful in the gown I made for her. All of her bridesmaids and the flower girl were picture-perfect as well. Some folks in town feel it's inappropriate to wear lavish gowns in this time of imposed rations. Momma asked why Mary's wedding had to be such a big deal. She said nobody in our family ever had a big wedding, and all of the marriages—except Thella's—lasted til death parted them. She warned me, "Don't make so much of the wedding day. Mary gon' care more 'bout making the day perfect than tryin' to make her marriage work fo' the rest of her life." But I didn't care. I've worked hard for enough rich white brides to do nothing less for my own pretty brown one.

I was determined for Mary to have the best wedding day imaginable. Still, I paid attention to the needs of our soldiers. After all, my dear Paul is training to serve as a pilot. I made Mary's gown out of rayon, since silk is in high demand for making parachutes, and cotton is needed for duffle bags and uniforms. I added embroideries and beautiful laces to make her gown, train, and veil as elegant as those seen before the war in *LIFE* and *Vogue* magazines. Mary's bridal gown is the most detailed and exquisite one I ever made. I attached hundreds of tiny pearls and seed beads by hand to her gown and made twenty-two covered buttons to fasten it down the back. The train was accented with pearl and rhinestone clusters like the ones I attached to the buckram crown under her veil. Mary chose to carry a simple bouquet of half a dozen lilies held together by periwinkle satin ribbon tied in a simple bow with thigh-length streamers. The ribbon was her "something blue." The pearl earrings Solomon gave me on our twentieth anniversary were her "borrowed" items. Her "old" item was her grandmother Juliette's embroidered handkerchief. I tucked it inside the base of her left sleeve. Of course, the dress, veil, shoes, and undergarments were all new. A shiny new silver quarter was placed on the inner sole of each of her shoes. That's supposed to bring money and prosperity into her marriage.

Mary made beautiful pastel gowns with matching turbans for her bridesmaids with help from Bessie, Cora, and Jean. The dresses are identical in design, but each is a different color—yellow, peach, lavender, and periwinkle. I made a pretty little white dress for the flower girl. Mary made the most adorable periwinkle knickers and tie with a white shirt for the ring bearer. Alvin and Solomon wore tuxedos. The groomsmen wore black suits with dress shirts Agnes and June made for them in colors corresponding to the bridesmaids they escorted. The one exception was my dear son—Paul. He had a weekend pass to come home from Tuskegee to be in his sister's wedding. He looked particularly handsome in his United States Army Air Forces dress uniform. I couldn't help but notice how much Paul has matured since he started training as a pilot. He's only twenty. But he has an air about him that makes him seem at least five years older. Solomon and I are both so proud of him, and he is thrilled to be flying. He says he can't wait to get into combat. I hope that the war ends before his unit is sent overseas. I didn't tell him that. I just confessed I pray every day for his safety.

The entire congregation of Allen AME attended the wedding. They were joined by Mary's and Alvin's friends and coworkers, and out-of-town AME lay people who are close to Solomon. The church was filled to capacity and beautifully decorated with flowers and bows at the ends of every pew. The reception at the town hall afterward provided a wonderful dinner buffet. Close friends and family helped by allowing us to use some of their meat rations. Mr. Parker allowed Solomon to purchase extra meat for the occasion. Others contributed homegrown vegetables and tubers to make the side dishes. Bessie, Cora, Jean, Agnes, and June combined their rations of sugar, butter, and milk to make the seven-tiered wedding cake decorated with white roses and light blue bows made from the butter cream frosting. The featured drink was everyone's favorite—frappé made from Vernor's Ginger Ale mixed with fruit sherbets and fresh fruits. We also offered homemade lemonade, iced tea, and water. The music was provided by a group of music teachers Mary knows. They play together at weekend events to pick up extra cash. There was a surprise appearance by Mary's jazz combo from Howard—Ebony Hues. They performed two of their hit records and a song they wrote for Mary and Alvin. It hasn't been recorded yet.

Mary's wedding is the talk of the town and beyond. Some guests said it was the nicest event they ever attended. Solomon said the visiting laymen from around the state thought everything was wonderful. Mary and Alvin were so happy. They thanked me before they left for their honeymoon. May Ethel was true to form with mean things to say after church services yesterday. Cora told me that May Ethel said, "That wedding must have cost a fortune. They should've bought war bonds to help our boys fighting overseas. All that showy stuff isn't necessary when two people are really in love. And that fancy white wedding dress can't 'white wash' the bride's past."

Cora did what she keeps telling me to do. She told May Ethel to shut up because she didn't know what she was talking about. Bessie told May Ethel that since I didn't ask her for any money to pay for the wedding, it was none of her business how much I spent "of my husband's and my money." Jean said May Ethel got all puffed up. She tried to walk away, but Momma's attendant—Mrs. Washington—let her have it. "You're the one that needs white wash for your mouth. Bea and Mary are both good people. You're just jealous and mean." May Ethel couldn't talk back to that sweet lady old enough to be her mother. I love my friends, and I did enjoy hearing how they hushed May Ethel. I honestly don't care about her. God gave us a perfect spring day. He helped me give my Mary a perfect wedding. And He brought her brother—my dear Paul—home safely to be a part of it. May Ethel can't say anything that will steal my joy.

Tuesday, July 4, 1944

Dear Friend,

The annual Independence Day barbeque was fun. Mary and Alvin came. So did some of Mary's friends from Detroit, but I missed Paul. The parade of veterans and soldiers home on leave made me look forward to seeing my brave son marching down Main Street in his uniform next year or the year after.

Paul came home for a few days at Christmas and again after he graduated from pilot training in February. I miss seeing his smile, hearing him call me "Ma Bea," and feeling his strong arms around me when he hugs me warmly. I wish he was still in college. He'd be home now for the summer. Instead, he's in some town in Italy I never heard of—Ramitelli. I know that he's in the Three Hundred Thirty-Second Fighter Group. They escort bombers. Paul says he won't be writing as often as before. He can't tell us any specifics about their missions when he does write. I understand. It was the same when Solomon was in France in World War I.

In the last letter he wrote before he went overseas, Paul told us he's in love with a Tuskegee coed from Birmingham. He can't wait for us to meet her as soon as the war is over. Solomon said he was likely to have many girlfriends before he's old enough to settle down. I'm not so sure. Paul dated girls in Parkersville but never had an actual girlfriend. The way he talked about his girl—Opal—I thought she might be "the one." Paul described her as "a good student, a devout Christian, and a kind and loving person." He met her family. He said they're very close. She has two elder brothers and a younger sister. Both of her brothers are soldiers but not airmen.

Solomon was shocked and upset when we received the first letter from Italy. Paul married Opal before he left the country. Solomon wanted him to finish his education before he got tied down in a marriage. I reminded him that he asked me to marry him before I got my degree. He responded that I'm a woman. My husband is supposed to take care of me. Paul is the man who is expected to provide for his wife. He has a lot of schooling ahead of him if he is going to be a doctor or a lawyer. It'll be harder to do that if he is married and working. I agreed it would be difficult, but reminded Solomon that he was a husband and a father working full time at Ford when he was in law school. He finished on time with honors. There's no reason to believe Paul is not capable of doing the same.

I'm anxious to meet Paul's wife. She sounds delightful. Still I want to judge for myself if she is a good match for my son. Paul wrote to Mary about her. Mary says Paul is the only one Opal has to please. It doesn't matter whether we like her or not. That's what Mary says, but I know she's just as concerned as I am. I want to be sure Opal loves Paul as much as he loves her. I hope she'll support Paul's goals like I did Solomon's. I'm praying she won't hold him back. Maybe her love will give Paul more encouragement to keep safe and come back home to her and all of us.

Tuesday, May 8, 1945

Dear Friend,

The newspaper headlines today announced the end of the war in Europe. They call it VE Day—Victory in Europe Day. There is rejoicing in a lot of houses. But there is no joy in this house. VE Day came forty-five days too late for my Paul. He died March 24. The news was delivered to Paul's next of kin—his wife Opal. She called us. Solomon, Mary, Alvin, and I went to Alabama for his memorial. We met our beloved Paul's wife only after she became his widow.

Opal is a lovely young woman. She spent hours with Mary and me talking about Paul. She said she loved him. He was a wonderful man, respectful and kind to her always. Their courtship was brief. But they knew they wanted to be together for life. They wanted to fully express their love before he left for war but not before they were married. So they wed in a simple ceremony at the local Catholic Church. Her parents and sister were there. They admired Paul and approved of the marriage. I studied her as she talked. I know why Paul loved her. I know that being with her made him happy. That comforts me, but nothing eases the pain in my heart.

It was such a sad mass. My grief was unbearable. Mary felt the same. Opal and her family were heartbroken. Solomon was overcome with grief and anger. He read the letter Opal got from Col. Benjamin O. Davis—Commander of the Three Hundred Thirty-Second Fighter Group. He wrote of Paul's bravery and his heroism in combat. He said Paul shot down several enemy planes that day before his plane was brought down by antiaircraft fire. Solomon read the letter from Colonel Davis over and over. He kept asking Opal for details she didn't know. He has written to everyone he can think of since we returned home to get more information about Paul's last days. He's devastated and wants answers nobody can or will give him.

I can't put into words the sorrow I feel. I don't care about finding reasons or blame for Paul's death. No information will bring him back to me in this life. I won't be reunited with him til God sees fit to take me home where I know he is. I wonder about his last moments of life. Did he know what was going to happen? He had no priest in the plane to give him last rites. Did he have time to pray? I know he didn't fear death. Still, I wonder if an angel—surely his mother Dorothy—came for him. It's hard for me to sleep most nights. I lie in bed wondering if my Paul was at peace as life left his body. I pray to Almighty God for his immortal soul. I pray he knows I loved him truly as my son. I'll cherish my memories of him forever.

I ache for my sons. Solomon Jr. and all the others I miscarried were with me so briefly. I loved them. But I can only imagine them as the men they might have become. Paul was with me eight and a half years. I helped raise him from boyhood to manhood. He wasn't my flesh and blood. Yet I loved him like he was. Losing him hurts even worse than the others. It's all so backward. Paul should be telling Opal and their children about his Ma Bea after my death. I shouldn't be telling his widow about him. I know God has a plan, and He knows best. But I can't imagine why He sent me Paul and made me love him only to take him from me. I don't know why he took away the four sons I carried inside me. My faith is strong, but it's being tested. Sweet Jesus, please help me accept God's will, even though I don't understand it.

Claudia's Maternal Ancestry

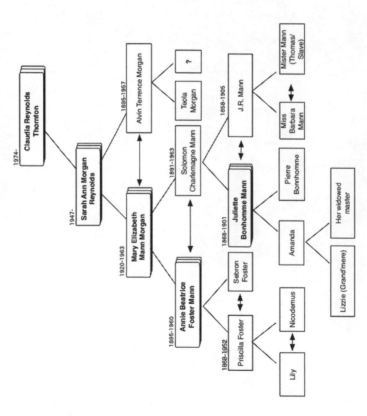

Claudia Reynolds Thornton
1974-

Sarah Ann Morgan Reynolds
1947-

Alvin Terrence Morgan
1895-1957

Mary Elizabeth Mann Morgan
1920-1963

Teola Morgan

?

Solomon Charlemagne Mann
1891-1963

Annie Beatrice Foster Mann
1895-1960

J.R. Mann
1858-1905

Juliette Bonhomme Mann
1868-1901

Sebron Foster

Priscilla Foster
1868-1952

Mister Mann (Thomas/ Slave)

Miss Barbara Mann

Pierre Bonhomme

Amanda

Nicodemus

Lily

Her widowed master

Lizzie (Grandmere)

Mother (left), Father(right)

Wife   Husband

Part 4

EXCERPTS FROM THE JOURNALS OF
MARY ELIZABETH MANN MORGAN

November 22, 1940

Another Friday night spent at home with Mama and Gran! A letter
came today from Gordon Johnson, the bassist in Ebony Hues, saying
that the group is under contract with Decca Records and has been on
tour since July promoting their first record, a song I used to sing with
them. Emma Randall is singing with them now. I knew her at the
conservatory at Howard. I believe that I'm a better performer than
Emma, and Gordon says the guys think that too. Nonetheless, Emma
has the record deal I wanted, and she is touring with "my" group. I
wrote back to Gordon, congratulating him and the group on their
success. I told him that I will try to come to see them if they play in the
Detroit area sometime after April, when I turn twenty-one. However,
I know that will not happen. I would have to lie to Papa because he
would not let me spend time with those men whom he holds responsible
for filling my head with foolishness and leading me astray, getting
myself suspended from Howard. He would not approve of me going to
clubs period. I am working too hard to earn Papa's trust to risk getting

caught in a lie. Besides, it would hurt me too much to sit in the audience watching Emma on stage in what should be my spotlight. I believe all things happen for a reason. Someday I'll find fame as a singer when the time is right. For now, I will remain focused on rebuilding the loving, trusting relationship I shared with Papa before he came to carry me home from Howard.

I haven't had much of a social life since I returned home last spring. Most of my time is spent working in the church and keeping up with my studies at Wayne so I'll get my degree in June. As soon as I came home, Papa assigned me a Sunday School class to teach, and I began singing in the young-adult choir at Allen AME. We rehearse Tuesday and Thursday evenings, and we sing at the service on second Sunday every month. It is now directed by my best friend since childhood, Gladys Renfroe Simpson. In April, Gladys asked me to assist her with the children's choir, and in September, I became its director. How things have changed since Gladys and I directed the children's choir when we were kids! We started that choir so we could escape sitting quietly through what we used to think were boring sermons. We took all of the other children our age and younger downstairs before the sermon started, and we ran their rehearsals until service ended. It was a winning solution for the children, who didn't want to sit quietly in church any more than we did; for their parents, who tired of the never-ending work of keeping them still; and for Reverend Gibson, who got to preach his sermon without the distractions of fidgeting children. Back then, the children's choir sang every fifth Sunday, which usually occurred only twice a year. Now, there are two choirs for school-age youngsters. The young children in elementary school are in children's choir. They still rehearse and sing as before, but now with two adults and two teens in charge of them during the service. Gladys and I direct the junior-senior high school students in the youth choir, which rehearses on Wednesday evenings and sings for service monthly every fourth Sunday. That works out well for me because I have come to enjoy attending church services every Sunday. I appreciate the sermons, and I like sitting in the choir loft. From there, I have a perfect view of the pastor and of the entire congregation. I like to look into the eyes of everyone, those who genuinely wish the best for me and those who whisper lies and speculations about me while they listen to sermons about love and forgiveness.

During the summer, Papa had me serve as a counselor and oratorical competition coach in Bible camp. He also hired me to assist him in his law office, where I did research for him and transcribed his barely legible notes from client interviews. Monday and Friday nights, I assisted Mama with her sewing and cooking classes at our house. It was clear to me that Papa was making sure that I was keeping busy and productive in plain sight of the good people of Parkersville and the church laymen who visited from around the state. It was his strategy for monitoring me and for restoring my reputation. Honestly, I don't care what people say about me. However, I do want Papa to trust me again. I know that Papa cares about my reputation and its impact on his own. I am truly sorry for any shame my actions have brought on him. He may no longer be mayor, but he is still the most influential man in town. Most people are indebted to him in one way or another. Those who don't owe him realize that they may need his help in the future. The current mayor, aware of Papa's continued relationship with Mr. Parker, consults him and curries his favor on almost every aspect of life in Parkersville. Papa is also the most influential layman in the church. He has served as Superintendent of Sunday School and head of the Trustee Board since Allen AME was established. He led the fund-raising that built and paid off the mortgages on the church building and the parsonage next to it (where Reverend Gibson and his family reside). Reverend Gibson knows how friendly Papa is with the presiding elder, bishop, and lay leaders in Michigan. So he seeks Papa's support in most church matters. There are those who think my father is too high and mighty. They relish any opportunity to whisper snide remarks about him. I won't give them reason to suggest that he shouldn't control so much of what happens in the town and in the church when he cannot control his own daughter. So I'm toeing the line now.

Since I started classes at Wayne University in September, I dropped most of my summer duties and continued just my choral and teaching activities in the church. Papa wants me to concentrate on my studies so I will graduate in June. Wayne is very different from Howard, but it is pleasant enough. There are only a few black students here, and I feel the prejudice. Yet I generally get along with most of the white students and faculty. Some professors grade my work lower than I know they should. I have seen the "A" work of some white students, and I know that my "B" work was much better. Other professors treat me fairly. One of those is

Dr. Fredrickson. He is my self-appointed advisor and has recommended me for a fellowship that will help pay the tuition for my master's degree. I enjoy my classes and the social scene I recently discovered in Detroit. Papa keeps me on a fairly tight leash. However, occasionally on a Friday or Saturday night, I ride to the city with girlfriends from campus. We go to block parties sponsored by local businesses like Wonder Bread. Large speakers mounted on big trucks play canned music, and everybody comes out to dance in the street. There are block parties most every weekend. They are free and lots of fun, but I rarely get to more than one in a month.

So my behavior since I returned home in April has been beyond reproach. Sunday and Monday evenings, I am at home. When I'm not studying, I play board games or cards with my parents and my adopted younger brother, my ba-bro Paul. On Tuesdays, Wednesdays, and Thursdays, I am in choir rehearsals at the church. Most Fridays and Saturdays, Paul goes out with friends, and I am at home chatting with Mama and Gran. Sometimes I visit with Gladys at her house with her family. Gladys married Charles Simpson right after she graduated from high school and is now a housewife with two young sons, Charles Jr. and Lester, four and two. She and I have remained close. Gladys and I used to be inseparable, but her husband, Charles, doesn't seem to want her spending too much time with me now. I guess he is worried that I will influence his wife to be as defiant and "wild" as the rumor mill says that I have become. Gladys pays no attention to her husband's urgings for her to distance herself from me. We are together three nights a week rehearsing at church. She also brings the boys with her to my parents' home at least once a week. Papa seems happy to see me maintain my friendship with Gladys. He says he hopes that she will have a positive influence on me.

Gladys and I are not concerned about influencing each other; we just enjoy being able to share our deepest feelings with each other. I told Gladys the whole story about Ebony Hues, Fletcher Henderson, Decca Records, and how much I still want a career as a professional singer. I also told her that I feel I owe it to my parents to finish college and become a teacher. Mama has worked so hard for me to become one, and Papa is so against my becoming a singer. As much as I hate to admit it, I need his approval and pride to make me truly happy. Gladys confided in me that while she does love Charles, she rushed to marry him to get out of her parents' home. Her father had turned to alcohol after losing his job at Mr. Parker's plant for chronic lateness. He was an abusive drunk, argumentative and demanding. He constantly berated her and her mother, calling them "ungrateful bitches" and yelling at them both for not taking better care of him and the house. He was always apologetic when he sobered up, but he got drunk again as soon as he found money to buy a bottle of bourbon. Her mother did clerical work at Parker's plant, and she also worked three nights a week and on Saturdays as a housekeeper at various homes in Detroit to pay the mortgage and to keep her family eating.

Marrying Charles offered Gladys a way to distance herself from her father's erratic behavior while staying close enough to her mother to get to her in an emergency. She wanted to go to college, at least part time. Charles had completed two years of college before they were married. He continued to take classes at night while working as a mailman during the day. Gladys says he initially agreed that she would go to college when he earned his bachelor's degree. However, when Charles Jr. was born eighteen months after their marriage, Charles said she needed to stay home to take care of their son. After Lester was born, Charles was even more determined for her to be a housewife. Gladys says Charles is probably more worried about me getting her excited about going to college than he is about me influencing her to act wild. Now that Charles has completed his degree, he says he wants to continue to get a master's or maybe a law degree like Papa. Gladys wants to get a degree now before he gets another one. She says he acts pompous enough already, talking down to her like she's ignorant and he knows more than she does about everything. He remains adamant about her not pursuing a degree yet. He says she should wait until Lester is in first grade. Then she can take classes during the day while the boys are in school. That will be four years from now. Charles will be a professional, maybe a lawyer, and Gladys will still have only a high school diploma. She does not want that. Gladys and I are both putting our dreams on hold for now. However, we know that, eventually, we will find ways to go after what we want to do.

January 27, 1942

My life is busy and fun again because I am an adult and I have more freedom. There are still some rules living in my parents' home but not as many as before, now that Papa trusts me. I have proven to him that I am responsible. I've decided to put my singing career on hold for now, at least until I complete my master's. Papa probably thinks that I have abandoned my plans to sing professionally, and I haven't told him otherwise. I like the way we are rebuilding our relationship, and there is no need to spoil it with talk of things that are not going to happen in the near future. I enjoy teaching music at the Trowbridge School in the Paradise Valley section of Detroit. I would rather teach in high school, but I like my students, and I've made friends among the teachers.

Teaching away from Parkersville, I feel less like I am under a microscope. I spend time with unmarried friends I made at Wayne and Trowbridge. Josephine "Josie" Robinson and Cassandra "Sandy" Simmons teach at Trowbridge, and Nancy Clark is my classmate at Wayne. At twenty-five, Josie is the oldest in the group. She graduated from Wayne University and started teaching at Trowbridge three years ago. Sandy, twenty-three, started teaching at Trowbridge last year. Like me, she attended a Negro college in the South, Tennessee State University, where she pledged a sorority. She's not a Delta like I am. She pledged Alpha Psi Chapter of Alpha Kappa Alpha (AKA) Sorority, Inc. The two of us share stories about Greek life on Negro campuses and engage in lightly competitive banter. Josie gets annoyed and calls us a couple of Southern belle sorority snobs. She says it in jest, but Nancy naively worries that we are all upset with each other, even though we explain it is just friendly teasing. Nancy, twenty-two, is a Wayne alum and non-Greek like Josie. We are all really close and spend most of our free time together. We go to dinner and movies together. Occasionally, we enjoy dancing on Friday or Saturday night at "black-and-tan" clubs in Paradise Valley and free block parties. Sometimes, we go dancing on Mondays, when it's colored night at the Graystone Ballroom.

I am so glad not to be married now. At twenty-one, I feel like my adult life is just beginning, and I enjoy being free to explore my options. Gladys is just two years older than I am, and I see how restricted her activities are. It is as though she traded living according to her parents' rules to living by her husband's. I am not ready to settle down. Now that Papa trusts me again, I feel in control of my life. I am free to come and go as I please without curfews, except that I cannot stay out all night. That doesn't bother me. Most of the parties and clubs close by 1 a.m. Mama and Papa have made it clear that if the sun rises before I am settled in my own bed, then I better not come home alone. I better return accompanied by my husband "with a ring on my finger and a marriage license in my purse." I have so much more I want to do before I get married. I want to finish graduate school and get a position teaching music in a high school. I also want to travel to places I have only seen in magazines. Along the way, I still want to see if I can make it as a recording artist.

October 24, 1942

I hate that the U.S. entered the war. A number of young men in Parkersville and everywhere else have been drafted or enlisted to fight, and possibly die, overseas. We've attended too many funerals this year, supporting families who lost fathers, husbands or sons in battle. My ba-bro, Paul, is in college, and I pray he does not have to fight in this war. I don't want anything to happen to him, and I don't want him to leave school. He has a bright future ahead of him as a doctor. He has a number of years of schooling ahead of him before he can practice medicine. I hope he won't have any interruptions, especially any that will put him in harm's way. For those of us not in the military, life is not dangerous but it is not normal. We don't have it nearly as bad as people in Europe who are being bombed and invaded by the Germans and Italians. We are dealing with adjustments and inconveniences due to the absence of so many young men and the rationing of certain foods and other necessities. I am glad that I got my car before Pearl Harbor was attacked. The automobile factories have been converted to build military vehicles and equipment, and they have stopped producing cars for civilians. I can't imagine how difficult it would be to get to work and campus without my car and my social life would be nonexistent. With gasoline rations in place, I can't buy enough gas to drive to work every day. I share driving with three other teachers who live in nearby towns. We each drive the others to and from work in Detroit once a week Monday through Thursday. My day is Wednesday. I also drive to work on Fridays so I can go out with Josie, Sandy, and Nancy in the city.

Last Friday, the sixteenth, the girls and I went out for a night of fun at Club 666 (The Three Sixes). We were sipping champagne poured from the bottle we ordered for our table. Josie directed our attention to a distinguished older gentleman sitting alone two tables away from us. I recognized him instantly as a man from my church. He usually sits near Papa, and he smiles at me when I'm singing. "Wow!" I muttered. "I'd never expect to see him here." Josie wanted to meet him, but before I could figure out a proper way to arrange an introduction, he recognized me and made his way to our table.

"Hello, Mary and ladies," he said in his sexy baritone voice with a slight Southern drawl lingering from his youthful years in Alabama.

"Hi, Mr. Mor—"

He interrupted me, "Alvin, please."

I felt silly. "Of course...Alvin Morgan. These are my friends: Nancy Clark, Josephine Robinson, and Cassandra Simmons. Josie, Sandy, and I teach at Trowbridge together. Nancy and I took classes together at Wayne. She teaches English at Northern High School."

He pulled a chair to our table. He sat and talked with us awhile and ordered another bottle of champagne for us. When no other men approached the table, he realized that he was probably being mistaken for the father of one of us, so he volunteered to move back to his table. Josie suggested that he dance with her instead. While they were dancing, Sandy and I were asked by other young men to dance. When we all returned to the table, Alvin asked me to dance. If he was feeling paternalistic and protective of us at first, he got over it when he realized that Josie was obviously flirting with him. He is rather handsome, standing almost six feet tall with a firm muscular physique. His tawny complexion and coal black wavy hair instantly attract attention from women of all ages. He has dreamy dark bedroom eyes, a chiseled nose, and a thick mustache that rests comfortably on his thick, juicy lips. His broad smile shows off his polished aligned teeth, yellowed slightly from smoking. He is suave and debonair, better dressed than most of the men we see at the clubs. He walks with a strong, sexy gait, and he is an incredibly smooth dancer. It is hard for me to believe he is around the same age as my parents. He looks and acts so much younger.

For the rest of the evening, Sandy, Nancy, and Josie danced and talked to different men in the club, but I spent all my time talking and dancing with Alvin. We discussed politics and the war. He wondered if the colored soldiers in this war would have experiences similar to those of colored soldiers in World War I. He wondered how many of them would see combat, if they would have adequate equipment and provisions, if they would be treated with respect by white American soldiers, and how they would be treated by the British and the French. Papa served in World War I, and he was angered by a lot of what occurred then. However, he won't talk much about it, so I was genuinely interested in hearing what Alvin had to say about the things that happened to him during that war. Alvin and I shared our views on how the current war would affect race relations, the economy, and women going to work. I told Alvin that I vehemently oppose double standards of behavior and opportunities based on gender. I find Alvin's views refreshingly similar to mine. Alvin says that women should not be expected to suppress their free will at home or in life. The more we talk, the more I like him. And I really like dancing with him. I like the way he turns and tosses me when we jitterbug, and I like feeling his chest expand and contract against my cheek when he is breathing in rhythm with slow music. Most of all, I like his thoughtfulness and gentlemanliness.

At the end of that night at the Three Sixes, Alvin wanted to ensure my safety getting home. So he followed me in his car as I spent almost forty minutes taking my friends to their homes in Detroit and then drove almost an hour back to Parkersville. I told Gladys about my encounter with Alvin, and I knew without asking her that she would not tell anyone else unless or until I told her that she could. At first, I wasn't ready to talk about my infatuation with Alvin to anyone else. I wasn't sure whether his feelings for me were paternal, friendly, or something different. Until I was certain that we were entering into a relationship, I saw no reason to mention that we spent time together. I persuaded my girlfriends to return to the Three Sixes last night, hoping to see Alvin there again. He was there and seemed happy to see us. During the course of dancing and talking, I mentioned that I am going to see some of my college friends when Ebony Hues performs at Broad's Club Zombie over Thanksgiving weekend. I was pleasantly surprised that he has heard their recordings played on the radio, and he would like to see them in person with me. I said that I would like that as well. Then Alvin told me that he wanted to ask Papa's permission to ask me out if I was agreeable. I told him that I would be delighted to date him and agreed that he should talk to Papa before calling on me at our home.

I know that Papa will be surprised that his friend wants to date his daughter. He may or may not approve. However, I am twenty-two, and I don't actually need his permission. I would like his blessing, but whether he likes it or not, I like Alvin. Papa says he is a good Christian man, and I want to spend more time with him socially. That really should be all that matters.

January 4, 1943

I haven't driven my Plymouth to Detroit on a Friday or Saturday night in two months. Alvin's 1940 Lincoln-Zephyr sedan pulls up in front of the house, and he comes to the door to take me on exciting dates. Sometimes we see Josie, Sandy, and Nancy at the jazz clubs in Paradise Valley: The Paradise, Broad's Club Zombie, Lee's Sensation, and, of course, Club 666, where Alvin and I had our first social encounter. Alvin and I are alone at most other venues like the Graystone Ballroom on colored night. That's where we enjoy the likes of Duke Ellington's and Jimmie Lunceford's orchestras battling local bands like McKinney's Cotton Pickers and the Graystone house band led by Jean Goldkette. Alvin introduced me to the Vanity Ballroom, where we dance to the big band music of Duke Ellington, Tommy Dorsey, and Benny Goodman. Sometimes he picks me up early so we can start our date seeing a movie at the Fox Theater downtown or the Fisher Theater further north before we go dining and dancing.

It is funny to me that the difference in our ages seems like such a big deal to my parents and most of the middle-aged population of Parkersville. However, none of my peers seem to care. They all like Alvin and accept him readily into our fold. Josie, Sandy, and Nancy have been comfortable with him since the night they met him. The same was true when I introduced him to Ebony Hues the Friday after Thanksgiving. It had been two and half years since I saw the guys I used to call my big brothers when we performed together. I had never seen Emma Randall performing with them in my place. I wasn't sure how I would react to watching Emma in the spotlight on stage, while I sat in the dark with the rest of the audience. It is one thing to hear their records on the radio and jukeboxes, but I thought it might be too painful to see them in a live performance. Nonetheless, I promised

Gordon, the bassist and my best friend in the group, that I would come to see them the next time they played in Detroit. So Alvin and I went to Broad's Club Zombie to see Ebony Hues perform.

The members of the group liked Alvin when they met him that night. Emma said he is charming, and all the guys said he is cool. They had no idea how old he is, and it never came up in conversation. During their last set, Gordon called me to the stage and invited me to sing "Jumpin' into Love," my signature song when I sang with them at Howard. It was the song that first impressed Fletcher Henderson and the Decca scout. An upbeat version of it became their first hit on Decca records with Emma Randall singing lead. Emma was gracious when the group and I performed the original slower version, my version, and the crowd went wild. Alvin jumped to his feet, starting the standing ovation I received from everyone, including Emma and the manager at Club Zombie. I felt wonderful, liberated from my longstanding jealousy of Emma for inheriting what I believed was rightfully my dream life. As I stood there on stage soaking in the applause, I realized that I am truly happy with my life now, happy enough to reject the manager's offer for me to perform there in the spring.

Alvin encouraged me to consider the offer. He says he will support me if I want to sing professionally, and I appreciate that more than he can imagine. Still, I do not think that the timing is right. I am just completing my master's, and I am ready to see how that will expand my opportunities in teaching. When I dreamed of a singing career, I was free of attachments, ready to travel and perform all over the world. However, in that moment before I left the stage, I realized that I have a different dream for now, a dream that involves a white dress, lots of flowers, and the man who was gazing at me with so much love and pride in his eyes. I was smiling the whole time I walked from the stage back to Alvin at our table. I didn't say anything about my dream to him. I just thanked him and kissed him when he praised my "extraordinary voice and stage presence."

I shared my epiphany with Gladys after church that Sunday and with my girlfriends after school the day after that. They all like Alvin, and they believe that he deeply loves me. So they are happy that I love him in return. I did not tell my parents when I realized that I want to spend my life with Alvin. I didn't trust myself to behave properly if they spoke against my hope of marrying him. Papa, in particular, has a vision of how I should live my life. He raised me to think for myself, but he can be judgmental and disapproving when my dreams and plans do not match the ones he has for me. He keeps trying to squash my dream of singing, and I know he will try to do the same to my dream of being Mrs. Alvin Terrence Morgan.

The only other person I told about my epiphany was my ba-bro, Paul. He didn't come home for Thanksgiving. Papa would have happily given him the money to take the train from Tuskegee to Parkersville, but Paul said it didn't make sense to spend two days riding on trains and have only two days to spend with his family, especially since he would be coming home for a whole month just two weeks later. On December 15, when he came home for Christmas and semester break, I told him of my secret love and desire for a union with Alvin. Paul spent time alone with Alvin and grilled him concerning his intentions toward me. Alvin says Paul is even more protective of me than Papa. Neither of them will tell me what was said during their conversation, but Paul says that he likes Alvin and thinks we are a good match. He says that Alvin is a man he can proudly call his brother-in-law. Alvin did mention that Paul inquired why he had never married. I, along with many others, have wondered about the same thing but never asked. Alvin says he told him that he is not a confirmed bachelor. "I just haven't found that connection with a woman that would make me want to get married." I am sure he could tell that I was disappointed with that answer before he added the words "until now."

After the New Year's Day service at Allen AME, Alvin walked me home to join our family dinner. As we strolled, he asked if I would ever consider marrying him. I said that I might consider it if he made a proper proposal and if he agreed to an engagement of at least three months followed by a church wedding. He said that he would consider my terms before seeking Papa's permission and making a proper proposal. I was truly excited, but I kept my composure at dinner. Uncles John and Peter, Aunt Agnes, Cousins June, James, and James Jr. came for the first family feast of the year and got their first glimpse of the man I hope to soon wed. However, there was no talk of marriage that day. Is Alvin being coy, or is he unsure?

January 17, 1943

Ba-Bro Paul left for Tuskegee Friday morning. Before he boarded the train, he whispered in my ear, "I love you, sis. I wish I could be here one more day, but I have to leave now. Be sure to be by the phone when Ma Bea and Dad call me, Sunday. I want you to tell me everything that's going on in town." I wasn't sure what he wanted to hear, but I promised to be home when Mama and Papa called him.

That night, I understood Paul's request when Alvin took me to his home and made a proper proposal to me by the fireplace. On bended knee, he spoke of his love and asked me to be his wife. Then he gave me a carat and a half diamond ring, which is, as Mama said when she saw it, matched by those of few white brides and no Negro ones around here.

He made such a long speech before asking me to marry him that I was afraid he might get a cramp and be unable to stand up. He swore his unconditional love and steadfast faithfulness to me, promising to cherish and protect me for the rest of his life. He said that he knew he wanted me to be his wife ever since our second date, but he did not dare believe that I would ever feel the same way about him. He hoped that I would, and he waited for signs that I did. He thought he saw one on the Friday after Thanksgiving when I turned down the offer to sing at Club Zombie. He felt more confident when I wrote a song for him and placed the lyrics in the pocket of the satin-lined vest I made for him as a Christmas gift. When I said I would consider a proposal from him, he felt the courage to buy a suitable ring and ask my father for my hand. He had to do all of that before he dared asked me to honor him by agreeing to become his wife. When I enthusiastically accepted, he stayed on his knee to slip the ring on my finger. Then he finally stood up.

Alvin held my hand and walked me to the stairs, where we kissed. Even in the three inch heels I wear most of the time, the difference in our heights makes it awkward for us to kiss standing on level ground. It's easier if I stand on the second step of a staircase while Alvin stands on the floor at the bottom. Sometimes he easily lifts me over a foot off the ground to bring my face closer to his. Both ways, our kisses are passionate, and I love the way his beautiful full lips encircle mine. We kissed a lot more until we had to force ourselves to stop.

I am overjoyed to be loved by a man I love so much. I am surprised by how much I want to be his wife and the mother of his children. Pursuing a singing career is a distant second on my list of priorities now. Before I got too carried away, I warned him that doctors told me that I might not be able to bear children because of how ill I was at the beginning of my life. Alvin didn't care. He said he is confident that I can do anything I set my mind to do. God has blessed me with good health since then. Only He will decide if we will be blessed with children. Even if I never give birth to a child, Alvin promises we'll have a lot of fun trying for me to conceive. And if I don't, we can adopt. A child we raise together will be just as precious to us as if we made it. It will be created and given to us by God. That's how my family feels about my ba-bro Paul. I am so happy knowing Alvin feels this way. It is no wonder that I love him so.

May 3, 1943

Now that our wedding is behind us, Alvin and I can transition into normal married life. But we'll be the primary topic of the town gossips awhile longer as they discuss every aspect of the nuptials. Before Alvin and I were dating, we were separate items in the verbal tabloids. Some old biddies, like Miss May Ethel, still believe that there is more to the story about why I was sent home from Howard. They wonder how soon my wild streak is going to show itself again. Alvin was grist for the rumor mill because he was an enigma—a fine man with enough money saved to buy a fancy house and car, as well as a very stylish wardrobe, didn't date any woman in Parkersville before he and I became an item. Many widows, divorcees, and single women tried to catch his eye, but he avoided them. That caused all sorts of speculations about him: Does he not like women? Did a war injury leave him unable to perform? Does he have a wife who lives away somewhere? Of course, Alvin dated plenty of women in Detroit, but he says that in a small town like Parkersville, if two people go out more than twice, the town has them in a serious relationship headed toward the altar. If it doesn't go the distance, the man is labeled a playboy and the woman is his victim. Mama and I laughed when I told her that he said that because we know that it's true.

When Alvin and I began dating, lips were flapping with commentary about our relationship. I was thought to be looking for a sugar daddy and Alvin was pitied because "there's no fool like an old fool." Alvin's a fool to think that marriage to a woman young enough to be his child has any chance of bringing him long-term happiness. Mama and Papa were asked what they thought about the two of us. Despite their actual misgivings, they always responded positively to others. They said that

Alvin is a fine Christian man and I am a grown Christian woman. Since we were exploring our feelings for each other in a respectable Christian manner, they had no qualms about our relationship. Once we were engaged, the talk focused on the large size of the diamond he gave me and the elaborate wedding Mama was planning for me in the midst of the war and rations.

Mama talked to me a lot about marriage as we prepared for the wedding. She asked me if I was prepared for better or worse, prosperity and poverty, and sickness and health, considering Alvin's age and the toll the foundry often takes on the men who work there. I tried to reassure her that Alvin is strong and in better physical condition than most men half his age. Whatever happens in the future, I'll deal with it. I'm not going to spoil the joy I feel right now with worries about what might or might not happen later on. Mama also warned me not to expect marriage to always be as fun and exciting as our courtship.

She and her friends talked to me about how love changes in a marriage. The initial feelings of romance and excitement begin to fade into deeper, lasting feelings of warmth, comfort, stability, and true friendship. It sounds so boring and sad to me. I said I plan to keep the romance in my marriage. They laughed and said that they didn't mean to imply that there would be no passion and romance. They just meant that marriage is more than nonstop passion. A couple builds a lasting bond as they learn to depend on each other and work together. It won't always be as thrilling as a roller coaster ride, but it will become as relaxing as a ride on a Ferris wheel. Both rides take you up and down. The roller coaster ride is over quickly, but the ride on the Ferris wheel lasts longer, and it is smoother and more romantic. Miss Bessie said that raising children together is a constant source of excitement. Miss Cora agreed, but Miss Jean said that issues related to children, money, and sex can cause problems in a marriage and even destroy it. So Alvin and I need to talk seriously and honestly before and during the marriage about our feelings related to those things. The others agreed with her. They all agreed that we should always keep God in our marriage and pray together to stay together.

As the wedding day approached, I became increasingly nervous about the wedding night. Mama and I finally had "the talk" the Friday night before I lay down to sleep for the last time as a single woman. May Ethel and others, maybe even Papa, had doubts about my virginity, but I knew and Mama believed that my first time would be after the reception. Mama listened as I shared my angst about the pain of the first time and about pleasing an experienced man like Alvin. Mama assured me that if I relaxed, I would be fine. She said that the pain was bearable and not long-lasting. I could feel some pleasure making love to my husband through my initial soreness, and my pleasure should increase each time afterward. As for pleasing Alvin, I should approach it like slow dancing: follow his lead and move my body in rhythm with his. Because he loves me, he will enjoy patiently teaching me things to do and how to do them, so we will both enjoy our intimacy. I will know how he feels by the sounds he makes and the excitement he will show with his face and body. Mama said that Alvin will want to please me as much as I want to please him. Pleasing me will be difficult at first because I won't yet know what I like during intimacy. We will have to figure that out together, and doing that is a big part of the fun that lies ahead.

I felt better after hearing Mama's advice. I knew from the kisses I shared with Alvin that I wanted to do more. I just felt unsure about what to do and how to do it. I remembered how horribly I messed up the first time I shared a French kiss with a boy my first year at Howard. I wasn't allowed to date while I was in high school. However, I shared more than a few kisses. They were all lip-to-lip. I knew from talking to Gladys and others in high school that in a real kiss, a French kiss, the boy would put his tongue in my mouth. So when I knew Kevin Hollis, a junior, was about to kiss me outside Truth Hall, I closed my eyes and opened my mouth wide like I was at the dentist's office. He looked bewildered and tried not to laugh when he asked me what I was doing. I pretended to be experienced and told him that I wanted a real kiss. He said that I didn't need to open my mouth for him to do that. Embarrassed, I closed my eyes and clenched my teeth. When his tongue hit the enamel wall behind my lips, he was even more amused.

"Keep your mouth closed," he said, "but open your teeth."

I must have looked like a complete idiot as I put my face through all sorts of contortions, trying to figure out how to look pretty and sexy with a closed mouth and open teeth. To say it didn't come naturally is a huge understatement. Finally, Kevin said we could wait and do it the next time. I couldn't believe that he intended to ask me out after that. However, I was glad, and I said, "Sure."

He opened the door to Truth Hall for me, and I took a step to walk inside. Before I reached the door, he called my name. When I turned back to see what he wanted, he pulled me close and kissed me before I realized what was happening. I didn't have a chance to think about what to do, so I wasn't nervous. I was relaxed. It was natural, and it was fine. Thinking back to my first kiss, I didn't want to be as awkward and ridiculous my first time making love. I didn't want to get confused trying to follow any instructions Alvin might give me. That's when I understood that Mama was right as usual. I just needed to relax and not think about what to do, just let things go naturally and follow Alvin's lead.

I didn't think about making love the next day. I was too busy preparing myself for the wedding, absorbing the vows we spoke in the wedding ceremony, and greeting as many of the guests as possible during the reception. When Alvin and I left the reception, it was far from over. Gladys came with us to my parents' home. We stopped there just long enough for her to help me out of my gown and veil and into the white suit and periwinkle satin blouse that Mama made for me to wear to the Gotham Hotel for our wedding night. Alvin waited in the living room, and as I descended the staircase, he watched me and smiled at me, just as he did when I walked down the aisle of Allen AME a few hours earlier. Gladys gave him the overnight bag I packed with Mama Friday night, and we left in his car. My anticipation of the night ahead of me grew as we traveled and reviewed the wonderful day we were blessed to enjoy. When we arrived at the Gotham Hotel, I felt pride knowing it is owned, managed, and staffed by Negroes and that I'd be spending my wedding night in a room where Negro celebrities from all over the country stay when they visit Detroit.

When Alvin carried me into the suite, we found champagne chilling in a bucket of ice, and there were red and white rose petals scattered across the pillows and sheets on the turned-down bed. I was so excited but tense. I calmed down a bit after sipping a glass of champagne. Alvin removed my suit jacket and laid it on a chair at the table for two. He untied the large bow at the neck of my blouse, unbuttoned it, and laid it neatly on top of my suit jacket. I removed my skirt while Alvin took off his tuxedo. I stood frozen before him wearing only my bra, panties, garter belt, and stockings. I could feel my heart pounding with excitement and a bit of fear. As he has done many times before, Alvin told me how beautiful I am and how blessed he is to have my love. He lifted me up to kiss me passionately. He continued to kiss me as he carried me to the bed. After a few more kisses and some fondling of my breasts and the pocket of moisture between my thighs, he eased on top of me to consummate our marriage.

Despite the difference in our heights, which always presents a challenge when we dance and kiss while standing, our torsos fit together better as we lay. His maneuvering through my inner passage and breaking the thick seal that blocked his journey caused us both a bit of pain. The horizontal dancing did not last as long as I thought it would. I didn't mind because I didn't enjoy it. I didn't say anything, but Alvin apologized. He said he was too excited to get inside me to properly handle himself as my lover. He asked if I was all right, and I said I felt sore, but I was fine. We finished the bottle of champagne, and he asked if I was okay to try again. I said I was, and that's when I understood what he meant before. He spent a lot more time massaging and kissing my breasts. He also massaged my private area until I was so excited that I tried to pull him on top of me. That time our dance lasted much longer than the first time. We moved slowly for a while, then faster and faster and more and more intense until we came to a screeching halt. I felt like I was having a heart attack. I felt myself screaming, but I didn't make a sound. My body was rigid and taut, soaking wet with perspiration. A thick liquid suspension flowed out from inside me. I think some of it came from Alvin and some of it came from me. The whole experience was frightening and wonderful all at the same time. I was so focused on my own feelings that I didn't take time to look at Alvin's face or listen for his noises. I think he must have been satisfied because as he lay beside me, he held me in his arms as we both fell asleep exhausted.

In the morning, he wanted to go at it again, but I awoke first and had taken my shower already. I was famished and needed to eat. By the time we came back from our delicious breakfast in the beautiful Ebony Room, it was time to pack and check out. It was then that Alvin saw the blood stains on his shorts and the bed sheets. I was embarrassed, but Alvin was delighted. "I knew it all along," he exclaimed. Coupled with the hurt and soreness he experienced the night before, he had the proof he needed to be convinced that he was my first and only lover. My normally discrete husband seemed determined to silence the liars and doubters who sullied my reputation and reclaim for me the respect I deserve as his pure bride. I really don't care what others think, and I'm sure the most hateful gossips won't believe him anyway. However, Alvin says he knows how to handle those folks and he will. In the next moment, he said that we should stop by my parents' home. I wondered if Alvin thought Papa was a doubter or if he was soliciting Papa's help in dealing with the doubters. When we arrived there, the men shared coffee and cigars in the living room. Mama, Gran, and I talked about the wedding upstairs in my room while I packed things to take to my new residence, Alvin's house. Alvin carried me over the threshold around 4:00 p.m., in time to unpack, have dinner, and make love in our own bed before sleeping.

July 6, 1943

Saturday, Alvin and I went to a barbeque with some of his friends from Ford's foundry. Josie and Sandy came, but Nancy had a prior commitment to go to her aunt's birthday party. It was the first time any of us had been to Belle Isle since the trouble that started there June 20. The park is all cleaned up and beautiful again. Negroes and white folks were both swimming in the river at the same time, and there were a lot of groups at the picnic tables. Most were all-Negro or all-white gatherings. Few were a mixture of both races. Everyone seemed comfortable, but I'm sure that some of them were as nervous as I was so soon after the rioting. Who would have imagined that the worst race riot ever would occur this close to Parkersville? What started in an integrated public park on a "beautiful island" spread into Detroit and lasted a week. According to the newspapers, police estimate around five thousand people were involved. Negroes and whites were fighting with fists and knives, throwing stones, and shooting at people of the other race. Reports say that more than thirty people were killed and over one thousand were injured.

Hundreds of white and Negro men fought on Belle Isle, and the violence spread into Detroit. I was glad that school was out, so I didn't have to drive to the city that week. Even though Trowbridge is in a Negro neighborhood, I drive through some white areas of the city to get there. I would have been afraid of having bricks or stones thrown through my windshield. Nobody knows for certain what actually started the fighting. White men claimed they heard that some Negro men raped and killed a white woman at Belle Isle. Negroes said they heard white men killed a Negro woman and threw her baby into the Detroit River. It has not been verified that either of those incidents actually occurred, but a lot of white people still believe that a white woman was attacked by Negroes and a number of Negroes believe the story about the murder of a Negro woman and her baby.

I have serious doubts about the first story, but see how white men would believe it. White men think that all Negro men want their women. Countless Negroes have been lynched because white men claimed they raped or acted like they wanted to rape white women. Sometimes all it took for a Negro man to seem like he wanted to rape a white woman was to look at her. "Reckless eyeballing" is what they call it. This myth of universal desire for white women is perpetuated in movies, magazines, advertisements, and worldwide beauty pageants with almost all white contestants and always white winners, even though most of the women in the world are not white. They push beauty products to help nonwhite women look more like white women so they can be more desired. The idea is carried to absurd extremes. In the movie *King Kong*, a gigantic gorilla chose the white Faye Wray over a beautiful Negro maiden offered to him as a sacrifice. Faye Wray's character was the size of a miniature doll to him, tiny enough to fit in the palm of his hand, so he couldn't do much more than look at her. But he was so infatuated with her that he died trying to protect her. It's pitiful that some Negro men have bought into the indoctrination that white and white-looking women are prettier and more desirable than darker Negro women. However, I don't think that most Negro men feel that way. When the girls and I go out, there are just as many men looking at dark-skinned Josie as there are focusing on Nancy, a fair-skinned mulatto, and Sandy and I hold our own with our milk chocolate and paper-bag brown complexions. Besides, even Negro men who prefer white or high yellow women are rarely crazy or violent enough to rape a woman, white or otherwise.

Riots have broken out in other cities like Chicago, Springfield, and East St. Louis. Negroes are tired of being victims and seeking justice through the legal system without success. They are subject to answer violence with violence. However, by the time these riots end, more Negroes than whites are dead and hurt and more Negroes get prosecuted. Still, people of both races have reason to be afraid. Throughout the week of rioting in Detroit, white people feared driving and riding buses and trolleys through the Negro areas of the city as much as Negroes feared traveling through the white areas. Alvin says a lot of workers at Ford's River Rouge plant called in sick that week, and while no fights occurred there, the tension between white and Negro workers was thick enough to cut with a knife. Workers of both races went out of their way to be polite, and they avoided discussing the riot going on in Detroit. When the riot was mentioned, white workers got uneasy. They said it was a shame that a few criminals could stir up so many good people. They wondered why the white people and Negroes in Detroit couldn't get along like the workers at Ford do, working together side by side without problems.

Alvin says that most of the Negro workers and white workers at Ford are not friends with one another. He says that when he returned to the U.S. from France, he was too used to being respected and treated as a man to go back to live among those crackers in Alabama. He came to Detroit like so many Southern Negroes did to work for the equal pay Henry Ford promised to men of all races. It sounded like there was no prejudice here. However, he learned quickly enough that the North was no panacea for Negroes either. Prejudice was evident but different from in the South. He couldn't work or live wherever he pleased. Negroes couldn't work as salespeople or elevator operators in the Detroit stores where they shopped. He couldn't buy a house in certain areas of the city and surrounding suburbs. Indeed, Parkersville was founded because towns like Dearborn wouldn't let Negroes live in them. Dearborn folks are still proud of their all-white town. At work, he learned early on that not all the white workers were happy working with Negroes. As more Negroes came to settle here, competition for jobs increased, and migrating Negroes were accused of taking jobs from white men who grew up here. Still, they all got along on the surface. That changed somewhat as white Southerners started coming North in increasing numbers. They brought their attitudes and beliefs about how to treat Negroes with them. They were more open about their resentment at working alongside Negroes and getting paid the same wages. They couldn't do anything about it, and they didn't talk about it to the Negro workers. However, they spoke frankly to some of the white workers who probably shared their attitudes but were used to the way things work at the plant. Conversations between white and Negro workers are pretty civil, and there is some mingling between the races during short breaks, but most of the workers sit and talk in single-race groups at lunch.

The barbeque we attended Saturday on Belle Isle was an all-Negro event. We had a good time, but we were mindful of the riot. We felt safer staying together, so nobody wandered off alone. Josie spent a lot of time talking to a guy that works with Alvin. He was at our wedding and remembered Josie. She didn't remember him, but they seemed to get along well. I hope it works out. I love Alvin, but I miss seeing my girls as much as I used to. Alvin and I usually go out alone or with other couples. I occasionally spend time with Josie, Sandy, and Nancy after school during the week. We're still friends, but I feel like I broke away or was pushed out of the group when I got married. I really miss my girlfriends, but I have no intention of spending too much time away from my husband. So I want Josie, Sandy, and Nancy to couple up too.

November 14, 1946

It seems that more than half of the young couples in town are new parents or soon-to-be parents. Every month, there are a couple of baby showers and babies are being christened or dedicated in all three churches. With six weeks left to go before the first day of 1947, Parkersville has welcomed more babies this year than in any of the twenty-three years since its founding. That seems strange because so many marriages are in trouble. Since the World War II veterans returned to town, Papa has received an unprecedented number of requests from their wives to help them get divorces. Most of them were married just weeks or months before their husbands left for war. They complain that after long separations, the husbands who have returned to them bear little resemblance to the men they married. They find their returning husbands irritable and quick-tempered, depressed, or, in a few instances, abusive. Some of the young men have developed negative habits, such as excessive drinking and gambling, staying out all night and coming home only after spending or losing their entire paychecks and valuables. Papa encourages the couples to try to work things out, seeking advice from their clergy and older veterans and their wives. He says he remembers returning home from World War I bitter, angry, and sometimes irritable and quick-tempered.

Thank God, Alvin and I have not been separated, and we don't have problems like those. In fact, he is such a good husband. Every weekend, we go to dine, dance, and see movies. In spring and summer, he sweeps me off my feet literally on the roller coasters, Ferris wheels, and tunnels of love at Edgewater Park and Bob-Lo Island. At home, we enjoy active, passionate, mutually satisfying lovemaking. He was a great teacher in the beginning, but he says that I have completed his course, and we are learning new things together. He supports my independence but allows me to lean on him whenever I need. He was my rock when I was frustrated in my attempts to get assigned to a high school music department in Detroit. When I was hired to teach at Central High last year, he was as happy for me as I was for myself. He bragged to everyone we know about my success in directing Central High School's choir when it took top honors in the citywide competition and placed third at the state level in May.

So I wonder why we are not part of the Parkersville baby boom. I haven't conceived a baby in three and half years of marriage. Mama says the doctor in Conant Gardens who tended to me as a baby told her that my growth was stunted and I might not be able to carry a baby to term in my tiny uterus. But he never said I would have a problem conceiving. Of course, this is the same doctor who didn't believe that I would live to see my fourth birthday. He was wrong about that, so he might be wrong about my chances of being a mother. But is he wrong about me not being able to carry a baby to term? Or is he wrong by not knowing that I am unable to conceive? Gran doesn't think I should try to have a baby. "Sick as you was as a baby, you ain't growed to nat'chal size. You so tiny inside, you might die if you try to carry a baby. Yo' husband is too old to be a daddy anyway. He prob'ly won't live long 'nough to see his chil' finish grade school. At his age, he should be a grandpa, not a daddy. If you die havin' the baby and he die raisin' it, the po' child gon' be an orphan."

Gran and I don't always see eye to eye, but she may be right about me. My irregular periods and severe cramps may indicate problems in my reproductive system. The doctors I have seen have not said why I have so much trouble with my periods. They just give me pills for the pain and tell me to have a stiff drink to make me sleep. There might be something wrong with me, but Gran is wrong about Alvin. He is more robust than most men half his age. I need to consult with a different doctor to find out about my chances of getting pregnant and carrying a baby to term. Josie's brother is a doctor who served in a navy medical unit during the war. His office is on Fourteenth Street, not far from Central High. I can easily go by there after work. Maybe I'll get his number from Josie and call him tomorrow for an appointment.

November 30, 1946

When Josie and I met today for lunch and shopping, I told her that I have an appointment to see her brother, Larry, in three days. Josie was happy that I took her advice, and she swears he's a great doctor. I'm also looking forward to meeting him because he is dating Nancy, and Josie thinks that they are headed to the altar soon.

"It looks like we're going to be in another wedding soon," she enthused. "You know how those dark-skinned men are. Larry met that high yellow mulatto, and he was a goner in a minute."

"C'mon, Josie, that's not fair. There's a lot to love about Nancy that has nothing to do with her complexion," I retorted. "I thought you got over your prejudice against fair-skinned women."

"Don't get me wrong. I love Nancy because she is such a good woman: compassionate, sweet, fun and smart...hmm, basically like us. I'm just saying that Larry wouldn't have been around her long enough to discover all that if she had been my color. I love my big brother, but he is color struck, like so many of our men."

"Now you do just fine with our men. A lot of them come after you, but you're so picky. They're too immature or too old, too stiff or too loose, not educated or refined enough, not good-looking enough . . . always something that they're too much of or not enough of for you."

"True, but I don't care about color. From the day Larry entered medical school at Meharry, a lot of the coeds at Fisk tried to get his attention. He always went for the light, bright, and damn near white ones. Some of them were so shallow, and it was obvious they would not have looked twice at him if he wasn't going to be a doctor. He passed on a lot of good women who weren't fair enough for his liking, and he wasn't the only one. Most of the fiancées and wives that showed up at Meharry's commencement were closer to Nancy's color than to mine."

"I wasn't there, but even if that's true, they may be fine women who just happen to be light-skinned. You're prejudiced toward light-skinned women. You didn't warm up to Nancy right away. It took you a while. She had to prove herself to you more than Sandy or I did. It was as though you were determined not to like her."

"I just get tired of the way some of our men are so foolish. They'll choose a high yellow woman with nothing to offer and pass on brown-skinned and dark women with everything going for them. The yellow women marry our successful men and then turn their noses up at the rest of us like they accomplished something. 'I'm Mrs. Dr. So-and-So or Mrs. Atty. This-and-That.' No, they're not. Their marriage license allows them to sleep with a doctor or lawyer, but it doesn't allow them to practice medicine or law. They're just Mrs. Whatever."

"Come on, Josie. We both know that becoming a doctor or a lawyer is a notable achievement for anyone but significantly more so for Negroes. Most of them have faced additional challenges of prejudice and hostility in getting to medical school, securing internships and hospital training, and setting up practices. Many doctors' and lawyers' wives supported them with money or hard work. I know Papa is the one who finished law school and passed the bar exam, but he is the first one to acknowledge that Mama's support was invaluable to him in doing so."

"I know how hard my brother worked to make it. But why should his wife take credit for what he accomplished on his own?"

"When Papa was mayor, Mama was proud of being the first lady. She wasn't appointed or elected to office. She was awarded that title because of whom she married. It is the way society is. Women get status not just for what they achieve but from the accomplishments of the men in their lives: their fathers and husbands."

"Mary Morgan, I don't believe you're saying that a woman's worth is based on who her father and her husband are! My father was a janitor without a high school diploma, and I am not married. Are you saying that as a teacher with a college degree, I'm not as good as other teachers with the same credentials whose fathers or husbands have money and degrees?"

"Of course not, Josie! My father is a lawyer and my husband works in a foundry. Neither of them defines who I am and what I'm worth.

I'm saying that I am not mad at women who "marry well" and enjoy the money and status they get for doing so. However, I do not think that their money and their husbands' titles make them better than me, any more than I think a white man's race or gender makes him better than me. They may think they're better than I am, but I don't care because I know they're wrong. I don't like snobs and prefer not to be around them, but I don't think all doctors' wives are snobs. You know Nancy is not going to be like that."

"I know, and I'm glad that my brother chose someone I genuinely like. I'm happy for them both because they are so in love. You know Nancy's a romantic. My big brother always treats his ladies special, and he goes all out for her. She spoils him too. She said after church Sunday that she wants you to be her matron of honor. Yeah, girl, she has him going to church, so I know this is serious. If you can get a man to go to church, it's easy for you to get him to go down the aisle."

I agreed, "That's the truth!" We both laughed.

December 4, 1946

Yesterday I drove to Larry's office as soon as I left Central High. His small office was more crowded than I would have expected for a cold, snowy Tuesday afternoon. I had to wait for him to see four patients whose names were ahead of mine on the sign-in sheet. He was running about an hour behind schedule. The waiting room was excessively warm and had a foul smell: a mixture of wet wool coats, sour milk on a baby's burping blanket, a soiled diaper, Vicks VapoRub, and assorted colognes and hair pomades blending with natural body odors. I felt sick, and after about half an hour, I went to the bathroom. I leaned over the toilet, and my stomach emptied its contents. I wiped my face and rinsed my mouth with water from the face bowl then chewed a stick of gum I confiscated from a student earlier. I refreshed my powder and lipstick. Even though Dr. Lawrence Robinson is probably used to bad breath in sick patients, he is Josie's brother and Nancy's boyfriend, so I didn't want to meet him looking and smelling bad. When I finally made it to his examination area, I was chewing my third stick of gum. I tried to talk and smile without opening my mouth too wide, just in case the gum had not been enough.

Larry was smiling as he entered. He said in friendly tone, "So you're the Mary I've heard so much about from my sister and Nancy. You're just as cute as they said you were."

"Well, Doctor, it's a pleasure to finally meet you. I have learned a few things about you from the same two people." We chuckled.

After a brief exchange of pleasantries, I told him why I came. "I wonder if you can find any physical impediments to my conceiving or bearing a child. I've been married over three and a half years. I haven't been trying to get pregnant, but I haven't done anything to prevent it."

He asked, "When was your last menses, or when are you expecting your next one?"

"I had one near the end of October, and I expect to have another one in a few days. I have an extremely irregular cycle, so I can never predict with certainty."

After he examined me, Larry said, "I believe that your uterus is large enough to accommodate a small baby to term or at least long enough for it to have a reasonable chance for survival."

"Thank you," I said with a smile. "That is good news."

He smiled and added, "I have more good news. You are about seven weeks pregnant now."

I was shocked. I was elated but cautious as I recalled what Mama told me about her history of miscarriages. I shared that with Larry and asked him, "Are there precautions I should take? Can I continue to work?"

"You should probably limit vigorous activity and get plenty of rest to lessen the likelihood of miscarriage. You can work through the end of the school year in June as long as you stay off your feet as much as possible. You should call me and rest in bed if you experience any cramping or bleeding. As long as all goes well, you should return here for monthly checkups, but you can come more often than that if you ever feel concerned."

Larry was calming and reassuring. I don't want to do anything to harm the baby, but I love teaching, and I want to adequately prepare the choir for the competitions that will begin in April.

Driving home, I was so excited and overwhelmed. I went to Larry to see if I could get pregnant someday. I learned that I can have a baby, and my someday is in about seven and a half months. When a policeman pulled me over, he asked why I was speeding. I responded that I wasn't aware that I was. He wondered if I was okay to drive, to which I responded happily, "Oh yes, Officer. I'm not sick or anything—I'm pregnant! I guess I was driving fast because I'm anxious to tell my husband."

"Well, all right, Mrs. Morgan," he said, smiling as he looked at my license. "Slow down and be careful. You don't want to hurt yourself or your baby." He let me go without issuing a ticket.

By the time I reached Parkersville, I was on top of the world. I wanted to think of a clever way to tell Alvin. Maybe I'd ask God to bless the food and the new life growing at the table. Maybe I'd tell him later in bed, asking him to be gentle when we were about to make love. All planning was wasted. As soon as I saw his face, I just blurted it out. Alvin hollered, "Yes!" He swooped me up and kissed me. Then he put me down gently as though I were a porcelain doll that he was afraid he would break. I was tickled by his reaction. I told him that I'm not fragile, but he told me that I am in a "delicate condition." He wanted to know everything Larry told me.

We wanted the world to know the news, but first, we wanted to tell my parents. Alvin drove me the two and a half blocks we usually walked to their house. Mama and Papa were excited but concerned. They also wanted to know everything Larry said. Even before I could begin to tell them, they insisted that I sit down. Mama put a pillow behind my back and propped my legs up on the ottoman. Then she went to make a cup of hot chocolate for me and Papa asked if I needed anything else. Gran was happy but said she was worried about me. She asked if I felt all right and told Alvin to take good care of me.

May 8, 1947

Mother's Day is Sunday, and I believe that next year, I'll be celebrating my first one as a mother. I'm only nine weeks from my due date, and my pregnancy is going well, except for my daily bout with morning sickness. It doesn't matter what time I eat my first meal, whether it's shortly after I rise or if I skip breakfast and eat only at lunch time. It also doesn't matter what I eat, a light fare of eggs over easy or a heavy one of pancakes or a sandwich. I am going to vomit all the contents of my first meal within a half hour. After that, I feel fine for the rest of the day. We're all beginning to relax because I feel like my baby and I are going to be just fine. Still, Alvin and my parents are still pampering me and hovering over me. Alvin is strutting around town like a proud peacock. His ego seems to be rising as my belly is expanding. Some of my dresses are worn in the front from Alvin constantly rubbing my tummy everywhere we go. When anyone asks how he is doing, he always replies that he is fine, adding, "I'm taking good care of my wife and our little gift from God." Then he rubs my abdomen as though he needs to point out my pregnancy, which is so very obvious at this point. Some of the older women think he is silly to be that proud of doing what any boy past puberty could do. However, Alvin knows that no pubescent boy made this baby and most of his peers aren't still making babies in their fifties.

Gran and I have grown closer during my pregnancy. For a change, she is not constantly telling Mama that she is doing too much for me. Mama asked Gran not to frighten me with talk about dying or having the baby before its time. So Gran tries to be encouraging. She asks Mama and me to describe in detail all of the sewing and embroidery we're doing to prepare the baby's layette and Christening outfit. She reminds us, "I'm blind and can't see nothin'." Monday, she called me to her room for a serious talk. She spoke matter-of-factly.

"I know you think I don't like you much 'cause I always tell yo' mama she spoil you too much. Truth is you my gran'chile and I love you. Always have. I think you had it easy, better'n my other gran'chillun. I ain't mad at you or yo' folks fo' dat. I just wished I coulda done as much for June. You think I love June mo' 'an I love you. That ain't true either. June's parents ran out on her when she was so young and she only had me. Sebron had done gone to glory. I was alone, and I didn't have 'nough money to give her all the things you had. She was a good girl and real smart. I wanted her to go to college like you. But she jus' wanted to feel loved and have a family. I'm proud o' her, and I'm proud o' you too."

I confessed, "I thought you favored June because Aunt Thella is your baby and your favorite. So you love her daughter more than you love me. Mama always took care of you, and you still seem to love Thella more, even though she has done nothing for you or June. I don't care if you love June more than me. But I think you should love my mother more than you do."

"I can't believe that y'all don't know how much I love Bea. She the first daughter I birthed. I love her much as I love Thella and all my chillun. I'm proud o' Bea too 'cause o' how she live her life—like Jesus taught us we ought to. She the only one of my chillun to go to college and the one what took me and June in her home. I always talk 'bout lovin' Thella so June know I love her and I thought she was special. Don't get me wrong. I love Thella, not more'n Bea but not less neither. I love her diff'ent 'cause she diff'ent. Mothers love all they chillun. Good or bad, smart or dum', pretty or plain, it don't matter. It don't even matter if they ain't come from yo' body. If you raise 'em, they all your babies. When they grow up or even if they die like my dear Bus, you still love 'em fo'ever."

I almost cried. I had never seen this side of my grandmother. She touched my heart and made me think about how much I already love the child growing inside of me. I feel closer to Gran than ever. We have talked every day this week, sharing our feelings about being wives and mothers. Gran admits that she wasn't happy about having to marry her late sister's husband and how it took her years to feel love for him. She knew he didn't love her at first either. Maybe he grew to love her over time, but it hurt her that he never once told her that he did before he died. Still, he was a good man, and she had a good life with him. She loved being a mother and raising all of their children. She is telling me stories I never heard before, some funny and a few sad, about Mama and her siblings when they were growing up.

June 23, 1947

Nancy and Larry wed Saturday, June 7. I was her matron of honor, and Josie was her maid of honor. I am still experiencing morning sickness every day. So Josie was a big help to Nancy and me. Sandy and two of Nancy's first cousins, one black and one white, were her bridesmaids. Larry's groomsmen were doctors he knew from Meharry Medical School, his residency at Detroit Receiving Hospital, and one from the navy. His best man was his best friend since childhood, Chester (Chet) Reid, who owns a successful barbershop on Beaubien Street. The dresses for the bridal party were purchased from J. L. Hudson's, except for mine. Mama made my dress, identical to Josie's, except for the modifications necessary to accommodate my baby pouch and oversized breasts. As usual, she did not need a pattern. She went to Hudson's with Josie, examined her dress inside and out to see how the fabric was cut and stitched. Then she purchased the material and trimmings at a fabric store on Woodward Avenue and made a maternity version of the dress to fit me. I was glad that I didn't have to make the trek to Downtown Detroit. I'm so big now that I barely fit behind the wheel of a car. So I need Alvin to drive me everywhere. Even as a passenger, long car trips make me nauseous. I don't like going to big department stores now. I can't see my feet, so I don't like riding on escalators. I've always felt claustrophobic on elevators. Thank God, Mama bought everything she needed and made my dress at home.

Love was in the air the day of Nancy's wedding. She and Larry radiated joy. Sandy and Josie were also feeling amorous. The girlfriends met Sandy's new beau, Walter Curtis, an attractive milk chocolate man with a solid frame. He's from Louisiana and went to Dillard University, where he was initiated into Beta Gamma Chapter of Omega Psi Phi Fraternity, Inc. Like my beloved ba-bro, Paul, he left college after his sophomore year to fight in the war. He moved to Detroit after he returned from overseas and works for Detroit Street Railways (DSR) as a bus driver. It is common to find colored bus drivers with college credits, even earned degrees, while white bus drivers might have as little as an eighth-grade education. There is no written policy related to race or color qualifications. However, all colored bus drivers have high school diplomas. The ones with no college credits are generally fair-skinned, while all of the dark-skinned drivers have completed at least a year or two of college, and some have bachelor's degrees. Obvious inequities notwithstanding, colored bus drivers are happy to have the pay, security, and good benefits of civil service and the promise of good schedules as they earn seniority. As Walt put it, "I had to work for three years after high school to save enough money to go to college. I don't mind working while I complete my degree. I was either going to work as a bus driver, postman, or garbage man. With my almost-flat feet, I don't like walking that much. I don't like heavy lifting and being surrounded by bad smells. So I appreciate the chance to get paid for doing something I like: driving around this great city. I get to help a lot of good people get to where they need to go without having to pay too much."

Walt told us that he works a swing shift: 6-10 a.m. and 5-9 p.m., and takes classes at Wayne during the day. He wants to teach history and government in high school, get a master's and become a principal. It was obvious that he wanted to make a good impression on Sandy's friends, and he did, not because of his ambition but because of his evident affection for Sandy. She is happy, and their relationship seems to be getting serious.

Josie was eyeballing the best man, Chet. She seems to be rekindling the crush she had on him when she was a girl. Chet is clearly impressed that Larry's little sister, whom he thought to be such a pest when he was a teen, has grown into an extremely attractive woman. The five-year difference in their ages isn't nearly as important to him now as it was back then.

Josie, Sandy and newlywed, Nancy, were still basking in the glow of romance two days ago at the surprise baby shower they helped Gladys organize for me. It was an incredible event. Not surprisingly, they were meticulous about every detail, from the giant watermelon carved like a baby carriage and filled with a fresh fruit salad to the unique cake, actually two cakes, which Mama made to look like giant alphabet blocks. One devil's food and one vanilla cake, each an eight-inch cube made from three eight-inch square layers held together and covered with buttercream frosting. Different letters of marzipan were on each side. The guests included women from Allen AME, Trowbridge, and Central High and a few of my classmates from Wayne University and Parkersville High. Josie, Nancy, and Sandy gave me the most exquisite baby carriage which was used to hold many of the other shower gifts. The remaining gifts were placed in the crib, the gift from the church choirs, and in the playpen from the women's club. I thought I was going to a women's club meeting in the church basement. Instead, I experienced such an outpouring of love for me and my baby. Alvin spent the day at Papa's. After the shower, they took the gifts, decorations, and leftovers there, and Alvin stayed with my parents for the rest of the evening. Josie, Nancy, and Sandy went home with me, and we laughed and talked for hours like we used to do when we were all single. Our lives have changed quite a bit over the last six years, but our friendship has remained constant.

July 15, 1947

July 4, I woke up with morning sickness as usual. I decided not to go to the church barbeque. Alvin delivered the charcoal he was supposed to bring to the park and then returned home to stay with me. Around 9:30 a.m., Mama and Papa were preparing to leave for the barbeque when Alvin called them to say that I seemed to be in labor and we were on our way to meet Larry at Detroit Receiving Hospital. Papa represented the family at the barbeque, and Bea rode to the hospital with Alvin and me. When Larry told Nancy that he would probably miss the barbeque at Roxboroug Farm because he had to deliver my baby, she called Josie and Sandy. I had a difficult labor, and Mama wanted Larry to give me more medication to dull the pain. I heard her raised voice outside my room. "It's 1947, and she's with a good doctor in a modern hospital. She shouldn't have to suffer like this." Larry understood Mama's frustration at not being able to take away "her baby's" pain. He explained that he didn't want to give me anything that would make the baby drowsy and lethargic, thus prolonging my labor. Mama and Alvin tried to keep each other calm by sharing stories about me and discussing everything else either of them could imagine to hold the other's interest for a few minutes. Josie arrived at the hospital around 4 p.m. She joined Mama and Alvin in the waiting area. At some point, Mama talked about how I survived four bouts of pneumonia before I was three. Josie was surprised, but she said that proved I had the will and strength to handle anything, including labor, just fine.

At 4:56 p.m., I delivered a healthy baby girl seventeen and a half inches long, weighing in at six pounds four ounces. When Larry went to the waiting room to share the news, Alvin came to see me, while Mama and Josie went to the nursery. Papa arrived a few minutes later, and Larry showed him to the nursery, so he could join Mama and Josie admiring my precious little angel.

Alvin and I discussed the Mann tradition of naming babies that has been passed down from Papa's mother, Juliette. The first name should be one from the Bible, and the middle name should be one of an historical figure admired by the parents. I suggested Sarah Anne as the name for our little girl. Sarah is the name of Abraham's wife, the mother of Isaac, in Genesis 17. Anne honors the woman I admire most in the world, my mother, Annie Beatrice. Alvin agrees that there is no woman finer than Mama. So he is pleased with my choice of names. Alvin left my room to join the others outside the nursery. He told them our baby's name and how we chose it. He said Josie repeated, "Sarah Anne, Sarah Anne, Sarah Anne, I love it. It's a beautiful name for a beautiful baby." Alvin stayed in the nursery with Josie for a few minutes so Mama and Papa could come in to see me before they left. Papa smiled when he told me that he came to see "the mother of Sarah Anne Morgan." Mama was so happy and honored that she shed tears of joy. Josie came with Alvin to my room. She stayed just long enough to say how happy she is to be "the Godmother of Sarah Ann Morgan." Alvin stayed with me until I fell asleep.

For the next week, Papa brought Mama to spend some time with me every day, and Alvin came by every day after he left work. Josie, Sandy and Nancy rotated days so that one of them would be there each day for an hour or so. Finally, Alvin brought me home Saturday with eight-day-old Sarah. I was surprised, but not shocked, that our living room was filled with family and friends: new grandparents, Mama and Papa; new grandaunt and granduncle, Agnes and Peter; cousins June, James, and eleven-year-old James Jr.; "aunties" Gladys and Sandy; and godmother Josie. Mama had prepared a feast with enough food to last for a week. It was another wonderful celebration of love. Alvin, Papa, James and James Jr. went to the church after they ate, leaving the house to the women. We talked and laughed, and they pampered me all afternoon into the evening.

Mama was the last to leave. She stayed until after Alvin returned and carried me upstairs to see the nursery and go to bed. The nursery is painted yellow because I like it better than pink. The ruffled white bassinette covering is beautifully embroidered with tiny yellow rosebuds and violets. It has yellow satin ribbon woven into the lace trim gathered at the bottom. A musical duckling mobile is attached. The chest of drawers, crib, nightstand and floor lamp are all white. A three-foot tall white cotton bootie-shaped hamper stands between the chest and crib. A note from the diaper service, which Mama arranged while I was in the hospital, is taped to the side. An antique oak rocking chair and pillowed footstool are the only furniture pieces that are not painted white. The drawers of the chest are packed with everything I need for Sarah, as well as beautiful knitted and crocheted sweaters and blankets made by Mama, Aunt Agnes, Miss Bessie, Miss Cora, and Miss Jean.

December 29, 1947

Sandy and Walter wed Saturday. Josie made a lovely maid of honor again. Nancy, five and a half months pregnant, and I were two of the four bridesmaids. The others were Sandy's cousin and a childhood friend. It was good to go out for fittings, the bridal shower, and a private gathering Josie hosted for Nancy and the ladies in the bridal party the night before the wedding. Mama kept Sarah so I could attend the prenuptial events. It was great spending so much time with the girlfriends again. We haven't spent as much time together as before, and when we do get together, we do so as couples. When Josie and Chet have their wedding in June, we will all be married. We are glad that our husbands and Josie's fiancé get along. Larry can be a bit aloof at times, but he seems okay being with the group. Josie is his little sister, and he and Chet were best friends growing up. Walter and Chet have become close friends and get together sometimes without Sandy and Josie. Although Alvin is much older than the other men and is closer to friends he made at Ford, he is comfortable with Walter and Chet and vice versa. Larry's not so subtle snobbery doesn't make it easy for Alvin to really warm to him. They are civil, but I think they tolerate each other because of Nancy and me. However, Alvin seems to enjoy going out with the group, and I just enjoy going out.

I love being a mother and spending time with Sarah. Still, as much as I love Sarah, I am bored. I am desperate for stimulating conversation. Most of the time, Mama and I only talk about babies and motherhood. Alvin is at work all day, and when he comes home, he wants to know all about what Sarah has done in his absence. He wants to be sure he hasn't missed any milestone in her young life. I want an adult discussion, but he wants to talk about how many times Sarah laughed and if she cooed or rolled over. I am often too tired to read the newspaper, but when I do, Alvin doesn't discuss it with me like he used to do. He takes care of Sarah when I enjoy a bath before going to bed. I appreciate that, but I wish he understood my need for intelligent conversation as well as he understands my need for rest. He has adult time all day and prefers to spend his evenings and weekends watching me breastfeeding, cuddling, singing lullabies, and reading and telling stories to Sarah. I miss going out dancing or to the movies with my husband.

I miss teaching and talking with colleagues during lunch. I can't believe I was forced to take maternity leave after the first semester ended last January because teachers aren't supposed to look pregnant in front of the students. I am married, and I'm sure that my adolescent students have figured out that I make love to my husband. It might be good to remind them that sex can result in pregnancy. Besides, it is an unfair practice because male teachers don't have to take leaves when they are expecting children. I know it's because men are not the ones who "show." I am going to voice my displeasure with this policy when I get back to work next month.

I admire Mama and other women who are content to stay home all day, caring for their babies and their homes. Yet I find pleasure working. I am thankful that Mama is delighted to be taking care of Sarah when I return to work. She is the consummate homemaker and enjoys making formula with evaporated milk and a touch of Karo syrup, preparing baby food with the grinder and strainer, and pushing Sarah in a baby carriage taller than I am. I like doing all those things, too, but not all day. I'll find joy cooking and attending to Sarah and Alvin when I get home from a day of teaching and learning. The satisfaction I'll get from working again will help me be a happier, better wife and mother.

November 18, 1950

Last night, Alvin and I were at Mama and Papa's as we have been every Friday for over a year. Papa bought a television at the Labor Day sale in 1948 so that he could watch television news every evening and on Fridays, *The Gillette Cavalcade of Sports*, which broadcasts boxing matches from Madison Square Garden in New York. Alvin and I, along with half the folks on their block, still come to watch the fights with Mama and Papa in their living room. It is a regular social event. Papa allows the men to drink beer but not to gamble on the outcomes of the fights. Whether they like his rules or not, they come every week because he still has the only television on their street. I remember how excited Mama was when their television was delivered. She called me to say, "Once again, your papa has done something that few white folks and no Negroes we know have done yet: he bought a television for our house." Mama likes to watch the boxing, but she prefers daytime serial dramas like *The First Hundred Years* on CBS. It is like the soap operas she loves on radio: *The Brighter Day* and *The Guiding Light*.

When everyone arrived last night and sat in their usual places in the living room, Papa turned on the television. Before the Gillette razor commercial at the start of the fight show, there was a commercial for KOOL cigarettes. That commercial ends with the character of Willie the Penguin standing next to a pack of the cigarettes, giving a high-pitched birdlike call of "KOOL." When Sarah saw that, she ran to the screen and pointed at the word on the pack. She was excited and proclaimed, "See, that's 'look' backwards!"

Mama said that history was repeating itself for her. She remembered seeing me excited when I discovered "dog" is "god" spelled backward when I was three like Sarah is now. Papa was the first to congratulate Sarah. As he extended his arms, he chuckled, saying, "Why yes, you brilliant child, that it is. I'm so proud of you for figuring that out. Come here and give your papaw a hug."

Gran laughed out loud and said she was not surprised. "I can't see it, but I know you got it right, baby. You smart 'cause you come from smart people. You get yo' smarts from yo' momma and yo' gran'momma. But I think you gon' be smarter 'an both of 'em." Showing respect for Gran's advanced age, nobody pointed out that Papa and Alvin are both smart and that Sarah probably inherited their intelligence as well.

Alvin and I had to wait our turn congratulate our daughter. Indeed, everyone was so happy to acknowledge Sarah's feat, each rewarding her with a nickel, that we missed the announcement of the first fight.

My darling Sarah is so precocious and eager to learn. I love reading to her every night after dinner and teaching her to find the notes on the piano. Alvin reads to her and plays silly games that amuse her and make her laugh until her tummy hurts. Papa likes teaching her to count forward and backward and to skip count by twos. Gran tells her stories about Great-Grandma Lily and Nicodemus and about Mama when she was a little girl. However, Mama is the one who teaches her more than the rest of us because she is with her every day while Alvin and I are working. She has been saying for a while that Sarah is ready to read at three, just like I was. But I don't like her being compared to me or anyone else. I just want her to develop at her own pace.

Alvin and I are still beaming with pride. I called Josie. She is giving us a set of reading pre-primers and primers with flash cards and workbooks for Mama to use teaching Sarah. Josie says that she'll bring them to me tonight when the girlfriend couples get together at Baker's Keyboard Lounge. I'm looking forward to seeing Sandy and Walter, and even Larry and Nancy are coming. They don't spend as much time with the group as they used to. Nancy didn't go out much during her pregnancies with two-and-a-half-year-old Larry Jr. and his one-year-old sister, Larissa. Lately, Larry has been taking her mostly to social events with Detroit's Negro elite, who are his professional peers, fraternity brothers and friends in various social clubs. Nancy joined The Links, Inc. and the Cotillion Wives Auxiliary, as well as Jack and Jill, Inc. She tries to play Bridge with us once a month but she is in other card playing clubs with Larry and her new friends. She says she wants to spend more time with us, but she wants to be with her husband wherever he goes. Larry appeases her by venturing out with us less fancy folks about once a month.

January 4, 1953

I had a difficult time getting through my solo in church today. I couldn't stop looking at Mama's stoic face. I know how deeply sad she is, but she is handling Gran's death with remarkable composure, as she finds comfort and strength through her unwavering faith. Although I felt like crying as I sang "It Is Well with My Soul," I thought about Mama and Gran. I know that Gran is at peace and Mama is accepting her mother's transition. So knowing that they are both okay makes it well with my soul.

Mama wept the morning after Christmas when she discovered that Gran had died in her sleep. She said that once again, the holidays had brought a sorrowful sting to pierce her joy. Mama always fears that something bad will happen to her between Thanksgiving and New Year's Day. Most years, nothing bad happens, but she seems to have lost all of her relatives, except our beloved Paul, around that time of year. Mama saw the signs that Gran was fading. For one thing, she was sleeping more each day. The night before Thanksgiving was the last time Gran stayed up until midnight. After that, she began to wake later in the morning and retire earlier at night. By the second week in December, she was sleeping more than half of each day, from 9:00

p.m. to past 10:00 a.m. Gran's doctor came to the house December 10 when she was too weak to get out of the bed. He told Mama that Gran didn't appear to have a particular malady. She was just old, and her body was getting weaker. She did not acknowledge any pain. She said she just felt tired. Mama gave her Geritol and vitamins, as the doctor suggested, and she massaged her body with oil several times a day. On Christmas Day, Alvin lifted her from her bed to the chair in her room, where Mama brought her dinner and we all visited with her after we ate. She grew weary, and Alvin lifted her back into her bed just before 9:00 p.m. Mama checked her at midnight. She was sleeping peacefully then and died sometime before morning.

Sarah was particularly close to her grannie. Since she was six months old, Sarah has been spending her days with Mama and Gran in their house while Papa, Alvin, and I were working. Nowadays, when Alvin brings her home for dinner every day, Sarah can't wait to tell us all about her day at "Bea and Papaw's house": what she read and learned, what story Grannie told her, and what happened on her favorite television show, *Howdy Doody*. Gran adored Sarah and thought she is a genius. "She smarter 'an any chile I been 'roun', got mo' sense 'an most adults too."

My five-year-old Sarah is the only one Gran trusted to walk her down the stairs from her bedroom to the living room (since my ba-bro Paul). Gran said Papa and I are too little to help her, and Alvin and Mama are too impatient. That's funny. Sarah is smaller than Papa and me, and she goes down the stairs much faster than Alvin and Mama, but Gran didn't seem afraid to keep up with her. Even when she let "that tall sturdy man" (Alvin) help her, Gran trembled and reminded him on every step, "I'm blind an' can't see, so go slow and don' rush me." Yet, holding Sarah's hand with her left hand and the banister with her right, she moved confidently at Sarah's quick pace. She said nothing until she reached the bottom and sat in a chair. Then she said, "Thank you, baby. You take such good care o' yo' ol' grannie."

During the two weeks before Gran died, she summoned Sarah to her bedside almost every day after school. She recounted stories about Lily and Nicodemus, Sebron (her late husband), and Mama and her siblings when they were growing up. She told Sarah to remember the stories and pass them on to her children someday so they will know that they come from good stock. Their ancestors weren't rich, but they weren't poor either. They were good people who believed in God, loved their families, and tried to help others. In her last days, Gran asked Sarah to tell her the stories so she could be sure that she remembered them correctly. Sarah was happy to comply. She liked telling the stories, and she was happy to make Gran feel better. Sarah says that Gran told her that she loved her at least a dozen times a day. Gran never said that to me until I was married and pregnant with Sarah. I don't think she ever said it to Mama or her siblings. As far as I know, my first cousin, June, was the only other child to hear Gran say she loved her.

It took me a while to realize that Gran loved deeply, but she had learned not to show her feelings. Most of her life, she was driven by duty, not feelings. She did what she was expected to do: to serve God, obey her parents and her husband, and take care of her nieces and nephews, her children, and her abandoned granddaughter. She loved them all, but she cared for them out of her sense of duty as much as because of her love. She was not afraid to die. In fact, she looked forward to it because she believed with all her heart that Jesus and her ancestors were waiting to welcome her to heaven. Sarah related to us that a few days before Gran died, she said that her mother, Miss Lily, came to her as she slept and told her that she would soon be freed from the prison her tired body had become. So when Gran died, Sarah knew that she must be overjoyed to "rise" during the night after we celebrated her Lord's birth. Sarah was fine, even happy, until the funeral, Friday. That day, she cried herself to sleep at the church and was upset even more at the cemetery. I guess that's when she realized that she wouldn't see her grannie again in this life. She hasn't cried since we left the cemetery, but she has been more quiet than usual the two days since.

Mama has been too busy to wallow in grief. First, she made several calls before choosing a funeral home. Mama was determined to have Gran's body handled by a woman. Gran took pride in the fact that no man, including her husband, had ever seen her naked as a woman. If she had lived her life that way, Mama wanted to respect her body, even in death. Mama decided on Stinson Funeral Home in Detroit because the co-owner, Mrs. Sulee Stinson, agreed to handle embalming and all other work on Gran's body until she was dressed. Mrs. Stinson came with the driver to collect her remains that afternoon. Papa drove Mama and me to the funeral parlor the next day (Saturday, the twenty-seventh) to complete the arrangements. Due to the holidays, we decided to delay the wake to Friday, January 2, and the funeral to January 3. Both were held at Allen AME instead of the Pentecostal Church where Papa used to take Gran for worship monthly when she first came here. Gran hasn't been there in over seven years. Reverend Gibson has come to read and discuss Bible scriptures with her monthly since then. So Mama thought it fitting for him to officiate at her funeral.

Mama's elder sisters (Birdie and Pearl), her living brothers (Genie and Billy), and their spouses arrived in Detroit by train from Mississippi Friday morning. Papa and Alvin picked them up and brought them to Mama's. Papa went back to pick up a lone Thella when her bus from Chicago arrived in the afternoon. The house was filled with family, mourners, well-wishers, and food prepared for Mama and her family. Mama's spirit was somber, but like her mother, she does not cry in front of others. However, her sisters were much more openly emotional. Mama was appalled by "all their carryin' on," especially since none of them has visited their mother in over five years. Most of them didn't call, write, or send cards to her, except at Christmas and Mother's Day and sometimes on her birthday. None of them had invited Gran to stay with them when she became blind. They said only Mama's house was big enough to make room for her and June. None of them ever volunteered to help Mama care for their mother, even when they used to visit and stay with Mama and Papa for days at a time. They enjoyed the food and hospitality Mama extended to them but did and said little to show any gratitude. They seemed to think that Mama was doing her duty like Gran did. As the most successful sibling, she was supposed to take full responsibility for their mother and for taking care of them whenever they made time to visit her.

Mama never spoke about how hypocritical Birdie, Pearl, and Thella seemed as they bawled in the kitchen and living room throughout the day. However, Sarah chastised them, asking, "Why are you all crying so much? Grannie is happy now. She's not sick and stuck in a bed. She is going to fly all around heaven with her Lord. You should be happy for her."

My aunts looked at Sarah in awe. They are not used to hearing a child speak to grown-ups in such a manner. They're no more ready for my precocious Sarah than they were for me when I used to visit Mississippi as a child. Mama hugged her and explained, "We are all happy for her. We are sad because we will miss her in our lives 'til the time comes for us to go home to heaven. We are being selfish, but we wish we could keep your grannie here with us a little while longer."

Birdie added, "Glory be! Bible say a little chile shall lead us. You right, baby. You's a good girl to remind us to have faith. We gotta accept God's will. He wants his chile Priscilla to come back home now."

"And she wanted to go home," Sarah informed them. "I know because she told me so last week. She said her mother, Miss Lily, told her she wouldn't have to wait much longer to be with her and Jesus. Grannie was happy to hear that."

"She been here a long time, eighty-fo' years." Pearl sighed. "She been blind fo' almos' twenty years, but now she can see again, see mo' 'an befo', see everything. Praise God!"

Thella offered only, "Amen." She was preoccupied by the entrance of June, James, and James Jr. Thella must have wondered if her estranged daughter would recognize her and speak to her. She has had little contact with June since she left her in Mississippi twenty-nine years ago. Gran told June Thella loved her, but Thella has never written or called to say that to June. Gran asked Mama to send pictures of June to Thella every year on her birthday and on special occasions. June has pictures of Thella given to her by Gran and Mama, but they were all taken years ago. Yet when June arrived at Mama's, she apparently recognized the woman who gave birth to her. She nodded and whispered something to her teenage son. He looked at Thella and then walked over to her.

"Hello, Grandmother," he said matter-of-factly. "How was your trip from Chicago?"

Thella seemed relieved that June was not trying to be unpleasant and that James Jr. had reached out to her. She answered tentatively, "It was fine. The train brought me to Detroit. Solomon picked me up from the station and brought me here. How're you doing? You're big now."

"I'm fine. I'm graduating in June, and I'll be going to the University of Michigan in September. I got other scholarship offers to play football, but Michigan gave me an academic scholarship. I don't want to lose the money for my education if I get hurt and can't play."

Thella smiled and said, "I know your parents are real proud o' you. They should be. You're a fine young man. You turned out real good."

James Jr. replied, "Thank you, ma'am." Then he walked back toward his mother, who was hugging an excited Sarah. Sarah ran over to James Jr. He scooped her up into his arms and kissed her on the cheek. She giggled with joy. Sarah loves her older cousin and is always glad when he and June come to visit about once a month.

Thella has no relationship with her grandson. She has only seen him in pictures sent to her by Mama at Gran's insistence. She doesn't write, and she seems to move around a lot, so Mama and June have not been able to contact her in over five years. June and her family are closer to Mama and Papa, her aunt and uncle. Gran was her "mother" since she was six years old. Thella shows no regret. She seems to have preferred partying a lot in the big city to raising a child in the "country South." She still likes to smoke and drink Scotch, but she didn't drink while she was here. Papa doesn't permit the consumption of hard alcohol in his home. She walks with a limp she got when she stumbled drunkenly into Michigan Avenue and was hit by a car four years ago. She says she is living with an orderly she met at the hospital. He has been taking good care of her since then. That's arguable. She's missing her front four top teeth and needs a bridge and more dental work. Thella knows better than to try to act like June's mother at this point in her life. Yet she claims that she wants to build a friendly relationship. She says that she cares about June and that she knows June was better off with her Grandma Priscilla and Aunt Annie than she would have been in "Chi-town." Only Mama's family from Mississippi calls her Annie. After Gran and June moved in with us, they started to call her Bea like Papa and everyone else here.

Mama's sisters were crying loudly at the funeral until Mama gave them that look she used to give me when I was acting up as a child. It seemed to work as well on them as it always did on me because they stopped hollering and cried quietly after that. When Pearl became hysterical at the cemetery, Mama was disgusted by her histrionics. She felt that such insincere dramatic behavior was disrespectful to her mother and to those who sincerely mourned her transition. When Pearl seemed determined to jump on the casket as it was lowered into the ground, Reverend Gibson and others looked on in shock. Her brothers grabbed her and tried to pull her away until Mama firmly told them, "Let her go." They turned to look at her as she repeated resolutely, "Let her go!" Mama says she knew that Pearl was showing out and had no intention of going with her mother's body into that hole. When Mama called her bluff, Pearl looked at Mama and saw that angry, disapproving "look." Pearl backed away from the open grave, holding on tightly to her husband. Then she returned quietly to sit in the folded wooden chair next to Birdie.

After the repast at the church, a school bus took the family from Mississippi to collect their luggage and then to the train station in Detroit. Before they left Mama's house, they told her how nice Gran's service was and how beautiful she was "laid out." They also commented on how smart Sarah is, just like they remembered Mama and I used to be when we were her age. Mama proudly boasted that Sarah skipped kindergarten and was sent to first grade two weeks after she started school in September. She told them how the first grade teacher wants to move her to second grade next month to finish out the year.

After the bus left, Thella pressed a piece of paper with her address on it into June's hand. Although June said nothing to her mother, she didn't throw the paper in the trash. When Thella was preparing to return to Chicago, James offered to take her to the depot to save Papa from having to drive into Detroit. However, although June seems open to trying to forgive her mother and make peace eventually, she seemed uncomfortable about making small talk with her for an hour in the car that day. Thella seemed to sense that and declined James's offer. She rode to the depot with Josie and Chet, who said they would be driving near the depot on their way home. It was after ten when the final people left the house, and Alvin, Sarah, and I went home. Still, we all made it to church this morning, and I managed to sing without crying. Now that everyone else has returned home, Mama and I can begin the real process of grieving, and our lives can get on to our new normal without Gran. Our lives will never be exactly the same as before, but God will comfort us and give us the strength to move on, remembering the joy Gran brought to our lives instead of our sorrow since she left.

May 22, 1953

I've been here in Detroit Receiving Hospital for almost two weeks now, and I want to go home so badly. Papa brings Mama to visit every day as soon as visiting hours begin. He stays for a while before going to work in the afternoon. Mama stays with me all day. Alvin visits after work and takes her home with him when visiting hours end. Sarah is staying with June and her family. June and James Jr. are keeping Sarah on top of her schoolwork, since Papa brought her books and assignments to June's. Still, I miss my Sarah, who is too young to visit me. Surely, the powers that be would bend the rules if they met my beautiful, bright, confident young lady. She is smarter and more mature than most children her age. She'll be promoted to third grade in September, since she is at the top of the second grade class, even though she just came into it in February.

I also long to sleep in my own bed with Alvin. I haven't been away from him at night since we married ten years ago, except for the week after Sarah was born. Now that we have our own television, I miss watching *Foodini the Great* with Sarah after dinner and I miss watching my favorite shows with Alvin after she goes to bed: *I Love Lucy, Dragnet, Arthur Godfrey's Talent Scouts, You Bet Your Life, Texaco Star Theater, The Jack Benny Show, Goodyear TV Playhouse* and *Fireside Theater.* Larry plans to release me Monday to finish recuperating at home for at least a month, so I'll miss the rest of the school year. I know that I'll be fit to return in September because Mama will take as good (or better) care of me at home than the fine nurses here. She always knows exactly what I need. After all, she is the one who first knew twelve days ago that I needed to come to the hospital.

It was Mother's Day, which was particularly difficult for Mama this year. June and I knew that Mama was going to be emotional facing that day for the first time after losing her mother. That is why we were both at her house by 8:00 a.m. to make breakfast for her as our first expression of love and honor that day. Still, we were surprised, and somewhat relieved, when Mama cried so hard for so long when she opened the white triple rose corsage Papa had bought for her to wear to church. She wept briefly the day Gran died but never since then, not even at the wake or funeral. The sight of her white corsage, symbolizing that her mother was deceased, triggered the release of emotions she had been suppressing for the past four and a half months. I made a cup of hot tea with lemon for her and sent Papa to church not knowing if she would make it or not. She decided to go. So June and I helped her get dressed, and Alvin came with Sarah to drive us.

Mama felt better after church. The service was uplifting. Reverend Gibson delivered a wonderful sermon based on Proverbs 31:17–31 about how good wives and mothers should be valued and praised for all they do for their families. I sang a song I co-wrote with Gladys, "A Prayer for Mama." There was a reception honoring all mothers afterward with a beautifully decorated cake, cookies, tea, coffee, and frappé. June and I stopped by the reception but left soon to go to Mama's to finish preparing her big Mother's Day dinner. Papa stayed at the reception with Mama for a while. James and James Jr. went home with Alvin. By three p.m., everyone sat down to eat the delicious meal of Mama's favorite dishes. That's when I started feeling queasy. I sat down in the living room. June made a cup of hot tea for me, and Alvin helped her get all the food to the dining room table: peach-glazed ducklings stuffed with wild rice, honey-baked ham, shrimp gumbo, candied yams, collard greens, and biscuits. Later, we planned to enjoy June's red velvet cake and the homemade vanilla ice cream I made the night before.

The smells from the dining room made me hungry, but I was experiencing cramps that were worse than usual. Alvin went home to get the pain medication that Larry prescribed for my painful cramps, but Mama noticed that I was pale and feverish. By the time Alvin returned with the medication, she insisted that he bring me to the emergency room here. I thought we should give the pills a chance to work, but she was emphatic. When I tried to stand, I fainted, and Alvin picked me up. Mama says that's when they saw the melon-sized blood stain on the back of my skirt. She went with Alvin when he carried me to the car and drove me here. She gave June Larry's number to call him. He met us at the hospital. June helped Papa put the food away and helped Sarah pack a little suitcase. She and her men took Sarah to their home in Ferndale, and Papa came to the hospital. June says that Sarah was worried about me, but everyone assured her that I would be fine.

I don't remember anything that happened when I arrived here. Larry says I was barely conscious. He was already here, waiting to examine me. When he did, he explained to Alvin and Mama that I had an ovarian cyst that had ruptured, causing sepsis and hemorrhaging to occur. Within the hour, I was in surgery after they were unable to stop the hemorrhaging and the spontaneous abortion of a tiny embryo in my uterus. Between my loss of blood and the rapid spread of a major infection, the best course of action was to perform an immediate hysterectomy. However, since I am under thirty-five, he needed to consult with my husband before proceeding. Alvin said all he cared about was saving me and signed the paperwork without hesitation. Mama begged Larry to do whatever was necessary to save my life. I could neither consent to nor refuse anything because I didn't regain consciousness until after the surgery. When Papa arrived at the hospital, I was already in the operating room.

Mama, Larry and Alvin were concerned that I would be depressed about the hysterectomy, but I'm not. I spent much of my life thinking I might not be able to have a child. I feel so blessed to have Sarah. The truth is I am ambivalent about having another child and certain that I do not want more than one more. If my pregnancy had gone the distance, I would have been happy, particularly if it had been the son I know Alvin wants. However, I didn't know I was pregnant and it is too early to know what sex the baby would have been. I am not devastated by the loss of a baby I didn't know was growing inside me. Sarah is so wonderful that she is all that I need to feel fulfilled as a mother. I never wanted a big family like I know Mama and Papa did. I am content to give my attention and resources to one child. I have the little girl I always wanted. I wanted to give Alvin a son. However, he says that he is content with Sarah. Getting such a late start in marriage, he is grateful for her. Honestly, I am glad I won't have to take another maternity leave. My family is my most important priority, but it is not the only thing that matters to me. I enjoy working and having some time for myself. Maybe that's selfish, but it is the way I want to live my life.

I can hardly wait to be released. I want to go straight to June's to get my darling Sarah and take her home with me. I know that she is being well taken care of at June's. However, I have missed her too much, and I need to be with her now probably more than she needs to be with me.

August 17, 1953

Yesterday I was so upset with Papa and even more upset with Mama. Papa was rude, ridiculous, and controlling, and Mama acquiesced to his foolishness. She says that she has her own way of communicating her displeasure with her husband's actions. After over thirty-eight years of marriage, she knows how to pick her battles and has her own strategies for winning them. But it's hard for me to keep silent, since I feel like everything that happened is my fault.

Last month, Larry said that I was ready to resume normal activity, including my wifely duties in bed. I was happy to hear that, but when

I bought some sexy lingerie to wear for my first time with Alvin since my surgery, I didn't like the way I looked wearing it. Childbirth and surgery have taken their toll on my abdomen, leaving me with a tummy bulge that I find unsightly. Mama teased me and said I sounded like Scarlett O'Hara in *Gone with the Wind* when she bemoaned the loss of her eighteen-inch waist after giving birth. I replied that I'm only four feet nine inches, and a bulge on my petite frame looks much larger than it would on Mama or any other taller woman. Josie told me that Nancy and Sandy both had full body corsets made to order at a shop in Downtown Detroit after they had their daughters. I asked Mama to go with me when I went for a fitting. Mama found the shop a bit pricey, but the difference in my figure before and after I tried on a corset made it worth every cent. I encouraged Mama to be fitted for one. I knew Mama could have a stunning hour-glass figure, but with poorly fitting bras that lack sufficient support, her 42DD breasts droop like flapjacks, hiding the inward curve at her waistline. She is still a beautiful woman at fifty-eight, but she dresses too matronly and looks older because of that. I know Mama isn't a vain woman, but she likes looking good for Papa and for herself. So reluctantly, she was fitted for a corset as well.

When Mama and I returned two weeks ago to retrieve our corsets, we were both amazed at our new figures. Mama admitted that she looked and felt more than ten years younger with her uplifted bosom, contoured waistline, and firm rounded hips and buttocks. She always downplays her breasts, which she considers to be too large. As a teen and young adult, she had bound them to make them flatter. But as she looked at them high and shapely in the corset, she realized that she looked as gorgeous as Jane Russell or Ava Gardner. I couldn't get over the transformation. "Oh, Mama," I said, "you look gorgeous! Papa is going to drop his jaw when he sees you. I bet you look just like you did back in college, maybe even better."

Mama was so excited that she hid the corset in her dresser drawer when she went home and immediately went to work on a pastel printed dress. It has a scooped neck bodice fitted to show off her bosom and trim waistline and a moderately flared skirt that lies comfortably on her hips before fanning out toward the hem two inches below her knees. She had to dramatically adjust the forms she uses to size clothing she makes for herself and for me. Even those headless padded pieces of metal look good with the expansions and contractions made to them to accommodate our new shapes.

I wore my corset for the first time when our girlfriend group, minus Nancy and Larry, spent an evening at the newly opened Twenty Grand. Sandy and I smiled knowingly at each other and Josie as our proud husbands compared us to fine wine, getting better with age. Later, when Alvin and I returned home, he could hardly wait to ravish me. Yes, that corset is worth every penny I spent.

Mama finally wore her corset yesterday. As usual, she got up early to make a hearty Sunday breakfast for Papa and only tea and a buttered biscuit for herself. She got dressed after Papa left to pick up Sarah for Sunday School. She later rode to church with Alvin and me for the 11:00 a.m. service. Alvin and I love the dress she made to go with her new shape. It's consistent in color and style with her other church dresses, but with her new undergarment, she looks amazing. Alvin told her she looked great when she first got into the car. From the moment she stepped out of the car at church, she and I both noticed the smiles directed at her by the men and women of the congregation.

Some men tried to be subtle. "Good mornin', Sister Bea. It sho' is a fine day, mighty fine."

Men and women liked her style. "That's a real pretty dress, Miss Bea." "Um hm, it sure is."

Some women spoke openly about her figure. "Why, Bea, you look great! Are you on a diet? My dear, you gotta share your secret with me."

When she entered the church, smiling ushers moved quickly to show her to her usual seat, two rows behind Papa and the other trustees. Even Reverend Gibson noticed something new and different about her as he stood at the pulpit. Looking out over his congregation and smiling at Mama, he exclaimed, "Praise God for this beautiful day and for this beautiful gathering of those who have assembled to worship Him!" After the service ended, several of the men, including Reverend Gibson, commented to Papa that Mama was looking especially nice today. They were not disrespectful in any way, just genuinely appreciative of her beauty.

"Yes, Brother Mann, Sister Bea is a fine figger of a woman."

"Mr. Mann, you are truly blessed with a good wife who is beautiful inside and out."

"Brother Mann, you're takin' good care of your missus. She's lookin' so pretty and healthy."

Papa generally likes to see others admire his wife. He proudly puffs out his chest with a look that communicates, "Yes, that fine woman is all mine, and I handle all of that woman." So he must have felt wonderful with all of the positive attention that Mama seemed to be getting. Yet he hadn't seen her when she entered the sanctuary, and she was seated behind him during the service. He didn't get a good look at her until the end of service when he turned around and saw her waiting to go downstairs with him for the usher board's fund-raising dinner. Mama and I expected him to have the same reaction to her new and improved look as Alvin and everyone else had. Instead, he gasped in horror. Quickly removing his suit jacket, he tried to hang it on her shoulders backward, covering her bosom. Observing that we were alone in the sanctuary, he blurted out, "Good god, woman! What were you thinking, coming to church dressed like that? And what have you done to yourself? You're throwing your breasts in everyone's face."

"Mary and I thought I looked nice," Mama replied, bewildered as I was and deeply hurt by Papa's reaction.

I added, "So did a lot of the ladies."

I couldn't believe Papa raised his voice to Mama. "And men! You got these good old Christian men acting like over-stimulated schoolboys. You are not the kind of woman who wants to attract that kind of attention, and I don't like men looking at my wife like that. I want them to respect you."

Perhaps Mama was too shocked to speak, but I wasn't. "Mama is respectable and respected. Can't she be attractive and respectable?"

Mama added, "Yes, there are a lot of pretty Christian women. Why is it wrong for me to be one of them?"

"You are pretty, Bea. More than that, you are beautiful. You don't need to push your breasts up in the air to be beautiful. You are naturally beautiful, and that's how I like you to look—natural. You look fine today, but you don't look like my Bea. My Bea isn't pulled in here and puffed out there, drawing too much attention from other men. I just prefer the way you usually look."

"Honestly, Dad," I said, seeing the disappointment in Mama's face. "Sometimes you can be so insensitive and so wrong. Are you okay, Mama? Even May Ethel is saying how lovely you are."

"I'm fine. I just feel a little tired. Could you take me home?" I knew Mama just wanted to go home and take off the corset that didn't make her more appealing to the person she most wanted to please. I obliged and picked her up in front of the church. Papa went downstairs alone.

Mama told me today that when Papa came in from church last night, he said that he was sorry if he had hurt her feelings by his tone with her. However, he stood by his opinion that it was inappropriate for his wife to look so provocative in public, particularly in church. He knows Mama well enough not to forbid her to wear the corset again. Such a directive would lead her to wear the corset to prove that he can't tell her how to dress. He'll get his way without saying more. His extreme displeasure will keep Mama from wearing the corset again. She said she didn't throw it away, but she stored it in the bottom of her cedar chest. That is where she stores Gran's dress, my baby shoes, and other things she will never use again.

I can't believe Papa used that disapproving tone with Mama. He used it with me when I had to leave Howard and when I started dating Alvin. He still uses it with me when I challenge him about his double standards for men and women. However, Mama sets the perfect standard of womanhood, against which Papa judges me and every other woman. Still, as shocked as I am by Papa's behavior, I am more upset by Mama yielding so readily to his wishes. She felt beautiful and happy until he spoiled her joy. She says she'll handle it in her own way. I hope so. She's a wonderful wife and mother, and she deserves to feel good about herself.

December 26, 1953

What an emotional holiday season this is for everyone! Mama and Papa are both sad, mourning the loss of loved ones. Alvin is ailing and frustrated. I am worried about my husband and angry at my father. Still, we are all trying not to spoil the holidays for Sarah. Christmastime is the most joyful, exciting time of the year for her. It is magical! Seeing Christmas through Sarah's eyes makes us all find happiness despite everything else.

Mama approached the season trying to hide the sadness she was feeling as she faced her first Thanksgiving and Christmas since Gran

died. As always, she gave more attention to the feelings of others than
to her own. She busied herself supporting Papa. He was worried and
frustrated when he learned that his eldest brother, John, was admitted to
Parkside Hospital the first week in November and that he had prostate
cancer. We learned that Uncle John had originally sought treatment at
Harper Hospital but had been referred by them to Parkside, a Negro-
owned hospital with a reputation for providing good medical care.
However, almost all the patients Harper Hospital refers to Parkside
are considered to be terminally ill. Folks say Parkside is "the place to
go when you die." Mama always feels apprehensive when anyone in
the family is ill during the holidays. She has lost most of her relatives
between Thanksgiving and New Year's. Still, she tried to help Papa hold
on to hope, although the doctors didn't give him and Uncle Peter any
cause for optimism, and Uncle John was accepting of what he knew to
be his imminent death.

Uncle John knew about the cancer for a while before he told his
brothers. The doctors at Harper had recommended surgery or radiation,
but John had refused both. So the cancer kept spreading. By the time
he went into Parkside Hospital, there was nothing that could be done
to save him. Papa and Uncle Peter visited him almost every day, and
Mama and Aunt Agnes went with them at least twice a week. Papa
wanted to have Uncle John moved to another hospital where other
doctors might not be so quick to give up. He suggested Burton Mercy,
another Negro-owned and operated hospital, where he thought different
doctors might keep trying to save his life. Uncle John wouldn't hear of
it. He was accepting of his fate and managed to stay in a good mood
right up to the end.

Papa was upset and frustrated watching Uncle John flirting with
the nurses and making jokes all the time. When Uncle Peter and Papa
tried to talk seriously with him about possible treatment to prolong his
life, he told jokes or funny stories to try to make them laugh. "Look,"
he told them, "I ain't never been too serious, and it's way too late to
start now. They say I'm lookin' at only a few weeks before I leave here.
So I might as well be the same as I've been all these years." Then he
told them a joke.

"Did ya'll hear the one about the man who wore a tuxedo to get the
operation they wanted to give me? He said if he was gonna be im*po*tent,
then he might as well look im*po*'tant." Uncle John laughed alone and

goaded his brothers. "Get it? He didn't understand 'impotent.' He thought it meant 'important' so he wore a tuxedo to look important. C'mon, y'all know that was funny."

Papa said he was angry at Uncle John because he seemed to be more terrified of losing his sexual potency than of losing his life. That was why he had refused the suggested treatments earlier. Papa said Uncle John was being "just plain foolish." John had his share of women and a whole lot of other men's shares as well. At sixty-seven, he wasn't fooling around all that much anyway, so why did he care so much about his potency? If he had acted sooner, he might have been able to wipe out the cancer. However, Uncle John said it didn't matter how often he had sex, he wanted to know that he could. Besides, the operation might not have helped anyway, and it wasn't worth the trouble of surgery for a few extra months to a year at best.

Uncle John died Sunday, December 13. He was on an intravenous morphine drip his last week, and he was asleep or semiconscious most of the time. Mama said that during one of his rare lucid periods near the end, he acknowledged how badly he treated his wife back in Mississippi, leaving her without a word, returning home eight years later, beating her for being with someone else during his absence, and then leaving her for good. He wondered if his fate was God's punishment for that and for all the women he had known biblically before and during his marriage. When Papa told him that Jesus had died so that our sins would be forgiven, Uncle John said he believed that, but he also believed that both the good and the evil that we do will come back on us. Uncle John believed that he would be forgiven in the hereafter, but he would first have to face some kind of hell on earth. He was never arrested for all the illegal things he did. He had been beaten up once, but the pain inflicted on him then didn't come close to what he did to his wife. So he believed his painful death was imposed on him by God Almighty.

Papa fell into deep despair when Uncle John died. Uncle John was barely four years older than Papa, and he is the first of his siblings to pass on. Mama lost a brother when she was in her teens. She tried her best to help Papa cope, but facing Uncle John's mortality made Papa contemplate his own. Mama says Papa has been telling her every day that he loves her. He says he always has and always will. It's as though he feels like he could be dying. She was glad to see him enjoy Christmas with Sarah and the rest of us. She hopes his lighter mood will continue.

Mama's concerns about Papa's emotional health have coincided with my concerns about Alvin's physical and emotional well-being. He has not been feeling well for a while. He developed a cough in early November, around the same time that Uncle John went into the hospital. Even Mama's special cough syrup (equal parts of freshly squeezed lemon juice, honey, and whiskey) failed to calm Alvin's cough for long. He sought medical advice from a doctor here in Parkersville, who said it was acute bronchitis. He recommended that Alvin drink a lot of fluids, use cough drops, and stop smoking until the coughing subsided. He also told him to avoid caffeine and alcohol, including Mama's special cough syrup, and get plenty of rest. Finally, twice each night, Alvin was to lean over a bucket of hot water with a towel covering his head and the top of the bucket. He was to do this as long as the steam from the hot water rose into his nostrils. Also, when Alvin got into bed, I was to rub his chest with Vicks VapoRub. We followed his instructions to the letter, and the cough subsided after five days. Alvin felt better but was noticeably weaker going into Thanksgiving. In previous years, when he and Papa shopped for Christmas trees, they bought the biggest Scots pine at the nursery for Mama's house and the biggest balsam fir for our house. Alvin carried the trees inside both the houses and held them up while Papa adjusted the screws on the bases and Mama and I gave directions to ensure that the trees were secured to stand erect. This year, Mama called June to solicit the help of James and James Jr. to help Alvin handle the trees. They also took over Alvin's usual chores of mounting the outdoor lights and tree lights at both of our houses. James put the angel on top of Papa's tree and James Jr., not Alvin, lifted Sarah up on his shoulders to place our treetop angel.

Alvin's cough returned around the first of December. It was worse than in November and lasted more than two weeks despite our strict adherence to the protocol the doctor had recommended before. He should have gone into the hospital, but he said he didn't want to add to everyone's stress during Uncle John's last days. When Uncle John died, Alvin was generally run-down and losing weight. He had a noticeable loss of appetite for food and for sex. However, his cough subsided by the time of Uncle John's funeral on the nineteenth, and Alvin was strong enough to serve as a pallbearer.

At the funeral, I met my aunt Rachel, the sister between Uncle Peter and Papa. She came north alone to represent the family still living in

Mississippi. She said they had contacted John's wife last month when they learned that he had cancer and was not expected to live much longer. John's wife did not respond. Aunt Rachel wasn't sure whether she told his children or not, but nobody heard from them either. Still, about fifty people attended the funeral services at Diggs Funeral Home on the east side of Detroit. Most of them were people Uncle Peter and Uncle John knew from the after-hours joint they ran at Uncle John's house in Paradise Valley. The rest were Papa's friends who came to support him, even though they didn't know Uncle John. The twenty or so mourners who traveled to the cemetery gathered afterward at Uncle Peter's and Aunt Agnes's home for a repast prepared by their neighbors and friends from Vernon Chapel AME.

The mourners and friends were in the living room and dining room. So when I went to the kitchen to get some iced water, I was surprised to see four women standing near the back door. They were smiling as they reminisced about Uncle John and didn't pay any attention to me. They didn't know me and didn't seem to care that I was there. I never spent much time with Uncle John, so as I went about my business, I listened to hear what they were saying about him. I quickly realized that the women had all slept with him, and they said that they would miss his charm and his jokes. They laughed when they agreed that most of his jokes were corny or just plain bad. Yet he was so funny when he told them that he made everybody laugh anyway. They described my late uncle as a lovable "scamp" who had his way with most of the women in Paradise Valley back in the day. They said that they couldn't imagine that the brothers made much money on the bedrooms they rented by the hour at their after-hours joint because Uncle John was usually using one of them. One of the women commented that Uncle John and Uncle Peter were both like the Studebaker Champion: "easy on the eyes, lightweight, and smooth-riding with a big powerful engine under the hood." The others laughed.

"Ain't that the truth!" said another. She was laughing as she added, "With them Manns, what you see ain't what you get. You see them little men, so you's real surprised at how big they is where it counts."

I became uncomfortable when Uncle Peter was added to the commentary. I know him and Aunt Agnes well. I also found it inappropriate for them to discuss his sexual activities while they were in his home. I started to speak up but was drawn to keep listening.

"And they some smooth talkers," a third woman chimed in. "They could sho' talk the pants off any woman, and once they got to her, they could talk her into jus' 'bout anything else. Umh, umh, umh!"

They all agreed that Papa is as cute as his elder brothers. They wondered if he is a scoundrel like them. They speculated that he's probably an even smoother talker because he's a lawyer. With all that education, he knows fancy words that his big brothers couldn't even pronounce. So he could probably talk the pants off a woman faster than they could.

"He could talk mine off for sure," one said with a smirk. "I'd like to find out what all that schoolin' taught him 'bout the laws in bed." The others shook their heads in agreement and laughed.

I was outraged that my father was brought into their conversation. Portraying him so crudely was an insult to him and to my mother, his wife. So I finally interrupted those shameful cackling hussies. "Excuse me, but that is my father you are talking about. He loves his brothers, but he is nothing like them. He is a devout Christian and a faithful husband who would not be interested in adulterous behavior with any of you or anyone else for that matter."

"We're sorry, honey. We meant no disrespect to you or your mother. We were just trying to have some fun on this sad day." Having spoken my peace, I returned to the living room.

When we returned home to Parkersville that evening, I told Mama what the women said about my uncles. I asked if she had ever heard talk like that. I had heard about Uncle John's shenanigans before but nothing to suggest that Uncle Peter was like him. Mama admitted that she and Agnes knew about Peter fooling around. As two grown married women, we can speak honestly about such things that she hid from me even as an adult before I married. I didn't tell Mama that the women at the house had also speculated about Papa's exploits. I just commented that I was surprised but not shocked that Papa seems accepting of his cheating brothers, while he was appalled when Mama merely dressed in a perfectly respectable manner that elicited compliments from men other than her husband. What an outrageous double standard! Mama said the Papa was raised to believe that women are supposed to be held to higher standards of virtuosity than men, in appearance and in fact. I told her that I don't think like that.

I asked Mama why Aunt Agnes puts up with Uncle Peter's infidelity. She said that Agnes never feels threatened by any other woman. Peter loves her the only way he knows how to love. He provides her with a fine house and plenty of food and clothing. She wants for nothing. He respects her at home and in public and never hides the fact that he is married. He doesn't respect the other women he lays with. They are only sexual partners, not lovers, to him. She said men are tempted to stray, especially when women act boldly and dress provocatively, shamelessly offering themselves to men like treats on a serving tray. As long as husbands don't get emotionally involved with those loose women, their wives learn to handle their misdeeds. They are hurtful but trivial incidents in the lifetime of a marriage built on love.

I wondered why Mama's explanation moved from being specifically about Uncle Peter and Aunt Agnes to more general commentary. I wondered why she seemed to understand how wives feel when their husbands cheat. I also wondered why Mama, normally a strong supporter of women, seemed to be blaming women for men's bad behavior. Mama doesn't fully support my intolerance for the double standard applied to men and women, but she generally shares my point of view that men and women are responsible and accountable for their own behavior. This conversation seemed out of character for her, and it was so personal that I became suspicious that Mama's statements were as much about her own experiences as those of Aunt Agnes. However, I didn't comment on that observation. I responded generally, pointing out that the other women had not taken vows of marriage to the aggrieved wives but the cheating husbands had done so. Thus, they were the ones accountable for breaking those vows. Their wives should call them to task, not passively accept their betrayal like they were the victims of wicked women. I always hate it when men blame Eve for Adam's trouble in the Garden of Eden. After all, God had given him the same free will and the same command that He had given to Eve. Adam was as much to blame as she for the wrath that was visited upon them.

Mama said that she did not mean to suggest that adulterous husbands are not responsible for their actions, just that wives also took vows to love them for better or worse. Uncle Peter's better far outweighs his worse, and that is why Agnes stays with him. As Mama spoke, it did not escape my notice that she had become uncomfortable and had shifted her comments back to the specific situation of her brother-in-law's marriage. I didn't want to ask her about her experiences with Papa. I was curious but did not believe she wanted to discuss it directly with me. Still, I wondered if Papa is the pillar of virtue I always believed him to be.

Later, as Alvin and I lay in bed, I couldn't stop wondering if Papa was a philanderer like his elder brothers. When Alvin stroked my breast as a prelude to lovemaking, I should have been excited. It was the first time in over a month that he had felt well enough to do so. However, instead of responding positively to his advances, I sat up and looked him in the eye, asking, "Do you know if my father has ever cheated on my mother?"

Alvin seemed startled by the inquiry. "Why are you asking me that?"

I repeated the question, adding, "You and my father are friends. I want to know if, as his friend, you have ever known him to be unfaithful to my mother."

Alvin's obvious awkwardness answered my question. He clearly did not want to betray his friend and father-in-law, but he did not want to lie to me, his wife. So he answered truthfully but cautiously, "I have never seen your father in an inappropriate situation with a woman."

I persisted. "Have you heard anything from him or anyone else that would lead you to *suspect* that he has been intimate with another woman?"

Alvin quipped, "Now, my love, you should know from your own experiences that people in this town like to gossip about things that may or may not be true. Your father has always said and shown that he loves your mother. He has never said or done anything that would cause me to question that."

Annoyed by Alvin's cagey choices of words, I boldly asked, "Do you suspect that my father has had sex with other women?"

Alvin admitted that there were rumors about women he might have been with, even that he may have fathered a child with one. Alvin said Papa never spoke of such activities to him, but he didn't deny the rumors when he was told about them. Of course, Alvin quickly pointed out Papa's failure to deny the rumors did not prove that they were true. Papa doesn't like people in his business. So he doesn't discuss any rumors or stories about him or his family. Alvin said, in all of his dealings with Papa, he found him to be a man who loved and respected his wife and who tried to live a decent life, serving God as well as he could. Papa is not without sin, and he would be the first to admit that. If he had ever yielded to temptation, it was because he was imperfect, as all men are.

Once again, Alvin reached out to me affectionately, clearly hoping to get my mind off Papa and on my husband and his needs. I was displeased with his insensitivity to my feelings. I pulled away and queried mockingly, "And what about you? Have you yielded to temptation? Have your imperfections led you to cheat on me?"

"My darling," Alvin began in a reassuring tone, "I can honestly say that I have never been tempted by another woman since our first date. I am an imperfect sinner but not when it comes to being faithful to you. I did my share of fornicating before we were together, but I have never committed adultery. I haven't even thought about being with another woman. Look in my eyes and you'll see that I'm telling you the truth. You can believe in me as I have always believed in you."

I did believe him. I also believe that Papa has cheated on Mama and that she knows it. I was angry, hurt, and dismayed by what I was feeling about Papa at that moment. I kept thinking about how badly he treated Mama when she wore her corset to church, so badly that she will never wear it again. All she did was try to look nice for him. Maybe she was hoping to jog his memory of how beautiful she is so as to turn his attention to her and away from other women. He was so jealous that other men found her attractive, or maybe he was just feeling guilty that men might lust after her as he does after other women. I remembered how he never stood up for me with Howard University, how he said I deserved what they did to me, and how what I did would cause rumors about me and our family here in Parkersville. If I had been a man, what I did would not have broken any college rule, and there would have been no cause for rumors. He was so angry with me then. I did all he asked of me to make amends, but he's never looked at me with quite the same adoration as before.

How hypocritical Papa seems to me now. His behavior is far worse than mine and causes more rumors. I love Papa, but I will never look at him the same way as before. I am so angry at him for betraying and hurting Mama and for confusing and hurting me. He raised me to be intelligent and independent, to think critically and fight for what I believe and desire. Yet somehow he expected me to turn out differently: unquestioningly obedient, respectful, and respectable, the way he believes a daughter should be. I tried to regain his respect and trust by being an obedient daughter, but I'm done with that now. I'm grown and married, and I don't need his approval. Besides, he's lost my trust and respect now. I wanted to confront Papa and yell at him right then. But when Alvin turned over, giving up on romance that night, I redirected my intense feelings into making passionate love to my faithful husband. Alvin matched my exuberance. Exhilarated and exhausted afterward, we fell into deep sleep in each other's arms.

Now just a week later, Alvin is feeling weak and worn again. He is not coughing much, but he has noticeably less strength and energy than he did a couple of months ago before he started having these repeated bouts with bronchitis. I am worried about him, and I am going to insist that he consult another doctor after New Year's.

I've managed to hide my worry about Alvin and my anger at Papa from Sarah. She has been excited about all of her roles in school, town, and church programs. She played Mary in the nativity play at church. She was the Sugarplum Fairy in the town of Parkersville production of *The Nutcracker Suite*. At the Parkersville Elementary School Christmas program, she sang lead on "O Holy Night" with the chorus and recited *'Twas the Night before Christmas* as the finale with children from kindergarten through third grade acting out the story in the background. Between rehearsals and decorating the trees at both houses, Sarah has been kept too busy to notice anything not related to the joy of Christmas. Sarah takes pride in helping Mama make the all edible decorations for the Christmas tree at her house: garland made of Cheerios strung on red yarn and shiny ornaments of sugar-sprinkled Christmas cookies, glazed gingerbread men, and colored popcorn balls. She also enjoys making the handcrafted papier-mâché ornaments that hang among the store-bought glass ornaments on the tree in our house. Her enthusiasm is contagious. I was too preoccupied making a good Christmas for Sarah to dwell on my angst and anger.

That is probably why it was evening when I realized how bad Alvin felt yesterday. Sarah woke us up around 7:00 a.m. to open the presents under the tree. Mama taught me to make gift wrapping as exciting as the gift inside. Alongside the bow, I attach a little toy and a sweet treat of chocolate kisses, candy canes, or clear-wrapped cookies. Sarah likes looking at the wrapping right up to Christmas Day. However, when it's time to open her presents, she rips through the wrapping, preserving only the edible treats, which she snacks on all week long. Watching Sarah's unbridled joy at home in the morning and later at my parents' house before dinner, Alvin and I laughed so much that we forgot about our cares and concerns for a while. I didn't notice that he hardly played with Sarah during the day. I first took note that he was hurting during Christmas dinner at Mama's. He ate very little and was less jovial than usual. Mama and June didn't notice the changes in Alvin. They kept looking at each other, missing Gran sitting in her special chair between them at the table. Papa was more subdued, no doubt remembering Uncle John. I felt so sorry for him that I started to think I might be wrong in assuming he cheated on Mama.

Then I observed Mama's unpleasant reaction when Papa added a sweet potato pie to the dessert table. He explained that it was a gift from Isabel Harris, a widow who was thankful for the help he gave her with insurance claims and other matters after her husband's death. Mama made "that face," obviously angered by a seemingly kind gesture. I wondered if Mama suspected that there were more "treats" that Widow Harris gave to Papa. I was livid at the thought that he would rub his indiscretion in Mama's face like that. I convinced myself that he wouldn't do that to her, so he must be innocent. Later, however, I wasn't so sure. Mama's reaction to the pie and something I remembered that Alvin told me after Uncle John's funeral got me thinking. I needed to ask Alvin some more questions.

Alvin and I brought Sarah home last night around 10:00 p.m. We were all exhausted from a long active day. After tucking in Sarah, I joined a half-sleeping Alvin in our bed. I pressed him to tell me more about the rumors that Papa had fathered children by other women. I asked him directly, "Where are these children, and has Papa contributed to their care?" I knew that Papa wanted a big family, especially sons. He readily adopted Paul, and it made him so very proud and happy to be his dad. If Papa has a son of his own blood, I can't imagine him not having a relationship with him. I thought Alvin was too sleepy to think of a convincing lie, so he would tell me the truth, whether he meant to do it or not. Yet my interrogation seemed to wake him up, making him as guarded as ever.

"Honestly, Mary, why are you asking me about that now? I told you before that the rumors were unsubstantiated. SC never acknowledged fathering any children outside of his marriage."

"I know that," I said, "but I still want to know what the rumors say about his children. Who are they, and where are they?"

Alvin was fidgeting uncharacteristically. "You know, my love, that I do not like repeating gossip. I don't pay attention to it and try not to even listen to it."

"C'mon, Alvin. You are my husband, and you promised never to lie to me. What are the rumors about Papa's children? I have a right to know if I have half siblings. I'd rather learn the truth from you than to hear it from some mean-spirited person trying to hurt me or my family."

"There was only one child mentioned. It was purely speculation, and to my knowledge, nobody ever asked SC about it. It didn't spread far back then and hasn't been talked about in years. Nobody cares anymore, and if you haven't heard anything about it by now, I seriously doubt that you ever will. It's long been put to rest. So let it be."

"Alvin Terrence Morgan, if you plan to get any rest tonight or any other nights hence, just tell me what the speculation was. Why are you so reluctant to tell me, unless you believe it to be true or unless I know the person? I know Papa cheats on Mama. Nothing can hurt me more than that. I'm not going to say or do anything rash based on gossip, and I will never admit you told me anything."

Alvin sighed. "All right. It was just that some folks said your brother, Paul, looked so much like SC that he could have been his actual son. Most people thought that was a preposterous idea. SC, Bea, and Paul's mother never spoke or acted like it was so. It didn't take long for people to dismiss the idea and move on to something else to talk about."

I thanked Alvin for telling me the truth. I said that it was silly gossip and that it didn't bother me. I know that this is a small town and folks are always looking for ways to chip away at the high esteem in which people hold my family. That's what I told Alvin before I let him sleep. Still, I did go through the photo albums today, and I was indeed struck by the strong resemblance between Papa and Paul. Except for height and coloring, Paul and I kind of favored each other. I also noted how his name fit the Mann tradition of Biblical first and historical middle names. Paul, a disciple of Christ, was his first name, and his middle name, DuBois, is the name of the man Papa reveres as the greatest Negro scholar and activist of this century. I'm not so ready to dismiss the idea that Paul could have been my half brother as well as my adopted brother. However, it is outrageous to think that Papa would move the progeny of his adulterous relationship into Mama's house and ask her to care for his mother and him. I'm upset with Papa, but I can't believe he would be that arrogant and cruel. I can't believe the idea to be true, not without proof. So for now, I am going to focus on other things, like trying to enjoy the rest of the holiday season and getting Alvin to consult another doctor.

January 3, 1954

New Year's Eve, Alvin and I went out with my girlfriends group, once again minus Nancy and Larry. They were at a lavish New Year's Eve party hosted by a couple they know from one of the various clubs or groups to which they belong. They are spending more time with that crowd these days than with us. We see them pictured in *The Michigan Chronicle* a lot, and sometimes in the *Detroit News* and *Detroit Free Press*, at posh affairs and in various community service and political activities in and around Detroit. Nancy has become friendly with other mothers whose children are near the same ages as hers. So her kids and she are often too busy to spend time with Kendra and Sandy and Sarah and me. When we do get together, Nancy is her same sweet self. Some of her new friends are very nice, but others seem rather snooty.

Josie commented that she and Chet rarely spend time with her brother, who is Chet's best friend since childhood. They don't blame Larry and Nancy for that though. Larry and Nancy often extend invitations for them to come to parties at their mansion-sized home on East Boston Boulevard and to other events which they attend. However, Chet and Josie don't always accept their invitations. Chet says that he still feels close to his childhood friend, and Larry still acts the same toward him. Larry's friends act friendly, but Chet says he doesn't have much in common with them. Chet makes good money with his barbershop, but he didn't attend college. They are accomplished doctors, lawyers, businessmen, and the accountants who keep all of them from paying too much in taxes. Chet doesn't have the money or time to "run" with them as they go across the river to the Surf Club in Canada and travel to each other's second homes in Oak Bluffs at Martha's Vineyard, Highland Beach in Maryland and Sag Harbor in the Hamptons, or when they vacation in Atlantic City, Las Vegas, Acapulco and elsewhere. Chet bowls but he doesn't play golf, tennis or croquet. He grew up in Detroit and is not much of an outdoorsman, like many of them who spent their early years in the South. They enjoy hunting and eating the likes of rabbit, pheasant and venison. Chet doesn't own a boat and has only been fishing a few times in fresh water. He knows nothing of fly fishing or fishing in the deep sea. Chet also doesn't feel he has anything to contribute to their casual conversations or their more serious ones. His experiences with prejudice in getting his barbershop opened seem far less interesting to him than all they encountered in white hospitals and the obstacles they overcame in establishing and administering Negro hospitals in and around Detroit. Chet says he is impressed by them and appreciates all they have done to improve health care for Negroes in Michigan. Most of them are self-made men, who worked hard to get where they are. They still work hard, and when they're not working, they have a lot of fun. He's just not in their league and doesn't fit with them socially.

Josie says that she doesn't feel their wives are "out of her league," but she doesn't feel like she fits in with them either. She loves Nancy and she finds most of the wives to be friendly enough when they get to know her or when they find out that she is Larry's sister. However, she has had a few experiences that have left her less than enthusiastic about socializing with some of them. She feels that she sticks out like "a fly in a bowl of rice" as one of the few dark-skinned wives in the crowd. Chet says that she is the darkest wife and undeniably the most beautiful and stylish. Josie says that apparently not everyone shares Chet's opinion about her appearance. She told a story about the first time she went to a party at Larry's and Nancy's home:

> It was some exclusive holiday shindig they hosted for one of their clubs. Each couple, including the hosts, could only invite one outside couple. Nancy and Larry invited Chet and me. I got out of the car in front of the house while Chet looked for the nearest available space, which turned out to be far away, almost to the end of the long block. While Chet was parking, I rang the bell at the front door. Nancy was in the kitchen talking to the caterer for the affair, and Larry was speaking with some of the guests in the foyer. So another member of the club answered the door. When she saw me, she smiled and politely told me, "The help is supposed to use the side entrance," as she pointed to her left.

I was taken aback by the comment, since I was dressed in a beautiful green silk suit with matching green lizard shoes and handbag, cultured pearl jewelry, dark green gloves, and a ranch mink stole draped over my shoulders. My hair was done earlier that day in a curly updo, and my makeup and lipstick were flawlessly applied. I wondered what there was about my look, other than my complexion, that would lead this silly woman to believe I was one of the "help." However, I quickly composed myself and replied politely, "I'll make a note of that." I saw Larry approaching the door, probably coming to open it, but he arrived too late to get to answer the bell in his own house because a guest took it upon herself to do it for him. When I saw him, I gently pushed past the woman and let her know who I was when I finished my sentence, "But I'll go through this door so I can kiss my big brother. Why don't you stay here and explain all of that to my husband. He'll be here in a couple of minutes."

When I ran into Larry's outstretched arms, he looked puzzled. "What was that all about?" he asked me. I told him that it was nothing important. For the rest of the evening, the woman tried to apologize, but I never let her engage me in conversation. I could not think of anything that woman could say that I would want to hear. So I walked away whenever I saw her trying to approach me.

Chet said that Josie never likes to finish the story. "The woman must have said something to Nancy because Nancy spoke to Josie about an hour later offering an apology on behalf of the woman, who said she was sorry about a misunderstanding she had with Larry's sister and hoped she had not offended her in any way. Josie told Nancy the same thing she had told Larry: that it wasn't important and she didn't get offended that easily." He said that truthfully, Josie was offended enough not to want to be with "her kind" again. "She was just one person, and we don't even know that she is one of Nancy's friends. None of the other women we met at Nancy's have said anything like that to Josie, but she hasn't wanted to be around them since."

Josie explained, "I'm not trying *not* to be around them. I just prefer to spend my time with people I like better, present company for example." Everyone laughed.

As usual, we had a great time ringing in the New Year. We stopped partying long enough to thank God for getting us through 1953 and prayed that He would continue to bless us with His love, grace, and mercy in 1954.

Alvin and I left earlier than usual. He was feeling tired and wanted to lie down. We were back on the road to Parkersville before 1:00 a.m. Alvin started coughing before we got in the car, so I drove. He was coughing all the way home. By the time we arrived at home, he was coughing so hard that blood was coming out in the sputum. The coughing finally subsided after we followed the protocol of steam and Vicks VapoRub. He was able to sleep peacefully after drinking a cup of hot tea. After two days of rest, he's still not up to par. He made it to church this morning but left right after the service ended. Before I went back to church with Sarah for the afternoon program, I prepared some chicken vegetable soup for him with plenty of garlic and some hot tea loaded with lemon juice and honey. I brought Sarah home as soon as the program ended, so we could check on him. He felt well enough to play Scrabble and Gin Rummy with us until she went to bed. I return to school tomorrow, so I didn't mind when Alvin wanted to turn in earlier than usual. He's already asleep, just five minutes after his head hit the pillow.

Alvin has finally agreed to see another doctor. Thank God! I'm afraid he has something more serious than bronchitis. I'll ask Larry to refer us to someone.

April 18, 1954

Happy Easter! Indeed, it is a very happy Easter for me. For the first time in three months, Alvin felt well enough to go to church. Ever since we learned that Alvin has lung cancer, I have been afraid of losing him. By the time we met with Dr. Evan Edwards, Larry's referral, he said that the cancer was advanced. He recommended surgery to remove the tumors followed by radiation therapy to kill any cancer cells that might remain. He urged us to begin as soon as possible. I took a week off from teaching and stayed at Alvin's bedside at Trinity Hospital from morning until evening every day. Sarah moved in temporarily with Mama and Papa. I was overwhelmed with shock, fear, and confusion. Alvin had been seeing a doctor for months. How could he have been so wrong about the true nature of Alvin's cough? Cancer is scary, and everyone I know who had it died within a few months to a year. All I could think about was getting Alvin to beat cancer and live. I couldn't imagine my life without him. I prayed with him at the hospital and alone at home every morning and night.

I was relieved and delighted that the surgery went well. They were able to remove all visible tumors, and the cancer did not appear to have spread beyond the lungs. Alvin responded well to the radiation treatments. He said that they were not painful, but they left him extremely tired. Less than a month after surgery, Alvin was released from the hospital. Dr. Edwards advised that he recuperate at home for at least another six to eight weeks. They further advised that he stop smoking immediately, which his local doctor had also advised him to do, and that he quit working in the foundry at Ford's auto plant. They explained that the combination of smoking and exposure to the chemicals in the foundry would dramatically increase his risk of more cancer or some other lung disease in the future. I wondered if the doctor in Parkersville should have known sooner that Alvin had cancer so it could have been treated before it was advanced. Dr. Edwards explained that it was not uncommon for symptoms of the cancer not to appear until it was advanced. They said that lung cancer often went undetected until chest X-rays were done to investigate symptoms of flu or pneumonia.

Alvin really wants to get better. He says that giving up smoking was easier than he had imagined it would be. By the time he was released from the hospital, he had lost his taste for cigarettes. Indeed, he hadn't had a cigarette since being admitted, so he quit cold turkey after forty years of smoking about a pack a day during the week and more on weekends when he was drinking socially. Mama has helped me a lot. She tends to Alvin and prepares a hot lunch for him while I'm at work. He has stopped losing weight, but he hasn't gained back all that he lost before the surgery. His face looks gaunt, and his physique is thin. For the first time since we met, he is beginning to look his age. However, he is still handsome. His old clothes don't hang well on his slimmer body, so I bought him a suit and shirt in smaller sizes to wear to church today. He looked as distinguished as ever in his new duds. Sarah and I are so proud of him and how hard he is trying to get stronger and better. He pushes himself to do more than he should because he says he doesn't want to be a burden on us. We don't find it a burden to care for him. Sarah and I, even Mama, love him and we don't mind.

Still, Alvin is frustrated and disappointed because he can't do some of the romantic and playful things he used to do with me and Sarah. He hasn't picked up either of us in over nine months. I admit that I miss him carrying me up to bed to have his way with me, like Rhett Butler in *Gone with the Wind*. Yet I have patience and faith that we'll get back to that or on to something even better when the time is right. Sarah is a different matter. Alvin wants to pick up his little girl, who at six is already almost as tall as I am. He hates that he's had to stop carrying her on his shoulders because he fears he will drop her. He doesn't want to appear to be less of a strong protector for Sarah and me. We both try to reassure him that we still see him as our strong and brave man, who is steadily beating a monstrous disease that has claimed the lives of so many others. Sarah and I want to spend as much time with him as possible, but he insists that we not alter our weekend schedule of a full day of lessons for Sarah (ballet and tap in the morning and piano and voice in the afternoon) in Detroit on Saturday and a full day at church most Sundays. We usually try to meet Josie and/or Sandy for lunch between tap and piano because we come home as soon as her lessons end. We no longer stay later to have dinner and see a movie with them as we did before January. Back then, we rarely got back to Parkersville before 7:30 p.m. I would take Sarah to Mama and Papa's, and I'd come home to get dressed to go out with Alvin. Now Sarah and I return no later than 4:30 p.m. and spend Saturday evenings at home with Alvin.

Alvin rarely leaves home, except to keep appointments with Dr. Edwards. I know he has missed attending church every Sunday. That's why it was so special that he went to church today and stayed after the service to attend the Easter dinner and program. He was tired when we returned home just before five, but he had enough energy to play Monopoly and Scrabble with Sarah and me before we all went to bed a little after nine. Alvin says he'll start going to church every Sunday again. Even if he only stays for service, that will get him out of the house at least once each week. I am feeling encouraged that he is on the way to recovering enough to go back to work. He really wants to be working again, for social reasons as well as economic ones.

January 2, 1955

For the first time, Alvin and I spent New Year's Eve at home watching television with Sarah until she fell asleep around ten thirty. I woke her just enough to walk upstairs to her bed, and I tucked her in with a kiss. Then I joined Alvin in our bed to watch New Year's Eve specials from New York on the television Alvin gave me for our bedroom as a Christmas gift. Alvin gave the money for the television to James and James Jr. They picked it up for him, just as they did everything else for him related to Christmas. They went with Papa to get the trees, set them up, and put on the lights. James Jr. lifted Sarah on his shoulders to put the angels on top at both houses. James and James Jr. did all of the outdoor decorations. Thanks to them, we have a beautifully decorated house, and now we have two televisions: one downstairs in the living room and one upstairs in our bedroom. As we watched 1955 ring in on our new TV, I opened a chilled bottle of champagne. Alvin and I kissed and clicked our glasses in a toast to love, health and happiness in the coming year. Alvin fell asleep within minutes without finishing his glass. I finished the bottle. It was enough to allow me to sleep but not enough to make me as happy as I should be.

I have a loving husband and a wonderful daughter. We're not rich, but we have a beautiful home, two cars, more than enough good food and clothing, and we have a number of supportive friends and family. I realize how fortunate I am, and I feel guilty about wanting more. Yet I'm in the prime of my life, and I feel like I'm missing out on the things I should be doing in my prime. I want to go out and have fun with my husband. I want to travel with him and Sarah to places I've never been. I want to make love with Alvin. I promised to love and cherish him in sickness and in health, and I do. Yet I miss the passion and intimacy we shared. My body and soul have needs and desires that only he can fulfill. I know the old saying that "sex is like a game of bridge. If you've got a good enough hand, you don't need a partner." But it's not the same. I want to feel Alvin inside me again, feel his heavy breathing, his warmth, his perspiration, and his nibbling on my ears and breasts. I've got good hands, but they can't do all that. Even after almost a whole bottle of champagne, my body knows the difference between my hand and my man.

As I try to find ways to bring passion back into my life, I am thinking more and more about my lifelong dream of singing professionally. When I had the opportunity to sing at Club Zombie, I turned it down. I was in love with Alvin, and I wanted to be his wife more than I wanted to pursue a singing career. I thought I had abandoned that dream, but now I wonder if I really let it go or if I just meant to postpone it. As much as I like teaching others to sing, I want to sing, not just in church but on stage. I want to sing on television and hear my records playing on the radio. I see many singers on TV variety shows, and I hear popular singers with records that top the charts. Some of them are really outstanding, but a lot of them don't have voices that are better than mine, maybe not even as good. Emma Randall is making records solo without Ebony Hues. She wasn't, and isn't, better than me, but she doesn't have a husband and a seven-year-old. I'm only kidding myself to think I can chase the dream of a singing career now. That's okay. If I had to choose between Emma's life and mine, I'd choose my family without hesitation or regret. So I guess I'll keep singing my solos with the choirs at Allen AME and teaching at Central High. I appreciate my life, Lord. Forgive me for wanting more.

It's just so hard to watch Alvin struggling so much and trying not to show his unhappiness. He's glad to be working again but frustrated about making less money in the general assembly line than he did working in the foundry. According to his medical checkups, he is improving steadily, and there are no signs of cancer cells in his body. However, his appetite, weight, and stamina remain lower than before he was sick. By the time he comes home from work, he's too tired to do much more than eat dinner and watch television for about an hour before going to bed around 8:30 p.m. Even on Sundays, he goes to bed by 9:15 p.m. right after he watches his favorite ninety-minute block on CBS: *The Jack Benny Program* at 7:30 and *The Ed Sullivan Show*, which lasts an hour, starting at eight. He and Sarah both go to bed then. I stay up to clean the kitchen, prepare everyone's lunches for Monday, and lay out their clothes. Then I watch *Alfred Hitchcock Presents* before retiring at ten. Saturday is Alvin's late night. He stays up until eleven. Sarah goes to bed at nine, after watching *The Honeymooners* with us.

Then Alvin and I get cozy in our bed to watch *Lawrence Welk's Dodge Dancing Party, Gunsmoke,* and *Your Hit Parade.*

Wednesday nights are special. That's when the whole family watches *Disneyland* together. I see how much Sarah is fascinated by Fantasy Land, Tomorrow Land, Adventure Land, and Frontier Land. When Alvin and I heard the announcement that Walt Disney is building a Disneyland park in California, we vowed to take Sarah there as soon as Alvin is up to the cross-country trip. Alvin thinks he might be feeling well enough to go on a family adventure by the time the park opens this summer. I can't wait to see Sarah's face when she meets all of her favorite Disney characters in person. That will be our surprise present to her for her eighth birthday in July.

July 24, 1955

Sarah was thrilled on her birthday when she got three presents that she wanted so very much. Her godmother Josie gave her a three-foot tall walking Suzy doll with red stitched hair that she can wash and set with rollers. Mama and Papa gave her a portable record player and some 45 rpm records and a 33 1/3 rpm album to play on it. Alvin and I gave her a twenty-six-inch Schwinn Starlet bicycle. We couldn't afford the trip to Disneyland that we wanted to give her, and Alvin wouldn't be able to handle a cross-country train ride now. I'm so happy that we never told her about our plans. So she's not disappointed like we are.

Alvin caught a cold in late January. It left him with another persistent cough and made him weaker and more lethargic. When it passed, he returned to work briefly but never regained enough of his former strength to work consistently. He had to retire in March. He planned to look for a different job when he felt up to it, but he never felt well enough to go back to work. At sixty, he had worked thirty-five years at Ford but was not eligible to receive a full pension based on the agreement between Ford and the UAW, which required one to be sixty-five with thirty years of service. Papa negotiated successfully with Ford Motor Company on his behalf and helped him get the full pension available to workers at sixty-five. Papa is also trying to get him awarded his Social Security benefits early, based on his inability to continue to work. Alvin had a healthy savings account at the start of the year, but it has been almost completely depleted now between his medical expenses and the period after his retirement when he had no income until Papa secured his pension for him. So our plans of taking Sarah to the opening of Disneyland this month had to be deferred.

I'm not abandoning that plan, just postponing it. I called the group together last week to make plans for a group-plus-kids cross-country trip to Disneyland next summer. Josie, Sandy, and even Nancy, who is eight months pregnant with her third baby, are on board with their husbands' blessings. Josie, still childless, is excited about sharing the cross-country adventure with her friends; her goddaughter, Sarah; and her niece and nephew, Larry Jr. and Larissa. We'll all do our part to help Nancy with her one-year-old. Last Saturday, we met to begin planning for our trip over lunch at J. L. Hudson's in its Northland Mall in the Detroit suburb of Southfield. Yesterday, we arranged for our children to play at Nancy's while we continued planning. We agreed to travel by train, exposing the children, and ourselves, to as much of the scenic American landscape as possible. Josie and I are in charge of investigating luxury trains and train routes to make the travel arrangements. Sandy will research historic sites and tourist attractions in California and suitable lodging for us when we are there. Nancy will get age-appropriate books about American geography to get the children excited about what they'll see along the train route. We are all excited about this trip. Nancy and her children have traveled to more places than the rest of us, but she has not traveled west of Chicago in the U.S., even though she has spent time in western Mexico. We're in our thirties, and we'll be learning about "America, the Beautiful" right along with our children: my Sarah, eight; Nancy's son Larry Jr., seven, and daughter Larissa, five and a half; and Sandy's daughter Kendra, also five and a half. Each member of the group is happy and enthusiastic about her assignment. We agreed to meet formally again at Nancy's in November, when her baby will be at least three months old. That's when we'll finalize our plans and bring down payments for our reservations. We are giddy, anticipating a marvelous summer vacation together.

September 16, 1955

I have been an emotional wreck for the past two and a half weeks, but I have to keep going. The group was devastated by two shocking deaths on August 31. Around ten in the morning, Josie called to tell me that Nancy had died an hour earlier, apparently from a cerebral aneurysm. The housekeeper arrived at eight as Larry was leaving to do rounds at the hospital. Nancy seemed fine as she bid adieu to her husband and welcomed the housekeeper. Half an hour later, the housekeeper found her unresponsive when she brought her breakfast. She called Larry, who sent an ambulance and followed immediately. He also called an obstetrician who lives around the corner from their house. He arrived before the ambulance and Larry. The doctor found her already dead. The baby was still alive, but he died before the doctor could deliver him by Caesarian section. Larry was inconsolable, blaming himself, even though Nancy had shown no prior symptoms. Sandy and I both came to help Josie with Larry Jr. and Larissa while Larry and Nancy's mother were making arrangements. We prepared food for the family to eat and made requested phone calls to relatives and friends. We were still in shock, and the reality that Nancy is gone didn't fully sink in, even after we each made over a dozen calls.

When I returned home that evening, I found Mama and Papa at the house with Sarah and Alvin. Papa was outraged and Mama was upset by a report on the evening news that the body of fourteen-year-old, Emmett Louis "Bobo" Till, had been discovered and retrieved by two fishermen from the Tallahatchie River near Money, Mississippi. Apparently, on August 27, the Chicago youth had been taken from his uncle's home, beaten severely, and had an eye gouged out before he was shot through the head and thrown into the river tied with barbed wire to a seventy-pound cotton gin fan. This heinous crime was visited upon him because he supposedly spoke to or whistled at a white woman in a local grocery store earlier that day. Papa said that Emmett Till's murder was a grim reminder to him of why he left Mississippi and why he hadn't visited there in so many years. Mama thought about all those summers she took me there as a child and how angry Gran was with me for not minding my tongue around white people. She used to say that my uppity Northern attitude was going to get me and June hurt or killed. Back then, I didn't really understand how much evil could be visited upon a colored child by white folks because of a word or gesture interpreted as a violation to the codes of behavior in the Jim Crow South. Alvin said it could just as easily have happened in Alabama or any other state in the Deep South. He said white folks in the South are still angry that the Supreme Court outlawed segregation in schools. He added, "Hell, ninety years after losing the Civil War, they're still mad we're not their slaves. They can't kill the lawmakers in Washington, but they can break the laws and kill Negroes in the South. They don't need good reasons for killing us. The reason is that they hate us. You can change the laws but not people's hearts. Their hate runs too deep."

Josie, Sandy, and I attended Nancy's wake on the fifth and funeral on the sixth. Our husbands were with us but not our children. Two consecutive days, Alvin left the house to go somewhere other than to a doctor's appointment or to Allen AME. Larry spared no expense in giving Nancy a fine service. She was dressed in a white satin and lace peignoir from Saks Fifth Avenue. Her long brown hair was perfectly coiffed in an upsweep style with a large roll across the top of her head like a crown or a halo. Tiny tufts of soft curls spiraled down both sides of her face. She wore simple pearl studs in her pierced ears. She was clutching her beautiful baby boy with his angelic face resting right above her heart. He was dressed in a tiny white Christening outfit. Nancy and little Nelson looked like they were sleeping peacefully, each smiling softly. None of the mourners had ever seen such a beautiful yet sad sight. The bronze casket was draped with a blanket of white roses. Larry and Larry Jr. wore white suits. Nancy's mother and Larissa wore white dresses. Attractive white floral funeral wreaths and sprays from family, friends, and hospital staff encircled the sanctuary of Plymouth Congregational Church. The sunlight coming through the stained glass windows added a glow to the white setting that made it seem heavenly.

The beauty of Nancy's funeral was in sharp contrast to the horror witnessed by mourners and curiosity seekers who crowded Roberts Temple Church of God in Chicago for the public funeral of Emmett Till, who was also buried on the sixth. Mamie Till, Emmett's mother, insisted on a public funeral service with an open casket so the world could see the brutality of the killing, in her words, "what they did to my boy." The pictures of Emmett's face, shown in yesterday's *Jet Magazine*, barely looked human. It was battered beyond recognition, bloated and partially decomposed from the time his body had spent under water. He had a bullet hole in his head. There had been thousands of similar murders in the South, but the television reports and graphic photos circulated in publications evoked visceral emotional responses to this case among whites and Negroes. Papa is disgusted that Negroes are still subjected to such outrageous treatment in the state of his birth, which he fled almost forty years ago. He says that he used to wonder from time to time if he could have changed things in Mississippi if he had stayed there. However, he no longer thinks that he could have made a difference. He's certain that his words and actions would just have resulted in Mama being widowed early and me never having been born. He and others in the Detroit-area Mississippi Club have been discussing the Emmett Till incident since it happened. A group of them went to Chicago for his funeral to show their support for his mother. This terrible tragedy has evoked their memories of other horrors they witnessed or experienced before they migrated to the North. They love their relatives who still live in Mississippi, and most are sending money regularly to help them out. However, none of them has any desire to move back there. Some still routinely send their children to spend summers with relatives there, but now they are wondering if they should stop doing that.

Because I attended Nancy's funeral, I missed the first day of school at Central. When I came the next day, I was amused by the eagerness of my new students, who were excited to be starting high school. My returning students were happy to see me, especially those in the choir, who were still riding high on our success in bringing home the state championship trophy again last spring. Looking at their bright smiles and responding to their hugs brought joy to interrupt my sadness. When I returned home, I was happy when Sarah greeted me with a broad smile and her excitement about going into fifth grade. I didn't let on that I already knew about it and that I told Papa that this is to be her last double promotion. I know that she can handle the academic work, but I have other concerns. She is fine now and has friends in her class. However, I don't want her to have problems adjusting to junior and senior high when her classmates are reaching puberty and beginning to date more than two years before she will be allowed to do that.

November 14, 1955

I am excited! I have my first performance as a professional singer scheduled for Thanksgiving. I'm not the headliner, and it's not on the weekend, but it is a holiday, and my name will appear on the sign outside the club. I thought I would never have a chance to see if I could make it as a singer, but an opportunity presented itself, and I seized it. My spirits are lifted, and I am happier about my life than I have been all year. I am getting paid to do something I would gladly do for free if I didn't need the money.

I was feeling low when school started in September. Even before Nancy died, I was saddened by the reality that I might not be able to take Sarah on our cross-country trip next summer. She and the other kids are so excited and happy about riding a luxury train across the country, seeing so many incredible sights and spending a day at the ultimate theme park. I got Josie and Sandy involved, and they are excited too. Still, if I couldn't find a way to make more money this year, I was sure that I wouldn't be able to afford such an expensive trip. Alvin's pension pays far less than his former salary, and insurance hasn't covered all of his medical expenses. So when I returned to school, I began giving private piano and singing lessons after school to supplement my teaching income. The extra money I made was not nearly as much as Alvin's prior income at Ford. Even when it was added to his pension, I still found it hard to save much after we paid all of our bills.

I thought a lot about that night almost thirteen years ago when I sang with Ebony Hues at Broad's Club Zombie and the manager offered me an opportunity to solo there. I wondered what would have happened if I could have persuaded Papa to sign the contract for me to record with them when I was about to turn twenty. I knew time was running out for me to try to get into singing professionally. At thirty-five, I felt I might be too old to break into the youth-oriented market of rhythm and blues (R & B). Even now, it's hard for me to see myself competing with younger R & B ingénues like Etta James and Zola Taylor of the Platters. They're both seventeen, the age of my senior students. Even in jazz and blues, the established stars started singing professionally in their teens. Ella Fitzgerald is three years older than I am but has twenty years of hits behind her. Sarah Vaughn and Dinah Washington are both four years younger than I am with more than a dozen years of popularity as jazz performers. Still, I had nothing to lose by trying, and any income I earned would be an added blessing.

I wrote a song to express my feelings about the deaths of Emmett Till and Nancy, as well as Alvin's slow decline, "Why Is Hatin' So Easy and Lovin' So Hard?" Gladys helped me write the piano accompaniment.

I shared it with Gary Preston, the band teacher at Central, who has a combo that plays in several clubs in Detroit and Windsor. He liked it a lot and arranged for me to audition with the combo's manager, Terrence Boone, known as T. Bone. T. Bone was impressed with my voice and my style when he asked me to sing some of the songs made popular by other female artists. He told me that he could get me work playing at clubs and after-hours jazz places around town, where customers often make requests to hear current and older hits by various artists. He said he would get me a list of songs that I should learn to sing in keys that suit my range. He and Gary arranged for me to sing a few songs with Gary's combo at some of their bookings. That would help club owners and managers get to see me and help me get a feel for performing in front of live audiences. I loved that idea.

T. Bone said that he would also see if he could get my song recorded, but I would have to be willing to travel around the country to promote it. I would have jumped at that opportunity a decade ago, but now I have a husband and child who need me to stay closer to home. I knew Alvin wouldn't like me being out late on the weekends. However, he would understand my desire to pursue my dream of singing professionally and my need for the extra money to help pay for the cross-country trip. Still, there is no way that I can travel around the country, sometimes for weeks at a time. I would have to quit my job, and I am not willing to give up my salary and my benefits on a career that might or might not pan out. I also don't want to burden Bea or hire strangers to take care of Alvin and Sarah in my absence. I would love to record my song, but I cannot commit to going on tour. T. Bone isn't pleased with the restrictions I'm putting on him and limits that he believes will stifle my potential career. Yet he agreed to manage me anyway.

For the past two months, I've been practicing with Gary and singing a few songs with his combo at their gigs around town. Now T. Bone has booked me for a "fill-in" appearance at the West End Hotel on Thanksgiving. I'll be singing between the sets of the resident artist, the fabulous flutist/saxophonist, Yusef Lateef. Between then and January, he has arranged for me to make guest appearances at the Minor Key and Blue Bird Inn, as well as at places I used to frequent with Alvin: Graystone, Vanity, and Twenty Grand. I can't wait to tell Josie and Sandy. I know they'll come with Chet and Walter to see me whenever they can. None of us are going out every weekend like we used to, and we all have parenting responsibilities. Josie and Chet have taken on much of the responsibility for Larry Jr. and Larissa since Nancy's death. Larry Sr. is working longer hours at the hospital, in part because he feels too much sorrow when he's in his house. He says that it doesn't feel like home without Nancy, and his bed feels cold and uncomfortable. He loves his children, but he doesn't feel that he's equipped to raise them alone. Nancy was the ideal housewife and mother with her background in teaching and her artistic creativity. Last month, Larry was going to hire a full-time nanny for his children, but he was relieved when Josie, who kept them in her home during the weeks following Nancy's death, agreed to continue to keep them awhile longer. Josie says the children need to be with family now, instead of a stranger so soon after losing their mother. Larry is delighted to have his children stay with his sister and Chet, their loving aunt and uncle. His children know and love them, and he trusts them. Josie is usually home from teaching in time to meet the bus bringing them to her from their private school. So they spend very little time with the housekeeper Larry hired to help Josie.

December 18, 1955

I'm angry with Papa and myself. For over a year, I have held my tongue and not spoken of what I know and suspect of my father's egregious infidelity and the hurt it causes Mama. However, I broke my silence tonight. Papa was furious with me, and I was livid listening to his sanctimonious, hypocritical commentary on what he considers to be my inappropriate behavior. I am not dishonoring my marital vows, and if his worst suspicions about me were true, they would still pale in comparison to his sins of lust and arrogance. I know he cheated on Mama, and I have come to believe that he threw it in her face when he brought his progeny into her home for her to adopt as her own. Where does he find the nerve to judge me as a spouse?

Although I never said anything, Alvin knew that I was feeling cooped up since we stopped going out together. He encouraged me to go out with Josie and Chet and Sandy and Walter, but I felt like a "fifth wheel" on a car when I went out with the two couples. However, now that I am singing, I don't feel like I'm imposing on their dates. They come to see the show and get an added bonus of spending time with one of the "stars." I haven't shirked my duties at home. Sarah always has her bath and is ready for bed before I leave to perform, and I'm always home hours before she wakes up in the mornings. Even when I'm out late Friday nights, I still take her to Detroit on Saturdays for her full day of lessons. We return home earlier, at least by 4:30 p.m. That gives me time to make and serve dinner and get Sarah bathed and ready for bed before I leave around eight for my Saturday-night gig. Alvin says he marvels at how I maintain such a demanding schedule without taking time off from teaching and church activities. He can't believe I seem more energetic now than when I spent almost every evening at home.

The truth is that I'm happy with my life now. Singing brings me fulfillment and helps me handle the frustrations I feel at home. I love Alvin and Sarah, but I had begun to feel like I think Gran did. I had lost control of my life. I was spending all my time doing my duty instead of going after my dreams. I enjoy playing board games and card games with Alvin and Sarah. However, I'm not cut out to be a nurse. Monitoring Alvin's medication is easy enough. I just don't relish helping to change him and washing the clothes and sheets he soils when he can't reach the bathroom in time or when his coughing escalates to vomiting. I do what is needed without complaint, even with comforting smiles and encouraging words, but I am hurting inside. I hurt because I hate what's happening to Alvin, and I hurt because I hate myself for not being happy just to be with him. I'm in the prime of my life, and I want more than just to look at my husband. I miss making love with him and, even more, experiencing his constant tenderness and displays of affection. He hardly kisses me anymore and only shows affection when he smiles at me and hugs me sometimes when we watch television together in bed. I miss the interesting conversations we used to have about current events, politics, and history. He isn't reading much these days, not even newspapers and magazines. He watches television or sleeps most of the time, and we rarely talk. Alvin used to seem so much younger than my parents, even though he's the same age as Mama and only four years younger than Papa. However, lately, he seems much older than both of them. I had begun to feel like I was aging with him, becoming old before my time. Singing on the weekends makes me feel alive, young, and in control of my life again. I am singing because I love it and I want to do it, not because I am obligated or duty bound.

If my husband is happy for me, why is Papa so against it? He has been urging Alvin to "take me in hand and stop me from running the streets and hanging out in juke joints until all hours of the night." Papa has the gall to say that my weekend singing is scandalous and unbecoming for a wife and a mother. Alvin defends me. He says that I spend so much time taking care of him and Sarah during the week that I need some time away from the house on the weekends. He says I'm not out any more than he was when he was my age. Papa disagrees vehemently with Alvin's thinking because I'm a married woman and mother, not a bachelor like Alvin was at thirty-five. Alvin knows how much I love him, and he trusts me as I have always trusted him. He admits that he worries about me being safe when I'm out late alone in the city. He wishes that he or someone he trusts could be with me to look after me as I travel about. However, he doesn't want me to feel pressured to stay at home all of the time because he's not well enough to be my protector. He has faith that God handles that.

Last night, I stopped by my parents' house to ask them to help get Alvin and Sarah to bed Christmas Eve because I have my first booking as a headliner to sing at Broad's Club Zombie. It is a wonderful opportunity that can lead to bigger things for me, and I'll make the most money I have yet. As usual, I'll prepare and serve dinner for Alvin and Sarah before I leave and I'll see to it that they are ready for bed. I just don't want them to have to retire so early when I leave. Mama said that she would be happy to help and wanted to know if I will be joining the family for Christmas dinner. I explained that I'm only singing at Club Zombie one night. So I'll arrive early to help with cooking and arrangements then stay with the family all evening.

When Mama left the room, Papa started in on me. "Why would you put more work on your mother than she has already taken on herself getting ready for Christmas? Not only will you not be here to help her like you usually do the night before, you want her to take time away from what she has to do here alone to go to your home to put your husband and child to bed while you're out carrying on in the city."

"Honestly, Papa," I responded, "I'll be working and earning money that Alvin and I need to pay bills and that I'm saving to take Sarah to California next summer. With all the money you spent on my singing and piano lessons when I was young, I'd think you'd be glad that it's paying off."

Papa became aggravated. "Every dollar you earn teaching music is paying back what we spent on music lessons and college. You and I both know that this so-called singing career you're pursuing is more about getting you out of the house than it is about the money. Now that Alvin isn't well enough to go gallivanting with you, you leave him behind, alone and weak, and ask your mother to take over your responsibilities while you're out and about having fun. You vowed to take care of your husband in sickness and in health. Don't you know how inappropriate your current lifestyle is and how embarrassing it is to your family? You don't care what people think, but we do."

His hypocrisy and self-righteous judgment of me brought out the anger I've been holding inside me for the past year. "I figure it's less inappropriate and embarrassing to the family than your adulterous behavior and the resulting added responsibility it put on your wife."

Papa was shocked, and the expression on his face confirmed my suspicion that Paul was my half brother. Still, Papa recovered quickly and arrogantly enough to answer me with ire instead of shame. "Watch your mouth, young lady. You don't know what you're talking about, and I am your father."

"You know I speak the truth, and I know you're my father, not my husband, praise God. How dare you talk to me about marriage vows when you've broken your own? Where do you find the nerve to talk to me about what people think when everyone in town knows what you do? What are you afraid of, that people will think I am my father's daughter—a cheating whore?"

I pushed Papa too far. He lost control and slapped me. As soon as he did it, I could see that he regretted it. He never hit me before. He taught me that a man should never hit a woman, no matter what she says or does, unless it is to save her life or his. However, he did not apologize. He just stared at me for a moment and then left the room. I left the house. Mama called me later to ask why I left so soon. I assured her that everything was all right. I just had so much to do at home before bedtime.

I am hurt that Papa disapproves of me so much, and I'm angry at myself for caring about his approval. I don't approve of his behavior, and I am angry at him for judging mine so harshly. I'm also angry at him for betraying Mama. When I finally expressed my anger and disapproval of him, I wanted to hurt him the way he hurts me. He lost control, so I know I succeeded. Yet, I don't feel victorious. I'm feeling sad, maybe even sorry, though I'm not sure exactly why. I'm infuriated with him and with myself for feeling that way.

April 8, 1956

Today after church, many people said how much they were moved by my singing of "What a Friend We Have in Jesus." It was my heartfelt testimony that Jesus saved me from the worst situation I ever faced. He alone answered my cries for help when I called on Him in prayer.

Thursday, I stayed late at Central to rehearse the choir for the spring music festival and the upcoming choral competition. I ran late for the piano lessons I give to my pupils Thursdays in their homes. I stopped by Josie's just long enough to shower and change for my night of singing at the Flame Show Bar on John R and Canfield. I don't usually perform during the week, but this was a rare opportunity for me to perform at the best venue on Detroit's "Street of Music." I performed two songs at each of the three shows and then left the bar shortly after midnight. I had driven only a few blocks down Woodward Avenue when my grumbling stomach reminded me that I had not eaten anything since lunch. I saw a diner open and parked right at the entrance, under a street lamp. I went inside and ordered a cheeseburger with fries and a Coke to go.

I opened my car door and gently tossed the bag of food onto the open newspaper on the passenger seat. I still had the bottle in my hand when I heard a man's voice behind me. "Excuse me, miss, how much for your time?"

I turned to see an obviously inebriated white man in his forties. His clothes were wrinkled and a bit dirty. His breath reeked of alcohol, and his words were kind of slurred but clear enough to be understood. I just did not understand their meaning at first. "I beg your pardon," I said.

He repeated, "How much for your time?" That time, I understood that he thought I was a prostitute and wanted to know my fee.

"I'm sorry, but my time is not for sale." I said, trying to be polite but clear that he was mistaken about my profession. When I attempted to enter my car, he became agitated and put his hand on my shoulder to stop me. I was paralyzed with fear and looked for help from the three white men, the white woman, and the Negro man eating in the diner. They were watching but did not move.

The drunk pulled out a wad of bills from his pocket, probably his week's wages from a factory. It was payday, and I know many workers cash their paychecks on site. He waved it proudly as he spoke. "What you think? I can't afford you? I know you ain't cheap. I got enough to pay you."

I tried to calm him. "It is not a question of money. My time is not for sale for any amount."

It did not help. He became enraged. I tried to slip into the car when he put the money back into his pocket, but he managed to grab me with both hands. I dropped the Coke, and the bottle broke into pieces on the street. "What you tryin' to pull? Any nigger bitch can be bought!"

Hearing those words and his tone, my fear gave way to pure anger. I tried to pull away from him. I couldn't put my knee to his groin because he was too much taller than me. So I kicked his leg as hard as I could. As he pulled me away from my car, I screamed and again looked into the diner. The people inside turned their heads, pretending to read their newspapers or examine the food on their plates. I could not believe it. The four men could have easily taken him. The woman could have screamed for help. Instead, they all just looked away.

He was staggering when he lifted me and carried me around the corner to the alley. I was kicking and screaming the whole way. He wrestled me to the ground. My head hurt when it hit the concrete, but I was not dazed. He pinned my arms and fell on top of me. I closed my eyes and prayed. He let go of my right hand to pull down the zipper of his pants. That's when I felt an empty liquor bottle on the ground beside me. I grabbed it and hit him over his temple as hard as I could. He held his head as he rolled onto his side, pulling back enough for me to squeeze out from under him and rise to my feet. Standing over him, I gave him a swift kick to the groin. I knew that would make him pause long enough for me to get a good head start as I fled from him. I did not look back to see if he followed me. I ran straight to my car, leaped inside and turned the key in the ignition as I locked the doors. I sped down Woodward Avenue toward the Edsel Ford Freeway heading home.

Before I could get to the freeway, two police cars were chasing me with their sirens blasting and their lights flashing. Apparently, I ran two red lights as I was speeding down Woodward. A police car from each cross street sped around the corner in hot pursuit of me. Two white policemen were in the first car, and one white and one Negro officer were in the second one. All four got out of their cars and approached mine. I was hysterical. I got out of my car screaming, "Where were you a few minutes ago when a drunk tried to rape me back there? I screamed but not one cop came to help me. Now I run a red light, and four cops come to arrest me! If I was white and a Negro man approached me, the men in the diner would have jumped him, and cops would have rushed there to haul him off to jail."

The Negro officer tried to calm me down. He asked me to tell them exactly what happened. The policemen in the first car went back to the diner and the alley, looking for the man I described. While they were gone, the Negro officer asked me about myself and why I was out alone at that time of night. I told him I teach music at Central and was singing at the Flame Show Bar. He believed me, but I could tell he and his partner did not approve of a teacher doing that. They said that many women who dress up and go out alone at night in that area are for hire. It sounded to me like they thought my attacker was justified in thinking I was a prostitute and I was somehow asking for what he did to me. Before I could ask if that is what they were implying, the other officers returned saying they did not find the man.

They asked if I wanted to make a written statement, but I declined. The Negro officer and his partner followed me all the way home to Parkersville. I prayed that nobody saw them. The rumor mill would be active with questions and speculations as to why police were following me. Papa and Alvin can never know what happened. Papa would say that appearances matter. "Gallivanting around alone at night, you look like a loose woman. So you should not be surprised when men treat you like one." Alvin would worry whenever I leave the house and feel bad that he cannot go to protect me. They would both want me to stop singing at night, and I will not do that.

I sat in my bathtub for hours. The water went from near boiling to cold while I tried to scrub all the filth of that man and that alley from my body and my mind. I sealed everything I wore that night in a garbage bag, from my underwear and stockings to my dress and jacket. Friday morning, I was shaking and holding back tears as I drove to work. I looked all around to be sure nobody was there when I stopped and got out of the car to throw the bag of clothes into a garbage can. I quickly got back in the car and immediately locked the doors. When

I parked the car, I waited for another teacher to walk with me into the school.

I will not stop singing, but I will be more careful. Someone always accompanies me to my car after I finish for the night. From now on, I will say a prayer when I start the engine. I know my Lord answers prayers. Once I leave, I'll stay locked in my car, making no stops until I am safely home. I will never tell anyone what occurred on Woodward Avenue in the wee hours of Friday morning. I pray that I will someday forget the details of what happened and only remember that Jesus sent me what I needed when I prayed. He is indeed my Savior and a perfect friend!

July 7, 1956

What a remarkable day this has been! Everyone else is sleeping soundly, exhausted from the first day of our cross-country adventure. Before Sarah fell asleep, she hugged me tightly and whispered in my ear, "Mommie, this is my best birthday present ever!" I whispered back to her that this was just the first day with fifteen more wonderful ones to come. I am so happy that Sarah is enjoying herself as I hoped she would be if we actually got to come. There were so many setbacks that I didn't think we would make it, but we're here, and so far, it is all I imagined it would be. It's one o'clock in the morning, but I'm too excited to sleep. Besides, I'm used to long days. Every Friday and Saturday for the past six months, I have worked for twenty hours straight with only four hours of sleep to recharge me for the next day. Today, I've been up for only eighteen hours so far, and instead of work, I have been treated like royalty while relaxing with my best friends and our children.

Papa brought Sarah and me to meet Josie with Larry Jr. and Larissa and Sandy with Kendra at the train station in Detroit at nine o'clock this morning. Since it's after midnight, I mean yesterday morning. We took a local train to Chicago's Union Station, where we boarded the luxurious Silver Star North bound for San Francisco. We're traveling along a scenic northern route that will take us through the heart of the Colorado Rockies with views of their snow-capped peaks, across the Mississippi River and other white water rivers, through dense forests and over the Sierra Nevada Mountains in California. En route, we'll have full-day stops in Denver and Reno, where we'll take a bus tour to Lake Tahoe.

As exciting as the itinerary is, the train itself is a big part of the adventure. It is a beautiful silver passenger train with all new four-passenger Pullman sleeping cars equipped with showers, toilets, and wash basins. Sarah and I are sharing one compartment with Sandy and Kendra. Josie is with Larry Jr. and Larissa in the adjoining one. The beautiful dining car serves delicious food that rivals the best restaurants where we've dined. There is a glass enclosed dome atop the beautiful observation car. The lounge car has tables where we play cards and board games with the children while we enjoy snacks available at the bar. Today, we plan to go to the theater car to see a recent movie at two thirty. We'll be at dinner when it shows again at seven. Sarah, Kendra, and Larissa are the only Negro girls on the train, and Larry Jr. is the only Negro boy. The Negro gentlemen who serve as porters took an instant liking to our children. The porters are going out of their way to treat them like little princesses and prince. They brought them extra food and special desserts at dinner and engaged them in conversation. They are so impressed by the children's knowledge and vocabulary that they want to introduce them to the people in charge. They asked our permission to take them tomorrow to meet the conductor and to go into the engine car to talk to the men who handle the train. Sarah and the other children have been having so much fun. That is why they were all asleep by nine. Josie and Sandy were tired also and retired around eleven, but I can't sleep.

I'm thinking about Alvin. I admit that I feel guilty having so much fun here, while he's home alone. I considered missing this trip to stay home and take care of him. He doesn't seem to be any worse, but he isn't much better either. I was concerned about leaving him for two and a half weeks. However, Alvin insisted that Sarah and I go, and Mama agreed that I shouldn't disappoint Sarah. She said she would "add his name to the pot" when she cooked for her and Papa every day, and she would make sure that he took his medicine and followed the doctor's orders I explained to her before we left. I'm sure that Papa disagreed, but he was silent on the subject once Mama encouraged me to go. I am glad that we came. I know that Sarah will remember this trip for the rest of her life, and I will too.

I plan to call Alvin when we arrive in San Francisco, again when we get to Los Angeles, and again when we board the train to return home. I also found a way for him to hear from us as often as he wants. I bought a tape recorder. Sarah and I made a tape of us performing his favorite things from our repertoires. Alvin has been too weak to attend most of the afternoon programs at church, but he enjoys listening to Sarah practice her recitations, piano selections, and solos before the programs, and he always requests an encore performance at home for him afterward. Sarah recorded her recitations of his favorite poems: "When Malindy Sings" and "In the Morning" by Paul Lawrence Dunbar, "Incident" by Countee Cullen, "Mother to Son" and "Merry Go Round" by Langston Hughes. I also recorded her playing his two favorite piano selections: *Claire de Lune* and *Moonlight Sonata*. Sarah and I sang a duet of "Mr. Sandman," and I sang the song I wrote for him the Christmas of 1942 before we married, as well as two of his favorite hits: "Autumn Leaves" and "Unchained Melody." We each also recorded a message to him, telling him how much we love him and promising to bring back pictures and souvenirs for him from every stop on our adventure. Alvin was surprised and very happy to get the tape. He promised to listen to some or all of it every day that we are away from him.

July 19, 1956

I made my third call to Alvin today. He sounded weak and tired like he did on the other calls. Still, he tells me that he is feeling better than he did when I left. I don't believe him. When I ask him if he has spoken with Dr. Edwards, he changes the subject and asks me for detailed accounts of our trip. Alvin says that he likes hearing about the places we visit and he can't wait to see all the pictures we've been taking. Alvin says that although he traveled around Europe and lived in France for a while, he has seen very little of the U.S. He has only traveled around Michigan on church business with Papa and to Chicago, Illinois, and parts of Alabama. So he presses me to give him detailed descriptions of everything we see and do.

I have shared with him our excitement and enjoyment of all we've seen and done so far. On the first call, I told him about the incredible cross-country train ride: the majestic mountains, amazing sunsets, exciting white water rapids and the feel of the air a mile above sea level. This is the first time Sandy, Josie, the kids, and I have traveled this far from Michigan. When I called him the day we arrived here in Los Angeles, I described what we did in San Francisco: how we marveled at riding cable cars up and down the steep streets, shopping along Market Street, walking down the "crookedest" street in the world, crossing the beautiful Golden Gate Bridge, dining on scrumptious meals at Fisherman's Wharf and in Chinatown, taking a boat ride around the Bay, passing near the infamous Alcatraz, and the unique experience of riding in our taxis through the huge trunk of a redwood tree in Muir Woods.

On today's call, I told him we were boarding the train back to Chicago and we'll see him in a few days. He wanted to know everything about our trip to Disneyland yesterday on the first anniversary of its grand opening. I shared how excited the kids were to see "in person" the characters they knew from Disney Golden Books and the *Disneyland* and *Mickey Mouse Club* shows on television. Within minutes after we arrived at the park, Kendra first saw her favorite characters, the Three Little Pigs, standing on Main Street. She was so excited that she broke away from Sandy and ran toward the pigs screaming, "Little Pigs, Little Pigs, it's me, Kendra from the book!" They shook her hand and hugged her then posed for pictures with all of the children. Sarah and Larry Jr. giggled at Kendra's and Larissa's naïve beliefs that those were the real pigs and that they recognized them. However, within minutes, they both started to believe in the magic as much as Kendra and Larissa. Yet, we all enjoyed so many other wonderful experiences in and near Los Angeles that I shared with Alvin. The "magic kingdom" and "fantasy land" for Josie, Sandy and me were Hollywood and Beverly Hills. We enjoyed seeing the homes of our favorite movie stars and shopping and dining in proximity of them as much as the children enjoyed shopping and dining near their favorite Disney characters. We all enjoyed the day we spent at the beach on the Pacific. We had all been to beaches along lakes and rivers in Michigan, but we had never been in salt water or been tossed about by cresting waves. We had also never been to a swim-through aquarium before we went to Marineland of the Pacific. It was fantastic! Alvin says that my descriptions are so vivid that he can close his eyes and imagine being here with us.

I told Alvin that I wish we had been able to follow through with our original plan to make this a family trip for Sarah, him and me. However, Sarah enjoyed playing with the other children, and I am glad to have shared so much time alone with Josie and Sandy. We booked adjoining rooms at the hotels in San Francisco and Los Angeles. In both, we opened the door between our rooms and let the children sleep together in one room, while we shared the other one. After the children were asleep, we stayed up for hours, talking like we used to do before husbands and children. This has been the most wonderful vacation imaginable for our group, not just because of all we have seen and done but because we have become even closer through our shared experiences and intimate conversations.

Last night, after we packed our bags for the train, we shared a bottle of champagne and talked candidly to one another until sunrise. We spoke about missing Nancy and about stressful situations at home that we were glad to escape temporarily but would be facing again in three days. I spoke of my concern with Alvin's health and its effect on his emotions and our relationship. That situation and the tension between me and Papa have been weighing me down for months. I didn't speak about Papa's indiscretions. That's his and Mama's business. I only shared the stress I feel from his negative judgments of me as a wife and mother.

Sandy shared how much she wants to have more children before Kendra is too old to be a real friend to her siblings. Sandy has a sister who is fifteen years older than she and is more like a second mother to her than a sister or best friend. However, Walter is insistent that they wait until he finishes school and they can afford for her to be a housewife and full-time mother. Sandy doesn't want to be a housewife; she enjoys teaching, and she feels that, as a teacher, she has enough time to spend with her children. She wants Walter to be more involved as a father. He finished his bachelor's degree, and he's teaching at Northwestern High School in Detroit. Now he is going to law school at night. He seems driven to become a man of influence and affluence. Sandy supports his ambition. She wants him to be happy, and she would enjoy living comfortably, but she isn't happy. Between work and school, Walter spends little time with her or Kendra. He's in class until late, and when he is at home, he's either studying or talking about the law, even to little Kendra. He's never relaxed, and she says that they are rarely intimate. He shares few tender moments with their daughter and even fewer with Sandy. Sandy misses the conversations they used to have over dinner and at bedtime, and the way he massaged her feet in his lap while they watched television. She misses him holding her when they are drifting off to sleep. He keeps saying that when he is finally able to set up his practice, it will be worth the sacrifices they are making now, but Sandy wonders if their relationship can survive until then. She says she is going to discard her diaphragm and start actively trying to have a baby when she returns home. She's not sure how Walter will react if she gets pregnant, but her body and soul are aching for another child. So she plans to have one as soon as possible. She says they have enough money saved to support her during a maternity leave and pay his tuition.

Josie's brother and husband are both contributing to her tension and grief. She worries about her brother, Larry, and the effects his behavior is having on his children and her relationship with Chet. Larry is still mourning the deaths of his wife and son. She says that he is feeling very lonely and sad, perhaps even depressed. She fears that he will remarry in haste to fill the void Nancy's death has left in his heart and in his big house. The nurses at the hospital, as well as the single and divorced ladies in his social circle, see him as "a great catch." If he would take his time, Josie is sure that he would find a good woman to be his wife and stepmother to his children. However, he seems to be eager to settle down and likely to settle on a woman whom Josie believes to be a poor choice for him and his children. She says the clear front-runner in the race to be the second "Mrs. Dr. Robinson" is Estelle Blackwell. Estelle is the twenty-five-year-old divorced daughter of Dr. and Mrs. Samuel Johnson. Josie says she is fifteen years younger than Larry and has two young children. Her son, Julius, is almost four, and his sister, Chloe, is two and a half.

Josie fears that if Larry marries Estelle, he will pay more attention to her and her children than to his own children with Nancy. Larry is already spending less time with his children than he should. They are living with Josie and Chet. Larry pays for their private school education and a part-time housekeeper/babysitter for them at Josie and Chet's. He only visits them on Sundays, and not every Sunday since he started dating Estelle. Larry Jr. and Larissa lost their mother, and they feel like they are losing their father as well. Josie tries to comfort them, saying that their father works six days a week and only has Sundays free to rest and to be with them. Larissa believes her, but Larry Jr. is not convinced.

He told Josie that he thinks his dad wants to make a new family with his lady friend and her children. Josie told Larry his son's comments. She says Larry tried to assure the children that he loves them, but he hasn't increased the frequency of his visits.

Josie says she loves her niece and nephew, and she wants what is best for them. She and Chet have accepted their roles as temporary guardians for the children. However, Chet wants Josie to keep trying to have a child. Josie wants children with Chet. She had been trying to conceive since they married, but she didn't. Now she's using a diaphragm because her hands are full caring for Larry Jr. and Larissa. Chet says his barbershop is successful enough to allow Josie to quit teaching. So she could handle three children. In heated discussions of late, Chet questions Josie's love for him, wondering why she no longer wants to have his child. She has tried to explain to him that she is not ready to carry and care for an infant while trying to meet the needs of two children who are going through difficult times. Also, she doesn't want Larry Jr. and Larissa to have to adjust to another change in their lives. Despite Chet's feelings and the strain that her use of birth control is putting on their marriage, Josie knows that now is not the right time for her to have a child. She says that she'll start trying again once Larry's children return to live with him, probably within a few months. She just doesn't want to argue with Chet about her decision every day until then.

We talked for hours. Sandy made us laugh when she said it was too bad that she and Josie couldn't switch husbands temporarily or at least have them switch some brain cells. It is ironic that Chet wants a baby and Josie wants to wait, while Sandy wants a baby and Walter wants to wait. We were still talking at dawn. We watched the sunrise together and woke the children to prepare to catch the train for home. We were happy that we still had a few days left to our vacation with other exciting first-time experiences ahead to take our minds off the unresolved issues waiting for our attention back home.

As I think about Josie's and Sandy's situations, as well as my own, I am reminded of something Gran said to me when I was preparing for my wedding. She asked me why I wanted to marry such an old man. She said he would get old when I was still young and I would wind up being his nursemaid. I told her that I would be fine with whatever happened down the road because I loved him. She said that people make too much about love in marriage. She and her husband were not in love, but they stayed together for life. She said she knew people who were in love when they married but didn't stay together. She said that marriages need a lot more than love to make them last. You have to want to stay together, and it helps if you think the same way about things like money and children. A saver and a squanderer will have problems. The same is true of people who disagree about having children and how to raise them. Neither money nor children can make a marriage work, but differences over either one of them can "mess it up."

I see some truth in Gran's words as I contemplate the concerns Josie, Sandy, and I are facing in our marriages. Alvin's illness has debilitated him and caused problems with money in our marriage. However, the sadness and disappointment I feel have far less to do with money than with my feelings of helplessness as I realize my inability to ease my husband's pain and frustration. I also know now that differences over the timing of children are causing my two best friends tension in their marriages. Still, I am confident that my marriage will last, and so will Josie's and Sandy's. This vacation gave us the opportunity to distance ourselves from our stress at home and to discuss our concerns with our best friends. We are all working through some things with our husbands, but we love them, and we plan to be with them "in sickness and health" and "for better or worse." The problems we are tackling are frustrating but not nearly the worst we could imagine. Besides, as Mama would say, in all of our marriages, "the better far outweighs the worse."

August 20, 1956

Sarah and I just returned from a weekend with the group and children at Larry's summer house in Idlewild. Sarah enjoyed playing with Larry Jr.'s friends and children of the other affluent Negro families who own or rent property there. Sarah and Larry Jr. looked at each other's vacation scrapbooks, made with pictures and mementos from all the places they visited last month. Larry Jr. was proud to show his book to his father yesterday, when he and Estelle drove out with Julius and Chloe. Larry seemed to enjoy looking at his son's book and listening to him expound on his two favorite places: Disneyland and Grand Canyon National Park. Larry Jr. was beaming when he told his dad how he walked along the rim of the canyon and saw it from different locations, and visited Grand Canyon Village. He was excited to share that we saw some remnants of two planes that collided in midair and crashed in the canyon three weeks before we visited it.

After Larry finished talking with Larry Jr., he spent a little time with Larissa. She showed him her Mickey Mouse toy and wanted him to play with her. He said he was tired from driving and he would play with her later. When she went to play outdoors with the other children, Larry took Josie aside to tell her privately that he and Estelle plan to be married Saturday with a small reception at Idlewild followed by a honeymoon in St. Thomas. He wants Josie and Chet to bring Larry Jr. and Larissa to the wedding. Josie was surprised at how quickly her brother was rushing into this marriage. She expressed concern about how and when he planned to talk to Larry Jr. and Larissa about his plans. They hardly know Estelle, and it's going to be another adjustment for them to move back to their home with a new stepmother and two new siblings when they start back to school. Larry said he was hoping that they could continue to stay with Josie and Chet while Estelle's children became acclimated to living in his house with him as their stepfather. Of course, he will continue to pay for housekeeping and babysitting support, as well as costs for his children's food, clothes, private school tuition and anything else they need.

I observed that Larry seems more attentive to the needs of Estelle's children than to those of his own. Of course, I said nothing to him or Josie, since it is not my business. Larry assured Josie that he is trying to be sensitive to the fact that Julius and Chloe have already been through so much with their parents' bitter divorce and their father's apparent lack of interest in them. When Josie countered that Larry Jr. and Larissa have also been through a lot between the loss of their mother and the limited time they spend with their father, Larry's response was that Larry Jr. and Larissa are older and have better family support than Estelle's children. Their father is an only child and Estelle's siblings live in Atlanta and Los Angeles. So they don't have any aunts and uncles around. The only men active in their lives are their grandfathers, both of whom are very busy and rarely visit them. Larry plans to be the father figure that is missing in their lives. Josie listened to her brother and did not voice her opinion that Larry should be more of a father figure for his own children. She only expressed her agreement to continue to keep them as long as Larry wants her to do so. She knows Chet will not be happy that she is going to continue to have an excuse for using birth control. Nonetheless, she loves her nephew and niece and is going to do what she feels is best for them. She admits that as much as she wants Larry to spend more time with his children, she enjoys having them with her. She will miss them terribly and worry about them when Larry eventually takes them to live with him and Estelle.

November 16, 1956

When the group met after work yesterday for our monthly girlfriends' dinner out, we had much to discuss as we sipped our pink lady cocktails. Josie is growing increasingly frustrated by her brother's lack of sensitivity and common sense as a father. Estelle seems to be the one in charge when it comes to running the house, including who lives there. She is pregnant and having a difficult time with nausea and fatigue, so she doesn't think that she can handle four children, even with the full-time housekeeper/babysitter he hired. He wants Josie and Chet to keep Larry Jr. and Larissa for the balance of the school year. Of course, if it is too much, he will make other arrangements. Josie didn't ask him what the other arrangements would be, but she knows that she would rather have Larry and Larissa with her. Josie can see the handwriting on the wall. When the baby is born in June, Estelle will have too much on her hands with three children under five including a newborn, so she will urge Larry to ask them to keep his older children through the summer. Josie says that she'd frankly rather keep them for good than to see Estelle and Larry put them on the back burner in their home. She says that Chet has come around and feels the same way. However, he still wants Josie to have a baby. Sandy joked again that she and Josie should trade husbands. She has stopped using birth control despite the fact that Walter still wants to wait at least two years to have another child. Alvin and I have no problems related to children. We can't have any more, and we are both content with that. Our dear Sarah is wonderful. She's becoming quite proficient at cooking (which she loves to do) and simple sewing (which she seems to enjoy far less). She helps me with household chores and caring for Alvin. She gets him involved in playing cards and board games with us. She's a competitive Scrabble player, and she shows shrewd business acumen when we play

Monopoly. When Papa comes by to discuss church business with Alvin, Mama joins the two of us in spirited games of Gin Rummy.

Mama has commented on the strained civility that Papa and I have shown toward each other this year. She sees that we barely speak to each other. Alvin knows I am angry about Papa's infidelity and hypocrisy. I don't intend to speak of that to Mama, and I won't share it with Josie and Sandy either. I only told Mama and my friends that Papa and I have irreconcilable differences about my singing professionally. I'm glad Sarah hasn't noticed the distance between me and Papa. She loves us both, and I don't want her taking sides or trying to make peace between us.

Alvin's health is continuing to deteriorate, and he is bitter with feelings of anger, anxiety, depression, and frustration. Alvin's cancer has metastasized in the liver. For almost two months now, I have been taking Alvin to get the chemotherapy that Dr. Edwards recommended for him. However, due to Alvin's size, even with his weight loss, I can't adequately support him when he walks to and from the car. I am blessed to get help from friends he made at work and at church. They won't accept money from us, though we are finally receiving disability insurance benefits from Social Security as a result of the law that went into effect in July. Alvin has always been so loving and so supportive of my singing, but since the recurrence of his cancer, he seems to resent the fire and ambition he previously admired in me. He is argumentative and critical of me for singing on weekends, accusing me of using my engagements as excuses for socializing without him. With his disability and pension checks now coming regularly, and the expensive cross-country trip done, he doesn't see why we need the extra money any longer. He says that if I love him, I should want to stop singing to stay home and take care of him. I know that Alvin is understandably reacting negatively to the recurring cancer, and I know Papa is feeding his feelings of insecurity. Yet it still hurts me deeply that Alvin wants me to stop singing, especially now.

My comments gave Josie and Sandy a perfect opportunity to bring up the topic they most wanted to discuss. They are really excited that I have made a record and that they hear it played a lot on the radio. They wanted details about how it happened. They said they really love the song "Love Is Not Enough" and they relate to the lyrics, especially the chorus:

I know you really love me, and I love you so much. I do.

But you don't give me what I need, and I can't do all you want me to.

We've grown apart, and I'm not happy. Pretending to be is just too tough.

And though the love is still so strong, love is not enough.

I was happy to tell them I wrote the lyrics based on the talks we had during our summer vacation and something Gran said. Gladys helped me write the melody, and Gary Preston did the arrangement. He and his combo played with me when I sang it for our manager, T. Bone. He liked it and arranged for me to record it at the Fortune Records studio in Detroit. He sent that recording to his contacts at Atlantic Records and negotiated a contract for me to sing on that label. They flew me to New York to record it in the Atlantic Records studios and began distributing it immediately. It's been playing on radio stations a couple of weeks, and it's quickly moving up the R & B chart. T. Bone and Atlantic Records want me to go on tour because they believe that I can successfully cross over to appeal to a wider (meaning white) audience. They want me to work with their staff on an act for nightclub and hotel venues. T. Bone has also booked me to appear on national television next month as a guest on Nat King Cole's new show. It's all happening so fast. This has been my dream since junior high school, and I really want to experience it. At thirty-six, I'm a late bloomer in the music business. This is my big break, and if I don't go for it now, I might never get another chance to have the backing of a major record company.

I feel that I'm in a no-win situation. If I take a leave from teaching to accept bookings across the country, Alvin will most likely resent me choosing to pursue a singing career instead of staying home to take care of him. I'm not upset with him about that. He is sick and I should be here for him. However, if I stay home, I'll be resentful that I missed the opportunity to see if I could be successful as a professional singer. If I was a man, nobody would expect me to give up a good job opportunity and stay home to nurse my wife. Once again, I feel judged on the basis of the double standard that I have been battling since college. I told Josie and Sandy that I have decided to make the most of this God-given opportunity. I haven't told my family yet, but I already know how they are going to react. Papa will disapprove, but he already disapproves of my choices, and I don't care any longer what he thinks. Mama might not agree with my decision, but she will understand it and support me any way she can. She'll be there for Sarah and Alvin, and I'll arrange a schedule with his friends to come by to help him move around the house and get to his medical appointments. Even if I stayed home, I couldn't handle him by myself, not even with Mama and Papa helping me. I'll send money and come home as often as I can. Josie and Sandy understand my dilemma and support my decision. They think that my guest appearance on television next month will help. Papa and Alvin are both huge fans of Nat King Cole. They will surely be watching me with pride when I'm performing with him on his show. That may soften their attitudes about my singing. I hope my friends are right, at least about changing Alvin's attitude. Even if Papa loves me and is proud of my success, I don't think he will ever respect me or my choices. Perhaps if I was in an opera company or symphony orchestra, he would approve of me as a classical musician, but never as a jazz or blues singer. That's not classy musicianship.

November 28, 1956

The night before last, Mama called me panicking because Papa knocked himself out when he walked right into the corner of the wall by the stairs. He was lying motionless on the floor, and she was afraid something was terribly wrong with him. I went over immediately, but Papa had already regained consciousness and walked to the sofa in the living room. I asked him what happened, and he responded reassuringly, "It was the darnedest thing. I just didn't see the wall there. I guess I wasn't paying attention to where I was going."

Mama thought it was more serious than that. "He had a bad headache last night. It came on really sudden like he was having a stroke or something. He grabbed his head with both hands and let out quite a yell. I tried to get him to call Dr. Baker, but he just wanted some aspirin. I gave him three, and within an hour, he said he felt fine."

"Papa," I chided, "you have to see Dr. Baker tomorrow and tell him what happened. What if it is really something serious with your brain?

The sooner they diagnose whatever it is, the sooner they can treat it. Ignoring it or waiting could be the difference between life and death."

"Sound familiar?" Mama asked him, adding, "I told him that last night. Maybe if he had seen Dr. Baker today, he might not have had this happen tonight. Don't worry, honey, I'll make him go to the doctor's office in the morning, or I'll call Dr. Baker and make him come by here."

I took yesterday off to take Mama and Papa to see Dr. Baker at Sidney A. Sumby Memorial Hospital in River Rouge. I was glad I did because Dr. Baker referred him to the ophthalmology group at Detroit Receiving Hospital. He called ahead to set up an emergency appointment for him. The doctors there concluded that he has glaucoma and has lost almost all of the vision in his right eye. They prescribed eye drops for him and want him to return for regular monitoring every three to six months. They hope to prevent loss of vision in the left eye, where his vision is still normal. Mama said that she was confused because her mother had glaucoma, but her blindness came about gradually in both eyes. The doctors explained that Gran probably had open-angle chronic glaucoma. Papa has closed-angle glaucoma, which is more sudden. Given our family history, they recommended that Mama and I both have regular eye examinations with glaucoma screening. If we show symptoms, we should be able to take preventative measures to avoid blindness.

We left the hospital feeling blessed. Papa is fortunate to have excellent vision in his left eye and will be able to read, write, watch television and movies, and do most things. However, he has no peripheral vision on his right side, and the range of his central vision is narrower than before. He should not drive and will not be able to renew his driver's license because he won't pass the required vision test. Papa says that he understands his limitations, but I wonder. Papa is stubborn and believes that he is capable of doing anything he chooses. Mama and I will have to force him not to drive. I told Mama to at least not ride with him if he disobeys doctor's orders. Papa made it clear that he doesn't want anyone else to know about the glaucoma. We know that he is a proud man who doesn't want to be seen as handicapped in any way. He abhors pity and resists assistance. He'll take his pills and eye drops as prescribed and keep his future appointments with the doctors. However, he will never again discuss the glaucoma or any recommended limitations to his activity, not even with Mama.

Papa likes being recognized as the most powerful and influential man in town. Everyone respects him, and most owe him for something he has done for them. Allen AME's new minister, Reverend Hardeman, owes him his job as well as the fine church where he preaches and the parsonage where he lives. Papa's friendship with the bishop and his fund-raising efforts keep the good reverend beholding to him. Papa has personally handpicked every mayor of the town since he stepped down from that job. He has the ear and trust of the Parkers, who own most of the businesses in the town. There are some who find him too full of himself and too much in control of almost every aspect of life in Parkersville. He would not want them to find any weakness in him that would allow him to be seen as less than perfect, physically or mentally. It is ridiculous to think that anyone would think less of him because of the glaucoma, but Papa's pride will make him keep it secret as long as he can.

In light of Papa's glaucoma, I found it difficult to tell Alvin and my parents that I am leaving town for a while. I met with T. Bone after school a few hours before Papa's accident. I agreed to take a leave from teaching to go on a three-month cross-country tour beginning right after the first of the year. I want to do this so badly, and I'm determined to pursue my dreams. Yet, I don't want to desert Mama. She never learned to drive and will need help getting around. Papa is more upset with me than ever and finds it shameful that I am willing to leave them now. I had to force him to tell June and her family about the glaucoma. Mama and Papa need their help, and they don't talk to anyone in town. James and James Jr. immediately agreed to come every Saturday to take Mama grocery shopping and anywhere else she needs to go. Papa will have to figure out how to maneuver during the week. However, if I stayed in town, I'd be working and wouldn't be available to him then anyway.

Alvin is not happy about my going on tour, but he knows that once my mind is made up, there is no changing it. He never forbids me to do anything, and he knows that he cannot use guilt to make me stay home. I have talked to Ron Barber, one of Alvin's friends from church. He has agreed to start coming by every day from noon to four. When the tour starts, probably in February, he'll be with Alvin daily from eight in the morning to eight in the evening, helping him with bathing and dressing for the day, monitoring his medications, and helping him prepare for bed. Once again, we are blessed that Ron is willing to accept low payment for his services. He says he and Alvin are friends and, like many people in this town, he owes Papa for helping him avoid jail many years ago when he was young and foolish. Ron is over six feet tall, around two hundred pounds, and strong enough to really help Alvin move around. Most important, Alvin likes him a lot. I promised to call Alvin at least every other day to assure him that I am fine. I won't be traveling alone. T. Bone is going to accompany me. Alvin is questioning my relationship with T. Bone. I assure my husband that my manager is a businessman protecting his financial interest in my success. I have no personal interest in him or any man other than my husband. Alvin believes me, but he says that I have needs that he has been unable to fulfill for a long time. I admit that I miss making love to him, but I have no desire for sex without love. I love only him. So he has no reason to concern himself that I will be intimate with anyone else. Alvin is insecure, and perhaps even jealous, that I seem to depend on T. Bone more than I do on him. I wish that I could spare him from his feelings and concerns. Yet, I have to follow my dreams to spare myself from feelings of frustration and despair.

December 31, 1956

What a perfect way to end an unbelievable year! I'm on an airplane flying home from New York City, where I just finished recording an album for Atlantic Records. I worked all day every day from the moment I arrived there the day after Christmas so that I could be finished in time to spend New Year's Eve in Parkersville with my family. A year ago, I didn't imagine that this would happen. I wanted to do more than sing in local clubs, but this is more than I dared hope for back then. I could not imagine that a major record label like Atlantic would have their songwriters write songs especially for me. Now they are going to work with me to develop a full nightclub act to perform in some of the finest hotels and lounges in the country, including some where I'll be the first nonwhite performer to appear there. That's much better than the tour T. Bone said they were planning for me when we discussed it last month. It seems that my appearance on the *Nat King Cole Show* was a catalyst for my career. Atlantic is making an investment in me. "Love Is Not Enough" is at Number 7 and still moving up on the R & B chart. Atlantic believes that with better exposure, it has the potential to make it high on Billboard's Top 100 without being covered, meaning rerecorded by a white artist. Lavern Baker's R & B hit single "Tweedle Dee" was one of the latest in the long line of covered recordings. Atlantic is sending her on tour to promote her new single, "Jim Dandy." T. Bone says that Atlantic is pushing several R & B artists to cross over in 1957. I am a fan of the others. I'm much older than most of them and newer to the business, so it is quite an honor for me to be considered in their league.

I took my first airplane ride to appear on the *Nat King Cole Show* three weeks ago today. It was so exciting to board the plane, and my level of excitement continued to escalate when I arrived at the television studio. I sang "Love Is Not Enough," and I got to sing "True Love" with Nat himself during the medley feature on the show. T. Bone picked me up from Detroit Metropolitan Airport when I returned and took me home to Parkersville, where I was greeted by a crowd of cheering friends and family gathered at Town Hall to congratulate and celebrate with me. The festivities were arranged by the mayor's staff, assisted by Mama and Gladys. Alvin came to the festivities with Papa and Sarah. Most of the town's residents were there. Josie and Sandy came from Detroit, and so did Gary Preston and several other teachers at Central High School. They were proud of my performance, and they liked the positive things I said about Parkersville and Detroit on national television. It was the first time Papa said kind words to me about my singing. He still doesn't think that I should go on tour. He says I should spend more time at home with Alvin and Sarah. However, he applauded the fact that I was on the first network television program hosted by a Negro man. He is glad to see Negroes presented as talented individuals rather than as buffoons like Amos and Andy or in positions of servitude like Beulah. He wondered if T. Bone could find me work hosting a local television variety show so I won't have to travel. He couldn't just compliment me without expressing some disapproval and commenting about what I should be doing differently. Yet, he acknowledged being proud of my appearance on the show.

A few days later, T. Bone called, excited to report that I am booked for a guest appearance on *The Ed Sullivan Show* in February and that Atlantic wants me to record an album. He told me about the changes to my tour and Atlantic's plan for me to cross over. That's when I arranged to take a leave from teaching at the end of this term in late January. Papa and Alvin are both urging me to back out of the tour. Since I'll be playing more upscale venues, I thought they would stop worrying about my safety. I told them that they will be too proud of me to be worried when they see me on *The Ed Sullivan Show* and when my album goes to the top of the charts. Alvin tried to be optimistic, but Papa warned me not to get my hopes up about becoming a star. "Blessed is he who expects nothing," he said, "for he shall never be disappointed." Papa doesn't trust white people, especially when they are in charge of Negroes. He's not as convinced as T. Bone and I are that Atlantic cares about my best interests. He says that he has experienced enough and read enough to be convinced that white people only care about how much money they can make off Negro labor and talent. From slave trading to cotton picking to Mr. Parker's economic motives for building a town for Negroes, Papa believes that white people exploit us for profit. He wonders how long Atlantic will "invest" in me if I don't win over white audiences on this tour, and he's skeptical about white appreciation and treatment of Negro talent. Stars like Ella Fitzgerald and Lena Horne are subjected to prejudice, not just in the South but in places like Las Vegas and Hollywood. In Las Vegas, they are barred from staying in the hotels where they perform. Even if they garner thunderous applause on the Vegas Strip, they sleep in segregated hotels in the poorest section of the city. The famous Mocambo in West Hollywood, where I'm scheduled to perform, featured Ella as their first Negro artist just eighteen months ago. Papa says he doesn't want me to be crushed if white audiences don't respond enthusiastically to me or if I'm not given the respect I'm due by the hotel and club management, even if the audiences love me. He's always taught me to respect myself and to demand respect from others. Now he fears those beliefs that he has instilled in me might put me in harm's way. He worries how I'll react to the kind of prejudice I'll face. He doesn't want me to be hurt or even killed for speaking up for myself.

I'm not dissuaded by Papa's fears. I listened to what he said and discussed his concerns with T. Bone. I know that many of the venues where I'll be appearing are in or near hotels that may not welcome me to stay there. T. Bone assured me that he will be with me as much as possible, and he is making arrangements for safe, suitable lodging for me in each city. However, an unexpected call gave me the security I needed. The call came from Marguerite Patterson, one of my line sisters when we pledged Delta together at Howard back in 1938. She lives in Detroit now, and I saw her ten days ago at the December meeting of Detroit Alumnae Chapter of the sorority. As always, my sisters were supportive and offered to spread the word about the album nationally through the sorority network. Marguerite called to tell me that after I left the holiday social, some of our sorors expressed concerns about my safety and comfort on tour. They said that if I get my itinerary to them, they'll contact Delta chapters in or near the cities where I'll be performing. Sorors in those places may allow me to stay in their homes. At the very least, they'll help me secure suitable accommodations nearby. I'm so grateful. I know I'll be safe on tour with my sisters looking out for me.

October 20, 1957

I'm riding in an airplane returning me home from Washington, D.C. after my performance as the featured star at the Howard University Homecoming Concert. It brought me such pleasure and a positive closure to my Howard experience. I am riding high literally and figuratively. High in an airplane and high in triumph, I feel differently than I did the last time I left the campus to return to Parkersville. When I left Howard in April 1940, my head was low and my heart was heavy. I felt so defeated. However, I feel victorious this time. Pres. Mordecai Wyatt Johnson, the same president who upheld the dean of student's decision to send me home in disgrace, hosted a welcoming reception in my honor Friday evening. He introduced me as an example of the intelligent and talented students who are nurtured at the university. He was quick to point out that I was an honor student in the conservatory there. My concert performance last night was well received by students and alumni, and I was filled with pride. I can't wait to tell Mama, Papa, Alvin and Sarah all about my triumphant return to what I still believe is the best university in the world. Having been so welcomed and well-received at Howard gave me an emotional victory over a demon that has haunted me throughout my adult life. I have finally lain to rest my feelings of embarrassment when anyone reminds me that I attended Howard. I feel vindicated for whatever mistakes I made there in my youth. I am proud of what I learned and accomplished in my years there. Now I know that the university is proud of me too.

Homecoming weekend at Howard meant more to me than any of my other experiences this year, and it brought me the greatest pleasure. Most people would find it hard to believe that it made me happier than my appearance on *The Ed Sullivan Show* in February, which gave a tremendous boost to my record sales. "Love Is Not Enough" rose to no. 3 on the R & B chart and to no. 20 on the pop chart. Two other singles on my album, the lighthearted "Oopsy Daisy" and the more serious "Why I'm Still with You," rose to the top 10 on the R & B chart and top 40 on the pop chart. My album, *Meet Mary Morgan*, exceeded a million in sales. I received rave reviews, and I was greeted enthusiastically by my sorors and their families, who opened their beautiful homes to me in every city of the tour. It's hard to believe that I am more ecstatic now than when I was appearing at the Copacabana in New York City and at the Mocambo in West Hollywood, where I saw so many television and movie stars in the audiences applauding me. I feel more pride now than I did in July, when I recorded a second album for Atlantic with five new songs I wrote and additional songs by Atlantic contract writers. Being touted by Atlantic Records as one of its successful crossover artists of 1957, I am honored to be in the company of artists like Lavern Baker, Ruth Brown, Clyde McPhatter, Ivory Joe Hunter, and Ray Charles. Yet I felt even more honored to be praised by the president of Howard University.

Even my overseas performances in Paris did not bring me as much satisfaction as I felt last night after my performance in Washington. The time I spent in Paris and other cities in Europe was amazing. I felt such joy being able to travel to where Alvin lived after World War I and being able to share my time there with Sarah, Josie, Larry Jr., and Larissa. Alvin's attitude improved in my absence, as he and Ron became even closer as brothers in Christ. They bonded as they read and discussed the Bible, and they prayed together. The anger and frustration eating away at Alvin's usually positive demeanor when I left on tour seemed to have lessened by the time I returned. He acknowledged his pride in me and encouraged me to take Sarah with me to Paris and to spend extra time abroad, exploring more of Europe. I tried to get Mama to go, but she did not want to fly in an airplane. Sandy was six months pregnant with Wallace, so she and Kendra couldn't go with us. However, Josie jumped at the opportunity to come. We spent a week enjoying the vibrant City of Light and a second week traveling by train to Versailles, to Geneva in Switzerland, and to Venice, Florence, and Rome in Italy. I had a marvelous time on our European adventure. It was an experience I'll remember for the rest of my life, just as I'll always remember this year's homecoming weekend at Howard.

November 10, 1957

I'm at the lowest point of my life now, just three weeks after being at the highest point. I was so happy when my plane from Washington landed in Detroit that I didn't think anything could bring me down. However, my euphoria ended abruptly. T. Bone met me at the airport. Before I could tell him how great I felt, I saw his face. He smiled when he saw me, but it was too late. I saw him first and noted his somber expression. I knew he was going to deliver bad news.

"What happened?" I asked as he hugged me.

"Alvin's in the hospital. His liver and kidneys are failing."

He drove me to Trinity Hospital. He tried to cheer me up with news that I was booked for Thanksgiving weekend at Baker's Keyboard Lounge in Detroit and for holiday engagements in Chicago and New York, including another appearance on Nat King Cole's television show. However, I couldn't think about my career then. I was only concerned about Alvin. I love him so much, and I couldn't bear to think that I might be losing him. T. Bone didn't say that Alvin was dying, but I saw it in his face and heard it in his voice.

When we arrived at the hospital, Papa was speaking with Dr. Edwards. Dr. Edwards said that the chemotherapy had slowed but not stopped the spread of cancer in the liver. Alvin was told in June, a few days before I left for Paris, that he probably had only a few months to live. Alvin forbade Dr. Edwards to discuss his condition with anyone, except Ron, who needed to know how best to assist Alvin in coping with the effects of his condition. Ron was also sworn to keep Alvin's condition a secret. When Alvin was admitted to the hospital, a few hours before T. Bone met me at the airport, he was confused, jaundiced, and in extreme pain. The only thing that they could do for him in this final stage was to give him morphine for the pain. He was in and out of consciousness, but he tried to communicate with me when he was awake.

I spent all day every day at Alvin's bedside for the fourteen days he held on to life. During his lucid periods, he told me that he loved me and that he was always proud of me. I told him that he should have told me what was happening to him. He explained that he didn't want me to feel pressured to stay home and miss golden opportunities to advance my career. He wanted me to find happiness in my singing and songwriting after he was gone. I told him that I did not want to miss the opportunity to spend as much time with him as I could. There will be enough time for me to concentrate on my singing later, and I would rather not have missed precious time being with him. Alvin said he was happy to hear me say that, but I hadn't missed precious time with him. There was nothing precious about my being sad, watching him lose weight and becoming increasingly weak and sick. He was happy knowing that I was having fun with Sarah in Paris and Italy. He did not want me or Sarah to have missed that, and he didn't want me to miss my triumphant return to Howard University. If I knew his prognosis, he was afraid that I might have traded those joyful experiences for ones of sorrow and pity at home. The less time I spent watching him die, the better, he said. "When I am gone, I want you to remember me as the strong, virile man who swept you off your feet and loved you passionately." He told me that he hated not being able to make love to me for so long and not even dance with me. Our earlier years together are the precious times he wants me to remember, the years of good times, fun, laughter, lovemaking, and the beautiful daughter we made together. I assured him that I would never forget those times. He was and will always be the love of my life.

Last Sunday, which turned out to be his last day, I persuaded Dr. Edwards to arrange for Sarah to spend time with her father. At ten, hospital rules say she is too young to visit him in intensive care, but Sarah is more mature than most people twice her age. Sarah was happy to be able to hug and kiss her father, even as he lay in the bed, and he was overjoyed to see her. He tried his best not to let her know that he was in pain, but she could tell he was uncomfortable. She stayed with him for only a few minutes before she came for me and told me about their conversation.

"Daddy," she said, "you look so tired. I think you should take a nap. I'll stay in the waiting room and come back here when you wake up."

"If I go to sleep, I don't think I'll wake up this time," Alvin replied in a raspy, almost breathless voice.

"Sure you will!" Sarah asserted. "You'll wake up feeling better, and you'll keep getting better so you can come home soon."

She said Alvin smiled and answered, "I'll either wake up here with you or with God. Even if it is with God, know that I'll always be with you and your mother. I love you both with all my heart. Only God loves you more than I do." Then he added, "I'll go to sleep if you get Mommie to come in with us. I want kisses from both my beautiful ladies."

We returned together to kiss him. He smiled, and all said "I love you" for what would be the last time. My beloved Alvin closed his eyes and was asleep in less than a minute. Mama took Sarah to the cafeteria, and I stayed by his bed, holding his hand. He died peacefully in his sleep about an hour later.

Almost the entire congregation of Allen AME came to Alvin's wake Friday and his funeral yesterday to celebrate his life and his work in the church. They were joined by some of his former coworkers at Ford Motor Company, T. Bone and some of my friends and fellow artists at Atlantic Records, teachers and staff from Central High School, and, of course, the group. Teola, Alvin's mother, died in 1954, so Alvin's sister, Sadie, came by train from Birmingham alone. I offered to pay her airplane fare, but Sadie won't fly. Papa read the obituary and spoke of Alvin's faith, hope, and love. Reverend Hardeman preached an uplifting eulogy, and the choir sang two of his favorite hymns: "Precious Lord, Take My Hand" and "The Last Mile of the Way." Sarah cried a lot, but I was quiet throughout the services in the church and at the gravesite. There was a wonderful repast in the church banquet hall after we returned from the cemetery. I thanked people individually for their support when they approached me, but I said little else. I felt numb. It was as though I wasn't present in the moment, like I was watching a movie about other people who were somewhere else.

When everyone finally went home and Sarah fell asleep, I finally faced the brutal truth that Alvin is gone from me in this life. Lying in my empty bed, my grief was almost unbearable. I was comforted by the knowledge that God will take wonderful care of my Alvin, His faithful servant. Still, I cried myself to sleep, holding Alvin's pillow in my arms. When I awoke this morning, Sarah was in bed next to me. We held each other in silence for a long time before we rose from the bed.

December 26, 1957

Two weeks—that's all the two men left in my life gave me to mourn my husband. Two weeks—is that enough time to move on, to perform, to make life-altering decisions after you bury the love of your life? Apparently, that's what T. Bone and Papa thought. They didn't know, or maybe they didn't care, that I spent every night of those two weeks sleeping on one tear-soaked pillow while I held the other one tightly to my bosom, pretending it was my Alvin. Sarah cared. When she awoke in the middle of the night and heard me crying, she came to me and slept in my arms by her dad's pillow.

T. Bone and Papa approached me separately the Sunday before Thanksgiving. They both wanted me to answer questions and make plans for handling my business and personal affairs in the wake of Alvin's death. Although their agendas were different, they were both sure that they knew what was best for me and they both wanted me to act quickly. T. Bone wanted me to get back to work, writing and performing. He believed that throwing myself into my work would help lift my spirits by forcing me to focus on something other than my loss. He believes I will find new depth in my voice and my lyrics if I express my feelings in the music. Before Alvin died, I was already scheduled to perform at Baker's Keyboard Lounge on Thanksgiving weekend and in New York City and Chicago during this week between Christmas and New Year's. He has since received calls from clubs in Hollywood and Vegas, as well as organizations like the NAACP and my beloved Delta Sigma Theta Sorority, Inc., who want me to perform at their national conventions in the summer. My second album is ready for distribution, and at least a couple of the tracks seem likely to be hit singles. He says that I am "hot," and I should "seize the moment." He says it's important for me not to cancel anything I have already agreed to do and I should make new commitments. I know that T. Bone is motivated in part by money. He gets paid when I do. Yet I do believe he cares about me and wants to help me through my grief in the only way he knows how.

I'm not sure about what is motivating Papa. When he approached me, he bluntly asked me to give him and Mama custody of Sarah. I was shocked by his gall and dismissive of what seemed a preposterous idea! Why would I consider doing such a thing? Was he judging me once again, declaring me unfit to raise my own child? He implored me to hear him out with an open mind and an open heart. He said that with me on the road so much, Sarah needs a stable environment. He and Mama have been caring for Sarah for almost a year since I left to record my first album then go on tour. Sarah can't move from place to place with me. It would disrupt her education. She needs love and constancy in her life, having lost her father and being away so much from her mother. Legalizing guardianship of Sarah will give Mama and Papa authority to make decisions in case an emergency occurs in my absence. Papa said that he and Mama will never try to take Alvin's and my places as her parents, but they will be there for Sarah when I can't be. Truthfully, Mama has helped me care for Sarah since she was born, more after I returned to teach and almost exclusively since Alvin became ill and I began to tour. She was always careful to remind Sarah that I am her mother and that I love her very much. I also know firsthand that there's nobody better than Mama to raise a child. Papa said that if I agree to let them keep Sarah, I will always be welcome to stay with her in their home or in my own home whenever I'm in town.

I told Papa and T. Bone that I wasn't sure what I want to do about Sarah or about my music career. I don't like being pressured to do what others want me to do. I am an intelligent educated woman, and I want to be in charge of my own life. Yet I knew that if I was to be in charge, I would have to take charge, acting decisively and quickly. I was so emotional and conflicted that it was hard for me to think clearly. Nonetheless, I had to sort through my feelings and pray for divine guidance to know the right things to do. I needed to get back to singing and traveling. Staying in my home was depressing. I miss Alvin, and I feel sorrow from losing him and guilt for abandoning him when he needed me the most. I wish I had been there to tell him every day that I loved him in sickness and in health. I also wish that I had been there for Sarah, who must have been frightened and sad watching her father slipping away from her. I selfishly avoided all of that while pursuing my goals away from the harsh realities Alvin and Sarah were facing. Though I will never admit it to him, I believe that Papa's assessments of me as a wife and mother are correct: I have performed poorly as both. However, no matter what I do now, I can't get a chance to erase the past year, and truthfully, I'm not sure that I really want to do that anyway. I'm proud of what I have accomplished in the music business, and I am enjoying the ride. Alvin was proud of me too, and I think Sarah is as well. I kept in contact with them wherever I was, and they knew that I loved them. They were not angry at me for my choices. Yet somehow, because they loved me, they deserved more from me than I gave them. Alvin always put my needs and desires ahead of his own, and I didn't reciprocate. Sarah loves me unconditionally, and I have not put her needs ahead of mine as a good mother is supposed to do.

Sarah, my beautiful kindhearted Sarah—I thought about her and her needs as I considered all that T. Bone and Papa said to me. She towers over me already in height and compassion. She is tall like the women on her father's side with the full round bottom characteristic of the women in her maternal line. She has Alvin's tawny complexion that some of the old folks call "dark or dirty yellow" and others describe as "light or honey brown." Her long, thick, dark wavy hair is also like her dad's. The high cheek bones and Indian-looking eyes have been passed down to her from Miss Lily through Gran, Mama, and me. Her perfect lips and her cute little nose are unique to her, perfect blends of both families. She inherited the best of all her ancestors and is the most beautiful of us all. Her beauty attracts smiles and compliments from people of all races. Yet she is oblivious to flattery because she sees beauty in everyone and because recognition of her intelligence means more to her. She is polite and respectful of adults, but she fears no one. She is comfortable sharing her thoughts in any setting, confident but not cocky. She is compassionate, supportive and protective of others. In a word, she is wonderful!

As much as I'd like to share the credit for how wonderful Sarah is, I know that Mama, Alvin, and even Papa have strongly influenced her development into the delightful human being that she is. I spent limited time with her the past year, and if I pursue my career, I will probably spend no more time with her next year. Popularity in the music business can be fleeting, and I need to take advantage of what could be my short period near the top. I can't change the past, but I must put Sarah's needs first as I decide about the future. I can't provide a stable home for her and pursue my music career at the same time. I can't get a handle on my emotions if I abandon my career and stay in the home I made with Alvin. I need to find my strength, and I can find it through my music. I need to get back to work. Sarah needs be in a stable, loving home. Mama and Papa love her as much as I do, and Mama is the best mother I have ever known. She will encourage Sarah to develop her talents and to follow her dreams.

I was confident once I made my decisions that they were the right ones for me and for Sarah. Still, I had some concerns. I've seen the tension between June and her mother and the uneasiness between Larry and his children with Nancy. I don't want Sarah to feel abandoned by me. We're close, and I don't want to lose that. I don't want Papa filling her head with his judgments of me, telling her that if I loved her, then I would be with her. So before I spoke to Sarah, I needed assurances from T. Bone and Mama. I had heard Papa's promises already. I wasn't sure that I could trust him, but I knew I could trust Mama to keep her word and to tell me how she felt about my decision. First, I summoned T. Bone to my home. I told him that I would keep my commitments and continue to work, but I needed him to ensure that I would have at least one weekend a month to spend with Sarah, at least a month off during the summer, and some time to spend with her between Christmas and New Year's Eve. T. Bone seemed thrilled to have me back to work. He said that he would arrange my schedule as I requested.

Then I went to talk with Mama to get her opinion about Sarah moving in with her and Papa. "Mama, I know that you have done so much for me when I fell short in doing my duties as a wife and a mother. I wonder if you think I'm being selfish in asking you to take responsibility for Sarah so that I can work."

As always, Mama responded without judging me. "I don't think you're being selfish. I think you want what is best for Sarah under the circumstances."

"I mean do you think I should stop singing and stay home to take care of Sarah myself?"

"Mary," Mama replied calmly, "the best way for Sarah to be happy is to be in a home where people are happy to be there. I chose to be a housewife because that's what I always wanted to be. I wanted to stay home caring for my family. That's never what you wanted. You wanted to work and be a mother. That doesn't make you a bad mother. You tried to be happy teaching because that's what you thought we wanted you to do. But you always wanted to sing professionally. You said so when you were in junior high school, and you never changed your mind. Education is supposed to make it possible for you to choose the kind of life you want to live. I don't think it's selfish to use your talents and education to choose a career that makes you happy. It would be selfish to uproot Sarah and drag her from pillar to post with you on the road. But you would be sad trying to go back to teaching so you could stay home. And seeing you sad would make Sarah sad too."

"I love you, Mama," I said, crying. "You get me and accept me for who I am without judging me. Why doesn't Papa?"

"Your father grew up believing that men and women had to fulfill certain roles in life. He wanted an educated wife to talk with him and to raise his children to be intelligent. He didn't believe wives should work. But if they want to work, they should find work that doesn't interfere with them taking care of their home and family. He got what he wanted in me because I wanted the same things for myself. He raised you to be smart and strong, and to think for yourself. He just thought you'd think like he does."

"But I do think like he does. He pursued his dream of being a lawyer, even though it meant that he was away from home going to law school, working and studying long hours. He left Mississippi, Ohio, and Detroit, following his dreams. He left you and me to go to church and lay conventions all over the state and across the country because he wanted to have influence in the church. He never thought he was being selfish. He thought he was doing the best things for his family by doing what made him happy. That is exactly how I think and what I am doing. He just doesn't think I get to act like him because I'm a woman. Well, he taught me to think for myself, and I don't accept his definition of a woman's place. I won't be confined by my sex any more than he allowed himself to be confined by his race. I am my father's child, and I will make my own place. I won't let white people or men tell me what I can and cannot do."

Mama was amused, and she smiled. "That is why the two of you butt heads so often. You are so much alike. You're both determined, even stubborn, when it comes to doing what you think is right. And each of you thinks that people who don't agree with you are wrong because you think you're always right."

I asked, "Am I really like that? I try to be open to others' opinions. I just don't want other people's opinions to control my life."

Mama explained, "That's not a criticism. I am glad that you believe in yourself. I believe in you, and I'm proud of all that you've accomplished. Your father is proud too. But he doesn't know how to tell you that without appearing to approve of your lifestyle."

"Is my lifestyle so wrong? Is it immoral, even though I'm not drinking to excess or carousing with men?" I took a swipe at Papa's adulterous shenanigans to see if Mama would react.

Mama assured me, "Your father has not voiced a judgment about what you're doing on tour. His objection is that you are on tour and not happy to be at home. But he can't decide what should make you happy. That's what I'm trying to get him to understand."

Still, I was adamant. "I just don't want him filling Sarah's head with criticisms about me as her mother, undermining my relationship with her and her confidence that I love her more than anything or anyone else."

Mama guaranteed that Sarah will only hear me discussed positively in their home. They will love her and take excellent care of her, and they will explain to her that her mother loves her enough to allow her to have a normal life with her grandparents. She affirmed what Papa told me, that I will have access to Sarah whenever I want to stay with her or travel with her as long as we travel when she will not miss too much school. I told her that I will continue to send money for Sarah's lessons and for her care so that she can have everything she needs and whatever she wants so long as Mama thinks it's in her best interest. Mama says that Alvin's friend, Ron, is going to take her and Sarah to Detroit every Saturday for her lessons and they'll have lunch at Sander's Bakery, the way we usually do. I trust Mama completely. I also trust Papa's love for Sarah and his brilliance as a lawyer. So on Monday morning, December 2, I signed the papers Papa prepared to give guardianship of Sarah to him and Mama. Before the ink dried, I felt griping pains in my stomach. I left Papa's office hurriedly and went home, where I spent a painful hour in the bathroom with intermittent fits of vomiting and diarrhea. Afterward, I cried, not from the pain in my stomach but from the pain in my heart.

I explained everything to Sarah that afternoon after she returned home from school. I told her how much I love her and how much I wish we could be together all the time. I promised we'll always have time together in the summer and during her Christmas vacation. I'll try to spend a weekend at home every month too. She said she wishes she could go with me or be with me all the time but she understands why she can't. She loves her Bea and Papaw, as she calls Mama and Papa. She'll be fine staying with them. She is so mature and so sweet. I love her so much.

We spent three more weeks in our home together. When Sarah came home from school, we sang together and played Monopoly, Scrabble, Backgammon, or Gin Rummy after she completed her homework and we ate dinner. Then after her bath, Sarah watched television and slept in my bed with me. Monday, we moved Sarah's things to Mama's home. I celebrated Christmas there yesterday with Sarah and the rest of the family before I left for New York this morning. Everyone, including me, acted like this was just another road trip. In fact, I'll be back in Parkersville for a week after the first of the year. Yet looking out on Times Square from my room at the Astor Hotel, I know that, having lost my husband and given up guardianship of my daughter, I can never return home to my old life again.

November 24, 1960

It's the dawn of Thanksgiving Day, but I am having a difficult time finding a reason to be thankful. I haven't slept since yesterday morning, and I've been crying with few interruptions since yesterday afternoon. Our former paperboy, James Moody, called me in Chicago to tell me that Mama and Papa were in a car accident and that Mama was going into emergency surgery. He has grown into a fine young man, and he has been so helpful to us since Alvin passed. I told T. Bone to cancel my shows for the rest of the weekend, and I took the next plane I could get to Detroit. By the time I got to the hospital, Mama was out of surgery. The doctors said they discovered she had cancer all throughout her body. She would have suffered great pain and died within a few months. However, they couldn't stop the internal bleeding from her injuries in the accident. So she would probably die before morning. I suppose I can be thankful that I got to say goodbye to her and tell her how very much I love her. She asked me to honor my love for her by making peace with Papa. She wanted me to forgive him for all the wrong I think he's done. That takes a lot of forgiving, but Mama never knew all that I hold against him. I never told her that I knew about Papa's infidelity and that I figured out the truth about him being Paul's natural father. She thought we just disagreed about me leaving teaching to pursue a singing career.

I tried to keep the peace with Papa last night because I promised Mama and because I didn't want Sarah to get involved in our issues with each other. She lives with Papa, and he has legal guardianship of her. She loves him. That matters a lot, especially now that Mama is gone. She will need to love and trust him to get through this loss. Yet Papa pushed my buttons. Thankfully, Sarah was asleep upstairs and her door was closed before we tangled because it got heated and loud. Papa commented that he found comfort knowing that his beloved Bea was spared months of pain and suffering from the cancer. If she had to leave us, shocking as it was, it was better for her and for us that she went this way. It was shocking to me that he seemed to believe he somehow served as her hero by causing her death. I had to speak out.

"You are self-centered and arrogant to think that you did my mother a favor by killing her. You took away months we could have shared with her and any possibility that doctors could have found a cure before she died. I hope God forgives you because I never will."

He fired back, "I did not kill Bea. How dare you accuse me of such a thing! We were in an accident caused by a drunk driver. I would never harm Bea. I loved her with all my heart."

"I know it was an accident. You didn't mean to kill her, but you share the blame for her death. The driver that slammed into you shouldn't have been driving drunk, but you shouldn't have been driving at all. You didn't see that car coming because you can't see anything on that side."

He said nothing for over a minute. Then he answered quietly, "I never drive more than a few blocks around the neighborhood. I haven't since I had that problem with my eye."

I couldn't believe he tried to soften the reality of his condition. "Problem with your eye? You're blind as a bat in your right eye! You knew you were putting yourself, Mama, and everyone else on the street in danger when you started the engine of your car!"

"I was just taking Bea to the supermarket because she said she had to have some whole cloves for the ham for tomorrow's dinner. Moody brought ground cloves for her when he took Sarah shopping. Bea insisted that she needed whole cloves. Moody was at work, and she didn't want to wait for him to get home this evening to start preparing the ham. It's only four blocks to the store, and we both thought I could make it."

"So it's her fault because she was impatient and let you drive her to the store?"

"No! I'm just saying that I was trying to help Bea. I didn't mean for her to get hurt."

"You never meant to hurt her, I suppose, but you hurt her many times anyway. Your catting around hurt her, and you weren't even discrete about it. You had the gall to bring proof of your infidelity into her home for her to face and nurture every day."

Papa became as furious with me as I already was with him. "Don't speak of your brother in that way. Your mother loved him, and she forgave me for how he came to be."

"Of course, she loved Paul," I said. "We both did. He was wonderful and innocent of the adulterous wrongdoing of his parents. Mama forgave you, but she wasn't immune from hurt. Your cheating ways made her feel undesirable, and the time she tried hardest to make herself feel beautiful, you ruined it. Everyone at church told her how great she looked, and she felt so happy until you berated her for dressing provocatively. You stole even that bit of joy from her. Why?"

I didn't give him a chance to answer. "You set a high moral bar for everyone, and you never forgive us when we fall short. You still have not forgiven me for what happened at Howard. I was a teenager then, and I didn't hurt anyone, except myself. You are a grown man, but you think you should be forgiven for all the hurt you cause others. You really have a lot of nerve."

"What are you talking about, Mary?" Papaw asked, sounding really surprised by my words. "I forgave you years ago for what happened at Howard. I admit that I still think you were selfish to leave your sick husband and young child to go gallivanting around the country, chasing your dream of a music career. However, I did all you would let me do to help you anyway."

"You make it sound like I was having fun instead of working very hard to keep up mortgage and medical bill payments and provide decent food, clothing and care for my husband and daughter."

"I would have helped you financially if you had wanted to stay home and continue to teach."

"I know you would have," I conceded, "but your help always comes at too high a price."

"I wouldn't charge you interest or even ask you to pay me back. Gratitude might be nice."

"Oh, you would expect payback. You help a lot of people," I admitted, adding, "but you demand a lot more than simple gratitude in return. You want to control them. When they don't live their lives according to what you think is best for them, you withdraw your support and turn away from them. I know firsthand how much that hurts. I wouldn't set myself up for you to hurt me again when I disappoint you or don't let you control my life."

"Honestly," Papa said, "I had no idea that you've become so bitter and disrespectful of me. I am your father, and I love you, even when you make it almost impossible for me to like you."

"Don't worry, Papa, this is the only night that I will be staying here. I'm taking Sarah home tomorrow, and I'm making plans to keep her permanently as soon as possible."

"You cannot have forgotten that I have custody of Sarah," he reminded me. "Your gadabout lifestyle is not suitable for raising a minor. She needs a stable home."

"I gave custody to Mama and you," I answered defiantly. "I knew she would be an excellent guardian for Sarah, but I don't trust you not to bad mouth me to her, and I don't want you trying to make her live up to your ridiculously restrictive double standards. You know that is contrary to everything I believe. T. Bone is negotiating with the local television stations for me to host my own show in Detroit. When that is finalized, I won't be traveling anymore, and I can provide a stable home for Sarah. That is when my lawyer will see you in court, if necessary."

Papa's reaction was surprisingly cooperative, though cautious and controlling. "Sarah graduates from high school in two and a half years. If you take any job that will keep you here until she leaves for college, you won't need a lawyer. I'll transfer guardianship back to you, but I need to know that you are not going to run off and leave Sarah again, at least not until she is living most of the year on a college campus. Nat King Cole's show didn't last long, and we haven't seen any other Negro variety shows since then. It could take a long time for you to get your own show, if ever."

"As usual, Papa," I noted, "you don't believe in me as much as I believe in myself. It is time for another Negro, a woman this time, to host a show. I will get my own show, and I will get my daughter back. It may take longer than I hope, but it will happen in less time than you think."

"I do believe in you," Papa said. "You are talented enough to host your own show, but I don't trust white people to give you the chance. They own all the networks, so they decide who gets on television. We won't see another Negro show until they decide it's time. I don't know when or if they'll decide it's your time, so I hope you consider other options."

Wow! Papa hasn't said that he believes in me since I was his obedient child. He told me then I could be anything I wanted. He meant that I could be a principal or professor, maybe even a lawyer, something he deemed to be a respectable profession. This is the first time he has expressed faith in me since I chose to become a singer.

December 19, 1962

What a good day! It has taken me two years, but I am about to make good on my promise to Sarah to stop touring and settle back into our home with her. After having every television station in the area turn me down, I finally got an offer to host my own show on radio. Today, after two months of negotiations, I signed and mailed a contract to Dr. Wendell Cox, agreeing to host *Teen Time with Mary Morgan* for a year. It'll be a half-hour show running weekdays in the station's sign-off spot from 5:00 p.m. to 5:30 p.m. My first air date will be January 2. I am so excited! I immediately called Josie to thank her because she set the whole thing in motion.

In July, when I vented to Josie about my frustration with T. Bone, I had no idea that she could do more than just listen to me. I told her that T. Bone and I were becoming increasingly annoyed with each other and I was thinking about dropping him as my manager. I didn't trust that he was putting enough effort into getting something for me on Detroit television. I felt that he was spending much more time and energy on his newer clients. He complained that I was being difficult, turning down engagements because I wanted to spend more time at home with Sarah. He said I was losing money for both of us and damaging my professional image. He said that with no recent hit record, I needed to keep my name on people's lips to attract sponsors for a television show. I questioned why I had to tour the country to attract local sponsors.

We were vacationing with Sarah, Larry Jr., and Larissa at Larry's house in Idlewild when Josie told me that Larry's close friend, Dr. Wendell Cox, is one of the owners of Detroit-area radio station WCHB, the brainchild of his father-in-law, Dr. Haley Bell. Larry and Wendell were classmates at Meharry Medical College, and they are active together in several groups, including NAACP, Omega Psi Phi, and Cotillion Club. Josie was sure that if Larry introduced me to Dr. Cox, he would help me find a spot within the R & B, gospel music, and jazz programming or maybe even let me introduce something new to the station. With my professional singing and teaching background, there could be a number of possibilities if I would consider radio. I asked her to get Larry to contact Dr. Cox for me.

Josie and I didn't discuss WCHB after that. She called me in September to say that Larry was willing to sponsor Sarah as a Cotillion Debutante if she and I were interested. We were delighted. I want Sarah to experience more culture and class than she generally sees here in Parkersville. Papa doesn't approve of what he calls pretentious pomposity, the black bourgeoisie trying to emulate rich white folks. Still, he isn't interfering because he sees that Sarah is enjoying the process. I thought WCHB was off the table until Larry called in mid-October to say I had an appointment to meet with Dr. Cox on November 6. At the meeting, we discussed several possibilities. We decided on a half-hour show targeting a teen audience. We have talked several times since then to iron out specifics. Now it is finally done. I have a signed contract to start January 2. Papa said he would relinquish guardianship of Sarah when I settled down. I don't want him to think about reneging on that. I have already agreed to do a New Year's Eve show in New York, but it will be my last one for a long time. I am so happy and excited, but I will wait to tell my news to Sarah and Papa together at dinner on Christmas Day. If I do that, Papa will definitely honor our agreement. He won't want Sarah to see him trying to prevent her from moving back home with me.

Claudia's Maternal Ancestry

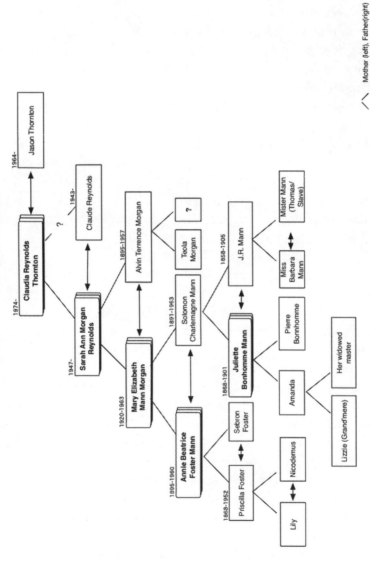

Jason Thornton 1964-

Claudia Reynolds Thornton 1974-

? 1943-
Claude Reynolds

Sarah Ann Morgan Reynolds 1947-

Alvin Terrence Morgan 1895-1957

Mary Elizabeth Mann Morgan 1920-1963

Teola Morgan

?

Solomon Charlemagne Mann 1891-1963

Annie Beatrice Foster Mann 1895-1960

J.R. Mann 1858-1905

Miss Barbara Mann

Mister Mann (Thomas/ Slave)

Sebron Foster

Juliette Bonhomme Mann 1868-1901

Amanda

Pierre Bonhomme

Priscilla Foster 1868-1952

Nicodemus

Lizzie (Grand'mere)

Her widowed master

Lily

＼ Mother (left), Father(right)

Wife ⟷ Husband

Part 5

(EXCERPTS FROM THE JOURNALS OF CLAUDIA REYNOLDS THORNTON)

Thursday, December 2, 2004
10:30 a.m.

I just finished reading the last of the journals of my grandmother Mary. Pouring through the pages of her journals and through those of Great-Great-Grandmother Juliette and Great-Grandmother Bea, I felt like a close friend, experiencing their lives and their feelings as they occurred. I had to remind myself periodically that the people and events they were describing were in the distant past, long before I was born. I wish they were here now and I could speak to them as I sense they have spoken to me. I would tell them I feel genuine affection for each of them and kinship with all of them. I am proud to have descended from them and hope they would be proud of me too.

Indeed, I observe many attributes and attitudes that Mom and I have inherited through our maternal lineage. Like Juliette, Bea, and Mary, we are strong educated women who live according to our convictions, and we deeply love our husbands and children. Our devotion to duty dates all the way back to my great-great-grandmother Priscilla. We strive to effectively discharge our duties as wives and mothers, but we do so according to our definitions of our duties in those roles. Our definitions are influenced by both the values passed down through our family and by the expanding opportunities for educated black women in contemporary society. I know that if anything happened to me, Cara would be a good and loving aunt to any children I left behind. However, she would not feel obliged to marry Jason and move in to be their stepmother, and nobody would expect her to do so.

Mom found fulfillment in educating others as did Juliette and Bea. Bea developed her own sewing business and, like Juliette, taught classes in her home. I know they would be proud to know that Mom built a successful private school and her home nearby on farmland reminiscent of their Mississippi roots. I hope they would be proud of me too for providing information to "educate" my viewers about the people and events of our day. I know Mary would be proud of me. Forty-four years ago, she wanted to host her own television show. She would have been the first black woman to host a television show locally in Detroit. She faced insurmountable obstacles and did not achieve her goal. However, her efforts and those of others paved the way for black women to gain a foothold in television news and variety programming. By the time I was pitching my ideas to television networks, there were already many black women reporting news and weather and serving as anchorwomen and talk show hosts, locally and nationally. With so many channels now available, I did not face nearly as much resistance or as many obstacles as my grandmother did. In fact, thanks to the phenomenal success of Oprah Winfrey, I found more than one television executive willing to give me an opportunity to prove myself capable of attracting and sustaining a following. Hosting a cable network talk show with a national audience, I have been able to fulfill Grandma Mary's dream and mine.

I learned more about my great-grandfather Solomon than any of my other male ancestors. He was a prominent figure in all of the accounts I read and heard. He was the son to whom Juliette felt closest, Bea's husband, Mary's father, and my mother's grandfather and guardian. I am proud of his accomplishments and his persistent struggle for equality for himself and others. He was better educated than most white men of his day but was denied the respect accorded to the least educated among them. He never sought favors, only what he was due if treated fairly.

He left a professorial position to accept an appointment as principal of a segregated school. However, he was forced to leave Mississippi when he tried to exercise the authority given to white principals. In Ohio, he found that his Southern credentials were devalued and he could not find employment as a teacher or even get the best factory work available. When he joined the army, he was trained and commissioned as a captain but never given the respect of white officers of lesser rank. Again, his work was devalued and disregarded. After returning from World War I, he did get to work in the steel mill, but he was paid less than the white men who worked alongside him, even though they were far less educated than he was. Trying to get equal pay for black workers, he was run out of Ohio. Only after moving to Michigan and finishing a Northern white law school did he gain respect and authority, serving as mayor and, later, superintendent of schools of a small, segregated (de facto), company-owned town.

If Solomon was alive today, I know he would be pleasantly surprised to learn that there have been many black mayors in Detroit and other major cities across the U.S., including New York and Los Angeles. Even in the Deep South, in his birth state of Mississippi, Charles Evers served as mayor of Fayette. Solomon would be stunned to learn that Virginians elected a black man, Douglas Wilder, as their governor. He would certainly be happy that Thurgood Marshall, whom he admired, served as an associate justice on the Supreme Court of the United States, and following his retirement, another black man was appointed to the highest court, albeit one I doubt he would have liked. If I told him that black World War I veteran, Freddie Stowers, was awarded the Medal of Honor posthumously in 1990, Solomon would probably say something like, "too little, too late." He would more likely acknowledge progress if he could see the number of black people being elected to state legislatures and to Congress. However, he would be discouraged that there have been only two black men elected to the U.S. Senate since his death: Edward Brooke III in Massachusetts in 1966 and, not until thirty-eight years later, Barack Obama, elected last month in Illinois.

I wonder what Solomon would say if I told him that the other black U.S. Senator, who served between those two, is a woman. Carol Moseley Braun was the mother of a teenage son when she was elected to represent Illinois in 1992, and she later served abroad as the United States Ambassador to New Zealand. How would Solomon feel about the number of mothers now serving in the military and in the president's cabinet or as astronauts, corporate executives, entrepreneurs, and the like, who travel the globe and beyond for their careers? I definitely wonder how he would react to the historic election in 2000 of the first woman bishop in the AME Church, Vashti Murphy McKenzie. She also serves as National Chaplain of Delta Sigma Theta Sorority, Inc. Despite his education and experiences, my great-grandfather seemed to cling to the unenlightened views of his grandfather and father regarding the roles of men and women. I understand why he and his daughter, my grandmother Mary, were often at odds with each other.

Grandmother Mary would be happy to know that I also reject the double standards of morality and decency. I reject notions of male superiority and entitlement in matters of sex, economics, politics, religion and other aspects of life and culture. I willingly give love, respect, honesty and faithfulness to Jason, and I expect the same in return. I don't share Juliette's view that it is the plight of women, wives and mistresses alike, to be hurt by the men they love. Like my great great grandmother, I prefer being a wife, but I won't accept Jason having a mistress, just as he would not accept me having a lover. Today, many people of both genders are opting out of marriage, and about half of those who do marry don't stay married for life. When I chose to get married, I did so with the expectation of a monogamous relationship. I also expect my husband's support as I pursue opportunities for advancement in the career of my choice. My career comes second to my family, but it is important to me to balance both.

I understand Grandmother Mary's disappointment, frustration, and even her anger, resulting from her father's seemingly hypocritical attitudes regarding her behavior before and during her marriage. Yet, I don't think she should have been so judgmental and angry at him about his relationship with her mother. It was their marriage, not hers. Individuals are complicated, and their relationships are even more so. Great Grandmother Bea said that she would not have tolerated J.R.'s ongoing relationship with Tessie. However, Bea didn't know him or Juliette. When Solomon asked her to care for his former mistress and the son she bore for him, she did it and learned to love their son as her own. She and Juliette had their reasons for how they handled their situations, love being one of them. Bea's mother, Priscilla, said that love is no guarantee of a happy or lifelong marriage. Her marriage began based on duty and obligation. Still, she found happiness and trust within it. Mom and Dad married for love, but they kept secrets from each other for more than thirty years. Still, they are happy, and exposing those secrets did not destroy their trust or their marriage.

I still believe in marrying for love, but I realize that other factors are involved in determining whether a marriage lasts or not. The gist is that only the two people in a marriage can decide whether the good in it outweighs the bad or if the better outweighs the worse. I sought time away from Jason because he should have told me about having dinner with his former fiancée. Compared to the situations I've read in these journals, that seems so trivial to me now. I don't have any reason to suspect he cheated on me in thought or deed. In the heat of our discussion, I said I wasn't sure that I could trust him. That isn't true. I do trust his love for me and his honor as my husband. I miss him so much, and I know I shouldn't have left home at all. However, I'm glad that I overreacted because the timing of my trip to Appleberry resulted in my illuminating discoveries about my family.

Vicki just called from the West Side Genetics Lab. She has the results of the tests she performed in my behalf and is sending them by messenger to me here. As promised, it took just three days. She thinks the information she has will help me with a story I'm investigating. She has no idea that she is holding the key to my identity. I became so engrossed in uncovering secrets about Juliette's, Bea's, and Mary's lives that I almost forgot about the revelation of Mom's secret that led me to have the tests done. For all I have learned about my maternal line, I know nothing of my paternal line, starting with who my father actually is. Although I'm confident that Claude Reynolds is my biological father, I'll feel better once the test results prove it to him and to Mom.

Thursday, December 2, 2004
11:30 p.m.

The messenger arrived at the condo with results of the DNA test just before 1:00 p.m. I stared at the envelope awhile. I wanted so badly to open it, but I felt that Mom and Dad had a right to know the results first, or at least at the same time as I did. I was convinced that the results would confirm Dad is my father. Still, I contemplated what would happen if I was wrong. I called Vicki to confirm my receipt of the envelope. She said the results were conclusive, and I thanked her before she could say more. Then, I called my parents. I told them that I had the results of the paternity test and would be taking the Metro North to bring them as soon as I went by the studio to confirm that all was in order for tonight's broadcast and by my office to confirm my plans for traveling to Chicago Sunday afternoon.

On the ninety-minute commuter train ride, my mind was racing through the events of the past week. It was hard to believe all that happened in the seven days since Thanksgiving. Delia's inappropriateness at the *BUMPN* affair seemed to have occurred so long ago and seemed so unimportant to me. Learning about my heritage made me feel closer than ever to my parents and to my ancestors. Although I never met my grandparents, great-grandparents, and great-great-grandparents, I feel as though I know them after almost seventy-two hours I spent reading firsthand accounts of their lives. Pouring through the pages of the journals kept me so riveted that I took only brief breaks when I called Jason every night and when I fell asleep with a journal open in my hands. I continued to reflect on the personality traits I have in common with my maternal ancestors. I wondered how I would have handled some of the situations they faced and how they might have handled things differently if they were living now. I thought about so much besides the fact that I would soon learn with my parents the results of my paternity test, which was the reason that I was on the train to Appleberry instead of to New Rochelle to be with Jason.

Dad picked me up at the train station and drove me to the house. Mom had prepared a wonderful dinner of roasted leg of lamb, wild rice, and asparagus. As soon as Dad opened the door, the delicious aroma traveled all the way there from the dining room table, which was set to perfection as per Mom's usual. Mom was sitting nervously on the living room sofa when we entered. She smiled and stood to greet me with a big hug. Then she returned to the sofa, and Dad sat next to her, holding her hand. I planned to open the envelope with the test results, which was sealed in my purse, and read the report to them. However, seeing them both looking so nervous and fearful as they clung to one another, I just blurted out, "The results indicate with 99 percent certainty that Dad is my biological father." Instantly, the apprehension I had seen in their faces changed to relief. Their desperate clinging softened into a warm hug. I smiled.

Mom gave a deep sigh and began to cry tears of joy. Dad kissed her, and they both thanked me. I was happy to see them exude the glow of contentment that I was accustomed to observing in their presence. Mom suggested that we eat because she was hungry, really hungry for the first time in days. Dad didn't say anything, but he nodded affirmatively. That's when I realized that I, too, was famished, having eaten very little since Monday. Throughout dinner, my parents smiled at each other and at me. Before we moved from the table, I asked Mom, "Have you made plans to go to Detroit to see Moody?" She said that she made reservations to fly there Monday. She'll be arriving at Detroit Metro Airport shortly before noon and should get to the hospital about an hour later. I told her, "Even though Moody is not my biological father, I want to meet him. I've heard so much about him. He seems to be a good man who loved you and helped you through the most difficult times of your young life. I'd like to see where you grew up with Mary, Bea, Alvin and Solomon, and I'd enjoy meeting someone who was close to you and them."

Mom and Dad both agreed that my visit might really help Moody because Mavis told Mom that he is one of my biggest fans. I said, "I'm flying to Chicago Sunday afternoon. I have meetings scheduled Sunday evening and Monday morning. I'll change my return flight to add a stop in Detroit, and I should be able to meet you at the hospital around three." So, it was decided that we'll both visit Moody and try to persuade him to fight to live. We'll take a late flight home, and Mom will arrange for us to ride around Parkersville so I can see the places she told me about and I read about in Bea's and Mary's journals.

Our plans made, I helped Mom clear the table, put away the leftovers, and load the dishwasher. Then we joined Dad in the family room to sip sparkling water with fresh lemon wedges while we watched my show on television. We sat down just in time to see the opening credits and hear the announcer say, "Once again, it's time to look past the headlines at the people making news across the nation as *Claudia Reynolds Reports*. Tonight, learn more about the man in headlines in Illinois and beyond when Claudia interviews U.S. Senator-elect Barack Obama and shares highlights of her interviews with those who are or have been closest to him. And now here's your host, Claudia Reynolds Thornton."

I enjoyed watching my show with my parents. They were beaming with pride throughout the hour. Watching them cuddling on the love seat, I was glad to feel that all is once again in divine order, and we can go on with our lives as they were before last weekend. With all I have learned about my heritage, I am more appreciative of the bond I share with my parents, which is even stronger than before. Though I still have not opened the envelope to read the test results, I am more convinced than ever that Dad is my biological father, as I told my parents he is. Mom's past can be put to rest, and she need never feel threatened by it again. Dad can let go of the guilt he harbored for not exposing Moody's fraudulent breakup with Mom. His silence allowed Mom to choose to marry the man she truly loved. Believing that Dad is my father, both of my parents are assured that they have not wronged Moody or me. They accept that their lies of omission hurt only themselves as they felt unnecessary guilt for so many years. I'm happy to have helped them finally find peace and renewed joy, even if I feigned knowledge of test results which I have not seen.

None of us has slept well in almost a week, since Mavis came and stirred up the past. So we turned off the television and headed straight to bed as soon as we heard me signing off: "That's all we have time to share tonight. We thank Senator-elect Obama, his family, friends, and associates for their candor and congeniality as we delved into the life of this man in the center of the headlines. Next week, please join us as we get up close and personal with exiting Secretary of State, Gen. Colin Powell. Until then, keep looking past the headlines at the people making news."

Tuesday, December 7, 2004
5:00 a.m.

I awoke from my first full night's sleep in days Friday morning at seven. Mom was up at least half an hour earlier and was making her usual full breakfast for everyone. I poured some freshly brewed decaffeinated coffee and hazelnut creamer into a sixteen-ounce thermos to take on the train to the city. Dad and I left in his car for the train station when Mom left in her car to drive across the field to the academy around eight. Jason called me at the office around ten to remind me that we had tickets to see *Wicked* on Broadway that night. He asked if I still wanted to go, and I said I did. We decided to meet for dinner at B. Smith's before the show. I was so happy to see him, and he apparently felt the same way. We talked briefly each night I was away from home, so he knew that I wasn't still upset with him. Nonetheless, he wanted to talk at dinner about why I left Saturday. He said he understood why he should have told me about his dinner with Delia. He realized that he would want to know if any man we knew ever made a pass at me. He trusts me, of course, but he needs to know who cannot be trusted. He understands that I have reason not to trust Delia, so we will never be friends. He promised to cut all ties with her after the photo shoot and have only minimal contact with her until then. I told him that he didn't have to avoid Delia on my account but that he should be careful not to give her any signs of encouragement that she could misinterpret as his interest in her. I trust that she is part of his past, BC—Before Claudia, and that she has no place in his present or future. That's AD—After Delia. He always smiles when I say that, and he acknowledges that it is true. I thanked him for understanding my feelings. I never want him to keep things from me because he fears they might upset me. He just needs to remember that what definitely upsets me is the thought of him keeping things from me. I admitted that I overreacted and should have stayed to talk things out. Jason seemed pleasantly surprised. He smiled and kissed my hand.

After a romantic evening with my husband, I slept late Saturday morning. I spent most of the day relaxing and packed for my trip to Chicago that evening. I called to finalize arrangements for my meetings. I advanced my Monday morning meeting to Sunday night at nine, following my first meeting at seven. I took my overnight bag in the car when Jason and I went to Mercy Baptist for the Sunday morning service. My whole family sat together: Mom, Dad, CJ, Cara, Jason, and I. On first Sundays, the service runs longer because of communion, so we had to hurry to Westchester County Airport in time for me to catch my flight to Chicago. Jason doesn't like me traveling alone in my condition, but he couldn't get away because he had quarterly meetings with both his editorial and directorial boards scheduled on Monday. I assured him that I would be fine. There would be a limousine waiting for me at O'Hare Airport when I landed and another would be at the hotel to take me back to the airport in the morning.

Everything went as planned. I arrived at the Talbott Hotel Sunday evening at six, an hour before my first meeting. A professor from Western Illinois University came to urge me to do a show about two families in Galesburg, Illinois. Three generations of both families were employed by the Maytag plant in Galesburg until it closed in September, following the growing trend of American manufacturers moving their production facilities to Mexico and elsewhere outside the U.S. He thinks that sharing the stories of these families will show the devastating impact of outsourcing on people and factory towns across America. Galesburg, a small factory town in the western part of the state, has been hit hard as its residents also faced the closings of National Seal and Bixby-Zimmer plants. The rising unemployment is taking a toll on local businesses and the economy in general. The professor pointed out that my most recent guest, Barack Obama, had mentioned that town and its unemployed workers in his speech at the Democratic National Convention in July. I found this story compelling, but a bit different from the usual focus of my programs. I promised to think about doing it and get back to him later.

My nine o'clock appointment was with a group of parents from Indiana and Illinois who hope I will bring national attention to seven African American adolescent girls between the ages of twelve and seventeen, all of whom are missing or have been found murdered in towns along Interstate 80 between Gary, Indiana and Joliet, Illinois. Local police are treating them as unrelated to each other, so there is no consolidated effort or sharing of information between the departments. The girls' parents believe this to be the work of a serial killer or killers. Furthermore, they believe that the police are not taking it seriously because the victims are all black. If the police acknowledge the possibility of a serial killer operating in two states, the investigation will receive federal support. While this is not the kind of story that I report on my program, I was deeply moved by the parents' pleas. I'll engage a private investigator to seek enough evidence to encourage the various police departments to collaborate and contact federal authorities. I pledged my support and various contacts I have to help the parents in their quest to uncover the truth behind the deaths and disappearances of their girls.

I called Jason and went to bed around eleven thirty Sunday night. I was up six hours later, preparing to make it to O'Hare for the eight o'clock flight to Detroit yesterday morning. All things ran smoothly, and I made it to Grace Hospital just before eleven, about ninety minutes ahead of Mom's scheduled arrival. Moody was sitting up in bed, watching television. He's in a semiprivate room but has no roommate at the moment, so we were alone. As soon as he saw me, he gasped and said, "Wow." Then he turned off the television and asked me to please come in. He wondered if I was really there to see him, and I said that I was. I told him that I heard so much about him, including that he is a fan. He readily admitted that he is. We laughed. I pulled one of the visitors' chairs to the side of his bed and sat down.

I said that my mother told me about how close they were and all of the sacrifices he made to take care of her after her parents and grandparents died. He said that he never thought of what he did as sacrificial because he loved my mother and he cherished the memories of the years they spent together. I told him that she loved him too and still held deep feelings for him. He smiled. He asked about my father and if I have siblings. I talked about our lives growing up and attending my mother's wonderful school. I brought him up to date on what we are all doing at the moment and showed him pictures of CJ, Cara and Jason, which I carry with me always in an accordion-style album of wallet-sized photos. I know that I will need a bigger one after my son is born. I asked Moody about his life, but he said that there was not much to tell. He continued to work at the plant where my parents met until he took ill a few months ago. He and Mavis have no children together, but he is proud of her son, Travis, whom he has helped raise since he was a young boy. He said that Travis joined the army after graduating from high school and is currently a police officer in Detroit, where he lives with his wife and their two young sons. His wife is an elementary school teacher, and Travis is taking classes at Wayne State. We talked and laughed for about an hour. I found him to be honest and humble with a wonderful sense of humor. I also know that he still loves my mother very much. He told me how glad he is that our family is so happy and successful. He said that it is what Mom deserves.

I changed the tone of the conversation. I spoke seriously and told Moody that I wanted to tell him something but only if he promised never to reveal it to anyone else, including my mother. If he did not want to accept the responsibility for keeping it secret, I said I would understand and say nothing more about it. He was surprised that I would trust him with a secret having just met him, but he was very flattered and agreed to keep whatever it was to himself, carrying it to his grave. I told him that I had learned only hours earlier that he is my biological father. I admitted that I wasn't happy with that discovery because I love my dad very much, and I wanted him to be my father. We are closer than close, and I don't need another father. I told him that I will keep the truth about my paternity from my dad and my mother for a few reasons. One is that I'm sure if Mom knew the truth, she would be consumed with guilt.

Moody was confused. I asked if he remembered Mom visiting him at the diner shortly before she and Dad were married. "Yes," he replied. "That was when I introduced her to Mavis."

"She went there intending to tell you that she was pregnant and that you might be the father," I told him. "But when she asked you if you thought that having a baby would have kept you two together, you said that you were glad that there was no baby to keep you tied to her."

He interrupted me, "I didn't mean that. I was lying to her. I had wanted a baby with her for a long time, and I still did."

"I know that, and she knows that now, but that night she took your words at face value," I explained. "She thought that you wouldn't want me, so she didn't tell you about me. She told Dad that same night that she was pregnant. He was overjoyed and wanted to marry her right away. So she married him and buried her doubts about my paternity."

"So what happened to make her think about it now, after all this time?" Moody inquired.

"Mavis didn't say anything to you back then, but she figured out that you might be my father when she first learned about my birth. She said that simple arithmetic made it evident. She also correctly surmised that Mom had planned to tell you that she was pregnant when she came to the diner. Mavis came to New York ten days ago to tell Mom that you were very ill and that she should finally tell you the truth."

Moody said that he did not know that Mavis had been to New York to see Mom. She told him that she was going to visit her sister in Philadelphia.

I continued, "Mom never knew whether you or Dad was my father, so I had a friend run a DNA test without telling her that it was my

DNA and Dad's. When she sent me the results, I didn't open them. I told my parents that I opened them and that they proved Dad is my father. That is what I wanted the truth to be, and it is what I believed Mom needed it to be. She had just learned that you only left her because you loved her and wanted her to be happy with Dad. She felt horrible about hurting you, and I knew she couldn't bear the guilt of denying you knowledge of and access to your child if that is what the test results proved to be the truth."

After a reflective pause, Moody conjectured, "I'm glad she didn't tell me back then. It was really hard for me to pretend not to want her anymore. If I knew she might be carrying my child, I would have told her the truth. She would've stayed with me and tried to make a good life for us. But she would've always loved Claude. He was the man she wanted to be with, and he made her happy. It was better for you to be raised in a happy home."

"My mother is blessed to have been loved by two good men," I said, holding back tears. "I'm proud to have ties to both of you. Even though I will not acknowledge you as my father, I am not ashamed that you are. I hope you will keep my secret and forgive me for asking you to do so."

Moody swore again that he would never tell anyone that he is my father. Yet, he was curious about my actions. "If you are so adamant that nobody else should know this," he said, "then I don't understand why you told me."

"Because," I explained, "I love my mother and I am doing what she would want me to do. When I finally opened the test results this morning on the plane and learned that Claude Reynolds is not my biological father, I wanted to tear them up or burn them and never tell anyone. Then, I thought about Mom. I knew that if she knew the truth, she would want you to know it. She would feel you have the right to know me and I have the right to know you. She would tell you now and ask you to forgive her for waiting so long."

"You are a wonderful daughter," Moody said proudly. He asked me to give him a hug. I was happy to oblige. We were both teary-eyed as we embraced. Just then, we quickly regained our composure as we heard a knock on the door by the young man delivering his lunch tray. The young man looked at me with recognition but said nothing as he placed the tray on the table and moved it from the foot of the bed to the middle so Moody could eat. I returned to my seat beside his bed. Moody asked if I was hungry and offered to request a tray of food for me. He said that the burgers and tuna sandwiches they served were actually "kinda" good. I told him that I would go to the cafeteria for something. I asked if he wanted a newspaper or anything else from the gift shop. He said that I had already given him the greatest gift he could imagine and he couldn't think of anything else he wanted.

Mom arrived as I stood up to leave. She was surprised to see me but happy that Moody and I seemed to be getting along so well. She asked where I was going. I said that I was going to eat a light lunch and would return shortly. I asked if she would like me to bring her something, but she said that she wasn't hungry. She brought a sandwich from home to eat on the plane. I left the room happy as I saw the smiles on Mom's face and Moody's. Mom wasn't looking at Moody the way she looks at Dad, but she showed genuine affection for him. He showed more than that for her.

While eating lunch in the hospital cafeteria, I was asked by a few staff and visitors for my autograph. Several told me that they were regular viewers of my program. A couple of staff asked if I was there to do a story on the hospital. I said that I was just visiting a family friend. I'm sure that they wondered who I know at the hospital, but nobody asked. I have never discussed my parents' Midwest backgrounds in interviews or on air. Most people only know that my family resides in New York. So there was no reason to associate my family with anyone in Detroit or Parkersville.

After responding to the questions and granting requests for autographs and photos with some of the staff, I had some alone time to reflect on my uncharacteristic behavior the past week. Objectivity and honesty are the principles upon which I base my work and live my life. Yet, from the beginning of my investigation into my paternity, I have been neither objective nor honest. From the moment I put together the packets of hair and nails, I was convinced that the test results would prove that Claude Reynolds is my biological father. My mind and heart could not conceive of any other possibility. Regarding honesty, I have always shown intolerance for lies and liars. I was so upset with Jason for not telling me about his dinner with Delia. Yet, I am finding it easy and natural to excuse, explain, and forgive my parents and myself for much bigger lies of omission and commission. Mom and Dad trust me because they believe that I would never lie to them. Yet, I did lie to them. I had not planned to do that. Last Thursday, I spent some time on Metro North contemplating how to support them in case the results showed Dad not to be father. I believed it was a remote possibility and didn't want to consider it. Nonetheless, I wanted to be strong and positive for them just in case I was wrong. Yet, when I saw the angst in Mom's face and recalled her near breakdown the previous Sunday evening, I impulsively blurted out a lie. I didn't know if I was lying about the results or not, but I was lying about knowing what they were. I want to think I did it to spare my mother the burden of guilt she would have felt if the results were not what we all hoped they would be. However, that was only part of the reason. I also had a selfish motive: to keep my family the way I want it. I know that I will always have Dad's love, no matter what, but I don't want to be his stepdaughter or my siblings' half sister. I want my place in my family to remain as it is: the firstborn child of Mom and Dad, conceived in their love. I lied to put an end to discussions of my paternity without including anyone else. However, once I learned the truth, I felt guilty about lying, not guilty enough to tell my parents the truth, but guilty enough to tell Moody once I believed I could trust him. My believing that so quickly is also uncharacteristic behavior on my part.

As I put the tray and dishes into the designated receptacles, walked through the hospital corridors, and rode the elevator back to the third floor, I thought of my attitude toward the people I interview. I have always been quick to judge those who lie to me and doggedly determined to publicly expose their lies. I felt smug and superior to them. However, based on all that has happened in the previous couple of weeks, I realize that I cannot paint all lies with the same brush. Lying is wrong, but to label and dismiss everyone who tells a lie, regardless of the circumstances, is also wrong. Just as I showed compassion and understanding to my parents, and now to myself, I know that I need to show the same to everyone else. It is not enough to uncover the truth. To tell the whole truth, I need to dig deeper to analyze how others perceive it and why some try to hide it. All of the people whose stories I tell are connected to families and people they care about and who care about them. I need to examine how those connections influence their behavior, as well as their perceptions of the truth and how much of it they reveal.

Mom and Moody were talking and laughing when I returned to his room. They included me in their conversation about people they knew "back in the day" and what they are doing thirty years later. I asked about the Fab Four, whom Mom had discussed with me. Moody said that they are all doing well. Since Bobby retired from the Cleveland Browns, he has become a commentator on ESPN. He works with his own local charity to raise funds to support school and community sports programs in and around Cleveland, including a summer football camp which bears his name. Ollie plans to retire from the school system in Lansing next June. Lenny and Phippsie divorced after five and a half years of marriage. Lenny married a social worker, and Phippsie married a professional basketball player on the Detroit Pistons but moved to the West Coast when he was traded to the Seattle Super Sonics. Moody said that Mom's childhood friend, Larry Jr., is a pediatrician here at Grace Hospital. We both encouraged Mom to see if he was in so she could say hello. My mother has not kept in touch with her godmother, Josie, who is Larry's aunt, and seeing Larry might be a first step in reaching out to her.

Larry Jr. came to see Mom and me a little before three, when he learned we were there. He called Josie, and Mom spoke to her. She promised to write and send pictures when we returned to New York. We found Mom's cousin, Aunt June, in the telephone book, and Mom called her. She is still at the same house in Ferndale, but she has not been well lately and has been living alone since her husband, James, died in 2002. James Jr., she told us, is living in California with his third wife, a white woman that June said is pleasant enough but kind of flighty. She said her "JJ" was always good at making money and making babies, but he doesn't seem to be able to make his marriages work. She asked us to pray for him. We decided to return to Michigan over the summer. I want to meet Josie, Sandy and Aunt June. I want to see the mansions on Boston Boulevard and visit Idlewild and Ferndale, which we didn't have time to do yesterday. It was interesting to me that nobody, except Moody, had realized that their Sarah has a daughter appearing on television. Larry heard me talk about my mother, Sarah, but he had never made the connection. Josie and Aunt June admitted they did not watch my show but promised to start. They all seemed happy and proud to claim me as family. I'm glad that they still care about Mom, although they haven't seen or heard from her in over thirty years. As Aunt June explained to me, "Families are like that. As the Bible teaches in Luke 15, when you return home, no matter how long you've been away, you will be welcomed with love and celebration."

Mom and I left the hospital around four and drove in her rented Chevrolet Impala to Parkersville. We didn't visit with anyone, but we drove by the houses where she had lived with her parents and with her grandparents. We drove by the plant where she met and worked with Dad. We stopped by Allen AME Church and saw the organ chimes with the plaque that showed they were dedicated to "SC and Beatrice Mann," my great-grandparents. We went to the town hall where I saw her papaw's portrait with the inscription, "S. C. Mann, Esq. / First Mayor of Parkersville 1923–1932. It is hanging in the large auditorium where town meetings are still held. We drove by the house where Dad used to live. The town is the way I pictured it to be as I read through Great-Grandma Bea's and Grandma Mary's journals. It is quaint, clean, and pretty, still a nice setting in which to raise a family. I could tell that Mom was remembering good times she spent there. She tried to blot from her mind the life of deception she led during the eleven years following the death of her papaw. She had also blotted out many of her wonderful childhood experiences in that town. They were all coming back to her as she drove through the streets of Parkersville, and she said that she felt surprisingly secure and serene.

Jason and Dad were waiting together for us at the airport in White Plains when we landed last night. We each exchanged warm hugs and kisses with both of them. We told them that we didn't mention Moody's illness but that we made sure that he knew how much we both cared about him and appreciated all he had done for Mom. Mom told them I had caused a commotion at the hospital, and Moody was proud to have a celebrity visitor telling everyone that he was a close and valued friend of her family. It was almost eleven, so we didn't talk long. We were all anxious to get home.

Part 6

(EXCERPT FROM THE FINAL JOURNAL OF CLAUDIA REYNOLDS THORNTON)

Sunday, April 29, 2034
11:30 p.m.

Mom died this morning. I am indescribably saddened by her loss, yet comforted by the knowledge that she is at peace with her Savior and with Dad, the love of her life. She has been anticipating this day for almost three years, since Dad died and she moved here with Jason and me, in their old home in New Rochelle. She gathered my siblings here yesterday and said her goodbyes to all of us, assuring us that she was ready for her impending journey and that she wanted us to celebrate her life rather than mourn her death. She left instructions for her funeral arrangements, along with her will, in the hands of her attorney daughter, my younger sister, Cara. So my thoughts today have not been cluttered with plans for her service and burial or handling financial matters associated with her passing. I focused on my precious memories of my phenomenal mother. She was my mentor, my counselor, my champion, and my friend.

I thought about the incredible love she shared with Dad. I remember her sadness when he died at eighty-eight on August 25, 2031, a few months after he and Mom celebrated their fifty-seventh wedding anniversary. Throughout their lives together, they remained quintessential lovers. They still went out on dates every Friday night and still beamed whenever they looked at each other, right up to that night when Dad died peacefully in his sleep. Mom awoke in his arms, which she said had become uncharacteristically cold, and she turned to see his face frozen in a tender smile. I remember the romantic scenes they used to create with each other. Once, I was riding in the car with Mom on a Saturday morning when we stopped on Old Church Road at the only signal light in Appleberry. Dad, returning home with Jason from an early round of golf, approached the light from the opposite direction. We were in the only two cars on the road at the time. When the light turned green, Mom and Dad pulled up next to each other in the intersection and stopped briefly.

Mom rolled down her window, motioning to Dad to do the same. Pretending not to know him, she said in a sexy voice, "Hello, handsome. Seeing you is a great way to start my day."

Playing along, he answered, "Thank you, miss. You are quite a lovely sight yourself."

"Well," Mom continued, "why don't you give me a call and let's see if we can brighten each other's days sometime in the future." She tossed one of her business cards into his open window.

Without looking at the card, Dad smiled at her and said, "Wow, you are certainly fine, but I'm happily married to the most beautiful woman in the world." He held up his left hand, proudly showing us his wedding band.

"My goodness!" Mom exclaimed. "So gorgeous and faithful too! Your wife is one lucky woman."

"Oh no," Dad responded. "I am the one who is blessed. She has outward and inner beauty that is unmatched on this earth."

They both laughed. As we started to drive away, Mom told him she had left snacks for him and Jason and we were on our way to the flea market for a couple of hours. Dad implored me to see that we didn't take any longer than that because he would miss her too much if we did. I saw many scenes like that one. My parents were indeed playful, romantic, and so much in love.

I recall how Mom grieved openly for Dad nearly a year. She found consolation and joy in spending time with her grandchildren and children at Mercy Baptist, and serving as a consultant at her beloved PEACE Academy. So many happy memories of her from my childhood days to the present raced through my mind today as Cara and I looked at still pictures in old photo albums, computer files and our phones, and watched videos with CJ, who is preparing the hologram tribute for her wake.

I spent much of today listening to Mom's friends, former colleagues, and others who stopped by as they shared their fondest memories of our wonderful mother and offered their condolences. During the times I was able to steal a few moments of solitude, I kept going over my last conversation with Mom. Yesterday afternoon, she called me to her room after she had spoken to CJ and Cara, whom she had me summon here to speak with her individually. As I entered her room, she motioned for me to close the door behind me.

She said, "And last, my firstborn, the one who made me a mother and taught me new and deeper ways to love. I tell you all the time how much your love has meant to me. You know more about me than anyone else, but you've always loved me anyway."

"Mom," I interrupted her, "please don't say goodbye to me. I don't believe that you are dying anytime soon. You are going to feel better if you start to eat more and take your medicines. In fact, it's afternoon, and I'm going to bring you your lunch now."

As I turned to leave, she said, "Please wait. Claudia, my dear, I need you to listen to me. I have missed your father every day for almost three years, and I'm glad that I'll soon be with him again. It is okay for you to miss me and to grieve my absence in your life. But know that I am so happy now, and I need you to be happy for me."

I was trying not to cry, but I couldn't stop myself. "I want to, Mom, but I can't, not yet anyway."

"Okay, I'll accept that if you promise to try. You've always kept your promises to me as you've kept my darkest secrets. That must have placed a burden on you, given your reverence for truth and your belief that withholding it is tantamount to lying."

"I never thought of it as a burden," I told her. "They weren't my secrets to tell. I was happy to help you bring closure after all those years you held on to guilt for no reason."

"Oh, I don't think it was without reason. I hurt someone dear to me. Still, confessing my sins to you made me feel much better. And when you told me the test results, I finally let go of the shame I felt for deceiving my husband and keeping a father and his child apart for thirty years. The truth really did set my heart and soul free."

"Mom, when you entrusted me with your secrets, I felt our bond grow even closer, which I would not have thought possible before then. That filled me with joy and gladness. I knew that we were more than mother and daughter—we were best friends."

Mom's eyes began tearing. "Yes, we are friends. And as your friend, I'm sorry that I made you feel you had to go against your principles, withholding information from your husband and siblings to protect me from embarrassment. I want to free you now. The truth cannot hurt me anymore. So let the truth free you of any guilt you have felt for lying on my behalf."

I did not respond. I couldn't tell her that telling her secrets could not free me because I had a secret of my own, a secret that I am not willing to tell, not even to her or Jason.

Before I left her room, I asked her a question about something that was puzzling me. Tuesday, after we came home from the hospital, I helped her get into the bed and brought her a cup of tea. I left the door to her room open, as well as the one to Jason's and my room, allowing me to hear her if she called me during the night. About an hour later, as I lay in bed reading an electronic book, I felt a breeze coming from her room as though a window had been opened for an instant and then shut back again. Of course, I knew that Mom could not have done that, given her condition, and nobody else was upstairs at the time. Then I heard Mom in quiet conversation with someone. When the voices ceased, I felt the breeze again for just an instant. Concerned, I arose from my bed and walked across the hallway to Mom's room. The windows were all shut tight, and Mom was sleeping peacefully with a beautiful smile of contentment on her face. I realized that I must have imagined the breezes and the muffled dialogue. The next morning, Mom asked me to summon everyone here Saturday. I asked Mom if there was a connection between the curious set of events Tuesday night and her request for me to gather the family.

Mom looked at me with an open-mouth smile, showing her beautiful teeth and raising her cheekbones so high that her eyes seemed to squint.

"Yes," she said beaming. "Tuesday night, Claude came to tell me that it was time for me to come home. He looked more handsome than ever. He was smiling, and he had a white glow all around him. I was so happy and excited. I wanted to go with him right then. But he said to be patient. My time would come very soon."

My eyes began to tear. I told her that I would miss her every day, and I would be profoundly saddened by the loss of her in my life on earth. However, I could rejoice with her because I knew how very happy she would be in her new life. Finally, I said that I thanked God for blessing me with her as my mother, that I would savor my precious memories of her and forever cherish the unconditional love she gave me. She responded that I could not have been a better daughter and her love would be with me always. I felt surprisingly calm and peaceful as I kissed her and went downstairs with the rest of the family.

Cara and I took Mom lunch, and we stayed with her while she picked at it. Cara encouraged her to eat more, but I understood her lack of interest in food. She was biding her time, trying to be patient as Dad had told her to be. I took her tray downstairs when she insisted that she didn't want to eat anymore. While I was gone, Cara started to help her get back in the bed. The covers were pulled back, and Mom was sitting on the edge of the bed when I returned. Cara was looking in her dresser drawers for a negligee to put on her. She found her favorite white silk gown with red lace trim. Cara and I helped her get out of her dress and into her gown. We sat with her for the few minutes it took her to fall asleep. It was three o'clock in the afternoon. She woke up around seven, in time to say farewell to CJ and his family before they left. Cara and I brought her dinner tray, and she picked at it much the same way she did her lunch. We talked and laughed with her until she fell asleep a little after nine. She slept through the night. Cara and her family left around midnight.

This morning, Jason and our daughters, Jasmine (Jazzy) and Jasinda (Sindy), went to Mercy Baptist, where they sat with our firstborn, our son Jason Claude (Jay). I stayed home with Mom. We watched the live webcast of the 11:30 a.m. service while we ate breakfast together in Mom's room. After the service ended, I took the breakfast trays down to the kitchen. When I returned, Mom was sitting up tall in her bed. She asked me to brush her hair into some kind of style. I brushed it all back, away from her face, into a low ponytail. I fastened it with a large sterling silver elephant barrette that I knew she had not worn in a decade but kept polished in her jewelry case. She smiled her approval when she saw it. She looked in the mirror and said, "Thank you. Now I don't look like a wild woman living in the forest." We both laughed, but Mom's laugh led into a horrible cough. I tried to get her to sip some water from the glass on the table by the window. She firmly yet gently pushed it and me away. I watched in shock as she put her left hand to her chest and raised her right hand toward the ceiling. She stopped coughing, closed her eyes, smiled, and said serenely, "Father, into your hands, I commit my spirit."

I screamed, "Mom!" and grabbed her as her body fell back on to the bed. I called 911 for assistance and performed CPR while I waited for the ambulance to arrive. But she was gone from her body. The paramedics took care of the formalities and made mandatory official calls. I called Jason's cell. Jazzy answered it and said that they were in the car and would be home within ten minutes. Jay was following them in his car. I asked her to call their aunt Cara and uncle CJ. I called the church and left a message for Pastor Ferguson to come as soon as he could. He arrived about half an hour later. CJ, Cara, and their families came within a few minutes of each other shortly after the pastor.

Pastor Ferguson has known Mom and our family since he was a little boy. He was among the first students at PEACE Academy and was in CJ's class. His father, the first Pastor Ferguson, was the pastor at Mercy Baptist when our family joined the church almost sixty years ago. Mom has spoken with him many times since he officiated at Dad's funeral, and he is well aware of her wishes regarding her own funeral and burial. She called him Friday, he said. They talked for quite a while, and they prayed together. So with the family assembled for the second consecutive day and her pastor present, it did not take long to plan the funeral. Her specific requests for family members were detailed in a letter enclosed in her will, which Cara brought with her. After the pastor left, CJ started working on the hologram, and the rest of us spent time with the many visitors who came throughout the afternoon and evening. The last group left around ten.

As I prepare to join Jason in our bed, my final thoughts are of those twelve days after Thanksgiving thirty years ago. I learned so much about my parents, my ancestors, and myself that challenged my previous views and attitudes. Colleagues and critics alike noted positive changes in my interviewing style and technique after Jay was born in the spring of 2005. Many speculated that becoming a mother brought more depth and compassion to my work. That is probably true. Yet I know that I was changed dramatically and permanently by all I heard, read, and did near the end of 2004 when I was still pregnant.

Mom, Dad, and I never spoke again of the secrets revealed over the weekend I spent with them. We also never mentioned the paternity test or the exact nature of Mom's history with Moody. We described Moody as Mom's "big brother." Cara met him when she went with Mom and me (toting six-month-old Jay) to Detroit nine months after our trip to see him in the hospital. We spent time with Mom's godmother Josie and her "aunt" Sandy and their families. We went to visit Aunt (cousin) June, who was preparing to move to California with her son James Jr. and his family. Sadly, we learned that she died in Michigan a few days after we returned to New York. Mom went to Detroit for June's funeral and later for those of Josie and Sandy. She rekindled her relationships with Josie's niece, Larissa, and Sandy's daughter, Kendra, who were her friends through high school. She and Dad vacationed together with them and their husbands a few times, and they attended a cotillion debutante ball, now presented by the Cotillion Society of Detroit, when Kendra's granddaughter was a deb. This evening, Larissa and Kendra expressed their sorrow when I called to tell them Mom passed.

I also called Moody, my biological father, with whom I have secretly corresponded since we met. There is a certain irony. Dad kept a secret about Moody from Mom for about thirty years, and I kept a secret about Moody from her for the next thirty years. Nobody knows that I call him at least twice a month and send him pictures of my children regularly, which he keeps locked in a box in his bedroom. Moody has kept our secret as he has kept my mother's secrets about her life with him in Parkersville. He came here for Dad's funeral. That is when he met the rest of our family and close friends. He called me after he returned to Parkersville to tell me how happy he was spending time with his grandchildren, even though he could not claim them as such. He is frail and weak now but plans to come to Mom's funeral with his adopted son, George, attending to him.

Mom gave me permission to tell her secrets now, but I will not do that. Nor will I tell the truth about Moody being my father. Revealing that truth now would hurt my husband and my sister. I don't think CJ and Cara would care that I am their half sister or that I lied about that to Mom and Dad. None of that would matter to Jason either. However, Jason and Cara would be hurt that I suffered the guilt of secrets and lies all these years and did not allow them to comfort me. Cara would also be angry that I didn't share the truth with her. We have always sworn that we are so close that we can tell each other anything. Yet she would argue that must not be true because I didn't share with her the biggest shock and hurt of my life. I did plan to tell her years ago, but the longer I waited, the harder it was for me to admit that I had been lying for so long. Now I see no good purpose to be served in ever telling anyone the truth about my paternity. The only person who has a right to know that already knows. I told Moody the truth within hours of learning it myself.

I used to believe that I was entitled to know the whole truth about everybody and to report it to the public. I still pursue truth. However, I am now convinced that some things are better left private and that some lies should not be exposed. The only one who has a right to know everything is God, and He already knows it without me or anyone else reporting it to Him. The truths I have told in my journals don't need to be shared with anyone, except perhaps my daughters after I am gone. Upon my death, I will leave them the journals I have written, as well as those of Great-Great-Grandma Juliette, Great-Grandma Bea, and Grandma Mary. They can read them and decide for themselves what wisdom, if any, can be gleaned from the experiences of the women in their maternal ancestry. They know that I maintained journals throughout most of my life, and I encouraged them to do the same. I no longer write in my journals regularly, only when special occurrences lead me to seek the comfort I find in doing so. I hope my daughters find pleasure and comfort in journaling. At least, I know their electronic diaries provide them opportunities to tell their truths, to freely express their private thoughts and deeds when they don't want to share them with anyone else, perhaps not even with each other.

Historical References

Actual people, organizations, places, and events are cited in the fictional journal writings. Following is a listing of some which you might be interested in researching.

People

Jim Brown (1936–)
Samuel "Ron" Brown, Esq. (1875–1950)
George Washington Carver (1864–1943)
Nat King Cole (1919–1965)
Frank Coleman (1890–1967)
Countee Cullen (1903–1946)
Benjamin O. Davis (1912–2002)
Elder Watson Diggs (1883–1947)
Frederick Douglass (1818–1895)
W. E. B. DuBois, PhD (1868–1963)
Ella Fitzgerald (1917–1996)
Fletcher Henderson (1897–1952)
Lena Horne (1917–2010)
Eunice Walker Johnson (1916–2010)
Edgar Love (1891–1974)
Benjamin Montgomery (1819–1877)
Isaiah Montgomery (1847–1924)

Mushulatubee (1770–1838)
Pushmataha (ca. 1760–1824)
Hiram Revels (1827–1901)
Willie Thrower ((1930–2002)
Col. Charles Young (1864–1922)

Companies/Organizations

Seventeenth Provisional Training Regiment (World War I)
  Fort Des Moines, Iowa in WWI
Ninety-Second Division, American Expeditionary Force
Ninety-Third Infantry Division, WWI
Three Hundred Sixty-Ninth Infantry Regiment/Harlem
Hellfighters
Atlantic Records (Atlantic Recording Company)
  Lavern Baker
  Ruth Brown
  Ray Charles
  Ivory Joe Hunter
  Ben E. King
  Clyde McPhatter
Bell Broadcasting/WCHB AM (1440)
  Drs. Haley Bell and Wendell Cox
Cotillion Club of Detroit (1946–1996)
  Cotillion Debutante Ball
  Cotillion Society of Detroit (est. 2007)
Department of Street Railways (DSR), Detroit, Michigan
Ebony Fashion Fair (1958–2009)
Fortune Records (1946–1995)
Greek Letter Organizations (historically/predominately black)
  Alpha Phi Alpha Fraternity, Inc., 1906, Cornell University
  Alpha Kappa Alpha Sorority, Inc., 1908, Howard University
  Kappa Alpha Psi Fraternity, Inc., 1911, Indiana University
  Omega Psi Phi Fraternity, Inc., 1911, Howard University

Delta Sigma Theta Sorority, Inc., 1913, Howard University
Phi Beta Sigma Fraternity, Inc., 1914, Howard University
Zeta Phi Beta Sorority, Inc., 1920, Howard University
Sigma Gamma Rho Sorority, Inc., 1922, Butler University
Iota Phi Theta Fraternity, Inc., 1963, Morgan State University
Ku Klux Klan (KKK)
National Association for the Advancement of Colored People
(NAACP)
Prince Hall Freemasons
Tuskegee Airmen

Places

Burton Mercy Hospital, Detroit, Michigan
    Drs. DeWitt T. Burton and Chester Ames
Conant Gardens, Detroit, Michigan
Davis Bend, Mississippi
Detroit Memorial Park Cemetery, Warren, Michigan
Gotham Hotel, Detroit, Michigan
Highland Beach, Maryland
Idlewild, Michigan
Oak Bluffs, Martha's Vineyard, Massachusetts
Paradise Valley, Detroit, Michigan
Parkside Hospital, Detroit, Michigan
Sag Harbor, New York
Sidney A. Sumby Memorial Hospital, River Rouge, Michigan
    Dr. Samuel B. Milton
Stinson Funeral Homes, Detroit, Michigan
    Sulee and Joseph Stinson
Surf Club, near Windsor, Ontario, Canada
Trinity Hospital, Detroit, Michigan
    Drs. W. Harold Johnson, Frank Raiford, Jr. and Chester Ames
Vieux Carre/French Quarter, New Orleans, Louisiana

Events

Lynchings of Black Women
    Maggie and Alma Howze
    Mary Turner
Murders of Black World War I Veterans, 1919
    Beating of Wilbur Little, Blakely, Georgia
    Lynching of Jim Grant, Pope City, Georgia
Red Summer, 1919
Steelworkers' Strike, 1919
Detroit Race Riot, 1943
Murder of Emmett Till, 1955
Detroit Riots, 1967

Edwards Brothers Malloy
Oxnard, CA USA
November 6, 2014